PARALYZED

J.R. LOVELESS

Jerking awake and gasping for breath, Nathan irritably swiped at the sweat pouring down his face, ignoring how his hand trembled. When would these nightmares stop haunting him? It had already been six years, but they only seemed to get more intense with the passing of time instead of fading. Glancing at the clock, he saw there were only thirty minutes until the alarm went off, and he got up instead of going back to sleep. The sheets stuck to his skin as he stumbled out of bed toward the bathroom, and they fell haphazardly across the floor behind him. Dark strands of hair tickled his cheek, and he brushed at them in frustration. They'd come free from the small band he used to tie his shoulder-length black hair back from his face.

His nightmares were always the same. Every detail of that night six years ago haunted him. The memory of his mother's face as she'd mouthed "I love you" just before the explosion disturbed him more than anything. If only things had been different. If his legs hadn't shattered in several places. Or if he hadn't been so angry at his parents and demanded that they leave the party. His best friend Troy would tell him to stop playing "What Ifs" because there was no way to change what happened, and Nathan was lucky to be alive. But he couldn't stop wondering if he should have died that night, too.

At only twenty-two years old, Nathan had seen more than his fair share of horrors. Every day, he struggled to not let everything envelop him and drag him back down into the dark abyss he'd been in following the deaths of his parents.

The pipes rattled in the walls as he twisted the handle for the hot water. Steam filled the small room in minutes. Nathan stared at himself in the mirror, studying his reflection. Dark circles were prominent beneath the green eyes gazing back at him. His mother had always said he'd inherited his grandmother's catlike eyes. Those same eyes were darker still with the memories never far from his mind. Raven's wing black hair, ragged from lack of proper trimming, hung around his slim face. His aunts were constantly nagging him because of how thin he was. He barely ate, and when he did, he hardly ever finished the food on his plate. His ribs stuck out against his skin, further proof of how little he consumed. A light dusting of freckles across his nose was the only color, and they showed clearly against his pale skin. He wasn't unattractive, but a little more weight on his five-foot-ten frame would help. A white scar trailed along his temple, about six inches long, but only two inches were visible; the other four disappeared underneath his hairline.

The mirror fogged over from the steam, slowly hiding his reflection. Once the mirror had turned opaque and he could no longer see himself, Nathan looked away and stepped into the tub, closing the curtain behind him. The hot water stung his skin, but he welcomed the momentary pain. It turned his skin a bright pink as he shampooed and washed for the day. His actions were routine and without thought while he showered, as he remained wrapped up in thoughts of his past and the nightmare he relived every time he slept.

His mother, the gentlest woman he'd ever known aside from the aunts who'd raised him after his parents died, had always smelled of peppermint and vanilla. It had been one of her favorite lotions. Whenever he caught the scent on someone else, it always brought sharp pangs of pain and loss straight to his chest. Memories of her hugging him and kissing his cheek when he'd been a child or of the last night before the accident, when she'd taken his arm to walk to the car, would overwhelm him, almost sending him to his knees in agonizing guilt.

Every day, he looked in the mirror and saw his father. Even if he'd wanted to, he could never forget the person his father had been. They both had the same blue-black hair, firm chin, and lightly flared nose. Nathan had only seen his father truly upset once—the night of the accident. Laughter was uncommon for Nathan these days. He could barely recall the last time he'd felt happy enough to let himself go. Guilt that he was still alive while his parents were dead kept him from being able to enjoy much of his life.

He finished his shower, turned off the water, and grabbed a towel to dry himself with. It didn't take him long to dress in his usual jeans and T-shirt, and he stuffed his feet into a pair of scuffed sneakers before leaving his bedroom to head into the kitchen for his morning coffee. The sun was just peering over the horizon as he filled his mug.

His apartment, though small, was perfect for a single person—one bedroom with a miniscule bathroom. Sparsely furnished, a simple couch rested against the wall of the tiny living room area directly across from a 27-inch television that his aunts had given him last year for Christmas. The dining area had a folding card table and two chairs. His bedroom contained a queen-sized bed he'd bought from a thrift store and a beat-up dresser to hold his clothes. The only personal effects he had lying around were his guitar and several pictures of his parents, aunts, and Troy. Anyone looking at it would think it a barren apartment, but to him, it was all his.

His aunts constantly begged him to let them pay for somewhere nicer, but he refused. Living in Myrtle Beach, South Carolina, wasn't exactly cheap, especially being so close to the beach, but he had to make his own way. Aunt Becky and Aunt Jessica had done more than he could have asked for in the last six years. He loved them with all his heart and wouldn't trade having them as his aunts for anything in the world. He just didn't think it was fair to rely on them so much. Especially after all the hell he'd put them through since his parents' deaths.

The one thing he couldn't live without though was coffee, his personal breakfast of champions, with lots and lots of sugar. Most would have asked if he wanted coffee with his sugar, that's how much he put in it. He had a major sweet tooth. Anything vanilla was his favorite. He felt pretty sure he'd inherited that from his mother. Vanilla ice cream with rainbow-colored sprinkles had always been his first choice at dessert time.

Rinsing out his mug once he'd finished his coffee, Nathan debated on having another cup, but with his hands still trembling slightly after the dream, he decided against it. He set the mug on the drying rack and then grabbed his backpack from the floor by the front closet. The door to his apartment stuck, and he had to tug hard sometimes to get it open. The landlord had been swearing up and down for weeks that he'd get it fixed. Nathan had finally tired of asking and just let it go. Closing the door behind him with a bang, he locked it and headed downstairs to find Troy sitting on the bottom step, crooning to a song he listened to on his iPhone. Troy smiled when he saw Nathan coming down the steps.

Troy Davis. No one could ask for a better friend. Troy had gone through hell helping him survive the last six years —the weeks spent in the hospital after the accident, six months in rehab, and then the year Nathan had spent in the institution because his aunts and the doctors had believed he'd snapped under the trauma of his parents' deaths. Troy had also helped him make up the work he'd missed from school so he could graduate on time. He would never forget how Troy had been there for him or how much he owed him for it.

Friends since middle school, he'd never really considered Troy anything else, despite how drop-dead gorgeous he was. Black hair with ocean blue eyes, a firm chin with an amazingly sexy cleft, toned physique, and being six foot two made for a sexy package. But Troy was like a brother to Nathan, and he couldn't imagine anything more developing between them—he knew Troy chased skirts like a dog chased cars.

Nathan had known he was gay since he'd turned thirteen, when he'd started noticing other boys instead of girls. At first, he hadn't realized, but his mother had. She'd helped him come to terms with it. Unlike some parents, who would have swept his sexuality under the carpet or even possibly disowned him, his mom and dad had accepted his sexuality as though he'd told them there were clouds in the sky. He supposed it was because of his aunts. Aunt Becky, Mom's sister, had lived with her life partner, Jessica, for almost his entire life.

"Hey, Nate! How's it hanging?" Troy asked as he stood, slipping his earbuds out and sliding them and his phone into his pocket. He adjusted his jeans, pulling them up slightly.

Nathan shrugged. "It's going. You think Professor Johns will try to humiliate us again?"

Troy growled. "That man seriously needs to get laid. He's such a bastard."

Nathan huffed a quick laugh, which died almost instantly. Johns really was an ass. "Did you finish his assignment?"

"Yeah. I'd love to tell him to stick it, though," Troy muttered as he walked around the front of his car to clamber into the driver's side.

Nathan climbed into Troy's beat up Chevy Malibu and leaned back, putting one foot on the dashboard. "You think you could give me a lift to the store after classes?"

"Sure. I have to go that way, anyway. Nikki's working today." Troy grinned cockily.

Nathan rolled his eyes. Troy's recent interest, Nikki, was a beautiful brunette who worked in a coffee shop near the music store. Troy had been trying to get her to go out with him for a couple of months now. She always refused. Nathan had a feeling she'd either been in an abusive relationship or maybe even still was because he could see a glimmer of fear in her eyes whenever a guy paid too much attention to her. He'd tried more than once to get Troy to give up on her, but he'd just laughed at Nathan's suggestion and brushed it off.

Six days a week, Nathan managed a store called True Music, where they sold vinyl records, new and used CDs, sheet music, musical instruments, and anything else music related his boss thought would sell. Nathan loved music—listening to it, singing it, and playing it.

On Saturday nights he played guitar at a local dive near the college. Students would come into the small café to drink coffee, listen to live music, and talk. It wasn't a lot of money, but he could do what he loved. Some would question why he wasn't going to school to study music, but he knew he had to finish his degree in business. He owed it to his aunts. They'd supported him entirely for three years without a thought of how it strained their own financial situation, cramped their romantic life, or what they could have done if he hadn't been there.

"So, I'll meet you at your car at three?" Nathan asked as Troy pulled into a space in front of Webster University.

Troy nodded, and Nathan climbed out of the car, limping toward the far side of campus. Despite months of rehab, the multiple pins in his legs, and the surgeries done to "fix" him, he still walked with a limp. He figured it was just another reminder of how selfish he'd been. He usually ignored the looks people sent his way, knowing they were sympathetic or curious, neither of which he wanted to deal with.

The morning passed by quickly for Nathan. He met up with Troy for lunch, eating almost a full sandwich and part of an apple. Later in the afternoon, Nathan slid into his usual seat in Professor Johns' class, pulling out his notebook, a pen, and the assignment the professor had given out a couple weeks ago. The assignment was simple: come up with a business plan and detail it out to where within five years a profit of over two hundred thousand was being made annually. It had been straightforward stuff for him.

Troy slipped into the seat next to him, greeting him casually and taking out his own homework. When the professor cleared his throat, Nathan looked up and finally noticed the man standing near the huge dry-erase board on the wall close to the window. His dream had still been weighing on him, and that's probably why he hadn't noticed him when he'd first walked into the classroom. Nathan clenched his jaw, trying to ignore his presence. Troy noticed immediately. "What's wrong?" he whispered, not daring to call the professor's attention.

"It's one of them," Nathan replied bitterly, his hand tightening around his pen. If it had been a pencil, it would have snapped in two. As it was, the case cracked under the pressure. The man was around Nathan's height, with dark blond hair and a body like Troy's but leaner in muscle. Nathan couldn't see his eyes since he was gazing out of the window.

A breath hissed from Troy. His eyes darted around, but he wouldn't be able to see him. "Are you sure?"

Nathan grimaced. "Of course. Standing by the window. No way Professor Johns would ignore a student standing there."

Troy's gaze flitted in the direction Nathan mentioned, trying in vain to see the man. "Just ignore him," he instructed softly.

Nathan snorted. He always tried to ignore them, but it was hard when they were right in his face and he knew what they were.

Professor Johns noticed them whispering to each other and stopped talking. "Mr. Bryant, Mr. Davis, is there something you would like to share with us? If it's enough to keep you whispering between yourselves while I am speaking, it must be quite stimulating."

"No, sir," Troy said. "We were just discussing how much fun we had putting together the business plan you assigned to us. It seems Nathan's plan is better than mine."

Nathan glared at Troy. Great. Now Professor Johns would zero in on him. "Oh, is that right?" The professor stepped forward, an eyebrow raised in skepticism. "Well, why don't you show me your plan, Mr. Bryant? I'd love to see what has Mr. Davis so fascinated."

Letting out a growl under his breath at Troy, Nathan stood and limped down the steps to hand the report to the professor. He turned to slink back to his seat, but Professor Johns stopped him. "Oh, I think you should stay here, Mr. Bryant. That way, you can show me exactly where you made a better business plan than your friend."

The man standing by the window moved closer to them, peering over the professor's shoulder. Nathan couldn't help but notice the dark brown eyes set above a slightly irregular nose. The slight musky scent of death wafted to Nathan's nostrils. He could tell whoever the ghost was, they couldn't have been deceased more than a few years.

Professor Johns started looking over Nathan's assignment, smirking as he continued through to the end. "Just as I expected. Inferior work. You haven't even considered the possibility that your target clientele might hesitate to use your products, as you are a newly established business. There is no way you'd be able to bring in those types of profits in the first six months."

A snort left the stranger behind the professor. "You are so full of shit, Johns. His plan is brilliant. He'd be making money hand over fist within months."

Nathan couldn't help it. He gave a small laugh, drawing the attention of both the professor and the man behind him. "You find something funny?" Professor Johns demanded at the same time the blond male asked, "You can hear me?"

Nathan's slight smile faded as he realized if he wasn't careful, he'd give his secret away. "No, sir. I just think that with proper advertising and the right sales representatives, it's not as far-fetched as you imagine."

Professor Johns took great offense to Nathan's response. "I have been teaching this class for well over twenty years," he blustered, face red. "You think you know better than I? Your paper is like reading that of a high school student. Shabby, poorly planned, and F material."

Shocked, Nathan exclaimed, "You can't seriously be giving me an F! I spent two weeks working on it!"

"That is so not cool," the blond murmured, shaking his head at the professor.

"Shut up," Nathan snarled, then drew back as he realized he'd just acknowledged he could hear the man. Of course,

Professor Johns didn't know Nathan wasn't talking to him, and he exploded.

"Excuse me? Did you just tell me to shut up, Mr. Bryant?" Professor Johns demanded.

Nathan kept his mouth closed. What could he say? How could he explain he hadn't been talking to the teacher, but to a person no one else could see? Sighing, he hung his head and waited.

"Please leave my lecture hall this instant. You are not to return to my class for a week. Do you hear me, Mr. Bryant?"

Scowling, Nathan nodded, stomped over to gather his things, and then slammed out of the room. Troy had given him an apologetic look he completely ignored. The rat had sent him into an ambush by bringing him to the professor's attention. Damn it! Stupid ghost! He knew the spirit followed him out of the class, but he kept walking, pretending he didn't see him.

"I know you can hear me," the man said caustically, still trailing after him.

Nathan knew the stranger wouldn't leave him alone, so he stopped, staring out the window into the courtyard in the center of the college. "Go away," he bit out between clenched teeth, his fingers digging into the handle of his book bag.

"Not going to happen. I need your help." The blond moved to stand in Nathan's peripheral vision.

"No. I can't. Please, just go away." He turned toward the stranger.

Shock slipped over the man's face. "You can see me, too!"

Nathan glared at him before stalking through him. He would just pretend the guy didn't exist. It was the only thing he could do. He couldn't help him because he had his own baggage to carry.

To his dismay, the blond continued to follow him. "My name is Alan. I really need your help. There's something I—"

Whirling around, Nathan shouted, "I don't care! Stay away from me."

Several students nearby turned to look at him. Surprise and fear all crossed their faces when they saw no one standing with him. Nathan closed his eyes, breathed deep, and smiled at them when he reopened his eyes before turning and hurrying away.

It wasn't fair. Why did this happen to him? Wasn't it enough that he'd lost his parents in the accident? His heart had stopped on the way to the hospital and during the surgery to stop the internal bleeding. When Nathan had regained consciousness, he'd first thought the people he was seeing were just other patients who'd wandered into his hospital room. It wasn't until the nurse had caught him talking to someone she couldn't see that he'd realized that when he'd come back from death, he'd come back wrong. Something had changed and he could see spirits—ghosts, as most would call them.

Nathan had insisted he could see and talk to them and had been transferred to the mental ward after his rehab. The doctors and nurses hadn't believed him. Even his aunts had thought it was the stress and trauma of the accident. It had taken time for him to come to terms with it himself. The months he'd spent in the mental ward had been the most terrifying months of his life. The things he'd seen, the ghosts that had lingered there, had left a huge scar across his soul. Those were things no one should ever see. It was horrifying. Finally, he'd learned to pretend they weren't there. He'd agreed with the doctors and told them what they'd wanted to hear. A full year later, they had finally released him.

Troy was the only one who'd believed him and hadn't thought he'd lost his mind. He'd been the one who'd suggested Nathan agree with the doctors. *Act like nothing is there,* he'd said. Nathan hadn't wanted to because they *were* there. He wasn't seeing things like they thought he was, but the longer he stayed in the hospital, the more he'd grown certain if he remained much longer, he would have a nervous breakdown. So, the lies and deception had begun.

Over the years, he'd learned to figure out when it was a spirit. They moved a certain way, acted a certain way, and there was always so much emotion around them. Their emotions were like a tangible living being to Nathan. Sometimes anger would hit him with a blast of heat across his skin when they were near. Or happiness brushed over him, a gentle breeze blowing through his hair, kissing his skin. Other times, despair and sadness would weigh him down under what appeared to be a thousand pounds suddenly resting on his chest. The sadness hit him hardest. It had taken months for him to train himself not to burst into tears the instant he felt the emotion. It ate through him, destroying him.

Anxiety struck Nathan as it rolled off the man. "Please, help me. I need you to see someone."

"No," Nathan muttered. Instead of heading for the library to wait for Troy, he detoured and was practically running by the time he reached the front of the building. He needed to get away from there. Now.

Thankfully, the spirit disappeared when Nathan exited, but he knew until he did what the blond ghost wanted, he'd be back. A shudder raced through Nathan as he stepped onto the bus, dropping change into the meter and then walking to the back to sit. He stared straight ahead, ignoring the woman who sat nearby, a dazed expression on her face.

Eventually, he'd understood that an item related to a spirit's death or a thing they had an emotional connection to was what tied the ghosts to the physical plane. Dried blood matted the woman's hair, and it stained one side of the dress she wore. She looked at Nathan. Her lips trembled as she cried. "Where's my baby?" she whispered repeatedly.

Nathan steeled himself against the onslaught of emotions flooding the small confines of the bus. He clenched his teeth so tightly his head hurt. "I can't find my baby."

He wanted to lift his hands to his ears, to cover them and block her out. He almost ripped his bag while opening it and frantically yanked out his outdated MP3 player. Stuffing the earbuds in his ears, he clicked on the first song he came to, and as the music started, he closed his eyes so he wouldn't have to see her. He raised the hoodie he wore up enough to cover his nose, the stench of death and decay gagging him. The stronger the smells, the longer they'd been deceased. If he'd been standing, the weight of her grief would have brought him to his knees. *Please stop,* he begged her silently. It wasn't until he stepped off the bus that he could breathe normally again. Once he got far enough away, he could no longer feel her energy.

CHAPTER 2

True Music's assistant manager, Quinn Jones, stood behind the counter when Nathan entered the store. Surprised, he said, "You're here early."

Nathan grimaced. "Professor Johns threw me out of his class."

Quinn knew his dislike for the man and shook his head. "For what?"

"For telling him to shut up," Nathan lied. He couldn't exactly tell him the truth.

Quinn started laughing and came over to slap him on the back. "Way to go, Bryant! Bastard probably deserved it."

Smiling slightly, Nathan shrugged. He had deserved it. "He told me the assignment I spent two weeks working on was high school quality and he gave me an F."

"You mean the one where you had to outline the five-year business plan?" Quinn winced when he nodded. "That is so wrong, man. Can't you do something about it? Maybe switch to another class?"

"No. I need the class. It's part of my required credits and he's the only professor. If I could do that, I would have done it already," he said as he started grabbing some CDs from the return box to restock.

"That sucks, dude," Quinn commiserated.

Nodding, he slid a CD into its place. Maybe if Quinn had been into guys, Nathan would have had a tinge of interest in the man, but Quinn was straighter than straight. He chased a new woman every night. It made Nathan's head spin with how many names the man dropped into a conversation.

Admittedly, Quinn was gorgeous, though, with bright blond hair, a killer smile that curved into two dimples, and dazzling blue eyes that always seemed to sparkle with mischief and humor. There were only a handful of times Nathan had ever seen him angry or upset, and it was usually after a difficult customer. A full head taller than Nathan, he had broad shoulders wide enough to be great for playing football, yet he held no interest in the sport.

"What are you up to this weekend?" Quinn asked while straightening out some records someone had been digging through earlier.

"The same as always. Saturday shift here. Gig at Java Bean afterward. Sunday, I've got some assignments to finish." Nathan frowned when he found a bunch of CDs out of place. He pulled them and added them to the pile he already held.

"Don't you ever take time to have fun?"

"Of course I do! I love playing at Java Bean. Music is fun for me!" Nathan exclaimed, letting a CD slide into place with a bang.

"That's not what I meant. You're always so serious. You act as though the entire world rests on your shoulders all the time. If you keep letting everything weigh so heavily on you, you're going to end up old before your time, Nate," Quinn said.

A scowl of discomfort settled on Nathan. "I don't act like I have the entire world on my shoulders, Quinn. I'm just trying to get through school so I can try to pay my aunts back for how much they've taken care of me."

"Do you think they'd want you to run yourself into the ground? I doubt they'd be thrilled if they saw you," he pointed out.

"It's none of your business," Nathan growled, brutally shoving a CD into a rack. His mouth tightened in anger. What right did Quinn have to say anything? What did he know?

They didn't speak again until they were behind the counter later.

"I'm sorry, Nate. I'm just worried about you," Quinn murmured.

Nathan's hand stilled while writing a sign for the CDs on sale that week. "It's fine."

"No. I shouldn't have pried into your life. Just know if you ever need to talk, I'm here." Quinn squeezed Nathan's shoulder briefly.

"Thanks," he said gruffly.

"No problem. Hey, we're having a party at the Alpha frat house this week. Why don't you and Troy drop by?" Quinn fairly bounced in excitement. He attended Coastal Carolina University, which was only about a half hour away from Webster.

"I don't think I'll have time, but I'm sure Troy would love to," Nathan said distractedly. His thoughts had already shifted back to the ghost at school. He knew if he didn't help the man, he'd never leave Nathan alone. It wasn't the first time a spirit had realized he could see them and talk to them.

Quinn dropped his hand on top of Nathan's unexpectedly, causing him to jump in surprise. "Nate, you seriously need to have some fun in your life. Come to the party, even if it's only for a couple of hours."

Nathan studied his hand on top of his for a few silent

moments before nodding. "All right, but only for a little while."

A brilliant smile broke out over Quinn's face. "Great! It's on Friday at seven. Oh, and there's going to be some smokin' hot chicks there."

The mention of women almost made Nathan snort in amusement, but he stifled it. "I have to close that night. Won't be until after ten for me."

Quinn shrugged. "The parties usually go all night, so it doesn't matter what time."

Maybe getting out of his apartment and having some fun might be a good idea. Nathan hadn't been to a party since before his parents died. Even his birthdays were quiet events —normally only his aunts and Troy were present. Birthdays held no meaning for him and were simply him getting another year older.

The sound of the bell tinkling over the front door disturbed Nathan from his thoughts. A good-looking man in a dark business suit stood just inside the doorway, glancing around the store. Nathan had a good instinct when it came to a person's taste in music. The elegant suit made him pretty sure the man enjoyed classical or jazz even. The way the jacket hugged his broad shoulders like an affectionate lover spoke of class and money.

"Can we help you find something, sir?" Quinn called from the back of the store.

The stranger's dark gaze suddenly locked onto Nathan, pinning him in place. He resisted the urge to fidget under the intense look. "Hello," the man said. Nathan's stomach twisted sharply when he heard his voice. It was deep and husky with a slight rasp Nathan felt all the way to the pit of his stomach. "Where's your classic rock CD section?"

Surprised, Nathan tilted his head quizzically. He'd rarely been wrong about someone. Curiosity got the better of him and before he could stop himself, Nathan stepped forward to help. He normally let Quinn deal with the customers while he stocked shelves and changed the sale signs. "This way," he offered quietly, beckoning the man to follow him.

He could sense Quinn studying him in question, but Nathan ignored him. The scent of a woodsy aftershave washed over Nathan the moment the customer came closer. "Are you looking for something in particular?"

While waiting for the man's response, he took the time to look the tall stranger over. Dark chestnut hair was brushed into a short, neat cut that made the strong angles of his face more prominent and his hazel eyes appear even more intense. A deep cleft in his chin had Nathan wondering what it would be like to trace it with his tongue, which caused him to startle in shock. He hadn't really had an interest in anyone since the accident, had never had an actual boyfriend or any experience at all, but to look at this man—a stranger—and have such lewd thoughts made him uncomfortable. Firm lips formed an answer he had to concentrate on hearing. "An album by Pink Floyd, actually. *Wish You Were Here.*"

Nathan's breath caught. That was his favorite album. "Right this way," he replied. Never had he been more aware of his slight limp than he was as he walked toward the rack holding the requested band's CDs.

Flipping through the compact discs, he could feel the man's eyes on him. "You seemed surprised by what I asked for," the stranger mused.

Lifting his shoulder in a shrug, Nathan explained, "I'm usually good at guessing a person's style of music. You didn't strike me as someone interested in classic rock."

A husky chuckle crashed over Nathan, sending him spiraling under a wave of desire. The hyperawareness racing through him made him nervous.

"Shouldn't judge a book by its cover."

Nathan reached the end of the section with a frown. "It seems we're out of that particular CD."

The man sighed and ran a hand through his hair in frustration, messing the neat style. Nathan thought that suited him better than the sleek look. "Seems all the stores I've been to have had the same problem."

"Why not just download it?" Quinn called from the front counter. "Would be faster and easier."

"Not much for downloading. I prefer the physical album."

"I can special order it for you and call you when it comes in. Shouldn't take more than two or three days." Nathan lifted his gaze to the hazel eyes, which had darkened with an almost sad gleam. He had to blink when they seemed to change colors to an almost light green.

"That would be great. Someone broke into my truck a week ago and stole the CDs in my glove box."

"Come over to the counter so I can take down some information," Nathan told him. "I'll put the order in this afternoon, and it should be here by Friday at the latest."

"That's perfect."

Nathan pulled out the order book from behind the counter, noting the name of the album before asking, "What's your name?"

"Erik Moore."

Strong name, Nathan thought as he wrote it. "Phone number?"

A white rectangle appeared in front of him. Moore Construction appeared in the upper left corner of the business card, along with the man's name and two phone numbers. The basic shape of a building under construction graced the right side of the card. Nathan's eyes widened a tiny fraction. Moore Construction was one of the biggest and most successful construction companies around. Everyone knew who they were. Taking the card, his eyes strayed to the long, calloused fingers extending it. They were tanned with blunt fingernails. He briefly wondered how they'd feel against his skin, and he promptly berated himself for having such thoughts.

"Thank you, Mr. Moore," he said by rote as he stapled the card into the book.

"Erik."

"Huh?" Nathan looked up in confusion.

"It's Erik. Mr. Moore sounds so stuffy." Those fascinating eyes were twinkling with what he could only define as mischief.

"Erik," he repeated hesitantly.

The man bid him goodbye with a small smile and a tip of his head. It was only after Erik had left that Quinn admonished, "I can't believe you never told me!"

Nathan looked at him quizzically. "Told you what?"

"That you're gay, dude. I don't care, but I feel like a real ass after trying to set you up with all those chicks." Quinn had tried several times to hook him up with girls he'd brought into the store on his days off. "Of course, I should have guessed when Tracey didn't catch your attention. Really pissed her off, too!"

"What makes you think I'm gay?" he spluttered.

Quinn smirked and propped his hip against the counter. "Maybe the line of drool down your chin? Or it could be the way you were practically stripping the guy with your eyes. I can't decide which."

Instinctively, Nathan swiped at his chin, causing Quinn to howl in laughter. He flushed in embarrassment, and Quinn slapped him on the back. "No worries, man."

"It's not something I talk about," Nathan mumbled uneasily. He didn't know he'd been so obvious about his attraction to Erik Moore. Had the man noticed as well?

"Don't worry, Nate. He was checking you out, too."

Nathan's dark hair practically slapped him in the face as he swung his head around quickly to look at Quinn. "You lie!"

"No way, man. He practically tripped over a rack of CDs because he wasn't watching anything but your ass when you walked by." Quinn held his hands out in a defensive gesture.

Nathan's breathing grew a little uneven. How could he even contemplate being with anyone when he was such a freak? But the idea of someone as gorgeous as Erik Moore being interested in him, even if just for a moment, brought a bit of warmth to his belly. "You think so?"

"I may not be into guys, but I know interest when I see it. Why do you think instead of answering me, he looked right at you?" Quinn took the book and read the guy's information before letting out a low whistle. "I'd take the CD to him personally. The man's loaded! Sugar Daddy for sure!"

Nathan gave a rough bark of laughter at Quinn's words and shook his head. "There is more to life than money, Quinn."

The conversation dwindled after that, and they went back to their normal companionable silence. Nathan had forgotten all about the spirit, at least for a little while, until Troy came strolling into the store. The almost content feeling dripping through him faded immediately.

"Nate, I am so sorry, man," Troy begged the instant he reached the counter.

Nathan scowled at his best friend. "That was royally fucked up, Troy."

"I really am sorry, Nate. It came out before I thought about it. I just figured if he thought we were talking about homework, he would leave us alone." Troy gave him his best sorrowful puppy dog face.

Nathan's anger had faded already, and he could only sigh,

running a hand over his face tiredly. "It's fine. I'm not really mad anymore."

Troy gave a relieved smile. "So, what really happened?"

Looking around furtively, Nathan saw Quinn had gone into the back for his break, and only one customer stood toward the other end of the store, digging through the bargain bins. "It was stupid. The one I saw in class had been talking while Professor Johns ripped apart my project. He wouldn't stop."

Realization spread over Troy's face. "That's why you said shut up."

He nodded miserably. "And now he won't leave me alone until I do what he wants."

When the spirits realized Nathan could see them and hear them, they refused to leave him be until he helped them find peace with whatever kept them earthbound. He'd done some research on ghosts after he'd gotten out of the psych ward, but after he'd read through accounts from other people claiming to see them and the things they'd had to do, he'd stopped digging and stopped wanting to help. The last one he'd made a mistake in acknowledging had been six months ago. Until now, he'd done exceptionally well at ignoring them.

"Tell him no then," Troy demanded. "Or just keep ignoring him."

"Easier said than done. You aren't the one hearing them yakking in your ear or seeing them standing right in front of your face. They aren't see-through, you know!"

In his incredulity, Nathan's voice had risen, and the lone customer glanced their way with a slightly freaked expression before scurrying out of the store. Nathan groaned and dropped his head onto the counter. He felt Troy's hand come down on the back of his neck and massage the tense muscles there.

"Let me help you, then. Find out what he wants, and I'll do it."

Nathan seriously considered it for a split second and then he grimaced and shook his head, looking at Troy again. "No. It's my problem."

Troy grunted in frustration. "You don't always have to take on everything yourself, bro. I'm your best friend. Let me help you."

Again, Nathan shook his head. "I can't rely on anyone anymore, Troy. It's not fair to do that. I need to take care of myself."

"I guess I can understand how you feel after the last six years, Nate, but you have to let people in. People care about you. At least know I am always here if you need me," Troy said sadly.

Hardening his heart, Nathan forced a flat smile for Troy and tipped his head in acknowledgement of his pledge. For almost three years, he'd relied on way too many people: his aunts, Troy, the doctors at the ward. He knew he'd hurt Troy, but he couldn't place any further burden on his friend, not after what he'd put on Troy since the accident. Troy left the store a half hour later to go see the girl at the café. Nathan watched him leave with a pensive expression and then got back to work.

The rest of the afternoon flew by and slowly faded into darkness. Nathan didn't have time to dwell on the ghost more until he was closing out the register, and then his thoughts started wandering again. The only emotions he'd gotten from the ghost had been nervousness and anxiety. It wasn't the usual fear, anger, or sadness. During his research, he'd found most of them didn't realize they were dead. The fear they felt was because of a sense of the unknown and being lost, without purpose. Anger or sadness resulted from the way they'd died or even, for some, the realization they were dead.

He still clearly remembered the first time he'd encountered one who'd known. The rage that had swamped Nathan had been so great he'd been unable to control his own temper, and the wall of his bedroom and his stereo had paid the price. His aunts had blamed it on the loss of his parents.

Only Troy knew the truth about the "ability" Nathan had returned with when the doctors had brought him back from death. Troy had saved his sanity more than once in the last six years. He may well have ended up back in the psychiatric ward if his friend hadn't been there for him.

The only thing he'd ever hoped to gain by having the curse was to see his parents. He wanted to tell them he was sorry for demanding they leave the dinner that night. If he hadn't been so selfish, if he hadn't been so mad at them for forcing him to go when he'd wanted to go to a party at a friend's house, they'd still be alive. Or if they'd left five minutes later instead of him rushing out to have the valet bring the car around so he could make it to the party for a couple of hours. He knew it was his fault they'd been going through that intersection when the drunk driver had run a red light. What right did he have to ask for their forgiveness? Not when he was alive, and they were dead.

Eyes burning, he finished closing out the register and locked the money in the safe for tomorrow's deposit. There were some nights where Nathan was too tired to bother dropping the money at the bank. He grabbed his book bag from the back room and turned off the lights. Approaching the front of the store, he realized someone was standing inside and frowned, stopping. "I'm sorry, but we're closed. You'll have to come back tomorrow."

When the person didn't speak, anxiety gnawed at the pit of his stomach. He edged forward until he could just make out the shadowed features, and he bit back a scream, swallowing hard. One eye stared at him, the other an empty socket. Half of the man's face was crushed, as if run over by a car or perhaps he'd fallen from somewhere up high. Nathan didn't know, but he knew the man was dead. Another spirit had found him. "Can you help me?" the man whispered. "Please, help me. I need to go home. My wife... She'll be worried."

"No," Nathan gasped, backing away. "No, I can't."

The smell of decay assaulted Nathan's nose, and he grimaced, bumping into a rack of CDs as he continued retreating, sending several cascading to the floor with a crash. "Go away!" Nathan shouted, bile rising in his throat. "I can't help you!"

An ear-piercing wail rose through the store, causing Nathan to cover his ears to stifle the sound. His eyes never left the disembodied spirit before him. The spirit rushed at Nathan, floating across the floor at lightning speed and disappearing just as he reached him in a blur of color. Nathan gasped and sank to his knees, rocking slightly, trying to grab hold of himself. Why? Why couldn't they leave him alone? He couldn't help them. How could he when he couldn't even help himself?

When he could finally breathe normally again, he struggled to his feet, cleaned up the CDs he'd knocked over, and then trudged out of the store. He locked the door behind him and slung his bag over his shoulder. He walked to the bus stop and sank down on the bench to wait, shivering and running his hands along his arms to warm himself. Sometimes when he refused to help the spirits, they grew angry, malevolent. None had gotten violent with him beyond screaming and scaring him, but he knew it was inevitable, knew one day there would be a ghost who would become so enraged they would physically lash out at him.

Throat still tight with fear, Nathan pulled out his MP3 player and slid the buds into his ears. Some of the horror dissipated as Disturbed blasted through his skull. He would have snorted at the irony of the band name if he hadn't been so distraught.

The bus pulled up in front of him a few minutes later and he stood, stepping onto it and then sliding the prepaid card through the machine. There were only two others on the bus, but he went to the back and sat near the window. He focused on the buildings and cars passing by, attempting to gather his wits once more. No matter how many times they came to him or how often he encountered them, the ghosts still scared the living shit out of him.

CHAPTER 3

Nathan left school immediately after his last class and headed to work, grateful the spirit from the day before hadn't appeared again. Maybe the man had taken him seriously. Once at the store, he straightened some CDs before manning the counter.

"I'm not going away," a voice huffed behind him.

Of course, he'd jinxed himself by thinking of the ghost earlier.

Nathan turned away from the counter and scowled. "Leave me alone," he whispered furiously, eyes darting toward the two customers browsing the vinyl albums. Thankfully, Quinn had stepped out for his break.

"Nope. Not until you talk to someone for me." The man, Alan, crossed his arms and grinned at Nathan.

"Excuse me, sir? Do you know if you have *The Wall* on vinyl?" one customer called out.

Ignoring Alan, Nathan scurried over to the customer and promptly dug out the requested album, handing it over. Damn it. He'd associated the spirit with his name instead of just a stranger who was a ghost. Alan had remained near the counter, watching him with a smirk as he returned to the register. "Why can't you just go away?" Nathan growled under his breath.

"Because I really need your help. There's something important I need to tell my fiancé." Alan frowned and rubbed his forehead. "The odd thing is, I can't remember what. It took me a while to figure out I'm dead. I can't even remember how I died."

Nathan swore quietly. "How can I tell your fiancé something if you don't remember it?"

"I was hoping you could help me," Alan replied sheepishly, giving Nathan a pleading look.

Nathan barked out a laugh, which promptly captured the attention of the customers nearby. He bent his head over the mailing list ledger near the register. "No. Now go away."

"Look, kid—"

"Kid?" Nathan replied indignantly, forgetting no one else could see Alan. "You can't be more than a year older than me, if that."

Alan rolled his eyes. "Fine, whatever. Sir. Is that better?"

Nathan wanted to hit Alan but knew it would do no good, since his hand would just go right through him. He opened his mouth to retort and saw Quinn standing in the doorway to the storeroom, staring at him as if he'd lost his mind. Snapping his jaw shut, Nathan snarled under his breath and stalked away from Alan. He brushed past Quinn and stomped through the stock room to the back door, slamming it open and then closed behind him. Breathing deeply, he tried to calm himself, pacing along the alley and muttering under his breath. "God damn it. Why can't they leave me alone?"

Frustrated, he ran his hand through his hair and glanced up to see Alan in front of him, but he couldn't stop his forward motion. A shiver trickled down his spine at the sheer coldness of walking through the incorporeal form. "Go away!" Nathan demanded, spinning to glare at him.

Alan gave him a sad look. "I can't. I wouldn't ask you to do this, but in the time I've been dead, you're the first person who's been able to see me."

Nathan slumped down onto an empty wooden crate and dropped his head into his hands. "I can't do this again. You don't understand what you're asking of me."

Alan floated closer to him. Nathan could just see the ghost out of his peripheral vision. Melancholy swamped him and he couldn't tell if it was his own or if it was Alan's emotions flooding through him. Finally, Nathan dropped his hands and looked at the spirit from under the fringes of his hair. "What's your full name?" he asked in defeat.

Satisfaction rushed through Nathan, and he knew Alan felt happy. "My name is Alan Grant."

"How did you end up at the college?"

"I used to go to school there. Majored in business economics. Mom always said I had a head for business." Alan smiled and drifted away from Nathan, crossing his arms and staring down the alley behind the store. "I had Johns as a professor two years in a row. He can be a real son of a bitch. My fiancé always said Johns probably had a very unhappy life and took it out on others around him."

"Do you remember when you died?"

Alan shrugged. "I have a vague idea. I saw the date on someone's planner. The last thing I remember is preparing for finals, so it's been around a year, maybe two. I can't quite keep everything clear in my head."

Nathan had heard it before. The dead never realized how much time had passed or remembered everything clearly about their death. They also got overly sentimental too. "What's your fiancé's name?"

An affectionate smile softened Alan's features. "Erik. I couldn't believe how lucky I was the day I met him."

Nathan started in surprise. "Your fiancé is a guy?"

Alan frowned at him. "You got a problem with that?"

Nathan snorted and shook his head. "No. Just didn't expect it."

The name Erik reminded him of the sexy man from the day before who'd ordered the CD. Nathan ignored the spiral of attraction. Even if Erik returned his interest, there wasn't a chance in hell Nathan could entertain the idea of being involved with the guy. Erik would run screaming the other way if he found out about Nathan's ability to see and talk to ghosts, believing him to be batty, most likely. Wasn't he crazy, though? Who else could see, hear, and feel the dead?

"What else can you tell me about Erik?" Nathan asked wearily.

Alan floated closer to his side and Nathan raised his hand, palm out. "If I'm going to do this, you need to stay farther away from me."

"Oh," Alan said, drifting back a few feet.

Nathan gave a sigh of relief and looked at Alan to encourage him to continue.

"He lives on Harwood Street in a big yellow house. He's an architect and built the house for us." Alan gave a soft smile. "We had so many plans. Wanted to spend our lives together. We even talked about adopting a baby."

Sadness crashed over Nathan, and he had to struggle to remain upright. "Stop it," he snapped at the man.

Alan frowned at him. "What?"

"Stop thinking about him or your plans," Nathan said harshly, his chest tight with the pressure of Alan's emotions. "You're dead. That isn't going to change."

Shock widened Alan's eyes. "No need to be a jerk!"

Nathan growled. "If you want me to help you, it's on my

terms, buddy."

"I don't know why you have to be such an asshat about it," Alan muttered. "What's so bad about my remembering how he made me feel or what our plans were?"

Nathan didn't want to tell Alan the truth about his abilities. It made him weak and could give a ghost control over him if they were strong enough. The depth of Alan's affection for Erik still tied him to the physical plane, giving him more power over what he could and couldn't do. "Just stop it."

"Fine," Alan grunted. "Jackass."

"Do you know how you died?" Nathan continued abruptly, ignoring the slur.

Alan ran his hands through his hair in frustration. "No. I've been trying forever to remember how. I can't seem to get a hold of it. It's almost as if it's just out of my reach."

That wasn't the first time Nathan had heard the explanation. When spirits tried to recall the exact moment of their death, they usually hit a blank wall. Nathan figured it to be their psyche protecting them from reliving the horror of dying. "Do you think you were involved in an accident?"

"I don't know," Alan said, shrugging.

Nathan sighed. "I can do some research and see if I can find an obituary."

"Now?" Alan replied eagerly.

Shaking his head, Nathan said, "I have to work. I need this job."

Alan huffed with impatience but relented. "Fine."

Nathan stood and then looked at him again. "Don't hang around the store, okay? You'll just distract me."

"Anything else, Master?" Alan muttered with a roll of his eyes.

"Yeah, if you want me to help you, then lose the attitude."

Alan raised an eyebrow at him. "I think you're the one who had someone piss in his Cheerios this morning."

Nathan scowled, his hand on the doorknob. "I didn't ask for this. It's not exactly like I want to drop everything and help you, you know."

Alan conceded his point. "You're right. I'm sorry."

Pulling open the door, Nathan glanced back to find Alan gone. He already knew he would regret agreeing to help the guy. After all, every time he'd done it in the past, he'd ended up being the one to pay for it. He thrust those thoughts away and returned to work. Quinn kept giving him strange looks the rest of the night, and Nathan hoped he could repair the damage. He didn't need the guy he worked with questioning his sanity.

At the end of the night, Quinn helped him close and sat on the counter talking about the upcoming party while Nathan counted the register. Nathan tuned out the inane chatter and concentrated on keeping his mind focused on the task at hand. He'd spent the rest of the evening in a sour mood, biting his tongue more than once when a customer asked a stupid question or when they came in expecting to return their opened CDs for their cash. Once opened, they couldn't take the CDs back per store policy. Too many people would buy them, copy them, and then bring them back to get the album for free. Nathan had faced down more than one disgruntled customer in his time as manager. The busy night and constant flow of people in the store had helped keep his mind off Alan, mostly.

"Earth to Nate!" he heard.

Nathan blinked and glanced up to see Quinn shaking his head. "Huh?"

"Where'd you check out to, dude?"

"Oh. Sorry. Just tired. Long day."

Quinn jumped off the counter and leaned against the side, propping himself on his forearms. "I asked you what happened earlier today. You were kind of talking to yourself."

Nathan tensed as he slid the night's profits into the bank bag and yanked the drawer out of the register to put in the safe. He had to think of something to tell him. "I was kind of still pissed off at Professor Johns."

Quinn gave him a skeptical look but didn't challenge his excuse. "So, you're still coming Friday night, right?"

He shrugged. "Sure. I guess."

"Come, Nate. Have a little fun and let go. You're too serious for someone who is only twenty-two."

It wasn't the first time Nathan had been told the same thing. Even his aunts tried to push him to go out, live life, but until he graduated college and started paying his aunts back for everything they'd done for him, he wasn't really interested in partying. "Just got a lot of shit to deal with," Nathan replied flatly.

Quinn sighed and shoved away from the counter, glancing at the clock. "You good to make the night drop on your own, dude?"

"Of course," Nathan said. He'd made the night drop many times by himself. "Take off. I'll see you tomorrow."

"Tomorrow is my day off. Thomas is covering my shift."

"Right. Forgot. Then see you Friday."

Quinn picked up his backpack and tossed Nathan a wave on his way out the front door. Nathan returned the gesture and nudged the safe shut with his foot before closing the register. He read over the special orders to see if any of them had come in. The business card of the man from the day before caught his eye, and he sighed. He'd forgotten about the previous day's encounter. He idly traced the elegant structure on the front of the card. What he wouldn't give to be normal and able to pursue someone like Erik Moore. The thought was nothing but a pipe dream, really. He'd never be anything except a freak, and thinking of having an actual relationship would only make him depressed, so he pushed the man from his mind. He made a few notes for the day shift employees on who to call and closed the book, leaving it on the counter.

Nathan spun the dial on the safe, ensuring it was secure, and stuffed the deposit in his backpack. The terrifying spirit from the night before didn't appear again to his relief as he shut off the lights and armed the security system. Maybe he could get home tonight without seeing any at all. Of course, hoping for such a thing jinxed him. Alan materialized to his left while he was locking the door. Nathan sighed and turned to look at the spirit. "Look, I agreed to help you, so why can't you just leave me alone?"

"Did you do any research?" Alan asked eagerly, ignoring his question.

Nathan gritted his teeth but held on to his patience by a thin thread. "I can't use the internet for personal use while I'm at work."

Alan floated along at his side as Nathan slung his bag over his shoulder and headed toward the bank. The street wasn't empty since it was only ten at night, with cars driving by at a fast clip, but the only people on the sidewalk were homeless or prostitutes. Nathan had always felt safe in the area despite the somewhat undesirable reputation. No one ever bothered him, really.

"You don't have a car?" Alan asked.

"No. Can't afford one."

"Oh. You could get a bike," Alan replied.

Nathan stopped and took a deep breath. "Is there a reason you're following me?"

"You aren't working anymore." He gave the spirit a blank look. Alan rolled his eyes and huffed. "Which means you can research how I died. Duh."

Nathan growled and balled his hands into fists. "I didn't say I would do it tonight!"

Alan grinned. "I know, but I want to keep you on track so you don't forget about your promise."

Giving a frustrated cry, Nathan swung his bag at Alan, uncaring that it only went through him and didn't really do any harm. It just made him feel better.

"You okay, son?" A voice came from the shadows at the side of a nearby building.

Nathan jumped and glanced in the voice's direction. A homeless man lay against the building, a bottle of booze in a brown paper bag in one hand. "I'm fine," he snarled.

"And they call me crazy," the man muttered as Nathan started walking again.

He tensed but said nothing. He'd heard it all before: the whispers of others in the hospital when they caught him talking to thin air, the frightened looks and wide berth people gave him when they saw him having a conversation with no one.

He's crazy.

What a whack job!

So sad about what happened to his parents. It must have driven him insane.

Maybe it's brain damage.

Such a pity.

Every memory echoed in Nathan's mind, and he blinked back tears. For so long, he'd been fighting the rumors and trying to forget the accident. The only friend who hadn't abandoned him had been Troy. Everyone else had grown scared of him, calling him a freak or weirdo. Nathan hid the pain of it all behind the wall he'd built after his parents died. Sometimes the wall slipped, and the despair shone through.

"I'm sorry."

Nathan realized Alan kept pace with him and he swallowed hard, forcing the shield back into place. "Doesn't matter."

"It does matter," Alan insisted. "I really am sorry. If I wasn't desperate for your help, I would have gone away like you asked."

Nathan shook his head. "No, you wouldn't. It's just what your kind does."

Alan frowned. "My kind?"

"Spirits. Ghosts. Whatever you want to call yourself."

"Oh." Alan fell silent for a heartbeat and then asked, "How long have you been able to see them?"

"Too long," Nathan answered tersely.

Alan sighed. "I know you don't want to help me, but I really can't shake the feeling that my fiancé is in trouble and if I don't get a message to him, he could get hurt or worse."

Nathan didn't answer as he crossed the street to the bank, approaching the night drop box near the ATM. He unzipped his bag and took out the deposit. Alan appeared in front of him when he went to open the small door. Nathan jumped and scowled. "Dude, space. I told you to stay away."

"I know, but I think you need to turn around. Now."

Nathan spun on his heel and his heart skipped a beat when he saw a guy, lean and mean looking, standing a few feet away and holding a dangerously sharp knife. A tattoo of a snake wrapped itself around the man's wrist and ran along the skin, disappearing underneath the sleeve of his black t-shirt. Hard brown eyes were set deep in a gaunt face with a hooked nose, obviously broken at some point. Nathan noted the goatee, but he couldn't make out anything else about the man's features. He stood just out of the light cast from the ATM and streetlamp.

Damn it. He'd been so wrapped up in trying to ignore Alan, he'd forgotten to pay attention to his surroundings. The music store wasn't in the best neighborhood and there were always break-ins happening. So far, the store had been lucky. Now he hoped he would be just as lucky.

The guy sneered at him. "Who the hell you talkin' to, kid?"

"What do you want?" Nathan demanded, ignoring the stranger's question.

"I should think that's pretty obvious, kid." The guy smirked, gesturing with the knife at the bag in Nathan's hand.

No way in hell would he give him the store's deposit. Nathan shook his head. "I'm not giving you anything, mister."

The smirk died. "You lookin' to die tonight? Give me the fuckin' bag."

Alan startled Nathan by saying, "Do it, Nathan. It's not worth dying over."

"Shut up," Nathan snapped at Alan.

The thief assumed Nathan's words were directed at him and rushed toward him in a rage. Nathan knew he had no chance in hell at getting away with the limp he had, so he held his ground, bracing himself for impact.

What happened next shocked the hell out of him. Nathan found himself shoved out of the way. He landed on the sidewalk with a surprised grunt. What the hell? Nathan looked up just in time to see the thief slam into the ATM. Alan appeared near his left shoulder. "Get up, Nathan. Now."

Nathan scrambled to his feet, grabbed the deposit bag he'd dropped, and turned to run. Only, he didn't get very far. He was airborne once more when the thief tackled him from behind. Nathan cried out when his wrists protested their combined weight when they slammed into the cement. Several layers of skin on his palms scraped off as they skidded along the sidewalk and his chin crashed into the concrete, his teeth snapping together with a sickening crunch. The blow stunned him for a moment and then he shouted, "Get offa me."

The guy grabbed Nathan's hair and yanked his head back, pressing the knife to Nathan's throat. Is this how he would die? Wasn't it what he deserved? He didn't have the strength to throw the bastard off him or wrestle the sharp blade from the guy's hand. Instead, he closed his eyes and waited for the end. Maybe he could finally see his parents again.

"Hey! Leave him alone! The police are on their way!"

The weight holding Nathan down to the concrete disappeared instantly, and he opened his eyes to see the guy grab the deposit bag and take off running. Swearing, Nathan watched his job going down the tubes right along with him.

"You okay, young man?" A warm hand settled on his shoulder and Nathan moved to a sitting position to find an old woman, probably in her late sixties or seventies, hovering over him.

"I'm fine," Nathan replied quietly. He touched his throat, fingers grazing the slight cut left behind by the knife.

She clucked and examined his chin, pulling out a tissue from her sweater pocket and pressing it to the gash. "The police should be here any minute. This neighborhood has become such an awful place in the last few years. Why didn't you just give him the money? It wasn't worth dying for or being hurt over it."

Nathan gave her a wan smile and leaned back against the side of the building behind him. He winced when he clenched his hands and looked down to see scraped skin, bits of dirt and gravel embedded in the cuts. Blood seeped from the deeper ones. His bad leg throbbed, and he knew tomorrow he would be in agony. Despite everything the doctors had done, the bones hadn't healed right during his long stay in the hospital and rehab center.

The sound of sirens cut through the night air and Nathan sighed, knowing he wouldn't be going home for at least an hour.

CHAPTER 4

Two hours later, Nathan finally collapsed into his own bed. The officers who'd arrived at the bank had wanted to take him to the hospital, but he'd vehemently rejected going there. He hated hospitals. He'd insisted his injuries weren't severe enough to require a doctor. They'd taken his statement and offered to drive him home when they'd found out he had no one to pick him up. He'd put some antiseptic on the scrapes on his hands and on his chin, as well as on the cut on his throat. There wasn't anything he could do for the cuts on his palms, but he'd put a small bandage on his chin. The one on his throat wasn't significant enough for him to feel the need to cover it. Especially since it wasn't bleeding still.

Sighing, he carefully pulled the sheet over himself and settled into the pillows. When Troy found out Nathan hadn't called him, he'd lose his shit. Nathan winced as he remembered the very uncomfortable call to his boss, Stuart Starr. The man had been livid, threatening to fire him and blaming him for the money being stolen. After groveling for several long minutes, Stuart had begrudgingly let him keep his job and demanded he be at the store first thing in the morning. It meant Nathan would have to miss class, but he could easily borrow someone else's notes.

His mind wandered back to Alan. Tomorrow he would research who the man was before he died and what caused him to lose his life. He wouldn't be able to shake the ghost until he did. Tonight proved the faster he got rid of Alan, the better it would be for him. If Alan hadn't been trailing him, the thief never would have been able to catch him unawares. His leg twitched at the memory of the attack and Nathan grimaced, reaching down to rub at the offending limb. He'd be lucky if he could walk semi-normal in the morning.

It took another hour of tossing and turning for his mind to quiet enough to allow him to sleep. The last thought on Nathan's mind before he slipped into unconsciousness was of the sexy man who'd come into the shop looking for a classic rock CD.

"What the hell, Nate?" Troy shouted when Nathan exited his apartment the next morning, locking the door and then hobbling down the stairs slowly.

Nathan winced and rubbed at his temples. "Don't shout. My head is killing me."

Nightmares of his parents' accident and the spirits he'd encountered over the last six years had plagued him the entire five hours he'd remained in bed. One dream had left him shaken as he'd jackknifed from the mattress, sweating and trembling. He'd seen Erik Moore running in the opposite direction of him, horrified by Nathan's abilities to see and speak to ghosts. What disturbed Nathan the most was how he already cared what the man thought when he'd only exchanged a few words with him in the store the other day.

Nathan didn't know why he felt so afraid of Erik discovering what he could do.

"What the fuck happened?" Troy demanded, gripping Nathan's chin and tilting his face to examine the bruises and cuts.

Nathan jerked away, biting back a groan of regret at the abrupt movement. Pain medication for the days his leg acted up was nothing stronger than ibuprofen. The doctors refused to prescribe him anything else, as they considered him a suicide risk. Not only were his leg and head bothering him, but the impact on the sidewalk the previous evening had left several large bruises along his chest and stomach. "Someone mugged me on the way to make the night deposit."

Troy swore ferociously. "I knew you shouldn't go alone! Not at night! From now on, I'm coming to the store and going with you."

"No!" Nathan protested. "I'm fine, Troy. It's only some scratches."

Scowling, Troy touched Nathan's throat. "You call these scratches?"

Nathan frowned and reached up. His fingers grazed the small scab on his throat and he flinched. "It's nothing."

"Bullshit, Nate! Whether or not you like it, I'm going to be there every night. Got it?"

Nathan protested, but when he saw the determination in Troy's eyes, he snapped his jaw shut. When Troy's stubbornness came out, nothing could change his mind. "Fine," Nathan groused.

Troy pulled Nathan into a tight hug, causing him to grunt in pain. "You're like my brother, Nate. If anything ever happened to you, I don't know what I'd do."

Biting the inside of his bottom lip, Nathan returned the hug, closing his eyes at the warmth from his friend's hard form. "I really am okay," he murmured.

Troy leaned back. "I just worry about you, Nate."

He knew Troy cared about him and how he feared one day Nathan would decide he couldn't handle everything anymore and just end it. Over the course of two years following the accident, he'd seriously contemplated suicide more than once. First because of the blame he carried for his parents' accident and then because he'd realized when they'd resuscitated him during surgery he'd come back wrong. Something had attached itself to him and wouldn't let go. Troy had talked him down every time. Now Nathan knew it would be selfish to take his own life instead of living through the pain he carried inside of him. It was his penance for killing his parents.

"I promise I'm not going to do anything stupid."

Troy stepped away with a sigh. "Doesn't mean I can't be there at night to make sure it doesn't happen again."

Nathan shrugged and looked past Troy, resignation setting in when he saw Alan. "It never would have happened if Alan hadn't distracted me."

Alan's eyes widened at Nathan's words and sadness swooped over Nathan. He gritted his teeth and held on to his own emotions by a thread. He didn't care if his words hurt Alan. It was the spirit's fault, after all.

"The ghost, the one from the other day, he's been bothering you?" Troy asked.

Nathan snorted. "You know the second they find out I can see and hear them, they won't leave me alone until I do what they want. He followed me from the store to the bank. I didn't notice the bastard approach because of him."

"Alan? That's his name?"

Nodding, Nathan once more locked eyes with his newest challenge. "Yeah. I have to help him, or he'll never leave me be."

Alan frowned and floated closer. "I'm sorry, Nathan. I never intended for you to get hurt."

"Doesn't matter now, does it?" Nathan said.

Troy spun around, trying to see Alan. "He's here?"

"Yeah. He's here."

"You have a lot of nerve, ass wipe," Troy snapped.

Nathan watched Alan turn toward Troy. "You're lucky I can't slap you."

Nathan grinned for the first time since Quinn had left the store last night.

"What did he say?" Troy growled.

"He said it's nice to meet you," Nathan lied.

Alan huffed and shook his head while Troy eyed Nathan.

"Look, Troy. I'm skipping class today. Stuart just barely agreed to let me keep my job after losing the money last night, but he wants me there first thing this morning. Most likely to resume yelling at me."

"What?" Alan gasped. "It's not your fault!"

Troy rolled his eyes. "Stuart is a grade A prick. I don't know why you just don't find another job."

"Because I enjoy working in the music store, and the pay, despite Stuart's tendency to be a dick, is good. Besides, Stuart knows no one else can run the store as well as me."

"Then why does he have to be a jerk?"

"Genes." Nathan glanced at his watch. "Go to class, Troy. I'll be fine."

"Let me at least drive you to the store."

"No. The walk will help loosen the knot in my leg, and Stuart doesn't get in until ten, so I have some time to run into the library to do a little digging on my newest problem. Besides, you don't want to be late for class."

Alan winced at Nathan's words. Nathan didn't feel guilty at all for making Alan feel bad, even if just a little, for demanding his help. If it hadn't been for him, Nathan never would have gotten hurt or kicked out of class for a week.

Troy grunted. "Fine, just be careful."

"I'll be fine, Troy. Go. I'll see you tomorrow."

"I'm picking you up after work and taking you home," Troy insisted. "You better be there."

Nathan scowled and tried to protest again, but Troy ignored him and tossed him a wave as he climbed into his car. "Stubborn ass," Nathan muttered, watching Troy drive away.

"He really cares about you," Alan said, drifting closer.

Nathan glared at Alan. "I know."

"I didn't mean to cause you so much trouble."

Shrugging, Nathan started limping toward the public library. He needed to use the internet, which he didn't have in his place because he couldn't afford a laptop. All of his studying took place at the college or nearby library. "Let's just get this over with as quickly as possible. Hopefully, I can hold on to my job and get back to my life sooner rather than later."

The walk to the library took about thirty minutes, a little longer than normal because of his leg. Nathan breathed in deep when he stepped inside. He'd always loved the smell of books. Old or new, it didn't matter. The librarian glanced at him when he entered the building but went back to her task at hand, and Nathan headed toward the bank of computers. There were few people in the library so early in the morning in the middle of the week. He wouldn't have to fight to keep the computer for longer than the allotted fifteen minutes.

Nathan sat down at the computer farthest from the librarian and clicked on the icon for the internet. Google popped up and he stabbed at the keys, punching in the spirit's name, Alan Grant, along with the state. The first result showed a link to a newspaper story, and Nathan breathed a sigh of relief. Maybe he could have this figured out before he headed to work, and Alan would be out of his life by the end of the week.

The article had an image of a wrecked vehicle, twisted and mangled, as if it had gone through a crusher at the junkyard. Nathan grimaced at the obvious violence in the crash and swallowed hard as memories of his parents and the accident which had claimed their lives washed over him. His fingers tightened on the mouse while sweat beaded on his forehead. Why did he have to acknowledge Alan's presence?

"What did you find?" Alan asked, startling him.

Nathan jerked and in a tense whisper said, "You died in a car accident."

Alan leaned in closer to the monitor, and Nathan resumed reading. Late evening a little over two years ago, the car had gone over the edge of a ravine, killing the single occupant on impact. They later identified the body as Alan Grant, twenty-four, and the police deemed it an accident, no foul play suspected. There were no witnesses, but the tire tracks left behind by the speeding vehicle suggested Alan had taken the curve in the road too fast and lost control of the car.

"That's bullshit," Alan burst out.

"You remember nothing at all?" Nathan said under his breath.

Alan sneered. "I've never been a reckless driver. There must be more to it than that. Is there anything else?"

Nathan clicked back and searched for another article. He found an obituary which listed roughly the same details and how Alan left behind his mother, father, younger sister, and his fiancé. The name of Alan's fiancé caused Nathan's blood to freeze in his veins and his breath caught. This couldn't be happening. No fucking way! Nathan wanted to stand and run out of the library. He wanted to refuse to help Alan. The man Alan would have married was none other than the man who'd come into the music store the other day. Erik Moore. Nathan struggled to get hold of himself.

"You were engaged to Erik Moore?" Nathan finally growled between gritted teeth.

"Yes. Why?"

Nathan closed the internet and stood. He stalked out of the library and down the sidewalk, stopping in a nearby alley to catch his breath. Alan followed him the entire way, demanding to know why Nathan had left. Nathan leaned his back against the building and bent slightly at the waist, his hands on his knees. Fate undeniably had it out for him. It didn't lack for irony or straight up aiming for his balls. How the hell could this possibly be happening?

"Nathan!" Alan said sharply.

"I've met your fiancé," Nathan replied, tone bitter.

Alan brightened. "Really? When? Where?"

"At my store a couple of days ago." He wanted to rage at the heavens, or maybe it would be more appropriate to rage at whatever hell lay beneath his feet. Had the devil gotten his claws into him when he'd died six years ago? Was the beast playing him as if he were a puppet for his amusement? Nathan finally collapsed down to the cement, bringing his knees to his chest and wrapping his arms around them.

Alan frowned, floating closer. "Why are you so upset? Did something bad happen when you met him?"

Nathan shook his head. "He came into the store to find a Pink Floyd CD. Someone stole his from his truck."

A sharp intake of breath caused Nathan to look at Alan in time to see pain cross his face, and Nathan closed his eyes, struggling to keep Alan's powerful emotions out. "Alan!" he said sharply.

Alan grunted and moved away from him. Nathan sighed in relief when the piercing fire pressing down on him abated. He opened his eyes to see Alan close to the opening of the alley. "What is the significance of that CD, Alan?" Nathan asked, not really wanting to know the answer but realizing mentioning the band had triggered Alan's emotional reaction.

Melancholy replaced the pain, and Alan hugged himself. "Our song was on it," Alan said, his voice hollow. "We planned it to be the song we walked into the reception with."

Nathan ignored the loss he felt. He couldn't differentiate if the feeling was his own or Alan's anyway. "I see."

"We met three years ago. Now it would be five years, wouldn't it? I was in my second year of college and—"

"You don't have to tell me," Nathan said, cutting him off.

Alan gave him a sad smile. "I want to. I need to."

Nathan bit back his irritation and nodded, turning his head to stare out into the street at the passing cars. "Fine."

"I've always been outgoing, unafraid of talking to strangers, and never even stopped to think when I saw him. He was beautiful. Big broad shoulders, tanned skin, and dark hair so thick my fingers just itched to run through it. I got the impression he wasn't much for malls with how uncomfortable he looked walking through the lady's clothing department. At first, I thought I was out of luck and he had a girlfriend, but it turned out he'd gone to the mall to look for a birthday present for his friend's wife."

Nathan heard Alan's tone soften as he spoke of Erik. "He looked so adorably out of place, and I took pity on him. We hit it off so fast my head spun. We made a date for the next night. When Erik proposed, I didn't even hesitate to think about it. We started making plans for the perfect wedding immediately. Everything was going to be flawless."

Swallowing, Nathan dug his fingers into his baggy jeans, wrapping the fabric around them to stem his disillusionment. Yet he found himself baffled at just how upset he truly was. He'd already convinced himself the man hadn't been checking him out like Quinn had said or how he himself would never be ready for any relationship. Even if it was only physical. The scars on his body from the accident would turn off anyone the moment they saw them. Nathan swallowed again, trying to force the lump in his throat to dissipate.

"Do you remember anything about the accident?" Nathan finally brought himself to ask.

Alan gave a frustrated shake of his head. "No. It never even occurred to me I died in a car accident, but I know I never would have been driving recklessly. Especially so close to the wedding. Something isn't right."

"Well, until you can remember, there really isn't anything I can do," Nathan said and stood. "I have to get to work before my boss fires me. Try to remember. Think. Go over everything as far back as you can and then do it again. Maybe something will trigger a memory. You also need to go to familiar places. Your place… Er—your fiancé's place."

"We lived together the last year before we were to be married," Alan replied distractedly.

Nathan ignored his stomach cramping at those words. Damn! Why the hell did it bother him so much? He couldn't understand how he'd gotten so attached to a man he'd met once and for only fifteen minutes.

Maybe he needed to go back on the antipsychotic the psychiatrist had prescribed him. The little bottle of olanzapine sat almost full in his medicine chest back at his apartment. He'd taken them for a very short amount of time and had hated the way they'd made him feel. They'd stuffed his head with cotton and his veins with heroin, or at least it seemed as if the pills had the same effect on him that heroin would. After almost walking into the street without realizing a car was coming, he'd promptly stopped taking them.

"Then visit the place you were living together," Nathan said and started walking.

Alan didn't seem to take the hint and remained at his side. "Jesus, would you just fucking leave me alone for a while?" Nathan snapped. "I need time to myself, ya know!"

Several people around him stopped and stared at him, fear and discomfort clear on their faces. Nathan growled under his breath. "Fuck."

Alan winced. "Sorry. I… I can't get there on my own."

"What?" Nathan whispered. "What do you mean?"

"I can't. I've tried already, but I just hit an invisible wall or something."

"For fuck's sake," Nathan ground out. He started walking as fast as his bad leg would allow. "So now I have to get you there? How am I supposed to do that?"

"Well, I can follow you."

Nathan halted mid-stride and gave Alan a harsh look. "Seriously, dude? You expect me to just go up to this guy's house and what? Walk in? Find a way for him to invite me in? How would you suggest I do that?"

"I don't know," Alan replied. "I'm sure you can think of something."

Whispers reached Nathan's ears, and he realized he'd once again been talking to Alan as if everyone could see him. People were crossing the street just to get away from him, and Nathan bit back the hurt. He buried the pain beneath disdain and sneered at some strangers, who startled and scurried away. Assholes.

Nathan resumed his trek toward the music store, this time ignoring Alan stalking him. He needed some time to think. "Just go away. I have to work and can't do that if you're there. Just… come back later."

"Okay, okay. I'm sorry." Alan put his hands up in a defensive gesture. "I'll come back when the store is closed."

Nathan tried to protest, but Alan disappeared before he could. The rest of the way to the store, Nathan brooded over the situation he once again found himself in. How the hell was he supposed to get into Erik Moore's house? Maybe he didn't need to get in there. Maybe he could just locate it and take Alan there. He could wait outside while Alan went in. Right?

CHAPTER 5

By the time the store closed, Nathan's headache had intensified, and his eyes ached from struggling to keep them open against the lights. The moment everyone else left the store and he'd turned over the Closed sign, Nathan shut off the overhead lights and sighed in relief. He leaned on the front counter and buried his head in his arms. He wished he could go back the last few days and erase ever having acknowledged Alan. If he'd just held on to his patience with Professor Jackass, he would have never let Alan get to him.

"You okay?" Alan asked.

Nathan tensed. "Just leave me alone."

"I'm sorry, Nathan. Really. I wish I could do this on my own, but I need your help."

Nathan lifted his head just enough to glare at the offending spirit. "Until you remember what the hell you need to tell your fiancé, there's nothing I can do."

A knock at the front door stopped whatever Alan would have said, and Nathan glanced out of the glass to see Troy standing there, waiting. Nathan breathed in and then out in a swift whoosh. He stumbled over to the door, unlocked it, and let Troy in, closing and locking it behind his friend.

"Jesus, Nate. You look like shit."

"Thanks," Nathan replied sarcastically.

"Did Stuart give you more grief?"

Nathan snorted. "When doesn't he? I just have a headache, Troy. I'm fine. It's been a long day."

"Well, close the register, prep the night deposit, and let's go. We'll drop the money and go grab some food."

The mention of food reminded Nathan he hadn't eaten all day and his stomach growled loudly. Troy gave him an exasperated look. "No wonder you have a headache, dumbass. You forgot to eat again, didn't you?"

Nathan shrugged. "Yeah. So?"

Troy shook his head. "If you didn't have a headache, I'd slap you on the back of the head. You need to take better care of yourself. You're already underweight."

"I wasn't hungry, Troy."

"If you don't start taking the time to eat, Nate, I'm going to make it my life's mission to shove food down your throat every chance I get," Troy threatened, guiding Nathan to the register with a gentle hand on his lower back.

Nathan rolled his eyes while rubbing at his temples. "It's just been a rough couple of days."

"Is *he* still here?" Troy glanced around the store with narrowed eyes as if he could see Alan.

"He's sitting on the counter," Nathan replied drolly and popped open the register to balance the drawer.

"I may not see you"—Troy gazed in the general direction Alan sat—"but if you don't stop stressing him out, I'm going to make you regret not crossing over sooner, got it?"

Alan snorted. "Does he realize how ridiculous he sounds?"

Nathan sighed and made a notation on the log. "As if it's

not bad enough that I have to listen to the two of you, now you expect me to play mediator? I don't think so. Now shut up and let me finish this so we can get the hell out of here sometime tonight."

Troy huffed and crossed his arms, leaning on the counter in front of Nathan. He kept glaring towards Alan. Nathan ignored them both while counting the money twice to make sure he had the total right before placing the cash in the deposit bag and prepping the drawer for the morning. Once he'd finished everything, he snatched up the night deposit and his keys. "Let's go."

After they stopped by the bank to make the drop, Troy headed toward their favorite diner for a quick bite to eat. During the meal, Alan disappeared, leaving Nathan to enjoy his burger and fries in peace. Nathan knew the moment the spirit faded away when the feelings of loss, melancholy, and confusion lifted from his chest. Sometimes he wondered how he could even still breathe under the weight of Alan's emotions. The man must have been extremely passionate when he'd been alive. Nothing else could explain how deeply Nathan found himself affected by Alan's feelings. He'd never been so… connected to the others he'd met or come across in the last six years. For some frustrating reason, Alan was different. Even if Nathan hadn't acknowledged Alan's presence at the college, he somehow sensed he wouldn't have been able to ignore him for long.

Nathan could barely keep his head off the table once he'd eaten. One of his rare moments of pure exhaustion overtook him. He usually slept three or four hours a night before the nightmares would begin, and he couldn't go back to sleep once he'd awakened. Sometimes the dreams were about the accident, other times they were of the spirits he'd encountered and the gruesomeness of their situations. Yet there were more he wasn't sure why he dreamed of them—images of faceless people standing in a line, begging for his help. Maybe they were a byproduct of his constant denial of helping the spirits he'd seen over the years. Tonight… Tonight he would sleep like the dead.

Troy helped Nathan to his feet once he'd paid their bill, and Nathan leaned heavily on him, yawning. "Sorry, bro," he murmured.

"It's fine, Nate," Troy said as he pushed the front door open with his free hand, directing Nathan through. Nathan was too tired to address the concern in Troy's voice and merely allowed his friend to do everything for him. He settled into the front seat after Troy opened the passenger door.

Nathan had almost dropped completely out of consciousness by the time Troy slid behind the wheel next to him. Just before nodding off, Nathan whispered, "Love you, bro."

The next thing Nathan knew, the ground moved, and he realized Troy had him cradled in his arms. "You don't have to carry me," Nathan mumbled.

"Just go back to sleep," Troy instructed, maneuvering the steps carefully.

Nathan sighed and snuggled in closer to his best friend's chest, closing his eyes again. He drifted, barely cognizant of Troy setting him on his bed and then covering him with a blanket. He stirred a fraction when he heard Troy give a heavy breath and then a hand brushed the hair back from his forehead.

"Good night, Nathan."

Giving an unintelligible mumble, Nathan rolled to his side and burrowed deeper into the mattress, his face stuffed into his pillow.

The daylight filtering through the windows woke him the next morning, and Nathan jerked upright in bed. Sunlight? He glanced at the clock and swore when he saw the time. He had exactly ten minutes to throw on some clothes and get the hell out of there before he'd be late to his morning class. Throwing back the blanket, Nathan scurried to his miniature closet while removing his clothes from the day before. He tugged on a random t-shirt and rushed over to the dresser to grab a pair of jeans. He hopped on his one good leg out to the living room while pulling on his jeans. His book bag sat near the couch, obviously dropped there last night. He tried to remember the previous evening and how he'd ended up back in his apartment. A flash of Troy carrying him came to mind, and he groaned. Damn it. He'd passed out and Troy had taken care of him. Again.

Stuffing his feet into a pair of sneakers by the front door, Nathan ran a hand through his hair and rushed out of the apartment, snagging his keys off the counter on the way. He locked the door and took the stairs down to the sidewalk. Troy sat on the hood of his car, earbuds in and shades on.

Nathan gave Troy a chagrined look. "Sorry about last night, Troy."

Troy waved his hand, smiling. "You were tired."

Nathan grunted and got into the car as his friend jumped off the hood and walked around to the driver's seat.

The morning passed rather quickly. Nathan still had a few days to go before he could return to Professor Johns' class. He spent some time in the library doing the required reading for his English class and then left to catch the bus to the store. Unfortunately, he ended up on the bus he'd ridden the other day.

Once again, the lady covered in blood, pleading for her baby, appeared in the same seat as before. Nathan jammed his earbuds in and brought one leg up to his chest, wrapping his arms around his knee while attempting to ignore her again. His stomach churned with the sorrow radiating from the spirit, and it was all he could do to hold out for the thirty minutes it took to get from the college to the stop near the store. He heaved a sigh of relief the moment he stepped off the bus and breathed in deep, eradicating the scent of dead, decaying flesh from his nose.

In the years since the accident, Nathan had grown to recognize the different smells some ghosts gave off. Dead, decaying flesh usually meant whatever object they were bound to was an instrument in their death. Soft perfumes or gentle musty smells showed the time period they'd died in. One scent scared him more than the others did—earth and dampness. The spirits surrounded by the odor of dirt were the bodies freshly buried. The recently deceased were more confused, more violent, and while they had never truly harmed Nathan, they still frightened him more than the others.

"Nate!" Quinn's voice interrupted his thoughts as Nathan entered the store.

Nathan saw Quinn giving him a wide grin and holding something in his hand. He gave Quinn a quizzical look and walked to the counter. "What's up, Quinn?"

Quinn winked and handed him the object, a compact disc. "The CD for your hottie from the other day just came in."

Nathan's breath hitched, and he quickly cleared his throat, ignoring the heat he felt in his cheeks. *Damn it*, he growled to himself as Quinn chuckled at his discomfort. "Cut it out, Quinn."

"Aww, I'm just having a bit of fun. It's nice to see you actually interested in someone for a change."

"I'm not interested in him," Nathan said.

"Pfft. Could have fooled me," Quinn said. "I saw the way you salivated over him."

"Quinn!" Nathan glanced at the two women near the front of the store. They were looking his way, giggling and smiling. Nathan flushed even deeper and turned back to his friend and co-worker. "I was not… salivating over him."

"Whatever you say, Nate. But I got the store covered for another couple of hours if you want to hand deliver the CD personally," Quinn hinted.

Giving Quinn an incredulous look, Nathan shook his head. "Stop. I am not delivering it to him. I'll call him and let him know it's in. That's it."

"Sure," Quinn said smugly.

Nathan growled, stalked to the storage room, and tossed his bag down near the time clock, where he punched in. Damn Quinn. Why did he have to make such a big deal out of this? It was impossible for anything to develop between him and Erik Moore. Especially now with Alan in the picture. Snarling, Nathan went back to the front desk and pulled out the special-order book for Erik's number.

Quinn pointed at the bruises and cuts from the attack the other night. "Man, I heard about what happened. He really did a number on you, didn't he? I should have asked this first, but are you okay, Nate?"

"I'm fine. It's not a big deal. Just some bruises and stuff."

Reaching out, Quinn tilted Nathan's head up and to the right a bit. He cursed softly and ran his thumb over the small slice on Nathan's throat. Nathan jerked back in surprise, his eyes widening a bit.

"Sorry, did I hurt you?" Quinn asked with a frown.

"No. I just need to make this call," Nathan said, brushing off the awkwardness of the situation. He turned back to the order book and grabbed the receiver.

Quinn began smirking at him as Nathan punched in the numbers. "Would you go find something to stock?" Nathan muttered at him.

Quinn raised his hands in a defensive gesture before grabbing the returns cart to restock. While Nathan listened to the ringing on the other end, Quinn kept looking back at him and smiling. "Erik Moore" came over the line, startling Nathan.

He didn't speak for a second and the deep voice on the other end queried, "Hello?"

A shiver trickled down Nathan's spine and he coughed to give himself a second to gather his wits. The cough garnered a choked laugh from Quinn, to which Nathan threw him a glare. "Oh, um… Mr. Moore, this is uh… True Music calling. The CD you ordered is in."

"Oh, perfect! Would you be able to deliver it? I'm afraid I have meetings most of the day today. I have another meeting at five this afternoon."

Nathan glanced at the clock. It was already three p.m. "Sir, we don't really offer delivery."

"What if I paid you a delivery fee?"

Frowning, Nathan scratched his chin, wincing when his stubby fingernails caught the scab from the mugging. "I'm sorry, sir, but I really can't."

Erik sighed softly. "I understand. How late are you open tonight?"

"We close at ten, sir."

"Erik."

Nathan started. "Sorry?"

"I thought I told you to call me Erik," the man teased, a strange note of something unidentifiable buried in his voice.

For a moment, Nathan grappled for words, uncertain how to respond to the fluttery feeling in his lower belly. If he were naïve, he'd almost believe that a man as beautiful and mature as Erik Moore was flirting with him. "Did I lose you?" Erik asked in a soft voice.

"No, I'm still here, si—Erik."

He saw Quinn's head whip around and his eyebrows go up as a grin spread over his lips. Nathan's face grew hot, and he knew he was blushing. Picking up a paperclip from the counter, he tossed it at Quinn, who deftly caught it in one hand. "I'll see you at nine fifty-five this evening then," Erik said smoothly and disconnected the call before Nathan could respond.

Nathan moved the phone away far enough to stare at it, dazed and completely confused. Quinn ambled over to the counter and leaned over to pluck the phone from his hand and put it back in the cradle. "You all hot and bothered just from his voice?"

Scowling, Nathan snapped out of his bemusement and slapped the special-order book closed. "No."

"Uh huh," Quinn said knowingly and sauntered back to the returns cart.

The rest of the afternoon went by too fast for Nathan's taste. He tried to will the clock to slow down as his stomach twisted and turned itself into knots, knowing he would see the man who'd dominated quite a few of his thoughts since he'd come into the store. The same man his recent spiritual attachment had been engaged to and was off limits!

Quinn reminded him of the party at Alpha Sigma's house before leaving at the end of his shift.

"I'll try to be there, Quinn. I can't promise I will, though," Nathan said.

"Just for a couple hours, okay, Nate? I think it would do you some good to relax and unwind," Quinn cajoled.

"I'll try."

Quinn sighed and nodded, hefting his backpack higher onto his shoulder. "Hopefully, I'll see you at the party, Nate. If not, have a good evening and be more careful when you drop off the night deposit."

Nathan waved him away, and Quinn left, leaving Nathan to his thoughts. Alan appeared a few minutes later, perching on the counter near him. "Are you on your own tonight?"

Nodding, Nathan reorganized the front counter display for the fourth time in an hour. His fingers twitched nervously as he tried to ignore the anxiety racing through him. The idea of closing early just to avoid seeing Erik again crossed his mind more than once, but Stuart would kill him. He resigned himself to the forthcoming meeting. "Your fiancé is coming in tonight," he muttered.

"Really? Fantastic! You can tell him I'm here!"

"Uh, no, I can't," Nathan protested. "He's going to think I'm nuts!"

"But you can prove it to him, right? You can tell him something only he and I would know."

"No, I'm not doing that. Look, I said I'd help you, but I'll do it on my own terms. When he gets here, just make your-self scarce, okay? I can't concentrate with you dancing around and talking at the same time."

Alan hopped off the counter, shaking his head. "No. I want to see him. I miss him."

"And that's exactly why you can't be there," he replied.

Alan frowned at him quizzically. "Why?"

Nathan sighed and rubbed his temples, his head throb-bing again. If he told Alan how he could sense the other man's emotions, Alan could use it against him later if he were smart enough. Another spirit a few years back had figured out how his emotions affected Nathan and had used that to his advantage. Troy didn't know that one time a spirit had caused Nathan's thoughts of suicide, and he intended to keep that bit of knowledge to himself. He didn't think Alan would do anything similar, but he couldn't really be sure. Ghosts weren't exactly rational beings.

"I-I can sense what you're feeling," he murmured anyway.

"What?"

"I said I can tell what you're feeling. I can sense it. If your feelings are powerful enough, they can affect my own."

"Seriously?" Alan asked incredulously. "That's why you want me to stay away from you, isn't it?"

Nathan nodded and glanced around the store. A guy and his girlfriend were digging through the clearance bin near the far wall while a couple of teenagers messed with the headphones for the sample music selections. Those people didn't know just how lucky they were, how ordinary their lives were. He'd give anything to be wandering through a music store with Troy or perhaps even a boyfriend. Instead, he stood at the checkout counter talking to a ghost no one else could see. "Yes. If you're here, it'll make it harder for me. I need you to go before he gets here tonight."

Alan protested again, but Nathan gave him a harsh look. "You want me to help you, don't you? Then you need to help me."

With an audible snap, Alan closed his mouth and gave a jerky nod. "Fine. I don't have to like it, but I'll do it."

"Good. He's supposed to be here right before the store closes."

"Fine. Can I at least hang around until then?"

Nathan wanted to scream no, but at least if Alan was around, it would distract him from the thoughts tying his stomach into knots. "I guess."

Alan smiled and hopped back onto the counter. Nathan tried to ignore the spirit while others were in the store, only truly acknowledging Alan's presence when the place was empty. He did some inventory of a few of the CD and vinyl racks and made a notation of which ones needed to be ordered, along with the new releases coming out on Tuesday. True Music carried everything from CDs to vintage vinyl to instruments and sheet music. Despite the rise of digital music, the store did pretty good business with the musical instruments and retro albums they carried. Nathan's first guitar, a blue and white Fender Strat, had come from True

Music while his parents were still alive. He'd done every chore imaginable for his parents, mowed the neighbors' lawns, and cleaned more gutters than he'd ever wanted to, just to save up for the guitar.

The clock seemed to mock him as each second went by at lightning speed. Before Nathan felt ready, the hands ticked to nine thirty, a mere twenty-five minutes until Erik Moore would step through the front door. Nathan breathed deep and balled his hands into fists. He berated himself for being so damn nervous. Why was he acting like a girl on her first date, for crying out loud? He glanced at Alan, who stood looking over the various instruments on one wall. "Time to go," Nathan said.

Sadness trickled over Nathan, and he pushed out the emotion. He couldn't let Alan's emotions control him. "You'll have your chance to see him another time," he said flatly.

A sigh lifted Alan's shoulders, and he turned to give Nathan a pleading look. Nathan ground his teeth together. "You're not staying. Go. Now."

"All right, all right," Alan said, rolling his eyes. "I'm going. At least tell me how he looks later."

Nathan gave Alan a pointed look and gestured toward the storage room. He watched as Alan stepped through the wall and out of sight. He heaved a relieved breath and started straightening a rack that had been left disheveled. If Nathan could admit it to himself, he looked forward to seeing Erik again. When he'd realized Erik had been the fiancé Alan mentioned, a ball of acid had settled into his lower belly and bitterness had welled up inside of him. Even if by some miracle Erik was interested in him, he couldn't, in good conscience, ever let anything develop. He wasn't sure why he even allowed these types of thoughts to dominate his mind.

The sound of the door opening brought him to his senses, and without looking, he said, "Welcome to True Music."

"Hi."

At the sound of the delicious, deep voice haunting him at every turn, he spun around and found Erik standing just inside the door. Nathan's involuntary intake of breath sounded loud in the silence of the empty store. Erik stood there clad in well-worn stonewashed blue jeans, which hugged every single inch of his long, muscular legs in loving detail, with a deep aqua T-shirt almost a size or two too small for his well-defined chest. Black work boots encased his feet. Nathan swallowed hard. Holy shit, the man was sex incarnate! If it wasn't for holding on to the bin he'd been reorganizing, his own legs may well have given out and he'd be nothing except a puddle on the floor. Sharp desire pooled in his groin and Nathan pinched himself, hoping it would cool the beginnings of a hard-on.

"Hi," Erik repeated easily, a smile on his firm, full lips.

He tried to return the grin but knew it fell flat. "Hi."

Erik walked closer to him, only to pause a couple of feet away, his eyes widening. Nathan tipped his head in question. "Something wrong?" he asked.

"What happened to you?" Erik demanded.

Nathan furrowed his brow for a moment, confused, and then remembered his cuts and bruises. "Oh. Uh… someone mugged me," he stated simply.

Erik strode forward, surprising Nathan by gently gripping his chin and tilting his head up to examine the cuts on his chin and throat. A bruise had formed where the knife had pressed against his skin. Erik slid his thumb over the tiny red slice in an almost soothing gesture. Nathan didn't know how to react to this man, a relative stranger—albeit a sexy one—touching him as if he were his lover. He blinked at Erik as he watched several emotions flit across his tanned, rugged features: anger followed by an almost tender look leading into the same one he'd seen on Troy's face more than once when he'd caught sight of some new girl he wanted.

Nathan couldn't stop the small sound he made, causing Erik to drop his hand, leaving him feeling somewhat bereft at the loss. Nathan stepped back and turned his head. "It's nothing. I'm fine."

"What happened?"

"It's really nothing. I got careless and didn't pay attention. Your CD is over on the front desk, sir, if you'd like to follow me." He convinced himself he was only seeing things and deliberately called Erik sir to put the wall back in place between them. Only, Erik seemed to have other ideas.

Erik wrapped his hand around Nathan's wrist, preventing him from walking away. Nathan glanced down at the tan fingers against his pale skin and then at Erik. "Let go." His mind flashed back to the times his wrists had been bound in the mental institution. They'd secured him to the hospital bed on more than one occasion.

Even though Erik wasn't gripping him tightly, Nathan felt handcuffed and unable to move. "Please let go," he begged, his breathing growing shallow.

Frowning, Erik dropped his wrist. "I'm sorry. I didn't intend to scare you."

Nathan put several more feet between them, eyeing Erik. "What exactly is your intention?"

Erik ran a hand through his hair in apparent frustration. "I don't know. Ever since we met the other day, I've felt as if we had a connection. Something I can't explain. I know that makes me sound like a crazy person, but I can't shake the feeling I *need* to get to know you."

Biting his tongue, Nathan wondered if maybe Erik could sense his tie to Alan. He didn't respond, simply walked to the register. He didn't know how to approach the situation. Normally, he would have done as Alan suggested and made the spirit's loved ones know they were there. Usually, it took a lot to convince them, and in the meantime, they thought him nuts. He'd never cared before, but the idea of Erik looking at him as though he'd lost his mind set the same ball of acid from earlier roiling in his stomach.

The man in question approached the desk slowly. "I'm sorry."

"It's fine," Nathan said quietly. God, he felt like such a dork. He was twenty-two with the experience of a second grader when it came to relationships.

"No, it's not. Please give me a chance to make it up to you?"

Nathan raised his brow at Erik.

"Let me buy you a cup of coffee or something. Please?"

"You don't have to do that," Nathan said. The album reminded him exactly why Erik was there and what Nathan needed to do. Coffee would be the perfect time to do it, right?

"I want to. Besides, I really would like to get to know you."

Nathan stilled. "Why?"

Erik smiled, the same smile which sent strings of lust straight to Nathan's groin. "Would it hurt my chances if I said it's because I think you're adorable?"

"Adorable?" Nathan squawked. "I'm a guy!"

Chuckling, Erik winked. "I know. Guys can be adorable, too."

Nathan fought the burning he could feel edging into his cheeks.

"One drink. Please? If you still hate me after that, I'll leave you alone."

"I don't hate you," Nathan protested. "I just don't—" He cut himself off.

"Don't what?" Erik prodded, leaning a little over the counter.

Nathan's hands shook as he put the CD into a bag. He tried to hide it, but he was pretty sure Erik couldn't have missed it.

"I don't bite," Erik said. "Just one small cup of coffee. My treat."

"I have to close up," Nathan replied weakly.

Erik placed his credit card on the counter and shrugged. "I can wait."

Nathan knew he would regret it, but his willpower broke. "Okay," he whispered.

A broad grin spread over Erik's face. "Excellent! There's a great diner a few blocks from here. I go there all the time for lunch."

"CJ's?"

"Yep. You know it?"

Nathan could have laughed as he swiped the credit card. CJ's Diner was the same one he frequented with Troy. How could he have never noticed Erik there before? It was probably because he and Troy were mostly there late at night. "Yeah. I'm a regular with a friend of mine."

"Huh. Surprised we haven't run into each other before now then." Erik signed the receipt and took the bag. "What time are you usually out of here?"

"Have to close out the register and make sure anything necessary is ready for tomorrow."

"Mind if I hang out while you do that?"

Despite the voice demanding he tell Erik no, Nathan agreed and hurried through his usual tasks of balancing the till and writing any notes for the morning shift. Erik spoke little, just watched him work, which made him feel nervous. Nathan couldn't quite calm his nerves. Excitement tinged with fear caused him to tremble slightly as he closed the deposit bag and placed it in the safe.

Once the register was closed out and everything straightened behind the counter, Nathan looked at the man who'd patiently waited. "I just have to grab my bag from the back, and we can go."

"Great," Erik said smoothly, smiling.

Nathan swallowed hard and went into the stockroom to get his backpack and punch out. Alan waited near the rear door with an eager expression. "Did you tell him?"

"No," Nathan whispered, glancing back toward the store. "I told you to leave."

"He's still out there?" Alan demanded.

"Yes. We're ah… going to get some coffee and talk."

"So, you're going to tell him, right?"

"I don't know if it's the right time yet," Nathan hedged, placing his backpack on his shoulders.

Alan sighed in disappointment, unaware of Nathan's intense attraction to his fiancé. Nathan felt a pinprick of guilt inside. He wondered if Alan would get mad if he knew Nathan wanted the man he would have married if not for his accident. "At least tell me if he misses me," Alan said sadly.

Nathan gritted his teeth at the almost overwhelming emotion from Alan. His eyes moistened, and it took effort not to let the tears fall. "Stop it," he snarled breathlessly. "Remember what I told you."

"Shit, I'm sorry, Nathan."

The sadness faded and Nathan let relief slide through him. "I've got to go before he comes looking for me."

He turned and walked to the stockroom door. His hand was on the knob when he heard Alan say, "Nathan?" Looking over his shoulder, he saw Alan had already begun to dissipate. "Thank you."

Nathan forced a small smile and gave a nod of his head.

He wrenched open the door and rushed out, almost barreling into Erik. "Ah, sorry."

"Was just coming to make sure everything was okay," Erik said.

"It's fine. I was just straightening some CDs someone knocked over. OCD," Nathan replied weakly.

"Ah. I thought you may have changed your mind."

"No!" Nathan could have groaned at how distressed his tone sounded. "I mean I ah… wouldn't back out on a promise I made."

Erik grinned, eyes twinkling. "I'm glad to hear it. Shall we go?"

Nathan nodded and preceded Erik out of the store, waiting until the man exited before closing and then locking the front door. God, he was such a dork! He slapped the sticky note he'd written for Troy on the front window to let him know that he had gone to grab something to eat and to go to Quinn's party without him.

CHAPTER 6

"Do you want to walk, or we can take my truck?" Erik gestured toward a nice dark blue F150 Ford pickup truck sitting at the curb.

Nathan imagined being enclosed in the very intimate cab and surrounded by the earthy smell of Erik's cologne. "I, um… think we can walk. It's a nice enough night."

Erik shrugged. "Okay."

They started toward CJ's Diner in companionable silence, one Erik didn't leave for long. "So, how long have you worked at the music store?"

"About three years now."

"You like music?"

Nathan nodded. "I love it. It's helped me through some rough patches in my life."

"Any specific genre or are your tastes eclectic?"

Nathan stopped at the corner, watching the cars go by and wishing the walk sign would appear faster. He felt very exposed now, though he couldn't have explained why for the life of him. Maybe because of the limp in his gait. He knew Erik had shortened his own strides to match his and wondered if he should have just taken the two-minute ride in the truck.

"I prefer soft rock, but I listen to everything. What kind of musician would I be if I didn't?"

"So, you play then?" Erik asked.

"Guitar, drums, and piano. Although I prefer guitar." The little white man appeared on the crosswalk sign and Nathan went to step off the curb, only to be jerked backwards into Erik's chest abruptly. A car swerved a bit and took the corner at a fast clip, narrowly missing Nathan. He trembled at the reminder of the accident which had claimed his parents' lives and scarred his own.

"Are you all right?" Erik questioned, his deep voice rumbling in his chest beneath Nathan's ear.

"I'm fine."

"Crazy idiot. He could have seriously hurt you, or worse."

Nathan peered from beneath his lashes at Erik, watching him glare toward the already long-gone vehicle. It wasn't until Erik looked down at him that he realized Erik still held him against his very muscular chest. Nathan blushed and jerked away, stumbling a bit from his bad leg. Erik caught his arm to steady him. "Thanks," Nathan mumbled.

"No problem," Erik replied.

They crossed the street and continued to the diner in silence. Nathan felt awkward. This was one of the main reasons he avoided people. He didn't know how to act around them. *Especially super hot ones,* the voice inside his head taunted. *Shut up,* Nathan growled.

There were only a handful of people in the all-night diner when they entered, and Nathan made a beeline for his and Troy's favorite booth. Erik followed at a slower pace. A sigh almost slipped free when Nathan removed his bag and slid across the cracked vinyl into the far corner. He pulled one leg up onto the bench and braced his back against the wall.

He frowned when he saw Erik smile, wondering what the older man was thinking.

"How often do you come here?" Erik asked after he'd settled into the seat across from him. More elegantly, of course.

"We're here pretty often," Nathan said.

"We?"

"My best friend Troy and me." Nathan glanced over at Erik in time to see an odd expression cross his face. He may have asked about it if they hadn't been interrupted by their server.

"Nate!" a bubbly voice cried. "When did you get here? Where's Troy?"

Smiling slightly, Nathan looked at Harriet. She was around the same age as his mother would be if she'd been alive today. "Hey, Harriet. Troy's at a party tonight."

"He didn't take you with him? I'm going to have to knock some sense into that boy," she threatened.

Nathan couldn't help but chuckle. "It's okay. I didn't really want to go, anyway."

"Who's your gorgeous friend here?" Harriet asked, batting her lashes at Erik.

Nathan bit back jealousy at her actions. Erik was gay, so even if she did flirt with him, it wasn't like she would get anywhere. Shit! What was he thinking? "This is Erik, a customer at the store."

Harriet raised a brow but didn't ask the obvious question Nathan could see on her face. "Nice to meet you, Erik. Now, what can I get you two?"

"Just coffee for me, thanks," Erik said.

"Cream and sugar?"

"Black."

Harriet turned to Nathan. "Usual for you, sweetie?"

Nathan had skipped dinner but didn't feel right eating in

front of Erik. He was nervous enough! "Just coffee for me, too."

She eyed him and shook her head. "Did you eat lunch or dinner today?"

"Not hungry."

"I'll bring you your usual plate of fries."

Nathan tried to protest, but she hurried off before he could. Shaking his head, he looked at Erik to see him with a grin on his face. "What?" Nathan asked self-consciously.

Before Erik could respond, the bell over the door tinkled and Nathan saw Troy walk in. Troy zeroed in on Nathan, and he could see the pissed expression on Troy's face. Nathan winced and gave a weak smile at his best friend stomping their way. Erik turned in his seat to see what Nathan was looking at.

"Nathan Bryant, what the hell is it with you and someone doing something for you?" Troy demanded, waving the sticky note. "I may have been a few minutes late, but that doesn't mean you can just leave. What the hell did we talk about earlier?"

Nathan flushed at being chastised in front of Erik. "I'm fine, Troy. Really."

Troy still hadn't noticed the man sitting across from him. "You got mugged the other night! That's not fine! I told you to wait for me, you stubborn idiot!"

"I don't think he really had much to worry about tonight," Erik said, interrupting Troy's tirade.

Troy immediately focused on Erik. "Who are you?" Troy demanded.

"Troy!" Nathan admonished his friend for being so rude.

Erik slid from the booth to stand in front of Troy, holding his hand out. "Erik Moore."

Troy sized Erik up for a moment before reluctantly accepting the handshake. "Troy Davis."

Nathan saw the power struggle between the two of them. They tightened their grips on each other, and Nathan wanted to groan in sheer embarrassment. What the hell was Troy doing? He didn't need a knight in shining armor for cripes' sake.

"Troy," Nathan snapped.

Troy finally loosened his grip and Nathan felt a bit of triumph when Troy gave a barely noticeable wince. He knew Troy only wanted to protect him, but sometimes it got to be too much. When Nathan had been released from the hospital, Troy hadn't left him alone for over a month. Finally, Nathan had to ask him to leave. It had triggered an argument, but eventually they'd stopped shouting at one another, and Troy had finally understood Nathan felt smothered. Sometimes, Troy forgot. Like tonight.

"Would you care to join us?" Erik invited, retaking a seat. Only this time, to Nathan's surprise, Erik sat next to him.

Nathan's breath caught in his throat, and he pulled his knee tighter to his chest, back still against the wall and his bag between his legs. A strong, muscular thigh rippled beneath jeans, scant inches from the end of his shoe. Nathan didn't even realize how long he stared at said limb until Troy plopped down across from them. He shook his head and dragged his gaze to his best friend, willing the heat in his cheeks to dissipate.

Troy gave him a strange look but merely said, "I'm getting you a cell phone, Nate. I nearly had a heart attack when I saw the note you left. You should have known I would never have gone to the party without making sure you got home okay if you really didn't want to go."

"I can take care of myself, Troy," Nathan said, embarrassed at being made to seem weak in front of Erik.

"I know you can, but even someone like me or your friend here couldn't stand up to a knife or gun."

"You're referring to him being mugged?" Erik asked.

Nathan glanced at Erik to find a tense expression on his face. Nathan frowned, uncertain what caused the look.

Troy nodded. "Nate can be extremely stubborn. He takes the deposit to the bank at night by himself, and the guy came from behind him. The bastard demanded the money and Nate refused."

Erik turned his head to give Nathan a hard stare. "You did what?"

"Hey!" Nathan protested at being ganged up on. "I need my job and my boss almost fired me as it was! I wasn't gonna let some jackass steal the day's deposit."

"Next time, just give it to him," Erik growled. "It's not worth your life."

Sorely tempted to shove Erik out of the booth with his foot and slap Troy for mentioning the mugging in front of Erik, he glared at both of them. "I'm not five years old and I'm not made of glass. So, I got a few bumps and bruises. Besides, if it wasn't for..."

He trailed off in horror. He'd almost revealed his secret to Erik.

"Weren't for what?" Erik demanded.

"Nothing."

Erik didn't ask again. "If you'd have told me about meeting your friend, we could have waited."

"I thought the note would be enough!" Nathan exclaimed.

"You said nothing about someone being with you," Troy accused. "I wouldn't have gotten so upset."

What the hell was happening? Suddenly, Troy and a man he'd just met were berating him. A sexy, gorgeous man, but that had nothing to do with it. Nathan shook his head. "Just go to the party, Troy," he begged.

Troy folded his arms across his chest and sat back in the booth. "No."

Nathan had the sudden urge to bang his head on the table. This entire night hadn't turned out like he'd imagined. Of course, he really didn't know what he'd thought, but he sure as hell hadn't expected this.

"Here we are," Harriet interrupted as she set down the coffee and fries. "Troy! You beautiful man! Nate here said you'd gone to a party."

Troy smiled at her and stood to give her a quick hug. "I'd never leave Nate behind, Harriet. You look gorgeous as ever."

She flushed and waved her hand at him. "Enough flirting. You know I'm married."

Troy winked at her. "You wouldn't consider leaving him for me?"

Harriet chuckled. "If I were twenty years younger, in a heartbeat. Now, you want the usual?"

Nathan couldn't help but laugh. This was their typical ritual—Troy flirted with her every time. Although Troy hit on any woman practically.

"Of course, Harriet. Although I'd rather have a cup of coffee instead of the shake."

"Coming right out."

Troy sat back down, and Harriet bustled off, a bounce in her step. Nathan laughed again. A smile crossed Troy's face, and he reached out to flick a strand of hair from Nathan's cheek. "Gets her every time."

Nathan looked at Erik to find a strange expression on his face. "You okay?" he asked.

"Fine," Erik grunted, picking up the mug Harriet had set down on the table moments ago.

Nathan furrowed his brow but kept silent. He took a sip of his own coffee, sighing at the taste. His stomach growled loudly immediately after, and Troy gave him an exasperated glare. "You didn't eat today, did you?"

Troy was out to make him look completely bad in front of

Erik. "I wasn't hungry."

Shoving the plate of fries toward him, Troy demanded, "Eat."

Nathan protested when Erik turned and called for Harriet. "Can you please have the cook prepare a cheeseburger?"

"Sure thing, gorgeous. How'd you like that cooked?"

"Medium."

"Won't take but a few minutes."

Nathan mumbled under his breath and grabbed the ketchup bottle, dowsing the fries in it. He popped one in his mouth and chewed furiously.

"So, Erik Moore, how did you meet Nate?"

"I came into the store looking for a specific CD. He helped me out."

"You two haven't known each other for long?"

Erik shook his head and took another sip of his coffee. "A few days."

"Your name sounds familiar," Troy said. "Are you the Erik Moore who owns the construction company?"

"I am."

"Nice," Troy replied. "My dad worked there for a couple of years before he retired and moved to Florida a few years back. Of course, it was before the company became so successful."

"Davis, you said?" Erik queried. "I remember him! Great worker. I was sad to see him leave."

"He said you were the best boss he'd ever worked for."

Surprise raced through Nathan. He hadn't known Troy's dad had worked for Moore Construction. Oh, he knew what Troy's dad had done for a living before his retirement, but he'd never really questioned where. "Your dad worked there?" he asked abruptly, even though they'd already confirmed the answer.

Troy nodded. "I think it was back when you were in the —"

Nathan interrupted him. "So, you started your company pretty young then, huh?" he asked Erik.

"I knew what I wanted from an early age and started saving and planning by the time I was sixteen. There weren't many men who would come work for a green newbie like me, but Bill was one of the few who gave me a chance."

"I'll have to tell Dad I ran into you."

"How is he doing?" Erik asked.

"Pretty good. He's enjoying the sun and beaches. He found a retirement place that you don't even have to leave to get groceries. The place has a built-in grocery store, movie theater, and everything. He's happy and living his best life."

"What about your parents?" Erik asked Nathan.

Nathan tensed, his cheerful mood disappearing in a flash. "They're dead," he said flatly.

"I'm sorry," Erik murmured. He reached out and laid his hand on top of Nathan's knee.

Nathan almost jumped out of his skin. He stared at Erik's tan skin against his dark jeans. "It happened a long time ago," he replied, his voice rough.

"I didn't mean to dredge up painful memories."

Shrugging, Nathan said nothing. Troy changed the subject then, to Nathan's relief. "Are you married, Mr. Moore?"

"Erik, please. Mr. Moore makes me feel like my father." Erik chuckled. "And to answer your question, no, I am not. I was engaged, but he passed away."

"Open mouth insert foot," Troy muttered. "I'm sorry."

"It's okay. He was in a car accident two years ago."

"So that means you're gay?" Troy asked.

Nathan whipped his head toward his friend. "Troy!"

Erik laughed out loud and patted Nathan's knee. "It's fine, Nathan. Yes, I am gay."

"Is that why you're interested in Nathan?" Troy asked, horrifying Nathan.

Nathan groaned and covered his face with both hands. "Yes."

"For sex?"

Nathan's stomach dropped, and he choked, coughing several times to clear his windpipe.

Erik squeezed Nathan's knee and then removed his hand. "Not just for sex. I want to get to know him."

"Why?" Troy asked.

"Oh my God, Troy!" Nathan finally broke in. "Stop it! Right now."

Erik ignored him. "Because he's funny, smart, and downright gorgeous."

Nathan wanted to crawl under the table. He was none of those things. Where the hell had the man gotten that idea? Had he really looked at Nathan at all? Gorgeous? Him? Not even a little!

Troy studied Erik for several minutes and then nodded. "Okay."

Nathan gaped at Troy. He couldn't believe the conversation they'd just had about him. Anger built, and he glared at them both. "I'm sitting right here, you know, and who says I want to get to know you?" he demanded of Erik. "Just because I accepted your offer of coffee doesn't mean I'm going to jump into bed with you."

"I didn't expect you to," Erik said. "Like I told your friend, I want to get to know you."

He stared at Erik. "Why?"

Erik gave him a patient look. "I just told you."

Once more Nathan opened his mouth to shout at Erik when Harriet came back with the cheeseburger Erik had ordered. "There we are, baby cakes. If you need anything else, just holler."

She bustled off and Erik pushed the plate in front of Nathan. "Eat."

"I'm not hungry!" Nathan protested.

Erik raised an eyebrow at him. "I'm not leaving until you eat at least half the burger."

Nathan huffed and folded his arms on the table. Erik shrugged and resumed talking to Troy. They chatted easily about Troy's major, Erik's business, and eventually Erik's fiancé. Nathan cocked his head a little to listen, hoping for some clue as to Alan's death. The only thing Erik seemed to know was that Alan had died in a car accident when the vehicle went over the edge of the ravine. Something about the situation nagged at Nathan. It didn't feel right. Usually when someone was in an accident like that, the ghost didn't linger, even with a sexy fiancé back home. "How did he go over the guardrail?" Nathan asked, forgetting his stubborn attempt to ignore the two of them.

"The police said he was driving pretty fast. He wasn't a reckless driver, but that night we were having our rehearsal dinner and he had been running late."

Nathan hadn't realized just how close to being married Alan and Erik had been. "You really believe that's what happened?"

Erik frowned. "The police investigated. Why wouldn't I believe what they found? You sound like you think there was something more."

Nathan furiously shook his head. "No. I'm just curious."

Troy gave him a look and then his eyes widened as what Nathan was doing hit him. He'd connected the dots and realized Erik had to be tied to the spirit haunting him. Troy gave Nathan a stern look but kept quiet, thankfully.

"You still haven't touched your food," Erik said.

Nathan sighed, moved to sit normally, and picked up the cheeseburger, taking a bite while rolling his eyes at them. "Happy?" he mumbled around the mouthful.

Erik smiled. "For now."

Glancing at Troy, Nathan said, "You should go to the party, Troy. I'm fine."

Troy shook his head. "Not in the mood anymore."

"Quinn's going to be disappointed if at least one of us doesn't show."

Troy lifted one shoulder in a half shrug. "He'll get over it."

"How long have you two known each other?" Erik asked.

"About twelve years," Troy said.

"Long time. Did you grow up here?"

Troy nodded. "I did anyway. Nate's parents moved here when his father started a job at a really prestigious firm."

"Your dad was a lawyer?" Erik looked at Nathan.

Nathan stuffed the last bite of cheeseburger in his mouth, surprised he'd finished the whole thing. "Uh huh," he garbled.

Erik gave a satisfied smirk when he saw Nathan had consumed the entire burger. "What kind of law did he practice?"

"Criminal prosecution."

"Did he have any televised cases?"

Nathan didn't answer right away. His father had been very successful as a lawyer. When they'd first moved here, Nathan had been angry at his dad for making him leave behind his friends. Over the course of the six years before his parents' deaths, Nathan had spent a lot of time resenting his father, especially during the Espinoza case, the only one his father had ever been on television for. "Only one I remember," he murmured. "Victor Espinoza, a bastard who raped and murdered a twelve-year-old little girl."

"I remember that case," Erik said. "It took several months to convict him because they could only find circumstantial evidence until the prosecuting attorney located a scrapbook Espinoza had stashed somewhere. That was your father?"

Nathan nodded. He hadn't cared about any of it back then. All he'd seen was his father breaking promise after promise and never being home. The case had concluded about a year before the car accident. Nathan had already felt as though the damage had been done though, and he'd either ignored his father or bickered with him, which led to their argument the night of the car accident.

Troy glanced at his watch. "We should go, Nate. We have to be at your aunts' house early in the morning to help them with the repainting like we promised."

With everything that had happened in the last few days, he'd completely forgotten about his aunts asking them to help move the furniture in their living room to paint the walls. They had to do it super early because of his shift at the music store. "Shit, I forgot."

"I can drive you home," Erik offered.

Troy jumped in instantly. "No, that's okay. I'll be staying at his place tonight, so I can take him."

Nathan gave Erik an apologetic look. "Sorry. We can take you back to your truck, though."

"No, that's okay. I'd rather walk. Nice night out."

"If you're sure," Nathan said hesitantly.

Erik smiled and bumped his shoulder against Nathan's. "I'm sure."

Nathan hadn't noticed, but Harriet had dropped the bill on the table at some point. Erik took out his wallet and set down a couple of twenties, way over what the bill was. Nathan tried to protest him paying the entire amount, but Erik waved his worries away with one hand. "I'm the one who offered to buy you coffee, and I ordered the cheese-burger. Don't worry about it."

"Thank you," Nathan said uncomfortably, sliding out of

the booth after Erik and putting his backpack on once more.

"You're welcome," Erik replied. "Can I call you tomorrow?"

Nathan glanced around for Troy, but he had gone ahead of them to the front door, where he stood waiting for them to follow. "I don't have a cell phone or a house phone."

"Are you working tomorrow?"

"During the day."

"Then I'll call you at work."

Nathan fidgeted. "Okay."

Erik grinned and placed his hand on Nathan's lower back, guiding him toward the front of the diner. Harriet called out a good night, which both Nathan and Troy returned. The hand on his back felt as if it was burning a hole straight through to Nathan's skin. He struggled to put one foot in front of the other, confused and excited at the same time while fighting off the guilt of wanting Alan's fiancé.

Troy walked to his car and unlocked the doors, sliding into the front seat. Nathan shifted from foot to foot in discomfort. "Uh, thanks again for the coffee and food. I… Uh…"

Erik leaned in closer, and for a minute Nathan thought the man intended to kiss him, but all Erik did was pull Nathan's jacket closed in the front and straighten out the edges of the hood. "I'd kiss you, but I'm getting the evil eye from your friend."

A thrill slid through Nathan at Erik's words before he glanced over to see Troy practically drilling a hole into them. "I gotta go," he squeaked and scurried over to the passenger side, almost wrenching the door off its hinges.

Nathan saw Erik laughing as Troy backed out of the parking space and pulled into traffic. He couldn't quite control his breathing and his chest hurt. He'd never felt this way around anyone, ever. Shame also mixed in with excitement and giddiness. Alan still loved his fiancé. Nathan knew it made no sense to worry about a ghost, but he couldn't help it. None of the spirits in the past had caused this much turmoil in Nathan's life, and he didn't know how to proceed. He didn't know if he could stand watching the smile on Erik's face turn to disgust when he told him the truth about what he could do.

"Nate!" Troy's sharp tone pulled him out of his thoughts.

"What?"

"Don't what me!" Troy snapped. "He's the reason that bastard spirit is still here, isn't he?"

Nathan didn't want to tell him, but he couldn't lie to the one person who'd always been there for him. He gave a small nod.

"Damn it, Nate!" Troy swore. "You haven't told him yet, have you?"

"No."

Troy slammed on the brakes at a red light, tires squealing a bit. He turned to look at Nathan. "I am happy you're finally showing some interest in someone, but why him? What do you think he'd say if he knew about your secret and the only reason you spent time with him was because of his dead fiancé?"

Nathan winced. A part of his friend's words was true, yet Nathan knew even if Alan wasn't in the picture, he'd have found himself attracted to Erik. Something about Erik made his body feel alive and made him see a future beyond the present day. It was stupid for him to think that way about someone he'd only just met, but Nathan sensed a connection between them and not just because of Alan.

"I know," he muttered. "You think I don't? I know it's not possible for anything to happen. He wouldn't want someone like me. Someone who has so much baggage and a terrible gift. I'm not an idiot, Troy."

"First, stop it! You're a great guy and anyone would be lucky to have you. But if that's how you feel, why put yourself through that kind of situation then, Nate?"

He was silent for a few breaths and then whispered, "Because it feels good to hope for once. To see a future for me that doesn't include horrible things. I know I don't deserve it and it's impossible for anyone to really want me, but it's nice to think it is possible. I'm being selfish, but I can't help it."

"You aren't being selfish! If anyone deserves a future, it's you. I've never understood why you think you aren't worthy to be loved, Nate. I love you. Your aunts love you. It's obvious Erik is into you. He couldn't keep his eyes off you as we were leaving."

Nathan flushed. "That's not true."

"Of course, it is. Have you looked in the mirror lately? I'm not into guys, but if I was, you'd totally be my type. You're hot, Nate." A horn honking behind them forced Troy to resume driving. "I'm just saying it's better if you tell him sooner than later. Don't wait because it's only going to hurt more if you let yourself get close to him and he finds out."

"I won't get closer to him, Troy," Nathan said. "It's a dumb idea, anyway. I'm a freak of nature and no one as successful and good-looking as him is going to want that in his life. This supposed gift of mine isn't going away, and I am always going to have other Alans who come along."

"You've done so well, though, Nate. This is the first time in over a year since one figured out you can see them."

Nathan gave a hoarse laugh. "No, it isn't. I didn't tell you about the last two because I knew you'd get upset."

"What?" Understanding dawned on Troy's face. "Last year, Christmas, you seemed withdrawn and preoccupied. That was one of them, wasn't it? And a few months back, you were distant, and I didn't see you for a couple of days. Damn it, Nate. We're friends! Why didn't you tell me? I can help you!"

"No one can help me, Troy. I don't want you to have to deal with this. It's my burden, my punishment for my parents' deaths."

Troy pulled to a stop in front of Nathan's building, roughly putting the car in Park. He turned in his seat and reached out to grab Nathan's arm. "You are not responsible for what happened to your parents, Nate. Some idiot ran a red light! You didn't put the asshole behind the wheel, and you couldn't have known the engine would catch on fire. None of it is your fault!"

Nathan winced as Troy's hand tightened the longer he spoke. "It is my fault, Troy! If I hadn't been such a brat about leaving the party, we never would have been at the red light! I should have died that night, too!"

Troy loosened his grip and sat back to stare out of the windshield, his hands on the steering wheel. "Now you're being selfish, Nate. It would have devastated your aunts to lose you along with your parents. And me... I'd be lost without you. You're my best friend."

Nathan covered his face with his hands and only then realized he'd started crying. He didn't want to hurt Troy, but he knew in his heart his parents were dead because of him. It wasn't right that he got to live a long life while they lay in a coffin. "I'm sorry, Troy," he whispered. "I really am."

Troy sighed. "It's okay. I didn't mean to yell at you. It kills me to hear you talk like that."

"I know," Nathan said.

"Let's just go inside and get some sleep."

Nathan nodded, and they got out of the car and took the stairs to his apartment. He knew with certainty his dreams tonight would be worse than ever. If he could even sleep.

CHAPTER 7

The alarm went off sooner than Nathan would have liked. His dreams were fractured, at best. He remembered reliving the accident and then seeing Erik with Alan. Erik had been angry at Nathan, screaming at him silently with words he couldn't hear over the roar of the fire consuming his parents' car. Somehow, Nathan sensed Erik had found out about his secret and Alan's presence. It only made his guilt triple, and he almost drowned in the emotion. Nathan could only watch helplessly as Erik turned to Alan and cupped the spirit's cheek as Erik leaned in to kiss him. The disturbing sound of the clock blaring its annoying beep had ripped him from the nightmare the second before Erik's lips would have met Alan's.

Nathan trembled beneath his sheets for several long moments after slapping off the alarm. The events in his nightmare only made him even more certain a relationship with Erik could never happen. "Nate, you awake?" Troy's voice came through the door.

"Yeah," he called back.

"See you in ten then," Troy said.

Dragging himself out of bed, Nathan stumbled to his dresser. He dressed in the dark, the moonlight streaming through the window providing enough light to see. His huge yawn echoed in the near barren room as he located his keys and wallet.

"Nathan?"

Nathan jumped about a foot off the ground. He swung around and glared at Alan. "Now you're in my apartment, too?"

"I'm sorry, Nathan. I needed to talk to you." Alan drifted closer.

"Stay back," Nathan growled.

"Did you tell him last night?" Alan asked.

Nathan jammed his wallet into his back pocket and the keys to his place in his front pocket. "No, I didn't have the chance."

Alan grew solemn and Nathan sucked in a breath at the instant melancholy inundating him. "You promised you would," Alan whispered.

"I said I would and I will. When it's the right time. It's not like I can go to him and say hey, guess what, your dead fiancé is here and he wants to tell you something. That's what got me locked up in a mental institution the first time!"

"You were in a mental hospital?" Alan asked in surprise. "Why?"

"Gee, I wonder why," Nathan answered sarcastically. "Because the doctors saw me 'talking to myself' and claiming I could see ghosts. They thought I was having a mental breakdown."

A knock at the bedroom door stalled whatever else he would have said. "You all right in there, Nate?"

"I'm fine," Nathan called out. "Just the friendly neighborhood ghost is here."

The door opened and Troy stepped in, frowning. "He

can't even leave you alone here? No sense of boundaries. Hey, jackass, why don't you stay out of Nate's apartment? You don't belong here. In fact, just leave all together and don't come back."

Alan glared at Troy and floated to his side. "You're a rude bastard, ain't ya?"

Nathan snorted and Troy growled. "He's smart mouthing again, isn't he?"

"Don't worry about it, Troy. He won't be around for long. I hope." Alan gave him a hurt look, which he ignored. "Let's just go. I only have a few hours before I have to get to the store."

"Going to stop for coffee on the way," Troy muttered, still looking around the room as if he could spot Alan.

"Wait," Alan demanded. "You haven't told me what happened last night."

"And I'm not going to. At least not right now," Nathan said. "I've got things to do."

Alan sniffed. "Fine. I'll be waiting for you at work."

"Oh boy, lucky me," Nathan said sarcastically.

Alan huffed. "You don't have to be so nasty."

Nathan rolled his eyes but didn't reply, walking out of the room behind Troy. They left his apartment and were on the road in less than a minute. Troy pulled into a drive-through to order coffee for them. The window attendant was barely awake as she handed Troy his change and the two cups with sugar packets and cream containers. Nathan sighed in plea-sure when he opened the little tab on the lid of his cup, and he poured in five sugars and two creams. A moan slid free as he got his first sip of the strong liquid.

Troy chuckled as he pulled forward and stopped long enough to add three packages of sugar and two creams to his coffee. "I don't know how you can enjoy it like that."

"Because it tastes amazing."

They'd had this conversation more times than Nathan could remember. It always came out the same. "Aunt Becky and Aunt Jessica are waiting for us. Let's go."

"Keep your shorts on," Troy said as he tossed his garbage into the compartment meant for change or some other such thing. He covered his coffee and put the car back into Drive. Nathan didn't even have to direct Troy on how to get to his aunts' house. They'd been there so many times it was routine.

There were several lights on in the two-story house when they arrived twenty minutes later. Troy turned off the car, and they exited the vehicle. Nathan didn't knock, just entered the house. "Aunt Jessica? Aunt Becky?"

"In the kitchen, sweetie," Jessica shouted.

Nathan and Troy walked into the kitchen to find Nathan's aunts sitting at the table eating breakfast. Becky smiled at them and jumped up from her chair to give them both a hug. "It's good to see you, Troy. Nate, you are still far too skinny," she chastised. "And what the hell happened to your face?"

Becky looked a lot like Nathan's mom. Tall and statuesque, she had dark hair down to her waist and bright green eyes that shone like emeralds when she was happy or excited about something. Nathan couldn't remember ever seeing her any way but bubbly except at his parents' funeral and the day they'd committed him to the mental hospital. They'd allowed him to attend his parents' funeral before, but he could still see the guilt and shame on her face as they'd taken him away.

"It's nothing, Aunt Becky."

"It's not nothing," Troy said. "Someone mugged him the other night."

"Mugged!" Becky screeched, and Nathan winced.

"I'm fine. I just got a little scratched up."

"A little? You look like hell," Jessica said drily.

Nathan huffed. "I promise I'm fine."

"He doesn't eat enough either." Troy moved around the table to give Jessica a hug and kiss as well. "No matter how often I try to shove food down his throat."

"You aren't working too hard, are you, Nate?" Jessica asked.

Jessica was the exact opposite of Becky: petite and slender with bright blonde hair and hazel-green eyes. She was moodier and quiet, a fact Nathan had appreciated when he'd finally convinced everyone he was no longer seeing things and had come to live with them.

Nathan wanted to smack Troy for feeding the fire, but he restrained himself and gave a weak smile as he hugged Jessica and kissed her cheek. "No, Aunt Jessica."

She leaned back to eye him and poked his stomach. "Going to bring you pastries and stuff to put some weight on you."

"You don't have to do that," Nathan protested.

"I certainly do. If you don't start gaining weight, I'm going to be there every day to make sure you eat."

Becky chuckled and took her plate to the sink. "I think you better listen to her, Nate. She doesn't mess around when she really wants something."

Jessica stood and went to the fridge, where she pulled out a box of guava pastries. She shoved it at Nathan. "Eat something. We still have a couple of hours before you have to leave for work, and I won't allow you to move furniture until you eat."

Nathan grumbled but sat down to eat at least one. It tasted like sawdust in his mouth, but he gave his aunts a weak smile as he choked the pastry down. Troy also snatched one from the box and munched on it as he chatted with Becky and Jessica. The conversation topic rolled around from Troy's classes to his latest love interest and then Nathan heard a name that made him lift his head in alarm.

"You finally have a young man, Nate?" Becky asked in excitement, her dark eyes glittering with intrigue.

Glaring at Troy, Nathan furiously shook his head. "No, Aunt Becky. He's just a customer at the store."

"Oh."

"A customer he had dinner with last night," Troy teased.

Becky perked up again. "Tell me all about him!" she demanded.

Nathan flushed. "There's nothing to tell," he said, trying to deflect the interest.

Becky slid into the seat next to him. "Of course there is! I want to know about the first person who caught your eye finally."

Nathan knew if he didn't give her something, she'd never leave him be. Sighing, he said, "His name is Erik. He's older than me by at least several years."

"Pssh." Becky waved off the age difference. "I'm almost ten years older than Jessica. Age doesn't matter when the heart is involved."

"The heart's not involved, Aunt Becky," Nathan said. "I met him at the store when he came in to buy a CD. Someone stole his out of his truck."

"Is he a cowboy?" Becky asked.

Nathan raised an eyebrow. "What would a cowboy be doing in a place like this?"

"He drives a truck, doesn't he?"

"That doesn't make him a cowboy, Aunt Becky. He works in construction."

"Ooooh, I bet he's got a nice body," Becky mused.

"Aunt Becky!" Nathan groaned and covered his eyes with one hand. "He's taller than me, with dark brown hair and hazel eyes."

"Does he have a nice body?" Jessica chimed in.

He sighed. "Yes."

Becky squealed and Nathan winced. "My baby nephew has finally caught himself a man!"

"I haven't caught anyone, Aunt Becky!"

Troy coughed to cover his laughter and Nathan snarled at him. He'd get Troy back. Somehow. "Can we just get this done? I have to get to the store by eight thirty to prep the register and put out the Saturday sale signs."

"I'll let you off the hook for now," Becky replied, smirking. "But don't think I won't have you back on it soon."

Nathan mumbled under his breath and stood from his chair, heading to the living room to move furniture away from the walls. He and Troy worked together hefting the heavier furniture. Then they moved to the dining room and into the hallways.

Nathan's aunts wanted to paint the entire downstairs except the kitchen and bathroom. They were the type of people who needed a change every few years. He'd spent many hours doing this same thing quite a few times over the last several years—and even before his parents' deaths. He could still remember his mom waking him before dawn and carrying him to the car when he'd been a child, then leading him yawning to the car as he'd gotten older. His aunts always had pastries and donuts waiting for them when they'd gotten there, much like this morning.

The memories saddened him, and he grew even more silent as everyone worked together. He missed his parents more than anything. He'd give his own life if he could go back and prevent them from leaving the party. It wasn't as though he had a lot to show for the six years since then.

Erik popped into his head immediately, followed by Alan. He never should have agreed to let Erik call him at the store. Maybe he should just have someone else answer the phone all day and have them tell him he wasn't able to talk. There was no way he had room in his life for the complications getting involved with Erik would cause. Aside from Alan, Nathan's life was a mess, and he had no right dragging a confident, successful person like Erik into it.

"Are you really that mad at me, bro?" Troy's question didn't register at first. "Nate?"

Blinking, Nathan glanced over at Troy. "What? Oh. No."

"Come on, Nate. You've been giving me the silent treatment for the last hour."

"I've just got a lot on my mind, Troy. I'm not mad." Troy gave him a skeptical look. "Seriously!"

"If you're sure," Troy accepted hesitantly.

"I promise I'm not mad."

Troy seemed satisfied with his answer, and they worked at a fast clip to finish moving the rest of the furniture. Nathan kept looking at his watch to make sure he would have enough time to get to work.

When they'd finished, Nathan rushed to say goodbye to his aunts. "Gotta run, Aunt Becky, Jessica. Only got thirty minutes to make it across town to the store. Love you both! Don't move any of the furniture on your own! We'll come back after the paint is dry to put it back."

Becky waved off his demand. "We're too old to try that again."

Jessica had put out her back the last time they'd tried. "Good!" Nathan said and kissed both their cheeks.

Troy gave them hugs and snatched another pastry from the kitchen before they headed out to the car. Nathan remained quiet on the way. He sensed Troy looking at him as he drove, knowing he was making Troy worry again. A headache began nagging behind his eyes. The more stressed he became, the worse it would get. Damn, if this kept up, he'd have to cancel his gig at Java Bean tonight. Sighing, Nathan rubbed at his temples.

"Headache?" Troy asked as he parked the car in front of the store.

Nathan nodded. "Thanks for your help today, Troy, and the ride to work."

"Of course, Nate. You know you don't have to thank me. I'm glad to do it."

"I'll see you later," Nathan said, opening the car door and then stepping out.

Troy leaned over the center console. "You think you'll be up for your set at Java?"

"I don't know. I hope so."

"Call me if not and I'll give you a lift home, okay?"

"I will. See ya."

Nathan slammed the door shut and walked over to the front of the music store. He undid the lock and entered, closing and then locking the door behind him. The usual activity of clocking in, setting out the sale signs, and adding the cash drawer to the register had a calming effect, and the headache dulled. Until Alan scared the crap out of him by popping out of the storage room when Nathan went to grab two more signs from the back. Nathan jumped backward, knocking over a small display.

Scowling, Nathan snapped, "Can't you give me one day of peace?"

The headache flared once more, throbbing behind his eyes and at his temples. Nathan set the shelf to rights.

"Sorry, Nathan," Alan said remorsefully.

Grumbling, Nathan finished putting all the CDs back on the rack and turned around to glare at Alan. "You are going to be the death of me."

"That's not true," Alan protested, floating behind Nathan as he entered the storage room to get what he needed.

Nathan pulled two of the sale signs from the usual drawer. "Yes, you are."

Alan frowned. "If you'd just tell Erik about me, maybe I'd be able to move on."

Nathan let out a snort. "Somehow, I have a feeling you're never going away."

"Am I really that bad?"

"About as welcome as a hemorrhoid."

"Ouch."

He left the back room to finish preparing the register and straightening the front counter. There were still ten minutes until the store officially opened for business, and he took the time to lean on the counter and rest his once again throbbing head on his forearm.

"You okay, Nathan?" Alan asked nearby.

"I'm fine," he mumbled back.

"Are you sure? You look a little pale."

"It's just a headache."

"My dad used to suffer from migraines, too. Do you have any medication for it?"

Nathan sighed. "No. The doctor at the hospital I was in won't sign off on a prescription for one unless I'm strictly monitored because of my risk of suicide. Or at least that's what he says is the reason."

"What the hell?" Alan demanded. "That's ridiculous."

"Is it? Most of the people in that hospital are supposed to be there. Wouldn't you think I was off-balance too if you saw me talking to thin air? When you were alive, I mean? I'd have been right there with you if it wasn't me."

Nathan raised his head and peered at the clock. "Please disappear for the day. I can't concentrate when you're here."

"You still haven't told me what happened with Erik last night. Did you tell him?"

"No. I didn't. It wasn't the right time."

"Nathan," Alan whined and drifted closer.

"Damn it. What did I tell you about space? And we're doing this my way. He's not ready to hear it."

Alan backed away and folded his arms with a huff. "When are you seeing him again?"

Never if he could help it. "I don't know."

"How are you going to help me if you don't see him?"

"I'll figure it out. Now leave."

Nathan heard a knock and glanced over to see Quinn standing at the front door. He could see the quizzical expression on Quinn's face, which meant he had seen Nathan talking to no one. Shit. This was getting more and more invasive by the day. Nathan gave a weak smile and headed over to unlock the door.

"Morning, Nate. Who are you talking to?" Quinn asked, looking around the store.

"Just myself," Nathan said.

He could tell Quinn didn't really believe him, but Quinn didn't press it. He walked into the back room to clock in. Nathan turned to Alan and hissed, "Leave now."

"Okay, I'm going. I'll be back, though."

"Great!" Nathan replied sarcastically.

Alan sighed with impatience but disappeared, much to Nathan's relief. His absence didn't really help the headache that was aiming for a full-blown migraine. Nathan narrowly missed knocking over a display in a wave of dizziness about halfway through the day. When Quinn called his name while he was restocking returns, he winced. He looked toward Quinn and saw him holding the phone, one hand covering the receiver. Nathan shook his head and went back to work. He couldn't deal with Erik right now.

Nathan's schedule had him at the store until five, but at about two in the afternoon, Quinn came to him and placed a hand on his shoulder. "You don't look so good, man. Maybe you should go home."

"No," Nathan replied through gritted teeth. It took every ounce of strength he had not to upchuck right in the aisle where he stood.

"Then at least go lie down in the stockroom for a while. I've got some Excedrin if you want it."

"It won't help."

Quinn grabbed Nathan's arm when he swayed. "Whoa, Nate. I'm calling Troy. Go sit down, now. I can handle things here until Tom gets in at five. It's been pretty slow today."

For once, Nathan didn't argue. Quinn helped him to the stool behind the counter, where Nathan promptly laid his head down and tried to breathe through the never-ending pain. He heard Quinn pick up the phone and a few seconds later, Quinn told Troy he needed to come get Nathan.

Damn, he really hated relying on anyone, but he couldn't even stand without wanting to pass out. When Troy arrived fifteen minutes later, Nathan could barely lift his head. Troy let out a loud epitaph and hefted Nathan off the stool and into his arms. "You should have called me sooner, Nate," Troy said with a grunt as he carried Nathan to the front of the store.

Quinn held the door for him. "Is he going to be okay?"

"He gets terrible migraines from time to time," Troy replied as Quinn hurried to open the passenger door of his car. "He'll be fine."

"If you're sure…" Quinn hesitated. "Maybe you should take him to the hospital."

"No!" Nathan burst out and instantly regretted it. His head almost exploded, and he groaned, closing his eyes in agony.

Troy set him down inside the car and stepped back, shutting the door. "He hates hospitals. Long story and not mine to tell, Quinn. I promise he'll be okay."

Quinn leaned in the open window. "I hope you feel better soon, Nate. Can't lose my wingman, huh?"

Nathan peered at Quinn through mere cracks in his eyelids and tried to smile, but his entire face hurt. "Never."

"What should I tell your guy when he calls back?" Quinn asked.

"He's not my guy," Nathan murmured. "Just tell him I had to go home."

"Sure thing, Nate. See you on Monday. Get some rest. I'll handle Stuart."

"Thanks, Quinn," Nathan said.

Troy slid into the driver's seat and started the car. Nathan had closed his eyes again and tried to will the migraine to recede. He didn't know why he bothered, since it had never worked in the past. The ride seemed to take forever and when Troy finally turned off the car, Nathan opened his eyes to find them parked in front of his aunts' house.

"Why'd you bring me here?" Nathan whispered. "Take me home."

"This is your home, Nate. Your aunts can take care of you."

"I don't want to be a burden on them."

"Shut up, Nate." Troy got out of the car and went around to Nathan's side. "Can you walk now, or do you need me to carry you?"

"I can walk," Nathan said as he climbed out of the car. He got about two feet before dizziness swamped him again and he almost crumpled to the ground. Troy caught him and lifted him into his arms. Nathan heard the words "stubborn" and "bullheaded" as Troy walked up the steps and hit the doorbell.

Jessica opened the door and went into action the minute she saw Nathan's face. "Upstairs. You know which room is his. I'll get Becky."

Troy nodded and took the stairs to Nathan's old room. He turned the handle and got the door open without dropping Nathan. Becky rushed into the room behind them. She yanked down the sheets and gestured for Troy to set him down. "Troy, can you get me a cold washcloth, please?"

"Sure thing, Aunt Becky." Troy disappeared into the adjoining bathroom to get the cloth.

Becky removed Nathan's sneakers and covered him with the quilt. She sighed as she brushed the hair back from his face. "I wish you'd come to me when you need help, Nate. I hate seeing you like this."

Nathan smiled weakly. "I already owe you so much, Aunt Becky."

"Oh pooh! You don't owe me a thing, sweetie. We're family, and family means loving each other through health and sickness."

Troy returned with the cloth, which Becky placed on his forehead. "Stay with him for a minute, Troy. I want to get the eucalyptus oil."

She hurried out of the room, and Troy grabbed the chair from Nathan's old desk and set it next to the bed. He straddled it and rested his chin on the back.

Becky couldn't have been gone more than a minute before she was back. Perching on the edge of the bed, she opened the little jar and placed her finger on the opening, turning it over twice. She gently massaged the oil into one temple, then the next, and along the forehead, with a small touch under his nose.

"That should help to calm it a little. I wish those damn doctors would at least prescribe you something! They can't let you continue to suffer like this."

"I'm fine," Nathan murmured and closed his eyes. He heard Troy stand.

"I'm going to leave you to rest, Nate. I'll call later to find out how you're doing."

Nathan huffed in acknowledgement. Becky leaned over and placed a kiss on the top of his head. "We'll let you be for now, sweetie. If you need anything, just call out and we'll hear you, okay?"

"'K." Nathan drifted into unconsciousness.

When Nathan woke sometime later, the headache was mostly gone. Twilight peeped in through the curtains and he could tell he wouldn't make it to his gig that night. He needed to call Java Bean and let Curtis, the owner, know. He reached out and snapped on the little lamp on the nightstand. The sudden light caused him to squint, and he waited a moment for his eyes to adjust before reaching to grab the phone near the bed.

It took more than one attempt to dial the right number, but eventually he got it. The phone rang twice and then a voice came over the line. "Java Bean."

"Bella, it's Nate. I need to speak with Curtis."

"Nate! How are you feeling? I heard you were sick."

Nathan frowned. How did she already know? "I'm doing okay. Is Curtis available?"

"Sure thing, Nate. One sec." Nathan heard her set the phone down and shout for Curtis. A minute later, Curtis' voice came over the phone.

"Nate, my man, how you feeling?"

What the hell? "Hey, Curtis. I wanted to let you know I can't make tonight's set."

"No worries, man. Troy called earlier to let me know. Told me about your migraine. My sister gets those, so I know how bad they can be. You doing any better?"

Nathan should have known Troy would call Curtis. "A bit. Not enough to make it in, though."

"Not a problem. I just changed it to an open mic night. Give me a shout tomorrow if you think you won't make it in for Sunday's set, okay? I hope you feel better soon. I gotta run, but we'll talk tomorrow."

"Sure, Curtis. See ya." Nathan set the phone back on the base.

Nathan stared at the ceiling. He kept trying to break free of the obligations piling up, and yet somehow, they always seemed to continue to place more strings around him. Erik came into his mind and Nathan groaned, yanking a pillow over his face. The man haunted him as surely as a spirit, even though he'd only met the guy twice. He recalled the shiver he'd experienced when he'd imagined Erik close to kissing him last night. Sad fact of the matter was, he'd never kissed anyone. Before the accident, there'd been several boys in high school he'd had a crush on, but none of them were gay. Then afterward, he'd never had the desire to be involved with anyone. As if any person in their right mind would want to deal with Nathan's issues.

He tried to shove thoughts of his current situation out of his mind. He wanted a break from reality right now. Rolling to his side, he hugged the pillow to his chest and zoned in on a tiny speck on the wall across from the bed. After about twenty minutes, he gave up and tossed the blankets back. His head throbbed at the sudden movement, and he groaned but still forced himself into a sitting position. Sometimes a shower helped. He dragged himself out of bed and into the bathroom, then he turned on the water, undressing while it heated.

Stepping under the spray, he stood there, letting the jets beat against the base of his skull. The doctors hadn't been able to identify where the migraines originated. At first, they'd worried the head trauma from the accident had caused them. There'd been multiple CAT scans and MRIs, but they'd always come out normal. His aunts had demanded pain medication, and the doctors had administered it while he'd been in the hospital. When they'd finally released him, they'd refused to provide a prescription, even with his aunts swearing to monitor his usage closely. Nathan supposed he couldn't really blame the psychiatrist who'd made the call. If he hadn't been the one seeing ghosts, he'd have thought he was nuts too.

The massaging of the water against his neck and shoulders helped relieve some of the tension. He tilted his head forward, allowing his chin to rest on his chest. He didn't even attempt to wash his hair or body. A knock at the bathroom door caused him to jump. He'd almost forgotten he wasn't in his apartment.

"Nate? You okay in there, honey?" Jessica's voice came through the wood.

Nathan shut off the faucet and watched the liquid swirling down the drain, wishing he could go with it.

"Nate?"

"I'm okay, Aunt Jess," Nathan called back.

"If you need anything, I'm right down the hall."

"Okay."

He heard Jessica's footsteps as she walked away. He debated on turning on the water again but got out instead. Grabbing a towel, he dried off as best he could and put his same clothes back on, his shirt sticking to his still damp skin. At least the migraine had died to a dull roar instead of the high frequency scream shattering his skull.

Nathan returned to his room, turned off the lamp on the nightstand, and sat in a chair near the window. His aunts would never allow him to return to his apartment tonight, but he supposed that was a good thing since Alan would be waiting for him. The street outside was quiet, a car driving by every once in a while.

Nathan thought back on the first spirit he'd encountered after they'd released him from the hospital—an old woman who'd lived a few houses down. At first, he'd ignored her as he'd learned to do, not wanting to go back to the psych ward. Each day he'd see her wandering, calling for someone named Peter, and each day he'd walk past her as though she didn't exist. Finally, a couple of weeks had gone by and he hadn't been able to stop feeling sorry for her. She'd seemed so lonely and lost. It turned out Peter was her son, and she'd needed to tell him something, to make him understand her death wasn't an accident. His wife had slowly poisoned her because she'd wanted the old lady's money.

He'd told her he wished he could help her, but without proof, the son wouldn't listen to him. The old lady had taken him to her house, which had still been up for sale, and told him to look in her room upstairs, underneath the bricks on the hearth of the fireplace. She'd pointed at the place she hid the key to her house and then disappeared.

Nathan had located the key, entered the house, and slowly taken the stairs to her room. There'd been the typical mothball scent in the home and apparently the son had wanted none of the furniture, for the place remained furnished. The item under the bricks had been a folder. The old lady had hired an investigator to investigate her new daughter-in-law when her son married. Multiple pictures of a blond lady in different wedding dresses with different men had fallen out and Nathan had picked them up, studying each one. The papers inside were reports from the detective and newspaper clippings of obituaries of several men.

Nathan remembered feeling sick knowing the woman in the photos had gotten away with murdering so many people. It had also made him feel even sadder for the old lady. It was the first time he'd really wanted to help a spirit. He'd located the woman's son and presented the folder without saying a word. He could still picture the son's face when the man had seen the contents of the file. Nathan had turned and walked away, letting the woman's son do what he would with the folder.

After that day, he'd never seen the spirit again. Nathan had seen a story on the news a few days later where the blond lady's image had shown up and the title Black Widow had appeared above her head. Vindication for the old woman had made him smile, causing his aunts to give him a look of puzzlement, but he hadn't elaborated and just kept watching the television.

It no longer took time for Nathan to figure out if the people he saw were spirits or not. Even the ones who appeared corporeal in form had an aura around them that Nathan now recognized. The energy they gave off wasn't a bright light, but more of a subtle tone that radiated outward. Sometimes the color of the aura changed depending on how the person died and who they were in real life.

White meant they were good people in life and had done a lot for those around them. Nathan hadn't encountered many of those, as they usually moved on after they died, since they had nothing left unresolved. Blue were ones who held a lot of influential power and they used that to get things their own way. Black auras clung to those who'd committed suicide, ones with mental health issues when they were alive and couldn't bear life anymore.

Nathan preferred dealing with either white or yellow, the color given off by normal people who'd been timid and unsure of themselves. Nathan steered as far away from the red ones as possible. They were people who'd been evil, committing crimes or even murders before they'd died. He'd learned that one the hard way.

Alan gave off a white light and Nathan knew the man had been a good person before he'd died. It didn't make it any easier to deal with the situation. He wanted to help Alan, but he didn't want to scare Erik away, either. The only problem was he didn't see a way to accomplish both. He had to make a choice, and the unselfish choice would be to tell Erik about Alan. His stomach twisted in knots, and he dug his fingers into the armchair at how much the idea affected him. Damn, this was exactly why he didn't want to become involved with anyone. They'd never understand his horrible gift.

"Why me?" he whispered into the darkness. "To punish me? Make me hurt even more than I already do for causing my parents' deaths?"

No answer came forth, and Nathan squeezed his eyes shut, tilting his head back against the chair. He'd never be able to have a normal life, and he couldn't subject another person to the awful future he foresaw for himself. "I'm sorry, Mom, Dad," he said hoarsely, hoping they could hear him on the other side.

CHAPTER 8

The moon had risen high in the sky and the night had moved into the late hours when Nathan returned to bed to sleep. Aunt Becky had come to the door once to ask if he'd like something to eat and when he'd refused, she'd hesitated for a moment before leaving. He knew his aunts were worried about him, and he felt terrible about it, but this burden didn't belong to them. No one else could help him carry it.

He fell into a fitful sleep, one where he dreamed of his parents and the devil chasing them. When he saw the devil's face, he cried out because it was like looking in the mirror. His own face peered back at him, a maniacal grin on the devil's lips. His mother turned to look at him, tears streaking down her face. She mouthed something he couldn't understand and before she could try again, the devil grew and grew, swallowing both of his parents in a shroud of darkness.

Nathan screamed and jerked upright in bed, gasping and sweating. Was the dream showing him his parents were in hell? Were they suffering because of him? "Oh God," he sobbed and covered his face with his hands.

A hand touching his shoulder startled him and he dropped his hands to his lap to find Jessica sitting on the edge of his bed, a sympathetic yet concerned look on her face. He felt his lip quiver like a little kid's about to cry and she wrapped her arms around him, pulling him into a tight embrace. "Shh, my little Nate, it was just a dream," she soothed, rubbing one hand up and down his back.

"I saw them, Aunt Jess." He wept against the side of her neck.

"Saw who, baby?"

"My parents. They were suffering... because of me." Nathan couldn't help but feel selfish for accepting her comfort when he didn't deserve it.

"Hush now," Jess murmured. "You know it was an accident, sweetie. We've gone over this before. It's not your fault."

"It is my fault. I never should have made them leave the party!" Nathan pushed away from her and tried to suck in air. His lungs felt constricted.

Jessica brushed his hair back from his face. "Breathe, Nate. Relax. It's okay. Just breathe."

Nathan couldn't stop the panic attack when it hit him. He struggled to breathe, to stop the bed from being yanked out from under him. His throat tightened and his screams echoed in his head, yet he couldn't make a sound. Jessica rubbed his hands between hers, but he couldn't feel her skin against his. His insides clenched hard, a giant fist wrapped around them, squeezing and squeezing. On more than one occasion, he'd missed a step on the stairs from his apartment and almost fallen, but the way his stomach lurched then never compared to the way it did when the panic attacks hit. His heart beat like furious bird wings at his rib cage, threatening to break free. It felt as though he were dying.

Minutes or hours could have passed by the time he could

breathe normally, and his aunts' voices filtered past the roaring sound in his ears. Nathan shivered and tried to calm himself.

"Nate?" Becky prodded.

"I-I'm okay."

"Maybe we need to call Dr. Schwartzer," Jessica said.

"No!" Nathan exclaimed. "No, I'm fine."

"I think maybe we should see if he could prescribe something for you, Nate," Becky argued, wiping his cheeks and forehead with a wet cloth.

Nathan shook his head furiously while grabbing her hand with the cloth to stop her ministrations. The pills always dulled his senses and made him feel as though he were underwater. "I'm okay, Aunt Becky. I just had a bad dream."

"It's been a while since you had a panic attack," Jessica pointed out. "Have you been under a lot of stress lately?"

Nathan almost snorted but didn't want to alert them to any changes in his life. "Just school and work."

"I really wish you'd move back home," Becky said.

"You know I can't, Aunt Becky. You've already done so much for me."

Becky sighed. "You don't owe us anything, Nate."

"Of course, I do!"

Becky huffed and stood. She glared at him angrily. "You don't and never will owe us a damn thing, you stubborn brat."

She stomped out of the room in a mood, and Nathan sighed. He knew he hurt her by insisting he owed them, but if it wasn't for him, they never would have had to take care of a teenage boy and put their own life on hold to do so. Jessica patted him on his shoulder. "She loves you, you know."

"I know," Nathan whispered.

"Then stop hurting her by saying such foolish things.

You're a part of our family and we wouldn't have it any other way, Nate."

Nathan looked at his aunt and then down at the bedspread on his lap. "I just feel responsible for you guys not being able to travel like you wanted."

Jessica made a *pfft* sound. "Big talk, Nate. We're two homebodies who prefer to be in our own place than romping the mean roads of different countries or states. The farthest we've ever gone, even before you came to live with us, was the next county over."

A smile danced at the edges of Nathan's lips. "Really?"

"Really," Jessica said. "I don't think your Aunt Becky could handle a sixteen-hour flight overseas. She'd be pacing the plane, making everyone nervous. You know she can't sit still for longer than five minutes. The air marshal would think she was a terrorist or something."

Nathan chuckled slightly. "You're probably right."

Jessica covered his hand with hers. "Stop apologizing and stop thinking you're a burden, Nate. You are far from anything except welcome here with open arms."

Nathan bit back the instinctual argument and gave her a weak smile. "I'll try."

"Good. Do that. Now, you think you can get back to sleep?"

"I don't know."

"There's still a couple of hours before daylight, so why don't you try? I'll make pancakes for breakfast, okay?"

"Okay."

Jessica kissed his forehead and stood. She gave him a comforting look on the way out of the room. Nathan lay back down and tried to sleep, but the memory of the nightmare kept him awake. He'd communicated with a lot of spirits in the last six years, some newly dead and some gone for years, but he'd never once seen his parents. He'd always assumed they'd just moved on to the other side, but the dream made him worry they were stuck in limbo, held by whatever demons haunted them. Maybe even the demons haunting him were responsible. How could he help them if they were? Could he help them?

Nathan spent the rest of the early morning hours staring at the ceiling, his thoughts chasing one another in an endless loop. He heard his aunts beginning to move around and getting ready to face the new day. Eventually the smell of frying bacon and the sweet scent of pancakes drifted up the stairs, causing him to give up the fight and drag himself from the bed. He didn't bother putting his socks from yesterday on and stuffed his feet into his sneakers, pushing the laces inside the shoe instead of tying them.

Arriving downstairs, he found Jessica at the stove and Becky setting the table. He walked up to her and gave her a hug, silently apologizing for upsetting her. She sniffled and returned his embrace. Nathan felt terrible.

"Enough blubbering, you two," Jessica interrupted, setting a large plate of pancakes in the center of the table and another with crispy bacon beside it.

Nathan released Becky and stepped back. Becky kissed his cheek, pulled out her chair, and sat down. "What are your plans for today, sweetie?" she asked, the events of the night before forgiven.

"Studying, and I have a session at Java Bean tonight." Jessica dished several pancakes onto his plate. "I'm not going to eat all this," Nathan protested.

"Try," Jessica said and placed two pancakes on her plate and another two on Becky's.

Grumbling, Nathan shook his head and poured syrup on them. He ate two before his stomach pained him. He sat back with a sigh. "I'm done."

"You barely ate anything," Becky said.

"I can't eat anymore, Aunt Becky."

Becky sighed and shook her head. "Troy was right. You aren't eating enough. I may end up having to come check up on you every morning."

"Please don't do that. I'm fine. I just don't have a large appetite."

Jessica chuckled and started clearing the table, and Nathan instantly jumped up to help her. He put away the syrup and butter and then started drying as Jessica washed. Becky wandered off to start the second coat of paint on the downstairs walls.

"She means well, Nate."

"I know, Aunt Jess. I am old enough to take care of myself now, though."

"If you don't start taking care of yourself better, they won't be empty promises, Nate. You know how she is when she gets something in her head."

Nathan knew only too well. There'd been many failed experiments on his aunt's part, and she'd often roped him into helping. The basement had several boxes of those attempts that hadn't panned out.

"I eat when I get hungry. Sometimes I just forget because I'm so busy. With the store and school, I don't have a lot of time to think of other stuff."

"You should make time, Nate. For our sake and your own."

"I'll try."

Jessica said nothing more on the subject and they finished the dishes without further chatter, listening to Becky singing in the other room as she painted. After they were done, Nathan glanced at the clock. "I should get going. I need to run home and grab my books before heading to the library."

"I'll drive you," Jessica offered.

"That's okay, Aunt Jess. I can take the bus."

"It's all right, Nate. I don't mind."

Nathan hesitated, but he knew he was still too fresh from last night's panic attack and the migraine to risk running into another spirit like the woman on the bus from the other day. "If you're sure it's not too much trouble."

"Of course not. Let me go grab my purse and tell Becky. Give me two minutes, hon."

Jessica left the room and Nathan made his way to the front door. He heard Becky and Jessica talking softly. Then they both appeared in the living room entryway. Becky had a streak of light blue paint on one cheek. He grinned. She always had been a messy painter.

Becky came to him and hugged him once more. "You take care of yourself, Nate, and please come over more often, sweetie. I miss having you around."

"Sure, Aunt Becky. I will."

"I love you," she murmured and stepped back.

"Love you, too."

Jessica kissed Becky. "I'll be back soon, baby."

"Be careful," Becky said.

A few minutes later, Nathan and Jessica were on the road heading to Nathan's apartment. Jessica fiddled with the radio for a bit until she found a station she liked. They spoke little, just riding together in companionable silence. When she pulled up to the curb in front of his place, Nathan opened the door. "Thanks for the ride, Aunt Jess."

"No problem, hon. Get some more rest when you're done with your studying," she commanded.

"I will," Nathan promised and shut the door. He waved as she left and then turned toward the front of his building, only to stop short. His eyes widened as he saw Erik sitting on the bottom steps, a coffee cup dangling in his hands between his knees. "What are you doing here?" he asked in surprise.

Erik stood and tossed the cup into a nearby garbage can.

"I called the store yesterday, and they said you weren't available. When I called a second time and they said you'd gone home, I went to the store because I thought maybe you were avoiding me. The young man, Quincy or something, told me you were ill. I was concerned."

"How did you know where I live?" Nathan ignored the thrill that went through him at hearing Erik's worry about him.

"Quincy gave me the address. You should really have a talk with him, giving out your personal info so easily," Erik admonished and came closer.

"Quincy? Oh, you mean Quinn." *Remind self to kill Quinn.*

"That's it. Are you feeling better?"

Nathan fought the urge to retreat. Erik stopped in front of him. "Much," he replied hoarsely.

"Good. I came by last night, but there was no answer. I was beginning to worry when you didn't answer again this morning. Who was that in the car?"

"My aunt."

Erik reached out and touched Nathan's cheek. "You were avoiding me when I called, weren't you?"

Nathan felt guilty, despite knowing it was best for them both. He tried to ignore the feeling of Erik's calloused fingers on his skin. "I wasn't avoiding you," he lied.

Erik gave him a skeptical look. "Why don't I believe you?"

"I wasn't!"

"It was just because you were sick, then?"

"Yes," Nathan said, grasping at the lifeline.

"What was wrong?" Erik stroked his thumb over Nathan's cheekbone.

"Huh?" Nathan had to struggle to understand what Erik was asking.

"You were sick. What was wrong?"

"Oh. Migraine."

Erik frowned. "Do you get those often?"

"Sometimes."

Erik dropped his hand from Nathan's face. "Have you seen a doctor about them?"

"There's nothing they can do." Nathan ignored the bereft sensation in his stomach at the loss of Erik's touch. "I just have to suffer through them."

"Well, that seems ridiculous. They can't give you any painkillers?"

Nathan shook his head. "No. They can't because I was—" He stopped himself, realizing in horror what he'd almost admitted.

"You were what?" Erik asked, frowning.

"Nothing. They just can't prescribe me anything that will help." Nathan limped past Erik, only to be stopped by Erik's hand on his arm.

Erik didn't say anything at first and then let Nathan's arm go. "Are you busy today?" he asked.

Nathan knew he should study. He should say yes and keep moving, but weakness stopped him. "Not until later," he mumbled.

"Spend the day with me, then."

Nathan hesitated, looking down at his shoes. "I need to take a shower first and change my clothes," he finally said.

"Okay. I can wait."

Crap, that meant he'd have to do the polite thing and invite Erik into his apartment. "Uh… would you like to come in while you wait?"

Erik smiled. "Sure."

As they climbed the stairs, Nathan tried to remember if anything was lying around Erik shouldn't see, but he couldn't picture his place from when he and Troy had left the morning before. He unlocked the door and entered, closing the door after Erik. He did a quick survey of the place as he dropped his keys and wallet on the kitchen counter. Somehow, the apartment seemed smaller with Erik there, and Nathan cleared his throat. "Why don't you have a seat? I won't be long."

"Don't rush on my account. I'm pretty easy to entertain." Erik nudged him lightly toward the hallway. "Go on. Promise I won't steal anything."

Nathan flushed. "I wasn't—"

"I'm teasing you, Nathan. I do that a lot, so you're going to have to get used to it."

Erik's words implied they were going to spend more time together, and Nathan tried to fight off the surge of anticipation the idea caused in his belly. "Sorry," Nathan said. "I'll be right back."

He hurried down the hallway as fast as his bad leg would allow and into his room. Alan was nowhere to be seen, which made Nathan happy. He couldn't handle another bout of guilt right now. Searching through his dresser, he found a pair of light stonewashed jeans with a couple of rips in the knee area and a plain blue T-shirt. They were some of the few "normal" clothes he owned. Most everything else he had was black and featured bands or skulls. He'd never needed to worry about his wardrobe because of the store he worked at, and Curtis didn't care what he wore during his sets at the Java Bean. Curtis said it showed his personality as an artist or some such thing. Nathan just preferred to wear what suited his moods regularly.

Nathan rushed through his shower, dried off, and dressed quickly. He brushed his hair and tied it back with a thin black band. Leaving the bathroom, he reentered the bedroom to put on socks and his usual sneakers. He took a deep breath and exited his room. Erik stood near the window, his back to him. Nathan couldn't help but wonder what Erik thought of his tiny apartment as he studied the man's broad shoulders and long legs.

Erik turned and smiled when he saw Nathan standing at the end of the hallway. "Ready?"

Nodding, Nathan snatched his wallet and keys from the bar separating the kitchen from the living area. He stuffed his wallet in his back pocket and waited for Erik to precede him out the door. Erik remained at the top of the stairs as Nathan locked up. They had to descend single file, as the stairwell was too narrow to go side by side. Nathan couldn't stop himself from studying the way Erik's jeans hugged every curve of his backside in a loving manner. Heat crowded Nathan's lower belly, and he had to take several deep breaths to calm down.

He was too busy struggling not to let his lust overwhelm him to notice his leg about to give out. When Erik reached the bottom, Nathan went to step down onto the last step and his leg crumpled beneath his weight. He slammed into Erik's back, almost knocking him over, and grabbed hold of the man's shirt. The minute his leg had stabilized enough to hold him, he stumbled backward. "I'm so sorry," he muttered in embarrassment, his cheeks hot.

"No harm done. Does that happen often?" Erik asked.

Nathan couldn't meet Erik's gaze as he struggled to form words. "So-sometimes."

Erik left it at that and didn't question him further. "Where would you like to go?" Erik asked.

Nathan shrugged. He didn't usually go anywhere to have fun. School, work, and playing at Java Bean consumed most of his time. "I don't really know."

"No favorite hangouts?"

Snorting, Nathan shook his head. "I rarely have a lot of time to hang out. I'm too busy studying or working most of the week."

Erik didn't respond, but Nathan could sense his words had upset Erik. "If you changed your mind, that's okay. I'll understand."

"Of course not!" Erik exclaimed. "Come on, let's go. I have an idea."

Nathan gave him a skeptical look but followed Erik to his truck. Erik opened his door for him, much to his discomfort. "I can open my door," he protested.

"I know you can, but I wanted to do it for you," Erik said. "Get in."

Climbing onto the seat, Nathan went to reach for the handle to close it, but Erik beat him to it. Nathan used the time it took for Erik to walk around the truck to look at the posh interior. Light tan leather seats with the latest state-of-the-art equipment on the dashboard screamed money. He kept his hands clasped together in his lap in fear of damaging anything. There was no way he could afford to fix any of the expensive gadgets.

Erik slid into the driver's side and started the truck. He pulled away from the curb and headed downtown. "So, Nathan, what are you studying in school?"

"Business."

"Any particular type?"

"Administration."

"That's a good one. It has a very broad range, so you aren't stuck with just one type of specialization. Also good if you intend to start your own business. Do you?"

"Do I what?"

"Plan on starting your own business?"

"Oh. Someday I suppose. I just need to get a better job so I can start paying my aunts back."

Erik glanced at him as he turned a corner. "Are they paying for you to go to school?"

Nathan tensed. Damn it. He seriously needed to stop

letting his guard down around Erik. This was the third time he'd slipped. Something about the man made Nathan feel so comfortable. Almost as though he were with Troy. "Something like that."

"I see. I'm sure they'll understand if you need a little time to return the money."

Shrugging, Nathan stared out the passenger window, watching the buildings go by. "So where are we going?" he asked, changing the subject.

"You'll see," Erik replied. "I started my business pretty early after college. It can be a very rewarding experience."

Yeah, if you have money to start it with, Nathan thought sarcastically. "I guess."

"What made you decide on business if you're so into music?"

Somehow, Erik had focused on the things Nathan couldn't answer without giving away his past. "Music is fun to play, but it doesn't pay the bills," he carefully said.

"But if you enjoy playing, that should be what matters. I've seen you talk about music. Your entire face lights up. Isn't that what you'd rather be doing?"

"It doesn't matter what I want to do."

"Of course it does! It matters a lot."

Nathan fidgeted in his seat, uncomfortable with the topic. Erik's words were like knives, sharp and unrelenting. He would give anything to be a musician. But what he wanted and what he needed to do were two entirely separate things. "Look, you don't know me, and you don't know my life. If you're going to continue to talk about it, please stop the truck and let me out now."

"You're right. I don't know you. Not yet anyway. I'm sorry. I'm sometimes more vocal about things than I should be. Forgive me, please?"

Nathan gave a stiff nod in acknowledgement of Erik's

apology. His acceptance had Erik smiling again and when they pulled up to the Oceanfront Boardwalk, Nathan raised an eyebrow. This is where he'd thought to come? "Ever been on the Skywheel?" Erik asked.

"No." They had built the Skywheel while Nathan had been in the hospital, and he'd never even thought about coming to the boardwalk to ride it. Troy had tried to get him to go a few times, but he'd always refused. The ride was a bit like a Ferris wheel with enclosed seats instead of the typical bucket seats. Glass windows allowed you to look out and see for miles in each direction. The thing went over two hundred feet above the beach.

"You're not afraid of heights, are you?" Erik asked as he climbed out of the truck.

Nathan shook his head. Heights were nothing compared to the horrors he'd witnessed over the years. He exited the truck on his side and slammed the door shut. Nathan immediately picked up on the presence of a spirit and tensed. A woman stood beneath a palm tree, staring out at the ocean. The white glow around her shimmered as her emotions shifted. Swallowing hard, Nathan tried his best to ignore her and followed Erik toward the Skywheel.

"You okay?" Erik asked, concerned.

"I'm fine." Nathan tried to paste on a smile, but the woman's emotions were so strong. They hit him like needles despite the distance between them. "Just a little tired."

Erik stopped and touched Nathan's shoulder. "Why didn't you say something? Do you want to go home and rest?"

"No! No. I'm okay," he said, trying to pull it back a notch. "I couldn't sleep even if I wanted to."

"If you're sure," Erik said, eyeing Nathan for a moment.

"I am. Let's go." Nathan didn't even stop to think before he grabbed Erik's hand and tugged him toward the Skywheel. Hopefully, being two hundred feet in the air would be enough distance to escape the woman's overpowering feelings. When they reached the ticket window, Nathan realized he still held Erik's hand and dropped it as if it was hot. "Sorry," he muttered.

Erik grinned and leaned in a little closer. "I'm not."

Nathan flushed and fumbled for his wallet. Erik immediately waved at him to put it back. "My treat," he said.

"But—"

Erik didn't give him a chance to finish his protest before he handed over his credit card to the woman behind the glass. "Two VIP please."

Nathan frowned. *VIP?*

The woman processed the transaction and handed him two black-colored tickets and his card. "Take the stairs to the right, sir. Our attendant will be right with you."

Placing his card back into his wallet and then stuffing it into his back pocket, Erik took hold of Nathan's hand again and held on tight, despite Nathan's attempts to pull away. Several people stared and whispered amongst themselves, causing Nathan to feel even more uncomfortable. "Erik," he muttered. "Let go."

Erik didn't pay attention to him, just handed the tickets to the attendant at the top of the stairs. Nathan kept his face turned away from the line of people they'd just skipped. He picked up on several people complaining about them getting to the head of the line when they were there waiting, but it wasn't that which made him stiffen. The venomous word one guy spat made Nathan tense. He jerked his hand from Erik's, this time successfully. Erik looked at him, forehead wrinkled in confusion. "What's wrong?"

"People are staring," Nathan whispered.

"So? Let them stare."

So easy for someone who'd never had people look at him with fear or hatred before. Nathan folded his arms and kept his head down, his gaze locked on the ground. Erik swore beneath his breath and wrapped an arm around Nathan's shoulders, leading him into one enclosure on the ride. Nathan sank onto a bench and pushed as far into the corner of the seat as possible. Erik sat next to him as the attendant closed the door and then the Skywheel began moving.

CHAPTER 9

At first, Nathan didn't notice the floor beneath them, but when he'd finally calmed down enough to look around, his breath caught. The floor was see-through. Glass allowed him to see straight to the ground. Nathan sucked in a breath. He raised his gaze to look out at the ocean and the beach goers bobbing in the waves.

Erik didn't ask him about his reaction from before and Nathan was grateful.

"Breathtaking sight, isn't it?" Erik asked.

Nathan nodded and continued to survey the surrounding area. The spirit's emotions were no longer weighing on him and he could enjoy the ride. He smiled and pressed closer to the glass, watching the boats sailing in the distance.

"Makes you feel kind of small, doesn't it?" Erik mused.

"Yeah," Nathan said. "I forgot how much I used to like the beach. Troy and I used to come here a lot in the summer before…"

Erik ignored his pause. "You and Troy have known each other for a while?"

Nathan smiled. "Since middle school."

"Somehow I can see the two of you getting into a lot of trouble together," Erik teased.

Laughing lightly, Nathan glanced at Erik for a moment. "We did. The principal was definitely glad to see us move on to high school."

"Caused a lot of trouble, did you?"

"Both of us liked to play poker, a lot."

"You take the other kids' lunch money?" Erik chuckled.

"We didn't steal it. We won it. Troy and I learned to play poker at an early age."

Erik leaned his head back and laughed loudly, a deep baritone sound that sent heat rushing to Nathan's groin. Nathan shifted in his seat to hide his reaction. "I bet the other kids' parents loved you," Erik said, eyes twinkling with mirth.

"We didn't force them to play. They wanted to win their money back each week. Wasn't our fault they weren't any good at it."

Erik had a knowing look on his face but kept quiet. Nathan returned to watching the waves and people who looked like ants. A glow resonated inside his chest, a feeling he'd never had before, and it made him almost giddy.

"Which college are you attending now?" Erik asked.

"Webster University. In my fourth year." He changed the subject. "What made you want to go into architecture and construction?"

"My dad was a contractor, and I used to hang out at the sites with him after school. I found I liked the smell of fresh cut wood, and I loved seeing the unique designs my father would help construct. They inspired me to want to create my own works of art."

Envy bit deep. Nathan would give anything to have had the same time with his own father. "Where was your mom?"

"Not in the picture. Dad told me she took off when I was a baby. Something about discovering herself in Hollywood."

Nathan couldn't imagine not being wanted. He looked at Erik with sympathy. "I'm sorry."

"Don't be. I looked for her later. She remarried and had a new family. I didn't even try to open communication with her. If she'd wanted to be in my life, she would have tried by then. My dad more than made up for her absence every way he could."

"Still pretty messed up on her part. I can't imagine not wanting to be a part of your life." Nathan realized what he said. "I mean uh… a mom not wanting to be a part of her son's life."

Erik smirked but didn't call him on the slip of the tongue. He shrugged. "Things happen. I may not be where I am today if she'd stuck around or taken me with her."

"Where's your dad?" Nathan asked curiously.

"Retired to Miami. He didn't want to, intended on working his whole life, but he had a heart attack about four years ago and his body couldn't take the strain anymore. I fly down there once every couple of months to spend time with him."

"That's nice," Nathan murmured.

"How long have you worked at the music store?"

"Almost four years now. I started working there right before college."

"You're a manager now?"

Nathan nodded and looked out over the water once more. "About a year and a half. I usually work after classes and on Saturdays, with a Sunday thrown in twice a month."

The Skywheel came to a halt to let passengers off. It wouldn't be long before the ride was over for the two of them. "What about Saturday and Sunday nights?" Erik asked.

"I actually play at a local coffee shop," Nathan replied.

"Play? Guitar?"

"Yep. The owner of the shop has been letting me set up every weekend for about a year."

"Is it just you, or do you have others with you?"

"Just me. I usually have about an hour or two of songs."

"Do you sing as well?"

"Sometimes. Depends on how I'm feeling."

Erik continued to ask him about his music as the Skywheel halted several times more before they reached the end of their own ride. Nathan stood a bit too soon and stumbled when the wheel stopped. Erik caught him and steadied him, a hand on Nathan's hip and the other on his waist. "Okay?" Erik asked, standing and bringing his body into full contact with Nathan's.

Nathan felt crowded and nodded, stepping back. "I'm fine. Stupid mistake on my part."

Erik led the way out of the car and down the steps. "Are you hungry?" he asked when they'd reached the sidewalk.

"Not really," Nathan said.

"Would you like to take a walk on the beach, then?"

Nathan shrugged. "Okay."

They headed to Erik's truck first to deposit their shoes inside the cab. The woman's spirit had disappeared, and Nathan couldn't have been more relieved. Nathan stopped at the edge of the sidewalk to roll up both pant legs until about mid-calf. When he straightened up, he noticed Erik watching him, a strange expression on his face.

"What?" Nathan asked.

Erik shook his head and the look vanished. "Nothing."

The waves crashed along the shoreline as Nathan waited for Erik to roll up his pant legs as well. He tried to ignore the way Erik's shoulder brushed against his as they walked toward the water. When they reached it, Erik turned to follow the shore. "Can I ask you something?" Erik asked over the sound of the ocean.

Anxiety hit Nathan, but he nodded.

"How did you injure your leg?"

Nathan swallowed hard. He glanced down and realized he'd forgotten the scars. No wonder Erik had been staring moments ago. He couldn't just brush off or ignore Erik's question this time. His throat felt like sandpaper when he choked out, "Car accident."

"How long ago?"

"Six years." Six agonizing years.

Erik said nothing for several minutes. They had gone another hundred feet when Erik asked Nathan the inevitable question. "Is that when you lost your parents?"

Nathan's eyes burned, and he blinked furiously, turning his head opposite the water. He cleared his throat. "Yes."

Erik halted and placed a hand on Nathan's forearm. "I'm truly sorry, Nathan."

Trying to act nonchalant, embarrassed at his reaction in front of Erik, Nathan shrugged. "It was a long time ago."

"Doesn't make it hurt any less. How'd it happen?"

Nathan looked down at the sand, watching their feet sink into the wetness, wishing it would swallow him whole. "Drunk driver."

Erik surprised Nathan again by pulling him into an embrace. Nathan didn't quite know how to react. He kept his arms by his sides until the warmth of Erik's body seeped into his, and Nathan hesitantly brought his arms around Erik's waist.

"I'm so sorry about your parents, but I'm glad you survived," Erik said, his voice rumbling against Nathan's ear.

Nathan didn't understand why Erik would care so much.

They'd only just met a few days ago. Discomfort set in, and he broke free of Erik's hug. He held on to the words he wanted to say. How he wished he hadn't lived. It should have been his parents who had. The water splashed over Nathan's toes, and he backed up a bit, refusing to meet Erik's gaze.

"I didn't mean to upset you," Erik said.

"You didn't," Nathan lied. "Can we head back now? I've got to get ready for my set at Java Bean."

"Are you sure you don't have time for lunch?"

"I'm not hungry," Nathan repeated his answer from earlier.

Erik let out a small sigh but didn't push. "All right."

Nathan ignored the sound. In order to clear his mind of the situation with Erik, he needed some time alone. He still hated himself for being attracted to Alan's fiancé and for not having the strength to stay away. There really was no excuse for his actions. Starting Monday, though, he wouldn't have any time to spend with Erik, so hopefully he could use that space to stamp out any feelings he had for him.

"What time do you play?" Erik interrupted his self-deprecation as they turned toward the truck and walked back.

"Seven." Nathan knew telling Erik the time his gig started revealed just how much time there truly was before he needed to leave for his set.

"I see," Erik murmured, barely discernible over the waves crashing along the shore. "May I come watch?"

Nathan didn't answer at first. He argued with himself to tell Erik no, but it wasn't like he could really stop the guy. It was a public coffeehouse, after all.

"You don't want me to," Erik said flatly.

"No! I mean… No, it's not that I don't want you to."

Erik's presence would definitely be distracting. The more time Nathan spent around him, the more he wanted to be normal and to have a normal life. If he were someone else or Alan had never realized he could see spirits, things would be different. Maybe. But things weren't different, and Alan had figured out Nathan's horrible gift.

Erik stopped walking and Nathan halted as well, looking at Erik. He could see hurt shimmering in Erik's eyes and his heart twisted. Before he could stop himself, Nathan blurted out, "You can come."

Damn it! What the hell was wrong with him? Hadn't he already learned his lesson? The happiness that overtook Erik's features, though, stifled any more of his silent arguments and Nathan returned Erik's smile.

"Great!" Erik resumed walking, a slight bounce in his step.

Nathan gave a small shake of his head and trailed after him. Somehow, the man wiped out all his survival instincts.

Once they reached the vehicle, Erik handed him a towel from the floor of the back seat to wipe his feet. Nathan worked quickly, dusting off the sand and perching on the edge of the doorjamb to put on his socks and shoes. He rolled down his pant legs and handed the towel to Erik, who also used it to remove the beach sand from his feet. Nathan climbed into the passenger side while waiting for Erik to finish. He stared out of the windshield at the ocean, wondering what the hell he planned on telling Alan when he saw him again.

Erik tossed the towel on the floor behind the driver's side and climbed in, and then he started the engine, backing out of the parking space. "So, where is this coffeehouse at?"

"Java Bean? You've never been there?" Nathan asked.

Erik shook his head. "Nope."

"I'm surprised. It's close to your office address."

"You know where my office is?" Erik prodded, interest buried in his tone.

Nathan flushed. "You gave me your business card at the store."

"Oh. That's right." Erik laughed. "I forgot. Here I was, hoping you were more into me than you let on."

"What?" Nathan stared at Erik, heart beating furiously.

Erik pulled to a stop at a red light and turned in his seat to look at Nathan. "You're not all that easy to read. Sometimes I can see you're attracted to me almost as much as I am to you, but at other times you're like a wall with a huge stop sign on it."

Nathan's mouth went dry. He tried to swallow. When he could finally speak, he said, "You don't have much of a filter, do you?"

"Not really. I don't see the point of not being honest with each other. Used to drive my fiancé nuts sometimes."

"I bet," Nathan muttered.

Erik laughed again. "See? You and Alan would have gotten along great. You both have similar personalities."

Nathan nearly burst into hysterical giggles. Erik had no idea just how much he and Alan wouldn't have been able to stand one another. "How long were you two together?" Nathan asked, even though he already knew the answer. He just really wanted to change the subject from being focused on his feelings for Erik.

"Three years."

"What was he like?"

"Fun and carefree, but caring. He had a big heart and helped anyone who needed it. He loved to dance and be spontaneous. You almost never saw him upset or sad. The only time I can remember ever seeing him cry was when I asked him to marry me. He also had a sarcastic streak to beat all hell."

"Oh yeah, we sound like two peas in a pod," Nathan replied drily.

Erik stopped the truck in front of Nathan's apartment, turning the engine off. "You sell yourself short, Nathan. I've seen the way you are with your friend. You care very much about him."

Nathan shifted uncomfortably in his seat. "That doesn't make me like your fiancé."

"You're also strong like he was," Erik said, leaning closer to Nathan. "Stubborn and fierce and full of pride."

Nathan couldn't do anything except watch as Erik moved toward him. His lips parted in a small catch of breath when Erik cupped the side of his face. Nathan's stomach twisted sharply the moment Erik's lips settled on his. Erik encouraged Nathan to kiss him back by breaking the contact long enough to surge forward once more.

Hesitantly, Nathan responded, copying Erik's actions. A gasp broke free when Erik slid his tongue along Nathan's lower lip, and Nathan struggled to control his reaction to the other man. Disappointment set in when Erik broke the kiss.

"Nathan..." Erik sighed and slid his hand down to Nathan's chest, coming to rest over his heart. The furious beating of said muscle tapped a rhythm against Erik's palm. "You should go in before I do something I'll regret."

Nathan didn't understand what Erik meant, but he felt too embarrassed to ask and kept his face averted, trying to hide the flush heating his cheeks. He fumbled for the handle, only to jump when Erik reached past him and opened the door. He climbed down from the truck.

"Nathan?"

Taking a deep breath, Nathan paused in closing the door and raised his gaze to Erik to find an amused expression.

"I'll see you tonight, okay?" Erik said.

Nodding, Nathan shut the door and tried to walk normally to the stairs. He took each one carefully until he reached the top, where he collapsed on the step. His entire body felt feverish, and it had nothing to do with the trip up the stairs. He lifted his hand to his mouth and ran a couple of his fingers along his bottom lip, his belly tightening in remembrance of Erik's mouth on his.

"Nate?" Alan's voice disturbed his dazed thoughts and Nathan started, horror setting in.

Erik had kissed him, and he'd kissed back. Good God, he was a glutton for punishment. What the hell had he been thinking? He should have pushed Erik away instead of responding. How would he be able to face Alan? Nathan cleared his throat but kept his gaze on the stairwell. "Hey, A-Alan." Nathan's voice cracked.

"Are you okay, Nate?" Alan asked, floating closer to stand near him.

Nathan closed his eyes. "I'm fine. Just tired."

"I saw you get out of Erik's truck. Did you talk to him?" Alan eagerly demanded.

"No, not yet."

"What? Why not?"

"Because I haven't." Nathan grunted and pushed himself up from the step. He spun around and unlocked his front door. He opened it and then slammed it shut behind him after he'd walked inside.

Alan didn't let up. He materialized through the wood and Nathan slapped his keys down on the counter. "Can you just leave me alone?" Nathan shouted.

"No! You promised, Nate! Why didn't you tell him I'm here?" Alan returned his shout.

Nathan didn't know what to tell him. "Because I'm not ready yet!"

Anger sliced through Nathan's nerve endings, and he stepped back from Alan, but Alan followed. "Back off," Nathan snapped.

"Why haven't you told him, Nate? What's stopping you?"

Nathan opened and closed his mouth several times, but he couldn't come up with an answer. Something must have shone on his face though, because jealousy bit into his skin, mingling with the rage building inside Alan. "You like him, don't you?" Alan snarled.

Nathan tried to step farther away, but his back hit the wall between the two windows at the front of his apartment. "Alan!" Nathan exclaimed in fear as Alan moved closer and closer, the spirit's emotions digging in deep and pressing on his chest.

His knees gave out, and he crumpled to the floor, falling to his side. He could barely breathe under the onslaught. "Alan," he choked out again. "Stop… please."

Alan floated over him, glaring at him in fury. "You're supposed to help me! You don't want to tell him because you know he'll think you're a freak."

Nathan cried out and curled into a ball, bringing his knees to his chest in agony. The word freak reverberated in his head repeatedly. Tears spilled down his cheeks as he sobbed, and his chest felt as if it would cave in. "Alan," he begged weakly.

Black spots danced before his eyes, and Nathan knew if Alan didn't let up soon, he'd pass out. "Please," Nathan said as the black spots got bigger.

Alan must have finally realized exactly what was happening and backed off. Nathan's sight cleared up slowly and he could see Alan standing near his kitchen, a horrified expression on his face. "Nathan… I-I'm so sorry," Alan whispered.

Coughing, Nathan dragged himself into a sitting position. "Get out," he spat.

"Nate—"

"Get out of my fucking apartment!" Nathan screamed. "Get out!"

Alan didn't try again and just vanished, leaving Nathan a shuddering mess on the floor. Nathan leaned his head against the wall and covered his face, scrubbing at the tears on his cheeks.

He couldn't do this anymore. The fire burning his lungs right then tasted acrid and metallic. He'd promised to help Alan because it was the only way to get the spirit to leave him alone, but it was all too much. His attraction to Erik only complicated things, made them worse. With every other spirit, he'd done what he'd needed to, and it was over.

Alan's words echoed in his ears, and he knew Alan was right. He couldn't tell Erik out of his own fear Erik would believe him to be a freak.

His emotions felt raw and frayed. Nathan dragged himself up from the floor and stumbled down the hallway to the bathroom. He opened the medicine chest over the sink and took out the prescription bottle of antipsychotics. Twisting the cap, he dumped two pills into his palm, then added a third one to ensure blissful oblivion for a while, and tossed them back, swallowing them without water.

Nathan stared at the contents of the bottle, the twenty or thirty some odd pills left, and seriously considered downing them all. Then it wouldn't matter—his attraction to Erik or his promise to help Alan. But he'd sworn to Troy and his aunts that he would never try to kill himself again. It was the only way his aunts would allow him to control the use of the meds himself. The psychiatrist originally had his aunts doling them out, but he'd begged them when he'd moved out to let him handle it on his own. Nathan dropped the open bottle in the sink and watched the pills roll around until they stopped. The plug kept them from going down the drain, the pills too big to fit beneath it.

He made it to his bedroom before collapsing on the bed. He returned to the fetal position and didn't move again, his unblinking gaze locked on the opposite wall. Nothing mattered. Not Java Bean or Alan or Erik. Not even Troy.

The pills set in, and his brain grew fuzzy. Sometimes the pills could last for hours, and Nathan prayed this dose would. His eyelids drooped and before long he was out cold, not knowing or caring about the hours passing by.

CHAPTER 10

Clouds enveloped him, keeping him warm and cozy. He never wanted to leave this place. Darkness was a comfort, a pillow supporting him. A banging noise brought forth a frown, and he moaned at being disturbed. He clung to the surrounding safety. The banging happened again, and then the sound of a voice calling his name.

"Nate! Shit, man, what the hell did you do?"

Nathan drifted between the clouds, burrowing deeper and refusing to let go. Hands gripped his shoulders and shook him. "Nate, wake up, bro."

Nathan groaned and reluctantly opened his eyes to find Troy hovering over him, worry etched on his features. Troy had turned on the light apparently, and he had a slight glow behind him. Nathan smiled groggily. "Troy," he whispered.

"Nate, you gotta answer me. How many did you take?"

"Many what?" Nathan asked, confused.

"Pills, Nate! Come on, wake up." Troy shook him again.

"Stop," Nathan grumbled.

"Then answer me, damn it! How many pills did you take?"

Nathan blinked heavily and gave his friend a goofy grin. "Three."

"You swear?"

"Promised, now go 'way." Nathan pulled his pillow closer and shut his eyes again.

He heard Troy sigh in relief, and a deep raspy voice asked, "What's wrong with him?"

Erik! What the hell was Troy doing bringing Erik here? Nathan struggled to surface from the fog smothering him. He heard Troy mention something about pain pills for his knee. Liar!

"I've never seen someone react to pain meds quite like that," Erik murmured.

Nathan wanted to smile at Erik's intuitiveness, but he couldn't feel his lips. "'Rik," he grunted.

"I'm here, Nathan."

He felt the bed sag and knew Erik had sat down on the edge of the mattress near him. "Go. Not 'posed to be here."

"He wasn't exactly taking no for an answer," Troy said dryly from somewhere to Nathan's right.

Nathan peered through miniscule slits in his eyelids at Erik. "Go."

Erik gave him a bemused look. "I'm not going anywhere, Nathan. Not until I know you're all right."

"Have to," Nathan insisted.

"Why?" Erik asked gently.

"Bad for you."

"What is?"

"Me," Nathan whispered and gave up the fight, sliding back into the comforting darkness.

~

When Nathan woke next, it was still dark outside, and Troy must have turned off the lamp next to his bed. He sat up and brushed his hair back from his face with both hands before leaning over to turn on the light. The soft glow chased away the shadows as he slid from the bed and padded down the hallway to the restroom.

At some point, Troy must have removed his shoes. He shivered at the cold vinyl on his bare feet as he entered the bathroom. Snapping on the light, he blinked several times against the harsh pinpricks on his corneas, the halogen bulb overhead crueler than the small wattage he used in the lamp near his bed. When he could finally see straight, he noticed the pills were no longer in the sink, and the bottle wasn't on the counter, either.

Nathan relieved himself and then looked in the medicine chest. Troy had stuffed the bottle behind several others. He knew Erik had been there, and he hoped Troy had cleaned it up before Erik could see what the bottle contained. Sighing, he flicked off the light and headed toward his kitchen to get a drink. He didn't even need to see to make his way to the fridge. He opened the door and reached in to grab a bottle of water, leaving the door propped open to put the bottle back when he finished.

The twist of the cap was loud in the silence of his apartment, and he took a long swig.

"Are you feeling any better?" Erik's voice whispered through the darkness, causing Nathan to choke on his water.

Nathan wrenched the bottle from his lips and turned to see Erik lying on the couch and Troy on the floor. Troy appeared to be fast asleep, from what he could tell. "What are you doing here?" he asked in a low voice.

Erik sat up and the sheet dropped to his waist, baring a muscular chest so beautiful Nathan had to let the fridge door close to hide his blush. "We were worried about you."

Troy… His friend would be lucky to live in the morning when Nathan got done with him. "I'm fine. You didn't need to stay," he whispered.

Nathan heard the shifting of blankets and the couch creak as Erik moved. He could just make out the sound of Erik's feet on the carpet and saw the shadow of his figure as he walked to where Nathan stood. Sawdust settled in Nathan's mouth, and he had to work to control his breathing when Erik stopped in front of him.

"I needed to stay," Erik murmured.

"Why?" Nathan frowned. "You barely know me."

"It doesn't take a lot to care about someone, Nathan," Erik said, reaching up to brush Nathan's hair back from his face. "Troy wouldn't tell me much, but I'm not ignorant. I could tell he was extremely worried. Why did he think you'd tried to kill yourself?"

Nathan tensed and jerked backward, dropping the water bottle. It clattered to the floor and water splashed across his toes. "I don't know what you're talking about."

Erik bent down and picked up the now half-empty bottle, placing it on the counter. "From the moment I met you, Nathan, I felt something between us. A connection. I know it's crazy considering we've only known each other for a few days, but I haven't experienced a feeling like this since Alan died. I didn't think I ever would again after he was gone." Erik placed his hands on Nathan's shoulders. "I need you to be honest with me. Did you try to kill yourself?"

"No!" Nathan protested.

"But you've tried before." It was a statement rather than a question.

Nathan tried to break Erik's hold on his shoulders. "Let go," he snapped.

Erik ignored his request. "Why, Nathan?"

"It's none of your business." Nathan attempted to free himself again.

"Maybe not yet. Someday I hope you'll want to tell me."

Nathan halted his struggle and stared at Erik. "Why do you care so much?"

"I already told you. You've awakened something inside me I thought I'd never feel again. I won't let that go so easily," Erik said patiently.

Nathan really had no response to Erik's words, but they struck him straight in the chest. His throat felt tight and his heart hurt. "I don't understand."

Erik smiled, his teeth flashing. "You will. I think you should go back to sleep and get some more rest."

Exasperated at Erik's unfailing confidence, Nathan shook his head. "You're really stubborn, you know that?"

"That's the pot calling the kettle black," Troy said sleepily from where he lay on the floor.

Nathan jumped. He'd forgotten Troy was there. Damn. He wondered how much Troy had heard. "Shut up, Troy."

Erik chuckled and nudged Nathan toward the hallway. "Go on. I'll take you out for breakfast in the morning."

"I have school," Nathan said.

"Before then. What time does your first class start?"

"Seven."

"Nine," Troy answered at the same time as Nathan.

"Troy!"

Erik laughed again. "So, let's get out of here by seven. There's a Denny's around the corner, right?"

Nathan sighed. "Yeah."

"I'll take you to school afterward."

"You don't have to do that," Nathan said. "Troy has class, too."

"I don't mind. Gives me more time to be with you."

Nathan was grateful for the darkness when he felt his

cheeks heat in a blush yet again. He mumbled under his breath and went back to his room, Erik's chuckles following him the entire way. He burrowed under his covers and closed his eyes, lips curling up at the edge in a slight smile.

~

Knocking at the door woke Nathan and he sat up, yawning. He wiped the sleep from his eyes and got out of bed, then opened the door and blinked at Erik.

Erik smiled. "Time to get up."

Nathan huffed and nodded.

"Not a morning person?" Erik asked.

Nathan shook his head.

"Get dressed." Erik reached out and ruffled Nathan's hair.

Scowling, Nathan grabbed Erik's wrist. "I'm not a dog."

"Of course you aren't." Erik didn't free himself from Nathan's grasp.

"Don't pet me like I am one," Nathan growled.

"Never," Erik said innocently. He slid his hand down until Nathan's was in his. Entwining their fingers, he brought Nathan's up to his lips, pressing a kiss to the back. "Better?"

Nathan sighed and stepped away, disengaging his hand from Erik's. "Let me get dressed in peace."

Erik pouted, literally. "Can't I watch?"

Gaping at Erik's outrageousness, Nathan shook his head and closed the door. He leaned his forehead against the cool wood to urge the heat in his cheeks to dissipate.

"Nathan?" asked a hesitant voice from behind him, causing him to jump.

He turned to find Alan standing near the window. Nathan glared at him. "What do you want?"

"I'm sorry, Nate."

"Not good enough. Get out." Nathan walked to his dresser

and wrenched open a drawer to take out a pair of jeans. He ignored Alan as he gathered the rest of his clothing in the early morning light filtering through the slats in his blinds.

"Nate, please," Alan pleaded.

Nathan snarled and whirled around to sneer at Alan. "I told you what happens when you get too close. I trusted you not to use that information, but you did anyway. Do you know what that did to me? Do you know what I almost did last night?"

Alan flinched with each word flung at him and Nathan felt a bitter sense of satisfaction. "I'm really sorry, Nate. I didn't mean to."

"It doesn't matter because I'm done. Figure out how to deal with your shit on your own," Nathan spat.

"What? No! Nate, please, help me," Alan begged. "Please! I can't do this on my own. You're the only one who can help!"

Nathan snorted. "You think that's enough? You've only been in my life a week and I've been mugged, suffered the first migraine I've had in months, and you almost pushed me to… You know what? Never mind. Now you expect me to just accept you're sorry and move on like nothing happened?"

"Then why haven't you told him yet?" Alan demanded. "If I'm such a damned inconvenience, why haven't you done what you promised and told Erik about me? Then I'd be able to move on and I wouldn't be causing you so much trouble!"

Anger caused Nathan to blurt out, "Because you were right! I am attracted to him, and I don't want him to think I'm a freak!"

Nathan covered his mouth in horror. What the hell had he just done? He waited for a repeat of the night before, but Alan didn't get mad again. In fact, Alan grew sad, eyes dimming.

"I heard what he said to you last night and how worried

he was about you. It's been two years for him, but it feels like only yesterday to me. He's moving on with his life, and I can't expect anything else. Only, I can't help but be sad that he's forgetting me."

Nathan dropped his hand to his side. He didn't know if the emotion inside him right then was his own or Alan's. "Erik isn't forgetting you, Alan. He misses you."

Alan gave Nathan a hopeful look. "Yeah?"

Nathan sighed and moved to sit on the bed, his clothes in his lap. "Yeah. I'm sorry I lied to you when you asked if I'm attracted to him." He glanced down at his hands. "It's stupid to even contemplate being with anyone, let alone anyone like him, but I don't want to let go yet. I'll tell him, Alan. I promise. Just… not yet."

Floating closer, Alan asked, "Why do you think you don't deserve to be with someone, Nate? You're an amazing person. You're kind and sincere, and you care deeply."

"I'm also a freak," Nathan replied. "Who in their right mind would want to be with someone who sees and talks to ghosts? Someone who can never have a normal life?"

"Erik would," Alan murmured, coming closer. "I didn't mean what I said before about him. He would never judge you like that."

Nathan looked at Alan. "Wouldn't he? He doesn't know me. He says he cares, but the minute he finds out about my past and what's wrong with me, he'll turn and run away as fast as his feet can carry him."

Alan shook his head. "That's not true, Nate."

"I don't have it in me to test that theory right now," Nathan said, standing. "Can you leave? I need to get dressed."

Sighing, Alan nodded. Just before disappearing he said, "I can wait, Nate. Until you know him well enough to have faith that he won't desert you."

For a moment, Nathan stared at the spot where Alan had

stood. Was he right? After all, wouldn't Alan know Erik well enough to say that with such confidence? Nathan's inner doubt slammed home, and he snorted. Yeah, right. As if anyone would be okay with someone with his "ability." Even the people he'd helped over the years hadn't been able to look at him without fear after he'd finally convinced them he could see their loved ones. Erik would be no different.

Yet Nathan knew he couldn't ignore the situation forever. Maybe he should treat it like a bandage and rip it off now instead of later, when it would only be worse. Courage didn't exactly run through his veins, though, and he wasn't ready to let go of the only good feelings he'd had since his parents died. His selfish side wanted to hold on a little longer, even if he didn't deserve to have it.

Dressing quickly, Nathan pulled on a pair of black jeans, ripped at the knees, and a dark gray t-shirt with a logo from a local grunge band. He put on socks and stuffed his feet into a pair of black-and-white Converse sneakers, pushing the laces inside without tying them. He stopped in the bathroom on the way to the living room to brush his teeth and comb his hair into a somewhat presentable fashion, tying it back with a black band.

Erik sat on the couch by himself when Nathan had finished. Nathan frowned, looking around. "Where's Troy?"

Erik stood, smiling. "Troy had to go home and change. Said he'd meet you in front of campus."

Nathan knew Troy had done it on purpose. There were a few items of clothing in Nathan's dresser for nights when Troy stayed over for whatever reason. "I see."

"Is that a problem?" Erik asked, a twinkle of mirth in his eye.

"Nope," Nathan lied. He fidgeted for a second, then moved to the front door where his book bag sat, along with his hoodie. He pulled on the jacket and zipped it up partially before putting his pack over one shoulder. "We should go. I can't be late for my first class."

"One second," Erik said, approaching Nathan.

Nathan couldn't move anywhere, his back almost against the wall already, and he swallowed hard when Erik stopped in front of him. "What?" he squeaked out, embarrassed at the rodent-like quality of his voice.

Erik leaned forward and dropped a peck of a kiss on Nathan's lips. "Good morning, Nathan."

Blinking several times, Nathan finally replied, "Morning."

"Now we can go," Erik said while opening the front door. He walked out into the entryway and stopped to wait for Nathan to lock up. When Nathan would have taken the stairs first, Erik stepped in front of him. "Just in case," he stated and started down first.

Nathan didn't comment and followed Erik. Thankfully, there was no repeat of the previous morning's stumble. They made it to Erik's truck and once again, Erik opened his door for him. Nathan gave him an exasperated look but climbed in, tossing his bag on the floor. Erik closed the door and jogged around to his side.

"Don't you have work today?" Nathan asked.

"That's the beauty of being the owner of the company," Erik said as he pulled into traffic after starting the engine. "I've already told my assistant I won't be in until later this morning, and she'll make sure it gets to the right people."

Nathan couldn't hold in his curiosity. "How many people do you have working for you?"

"About fifteen in the office and another forty or so on the construction sites. Sometimes I pull in contractors if need be."

"How many sites do you normally have at once?"

Erik stopped at the corner for the red light briefly before turning. "I don't like to take on more than one or two at a time. I prefer to set realistic expectations on a completion date, and I can't do that if I overextend my crew."

Erik turned the truck into the parking lot of Denny's and pulled it into a space. Their conversation halted for a few minutes as they exited and walked to the entrance. Once the hostess had seated them, Nathan continued his inquiry. "What was your first job?"

"A little place over on 9th Street called Sariano's."

Nathan had never heard of it before. "Is that a restaurant?"

Erik nodded. "A rather upscale Italian restaurant."

The server stopped at their table. "Welcome to Denny's. My name's Cheryl. What can I get you boys to drink this morning?"

"I'll have orange juice and coffee," Erik said.

"Just coffee," Nathan supplied.

"Do you two know what you'd like to eat yet, or do you need a few minutes?"

"Give us a few minutes," Erik said.

"Sure thing, sugar. I'll go get your drinks and be right back."

Nathan laughed under his breath, drawing a curious look from Erik. "She reminds me of Harriet."

"Yeah, I guess you could say that." Erik grinned.

They both looked over the menu and chose something. The server returned a few moments later and set down two cups of coffee and a tall glass of orange juice. "You ready?"

Erik glanced at Nathan, who nodded. "I'll have the mushroom and Swiss omelet with bacon on the side and whole wheat toast."

Nathan couldn't imagine eating all of that for breakfast. "Just an everything bagel with cream cheese. Toasted, please."

"That's all you're going to eat?" Erik demanded.

"I can't eat that much in the morning. It's actually more than what I usually have."

Erik eyed him skeptically, but thankfully he didn't force Nathan to order more.

"I'll have that right out in a jiffy, boys. If you need anything else, let me know," Cheryl said after jotting down their orders and then walked away.

Nathan grabbed the sugar container and poured several teaspoons into the cup, then dumped in a couple of creamers. He picked up his mug and took a small sip, sighing as the coffee flavor exploded over his tongue.

"You live off coffee, don't you?" Erik asked as he dumped a couple packets of sugar into his.

"Mostly coffee and either toast or Pop-Tarts."

"You're going to develop an ulcer at this rate," Erik muttered.

Nathan frowned. "Why do you say that?"

"Because you barely eat anything to combat the caffeine running through your veins."

"I'm just too busy to be hungry most of the time. Even before… I mean, I've never eaten a lot," Nathan said and took another drink of his coffee.

"I'm going to have to work at getting you to eat more often."

"Not going to happen," Nathan said. "Troy is constantly shoving food at me and he hasn't gotten me to eat more yet."

"I have powers of persuasion that he doesn't," Erik taunted huskily.

Nathan felt his mouth go dry at the outright flirting and promise behind Erik's words. He took another sip of his coffee, struggling for a response. Erik winked at him suddenly, and Nathan groaned. "You're shameless."

Erik smirked. "Whatever it takes to get my way."

Nathan ducked his head down to hide his own grin.

"So, what classes are you taking right now?"

They spent the rest of breakfast talking about Nathan's classes and the professor who had kicked him out the week before. Erik offered to look at his assignment, but Nathan declined. It wouldn't matter anyway, since the professor had already given him the grade he felt the project had earned. When they'd finished their food and the server dropped the check, Nathan went to take out his wallet, but Erik waved him off. He gave Erik an exasperated look, but he ignored it.

When they stepped outside, Erik gave a satisfied sigh and patted his flat, muscular stomach. Nathan fought to keep his gaze on Erik's face instead of said body part. "Thank you for breakfast. I really wish you'd let me pay."

"I invited you, remember? That means I pay." Erik started toward the truck, Nathan following behind him at a slower pace.

He felt uncomfortable at just how much Erik was doing for him. "I can do things for myself," Nathan said as Erik opened his door for him.

Erik turned and looked at him, a patient expression on his face. "I know you can, Nathan, but I enjoy doing things for you."

Nathan shifted. "You just shouldn't."

"Why not?" Erik asked.

He debated on repeating what he'd already said but went with the truth. "Because you won't always be there, and I have to take care of myself. Too many people have already wasted too much of their lives doing things for me."

Erik let go of the door and took hold of Nathan's hand. Nathan glanced around, worried people would see them. He tried to pull free from Erik's grasp, but Erik wouldn't release him. "One day you will have to explain what that second part means, but people do things for each other because they care about one another. I can't say if I will always be here. The future is unknown to anyone. I do things for you because I want to, and my father raised me as a gentleman. When I take someone out, I am the one who opens the door and takes care of the bill. You're going to have to get used to that because it isn't going to change, and I'm not going to stop trying to get to know you."

Nathan didn't know how to respond to all of that. He glanced down at their hands and wondered just how his life had become so messy lately. For the last two years, things had been relatively calm except for the few spirits who'd realized he could see and hear them. Erik was a complication he hadn't expected. "I can't give you anything," Nathan whispered.

"I'm not asking for anything from you, Nathan. I'm only asking you to spend time with me."

Several moments went by—cars whizzed past on the street, and people shouted somewhere nearby. When Nathan finally could answer, he replied, "Okay."

Erik smiled, a bright face-splitting grin. "Good. Now let's go. Don't want you to be late for class."

Nathan nodded and climbed into the truck, this time knowing not to bother with trying to close his own door. Erik joined him inside a few seconds later. "Webster, right?"

"Yeah."

Nathan spoke little on the way to campus, and Erik put on the Pink Floyd CD as he drove toward the college. Nathan pulled the hood of his jacket over his head and leaned against the door, watching the people and other cars go by. He needed time to think through the last week and everything that had happened. When they reached the school, Erik stopped the truck at the curb and Nathan opened the door.

Erik touched the back of Nathan's hand resting on the seat. "When can I see you again?"

Nathan extricated his hand from beneath Erik's and picked up his backpack. "I have to work after class."

"What time do you get off?"

"Late."

Erik sighed. "Nathan?"

"Ten o'clock."

"Great, I'll be there at ten on the dot."

Nathan went to protest, but Erik leaned over and kissed him on the cheek. Nathan jerked backward and stared at Erik, completely flabbergasted by his boldness. Erik chuckled and gently nudged at his shoulder. "Go on, before you're late."

Climbing out of the truck in a daze, Nathan shut the door and turned toward the front of the school. Troy sat on a bench watching them, a smirk on his face. Nathan glared at Troy and went to stomp past him, and he heard Troy following him and whistling. Damn him!

CHAPTER 11

Classes went by fast, with no sign of Alan. Nathan was surprised Alan hadn't made an appearance. Professor Johns gave Nathan the cold shoulder when Nathan entered the classroom, but at least Johns didn't call him out in front of everyone. Troy had supplied him with all the notes from the lectures, and Nathan had managed not to fall behind.

At lunch, Troy surprised him by handing him a small black cell phone. Nathan instantly protested. "Troy! I told you not to do this!"

Troy shrugged. "It's prepaid, Nate. At least this way I can get a hold of you when I need to, and you have it in case of an emergency. I told you the other day I was going to get you one, and I did. Deal with it."

"Damn it, Troy," Nathan growled, still trying to hand it back to Troy.

Refusing it, Troy picked up the sandwich he'd bought from the campus café and took a bite. "I'm not taking it, Nate. Just accept the damned phone," he mumbled around his food.

Nathan grunted and stuffed it in the pocket of his hoodie. "I'll pay you back for it."

"I won't take it," Troy said.

"Damn it, Troy! Why are you so pigheaded?"

Troy swallowed the bite and laughed out loud. "There's that pot calling the kettle black again."

Snarling, Nathan took a vicious bite of the sandwich he'd also gotten, chewing furiously.

"Come on, Nate. It didn't cost that much, and I feel safer knowing you have one. Okay?"

Nathan looked down at the tabletop and then sighed. "Fine. I don't have to like it, though."

Troy reached out and patted Nathan's shoulder. "Thanks, Nate. It has about three hundred minutes on it. When you get close to running out, it'll notify you."

Nathan nodded and continued eating in silence. He didn't feel comfortable accepting the phone from Troy, but he knew Troy was worried about him.

"So, you want to tell me what the hell happened yesterday?" Troy asked. "Curtis was not happy. I told him your migraine came back. He took the excuse, but I'm not sure he believed me."

Wincing, Nathan set the last couple of bites of his sandwich down. "I'll go see him before work to apologize. I know I deserve to lose the gig. Last night…"

"What happened, Nate? Come on, man, we tell each other everything, and ever since that bastard Alan came into the picture, you haven't been honest with me. Talk to me."

Nathan hesitated to tell Troy exactly what went down the night before. He knew his friend would get angry. "I'm sorry, Troy. This whole thing has me confused and I don't know what to do. Alan wants me to help him by telling Erik something he can't even remember."

"And you don't want Erik to know about your gift," Troy interjected.

"I know it's wrong," Nathan said. "But I don't want to let go of how I feel when I'm around him. It's so selfish, and I'm an asshole for not keeping my promise to Alan."

"You aren't selfish, and you aren't an asshole, Nate. I've seen the way you look at Erik and the way he looks at you. I thought he was going to pick you up last night and take you to the nearest hospital. It took a lot to keep him from doing that, and even then, he insisted on staying until you were better." Troy touched the back of Nathan's hand. "Did Alan find out?"

Nathan jerked his head up. Troy had always amazed him whenever he guessed things so easily. "He did."

Fury built in Troy's expression. "What did he do, Nate?"

"It's nothing, Troy. It's over. I didn't do anything stupid. I just… needed to get away for a little while."

Troy knew Nathan's aversion to the olanzapine and how it made him feel. "It wasn't nothing, Nate. Whatever he did made you do something you normally wouldn't. I swear, if he wasn't already dead, I'd kill him again myself."

"Troy!" Nathan admonished quietly, gaze flitting around to see if anyone had overheard him.

"I'm torn whether to tell you to just get it over with so that prick can go away, or to keep it to yourself for now," Troy muttered.

Nathan could deeply relate to Troy's words. He'd been struggling with that very thing for the last few days. "Maybe I should just tell Erik," Nathan said. "I mean, I only met him a week ago. It's not like I'm in love with him or anything."

"Maybe not yet," Troy said. "But in the entire time I've known you, Nate, I've never seen you show interest in anyone, and you've smiled more in the last three days than you have in the last six years. Your entire face lights up when you see him."

Nathan blushed. "I do not!"

Troy chuckled. "Yeah, you do, dude."

Covering his face with his hands, Nathan groaned. "Stop! Guys aren't supposed to talk about shit like this."

"Why not? We're best friends. Don't I talk about the girls I like all the time?" Troy asked.

"That's different."

Troy snorted. "Why?"

"Because… it just is," Nathan said.

When Troy didn't respond, Nathan dropped his hands back to the table to find Troy watching him with a strange expression. Nathan fidgeted in his seat a bit. "What?" he finally demanded.

"I'm just happy for you, Nate. I think he's good for you. Just promise me one thing," Troy said.

Nathan raised an eyebrow at him.

"Be careful. I don't want to see you hurt again."

It may be too late for that.

The rest of the day went by quickly and Nathan later found himself on a bus to Java Bean. He needed to apologize to Curtis in person for missing last night's gig. When he arrived, the coffee shop was busy, and he couldn't see Curtis anywhere. Bella waved when she saw him and hurried over to him.

"What happened to you last night?" Bella demanded. "Curtis is pretty pissed."

Nathan winced. "I figured he would be. Is he in the back?"

"He's in his office."

"Thanks, Bella."

Small tables filled an area around a short platform on one side of the café, while the main counter and kitchen area were directly across from them. More tables littered the sidewalk outside. Nathan had never been overly fond of the varying shades of oranges and browns used to decorate the shop, but Curtis loved the colors, saying it reminded him of a place he'd visited in Spain during his youth.

Nathan headed to the back, passing the restrooms and making his way to the stockroom. A shoebox-sized office took up part of the space. The door stood cracked open, and Nathan could see Curtis sitting at his desk through the slit. Taking a deep breath, he knocked, wondering what he planned on telling Curtis.

"Come in," Curtis barked, causing Nathan to flinch.

Curtis was most definitely pissed. Nathan slowly pushed the door open. "Hey, Curtis."

A glare froze him in place. "What the hell, Nate?"

"I'm really sorry," Nathan muttered.

"One night I could understand, but you didn't even bother to call last night. You better have a damned good excuse!" Curtis slammed his hand down on his desk.

Nathan didn't know what to say. He couldn't exactly tell Curtis the truth.

"Well?" Curtis demanded. "Was it the migraine again?"

Figuring he better give Curtis something, he nodded. "I really am sorry, Curtis. You know I would never want to jeopardize my gig here, but if you don't want to keep me, I can't blame you."

Curtis sighed, his anger dissipating, and leaned back in his chair. "I'm not going to fire you, Nate."

"Thank you!" Nathan breathed.

"What's going on with you? You've never not shown up or called before."

Nathan shifted in discomfort. "Nothing's going on, Curtis. I passed out and by the time I woke up, it was too late to call you. I feel awful about leaving you in the lurch like that."

Skepticism shone on Curtis' face. "Why do I think you're hiding something?"

"I'm not!"

Curtis still didn't seem to believe him, but he didn't press the issue. "Try to be here on time Saturday, okay?"

"I will! I promise!"

Nathan scurried from the office before Curtis could even contemplate changing his mind. He didn't want to give Curtis a chance to fire him. Troy was at the counter when he exited the back room.

"Everything okay?" Troy asked before taking a sip of the coffee he'd ordered.

"He didn't fire me," Nathan said.

"That's great. Isn't it?"

"It is. I still feel terrible, though."

"Don't. Shit happens, Nate. You've done nothing like that before, and I'm sure you'll never do it again. Curtis knows it too. He's just being a dick." They walked to the front door, and Troy held it open for Nate. "Come on, I'll give you a ride to work."

"Thanks."

"Anytime." They got in Troy's car and buckled up. "You off at ten as usual?" Troy asked once they were on their way to the music store.

"Yeah, but you don't have to worry about picking me up. Erik is going to be there."

"Oh?" Troy raised an eyebrow.

Nathan flushed and fingered the zipper on his hoodie. "Stop."

"What? I told you already I think he's good for you, bro. Just make sure if he doesn't show up to call me to come get you, okay?"

"Yeah, yeah. I can take care of myself."

Troy grunted. "I know you can. But if you're making a trip to the bank, you better not go alone."

Nathan scowled. "I'll be fine, Troy."

"We've already talked about this, Nate. Do you want me to show up at ten, anyway?"

Rolling his eyes, Nathan huffed. "No, *Dad*."

Troy pulled up to the curb in front of the store and mock punched Nathan's arm. "Don't forget, *Son*."

"Pfft. Anyway, thanks for the ride. I'll see you later, okay?"

"Tell Erik I said hi!" Troy grinned.

Nathan sighed and opened his door, climbed out, and slammed it behind him. He entered the store to find Stuart waiting for him so he could leave. "Hey, Stuart."

Stuart didn't cover the store often anymore. He only came in when the day manager couldn't make it in and no one else could be there to handle the shift. A short, rotund man, Stuart preferred to sit on his laurels at home and see the money hit the bank rather than do the work himself. "'Bout time you got here," Stuart replied nastily as he came around the counter in preparation to leave.

"I'm a few minutes early, Stuart." Nathan couldn't help but point it out as he headed toward the back to punch in.

"It'll make up for the other day when you left early, then," Stuart snapped as he scurried behind Nathan into the storeroom.

Nathan bit back a retort and set his backpack down out of the way before grabbing his time card and sliding it into the old-school time clock. Stuart was too much of a cheapskate to upgrade to something more state of the art. Even online time sheets would probably be easier than this shit, but Stuart claimed he didn't want to change because the employees could punch in from anywhere and take advantage. Secretly, Nathan felt pretty sure it was because it would cost money to set up that type of system. Money Stuart wasn't willing to spend, even if it would save him more in the long run.

It didn't take long for Stuart to gather his things and leave, much to Nathan's relief. Nathan returned to the front and sighed when he saw the mess Stuart had left behind. He got to work putting away the items customers had left in the wrong place or returned. Then he reorganized the front desk since Stuart apparently had felt it necessary to move things around. He'd just finished helping a customer when Quinn strolled in.

"Hey, Nate! How's it going?" Quinn greeted.

"Hey, Quinn. Good. How're you?"

"Great! Had an outstanding weekend!" Quinn launched into a detailed description of the girl he'd met at the party on Friday night and how they'd hung out all weekend, along with how amazing she'd been in bed.

Nathan rolled his eyes. "I don't need to hear that, Quinn."

Quinn chuckled. "Does the idea of girly bits gross you out?"

"Girly bits?" Nathan raised a brow.

"Yeah, you know, since you're into dudes, does thinking about boobs and a pu—"

"Quinn!" Nathan shouted, eyes widening.

Quinn hooted with laughter. "Oh man, you should see your face."

"That is so not funny." Nathan shook his head and stalked off toward the other end of the store with a stack of vinyl albums to restock.

"Aww, come on, Nate. I was just teasing," Quinn called after him.

Nathan huffed and ignored Quinn, going about his work. When he returned to the front desk, Quinn leaned against the counter near him. "So… wanna tell me how things are going with the hottie?"

That reminded Nathan how Quinn had given out his home address to Erik. "What the hell are you doing giving out my personal information, by the way?" Nathan demanded.

"Hey, I wouldn't have given it to just anyone, Nate!" Quinn protested, straightening from the desk. "He was really worried about you, and I knew you were into him, so I didn't think it would hurt. Why? Did he do something wrong? Do I need to kick his ass?"

Nathan spluttered and shook his head. "No, he didn't do anything. Just don't go giving people my information, okay?"

"Okay, sure. I didn't think you'd mind, considering it was him," Quinn muttered. After a couple seconds of tense silence, Quinn said, "Well? Did you see him?"

Nathan didn't know why Quinn was so interested. He lifted one shoulder in a half shrug. "Yeah. He came by. We went to the boardwalk."

"And?" Quinn demanded. "Did you hook up?"

"What?" Nathan almost shouted, eyes bulging. "Of course not! What the hell, Quinn?"

Quinn laughed and clapped Nathan on the shoulder. "I'm kidding, dude. Relax. I've just never seen you smile like that."

"Like what?" Nathan asked, curious.

"We've known each other for a couple of years now, Nate. I like to think we're friends, right?"

Nathan nodded. "Of course."

"Even when you're laughing, you seem sad. I've only ever seen my mom like that, and it was after my dad died. Until she met my stepdad. I could always tell she didn't really feel what she showed to everyone, including me."

Quinn shifted his gaze away, clearly uncomfortable talking about something on such a personal level. "You're a lot like her. I don't really know what made you so sad, but whenever you hear Erik's name or you talk about him, it's like you're a completely different person, Nate. It's as if you forget, even for just a split second, and you allow yourself to truly be happy."

Nathan stood there, stunned. His lips parted slightly in shock and his eyes widened a fraction. Was Quinn right? Did he forget about his parents? About the accident? Guilt stabbed him straight in the heart and he felt a roaring in his ears. He grabbed at the counter, knees weakening. He heard Quinn calling his name from a distance and sensed him guiding him to the nearby stool, but he couldn't see or hear anything past Quinn's words. How could he have allowed this to happen? He couldn't forget his parents, couldn't forget the part he'd played in their accident or how he didn't deserve to be happy. Not when they were dead and it was his fault. How could he be so selfish?

"Dude, if you don't talk to me, I'm going to call Troy."

Shaking his head, Nathan grabbed Quinn's wrist with trembling fingers. "No," he whispered. "I'll be fine. I ju-just need a couple of minutes."

"You sure, man? You're as white as a sheet."

"I'm sure."

"Why don't you go in the back room and lie down for a bit?" Quinn suggested. "I can watch the store for a few."

"No," Nathan said. It would give him too much time to think. "I'll be fine. Just give me a minute."

Quinn eyed him skeptically. "If you're sure…"

"I am."

Nathan released Quinn's wrist and Quinn left him alone, thankfully. He breathed in and out, deep and even, working to gather himself. God, how had he been so stupid not to have noticed what Quinn saw without even being around him and Erik? Nathan ran a hand through his hair, not caring that he was messing up the strands. He needed to tell Erik he couldn't see him anymore. Then he needed to tell

Alan to find someone else to help him. There had to be others who were able to see spirits. Right? There was no way he could continue to be around Erik, and he knew there was no way he'd ever be able to tell Erik the truth about his ability. His cowardice at not wanting to see the affection Erik had for him turn to disgust and horror would beat out his desire to help Alan cross over every time.

With a set plan in mind, Nathan watched the time fly by so much faster than he'd ever wanted. Dread filled him the closer the clock crept toward closing. He didn't want to tell Erik goodbye, but he knew he had no choice. He wouldn't be an anchor around Erik's ankle, tying the man to him—a skinny freak with blood on his hands—for the rest of Erik's life, and he knew it would be selfish to keep holding on to Erik when he didn't deserve to have Erik in his life.

Quinn left an hour before the store was due to close. "You sure you're all right, Nate?" Quinn asked, hesitating near the counter.

"I'm fine, Quinn. Just a temporary glitch." Nathan attempted to brush off his earlier panic attack.

Quinn didn't seem convinced, but he didn't press the issue. "Well, have a good night then. See ya tomorrow."

"You, too, Quinn."

Nathan watched Quinn leave and tried to keep busy for the last hour, but his mind kept straying back to Erik and the upcoming conversation. Alan hadn't appeared at all that day, and it made it easier to stick to what he intended to do. Maybe his earlier blowup had made Alan feel guilty. He didn't really know, but he knew he'd have to tell Alan he couldn't help him after all when he eventually showed up again.

Two minutes to ten, the front door opened and Erik walked in. Nathan swallowed hard at how beautiful the man looked. Tight faded blue jeans clung to Erik's long, muscular legs, rippling as he took the short walk to the front counter. The sleeves of a white button-down shirt were rolled up, the hem tucked into his jeans. A smattering of chest hair peeked through the first couple of undone buttons, tempting Nathan's fingers to run through it.

"Hi," Erik greeted, leaning over the counter and brushing his lips across Nathan's cheek.

Blinking in surprise, Nathan managed a breathless "Hi" in return.

"Busy day?" Erik asked, leaning on the counter.

Nathan swallowed hard. "A bit."

"How were your classes?"

The inane question threw him, and Nathan had to really think to gather an answer. "Uh… they were okay. The usual. Thankfully, with all of Troy's notes, I didn't fall behind in Professor Johns' class. Although he would love to have another reason to fail me."

Erik frowned. "The man sounds like a pompous ass."

Nathan chuckled. "You could say that again."

"The man sounds like a pompous ass," Erik repeated, this time grinning.

Nathan outright laughed. He shook his head and wrinkled his nose at Erik. "I just have to close out the register and then we can go."

"No rush on my account," Erik said.

The smile faded from Nathan's face as he reminded himself of what lay in store for the evening and what he had to tell Erik. His tension ratcheted back to a ten and his movements were jerky as he went through the motions. He dropped the day's cash into the deposit bag along with the slip and sealed the bag. "Would it be all right if we stopped at the bank to drop this in the night deposit?" Nathan asked.

"Of course!" Erik said.

"Thanks," Nathan replied, still nervous. "Just have to grab

my bag from the back and punch out. I'll be right back, okay?"

"I'll be here."

Nathan hurried into the storeroom, stamped his time card, grabbed his bag, and went back out to the front. Erik smiled and straightened from the counter as Nathan came around to meet him. Nathan almost jumped out of his skin when Erik placed a hand on his lower back as they walked toward the exit.

"Are you all right? You seem kind of jumpy," Erik said.

"I'm fine," Nathan said.

"You sure?"

"Yeah."

Nathan locked the store behind them and followed Erik to his truck. "Which bank is it?" Erik asked.

"Space Coast Credit Union," Nathan answered without looking at him.

A minute later, they were on the street heading toward the bank. The silence stretched between them. Nathan did nothing to break it, merely staring out at the passing storefronts.

Once he'd made the drop at the bank and they were back on the road, Erik asked, "Is something bothering you, Nathan?"

"No, I'm fine."

"You're not fine. Something is obviously on your mind. You've been tense since I came into the store, and you've barely said more than a handful of words. Talk to me."

Nathan didn't want to tell Erik what he needed to while Erik was driving. He didn't want to take the risk of distracting him from the road. Not after what had happened with his parents. "Can we go somewhere and talk?"

"Of course. Anywhere in mind?"

He shook his head.

"Okay. I have an idea."

They didn't speak again, and Nathan hugged his back-pack to his chest as he gazed unseeingly out the passenger window. He didn't realize until Erik pulled into a driveway that they'd gone somewhere other than a coffee shop or something.

"Where are we?" Nathan asked, sitting up straighter.

"My house."

CHAPTER 12

"What?" Nathan squawked.

"Relax. I don't bite. I figure this way we have privacy to talk. Okay?" Erik soothed.

Nathan bit his bottom lip and fidgeted with the strap of his backpack. Erik climbed out of the driver's side and went around to him. Nathan flinched at the sound of the passenger door opening but didn't move right away.

"Nathan?" Erik prompted.

He tentatively stepped down out of the truck, carefully avoiding brushing against Erik, and moved away to wait as Erik closed the door and started toward the front porch. Nathan cautiously followed along the cement pathway, eyes darting everywhere, taking in the neatly landscaped yard and the gleaming original color of the wooden railing leading up to the porch. There was a swing he could see himself sitting in and maybe writing a song or two.

The house was a light yellow, and Nathan felt as though each detail had been lovingly chosen by Erik as he'd built the home he'd intended to share with Alan for the rest of their lives. The knowledge left a sharp pang in his chest and reminded Nathan of what he'd come here to do. With that in his head, he pulled himself together and held himself tighter as he trailed Erik into the house.

The inside was as nice as the outside. Nathan couldn't help gawking at the light oak-colored hardwood floors, matching furniture, and beautiful riverbed stone fireplace which dominated almost half of one wall in the living room Erik led him into. Erik gestured for him to have a seat on a large brown suede sectional sofa in front of the fireplace. A low wooden coffee table squatted in front of the sofa.

"Would you like something to drink?" Erik asked.

Nathan sat, instantly swallowed into the soft cushions of the couch, and shook his head. "No, thank you."

Erik took Nathan's bag and set it beside the sofa before choosing to sit next to him, angling his body slightly toward Nathan. His leg was close enough to Nathan's that he could feel the heat from Erik's thigh seeping into his. Suppressing a quiver at the almost intimate situation, Nathan swallowed and tried to look anywhere except at Erik.

"You wanted to talk?" Erik prodded.

Nodding, Nathan cleared his throat. "I uh… I don't think we uh…" His voice trailed off when Erik slid his hand over Nathan's. He hadn't even realized he was twisting his hands together in his lap in nervousness until Erik halted his movements.

"Nathan," Erik said in a gentle tone.

He looked down at where Erik's hand rested on top of his. The warmth of Erik's skin heated the clammy coldness of his own and trickled up through his forearms to his chest. He nibbled on his bottom lip, knowing he needed to push the words out, to stop himself from giving into the cowardice of not saying them. "We shouldn't see each other anymore," he whispered.

Erik tightened his hold for a brief second before relaxing. "Why?"

"Because we just shouldn't," Nathan muttered, trying to pull his hands away from Erik, but Erik wouldn't let him go. Instead, he firmed his grip and moved to sit on the coffee table, peering into Nathan's face.

"Nathan, look at me."

Nathan resisted at first, keeping his eyes on their hands.

"Please, Nathan."

Giving in and knowing he shouldn't, Nathan lifted his head and raised his gaze enough to look into Erik's eyes. Erik's expression was soft, affectionate, something he'd only ever seen on his mother's or aunts' faces before. It surprised him, and Nathan tried to jerk away from Erik again. "Why do you think we shouldn't see each other anymore?" Erik asked.

"Let me go," Nathan said.

"Tell me."

"You wouldn't understand."

"You can't know that unless you talk to me, Nathan. Try me."

Nathan's heart beat a rapid dance of hope and anguish against his rib cage. He wanted to believe so badly that Erik could accept him, accept everything about him, but he knew he couldn't trust in that hope. "I can't," Nathan replied, his voice cracking.

Erik reached out his free hand to cup Nathan's cheek. "Why do you carry so much on your own? You were so ready to give me a chance this morning. What changed?"

For a brief selfish second, Nathan leaned into Erik's touch, eyes closing halfway in pleasure at the caress. Then reality came back. Quinn's words from earlier echoed in his ears and he gave Erik a sad smile as he turned his head away from Erik's hand. "Nothing changed."

"Bullshit. If you aren't lying to me, then you're lying to

yourself, Nathan. I can't tell which it is." Anger vibrated in Erik's tone.

Surprise held Nathan's tongue for a moment. He hadn't expected Erik to get mad. He freed himself and stood, pacing away from the couch to stop near the front window, staring out onto the street. "Even if I am, it's none of your business!"

A frustrated grunt came from behind him and then Erik was next to him, grabbing his upper arms and spinning him toward him. "Is it so wrong having someone care about you? Why is that a bad thing?"

"Because it is!" Nathan exploded, knocking Erik's hands off him. "Because I don't deserve it! I'm damaged, okay! You shouldn't even be touching me!"

"What?" Erik asked, a stunned look on his face.

Nathan's eyes burned and he could feel his cheeks were hot. He turned his back to Erik, not wanting Erik to see him so upset. "Just forget it. It doesn't matter. This was a mistake. I'll call Troy to come pick me up."

Nathan went to retrieve his bag, to leave, but Erik stopped him, his arms closing around him from behind. Shock held Nathan immobile, and his breath froze in his lungs. "Wh-what are y-you doing?" Nathan wheezed.

Erik ignored him and just held him. Nathan remained stiff for several long minutes until finally he gave in and went limp, a shudder racking his body and a sob sticking in his throat. Tears spilled over, silent and steady, dripping down his cheeks and onto his shirt, soaking the material. Erik rested his chin on the crown of Nathan's head and never let go, anchoring him as the storm raged through him. Nathan gripped Erik's forearms, his pale fingers shining bright against the tanned furred skin.

"I've got you, angel," Erik murmured almost unintelligibly.

Even during the months after his parents' deaths, Nathan

had barely accepted comfort from Troy or his aunts, and yet being there in Erik's arms felt so right and made him feel whole in a way he hadn't in a long time. At some point, Erik moved them to the couch and Nathan found himself curled up in his lap, his head resting on Erik's shoulder, but his tears were gone. Doubts and knowing he shouldn't be allowing Erik to comfort him set in once more and Nathan tried to find it in him to pull away, but he couldn't. He wanted to be selfish, to cling to Erik for just a few more minutes. For later, when he'd be all alone again and he'd need something to remember in the darkness, when the pain became too much to bear on his own.

He realized he'd burrowed his face against Erik's throat, the woodsy scent of his aftershave tickling the hairs of his nose and the sweet draft of Erik's breath whispering over his cheek. Nathan swallowed audibly when Erik moved, and he could feel Erik's hard thighs flex beneath his bottom. Their combined breathing sounded loud in the silence of the living room, reminding Nathan of just how alone they were. He tried to move from Erik's lap, but Erik tightened his hold, bringing one hand up to slide his fingers through Nathan's hair briefly before cupping the side of his neck, encouraging Nathan to look up at him. At first, Nathan fought him, but eventually he gave in, lifting his gaze to meet Erik's.

The brush of Erik's lips over his caused his heart to speed up, beating fierce and fast against his rib cage. Erik broke away for a split second. Long enough for Nathan to notice a tiny scar at the corner of his mouth. He vaguely wondered how Erik had gotten it, but the thought flitted away as Erik leaned back toward him, covering Nathan's mouth once more. Nathan couldn't stop the low moan he let out, warmth surging through him, sending an electrical current spiraling along his nerve endings straight to his groin. Slipping the arm not trapped between their bodies around Erik's neck,

Nathan tangled his fingers into the dark hair at the back of his head. He gave himself up to the taste of Erik's kiss, the firmness of his lips, and the soft, slick tongue sliding in to glide over and explore the depths of his mouth.

He felt Erik reposition him until he sat straddling Erik's lap, bringing their erections flush with one another, wrenching a gasp from him. "Oh!"

"Nathan," Erik growled into their kiss. His hands, which had been gripping Nathan's waist gently, slid underneath the hem of his hoodie and splayed out along the width of his back. Nathan could feel the heat of Erik's palms through his shirt, practically burning him through the material. He gripped at Erik's shoulders, steadying himself, fingers digging into the hard muscles beneath the shirt Erik wore.

Nathan let out a moan when Erik began trailing kisses along his jaw toward his ear. Shudders tore through him the moment Erik's lips touched the soft skin of the lobe. He couldn't control the panting breaths escaping his lungs.

"Er-Erik."

"So sexy," Erik murmured into his ear before nipping at the flesh there and then soothing it with his tongue.

"Ah!" Nathan cried out, trembling at the pure fire suffusing his entire body. The unfamiliar sensations raging through him were overwhelming, leaving him lost in pleasure and lust. His entire body throbbed with need. "I-i-it's too much," Nathan panted.

"What's too much?" Erik asked, still touching and exploring, his mouth and tongue continuing to tease Nathan.

Nathan shook his head. He didn't even know how to explain it. Erik rolled his hips upward, grinding their cloth-covered cocks together, causing a delicious friction Nathan could feel deep down in his belly. All the while, Erik never halted his assault on Nathan's exposed skin with his heated mouth, this time targeting the tender flesh of his throat. A scrape of strong teeth over the racing pulse just beneath the skin sent tingles straight to Nathan's balls. But it was the way Erik latched on and suckled at his neck that sent Nathan over the edge, come pulsing from his cock and coating the inside of his boxers and soaking the fabric. Nathan couldn't contain his cries or the trembling of his body, his eyes squeezed shut tight, arms clutching Erik closer to him, hips thrusting forward.

Erik groaned, the sound rattling against Nathan's throat, and Erik laved at Nathan's wet, bruised skin, soothing the mark he'd no doubt left behind. His hands caressed along Nathan's back and down to his rear to grip him tight, urging his erratic movements to continue. Nathan made a keening sound and arched his back. It felt as if his entire soul was being wrenched from his cock and he couldn't stop it.

"Oh God," Nathan said with a whimper.

Finally, the last spurt spilled from him, and Nathan collapsed boneless against Erik, his breath wheezing from his lungs, his body quivering. As Nathan came down from the high of his orgasm, the knowledge of what he'd done hit and embarrassment rocked him. He couldn't believe he'd just come in his pants like a teenager. He struggled to get away, to run and hide, to never have to face Erik again. Erik refused to release him.

"Let me go," he pleaded, unable to meet Erik's gaze.

"Nathan, it's okay," Erik said huskily.

"No," Nathan sobbed. "It's not. I'm sor—"

"No. Don't apologize."

Nathan reddened even more as he dropped his forehead down to Erik's shoulder. Erik ran a hand along his spine.

"There's nothing to be embarrassed of, Nathan. It felt good, right?"

He managed a shaky nod.

"Then that's all that matters."

"But—"

"Stop," Erik murmured. "It was beautiful watching you come apart in my arms like that."

Nathan's breath caught at Erik's words. He didn't know how to respond. His body still throbbed from the high he'd experienced, his crotch felt wet and sticky, and the heat from Erik's long length against his heightened his awareness of Erik even more. When he shifted in discomfort, he could feel Erik was still hard beneath him and bit his lip. Curling his fingers around Erik's shoulders and gathering his courage, Nathan asked shyly, "Wh-what a-about you?"

A light tremble went through Erik, and Nathan felt him brush a kiss to his temple. "I'll be fine," Erik rasped.

Nathan frowned and sat back to see Erik's face, forgetting his embarrassment and the uncomfortableness of his damp clothes. The movement caused his bottom to press harder into Erik's lap, and Erik let out a small groan. "But that's not fair to you," Nathan said.

Erik chuckled, albeit a bit breathlessly, his face flushed from what Nathan could see beneath the deep tan. He cupped Nathan's cheek. "What happens between us, Nathan, isn't about returning the favor. Just because I made you come doesn't mean you have to do something you don't want to, understand? You never have to feel like that with me. Ever. I got pleasure just from getting you off. Okay?"

Nathan chewed on his bottom lip for a moment and then nodded. "Okay," he whispered.

Smiling, Erik leaned in and kissed Nathan, running his tongue over Nathan's bruised bottom lip. When he broke away, he slid his hand to Nathan's neck and touched at the spot he'd abused during their passionate moments. "Although I think Troy is going to want to kick my ass tomorrow when he sees you."

Eyes widening, Nathan immediately brought his hand up to cover the spot. "What? Why? Is it bad?"

Erik laughed gently and tangled his fingers with Nathan's, lowering their entwined hands to their laps. "A little. I'm afraid I got carried away."

Heat flooded Nathan's face, and he knew he must be as bright red as a tomato. Troy would tease the shit out of him when he saw it. But a bit of pride and happiness settled into Nathan's chest. He'd never had a hickey before.

"Will you stay here tonight?" Erik asked him, pulling Nathan from his thoughts. Surprise caused Nathan's breath to catch, and his gaze snapped to Erik's. "Just to sleep," Erik rushed on. "Nothing will happen that you don't want to, Nathan. I promise."

Nathan's head spun with the abrupt turn of events. The entire night hadn't gone as planned. He'd fully intended on breaking up whatever they had started and insisting on never seeing Erik, and now he'd not only made out with him, but he'd had a full-on orgasm in the man's lap! Now he wanted him to spend the night! Nathan opened his mouth to say no, to tell Erik to take him back to his apartment, but the word that tumbled out shocked him. "Okay."

Erik smiled, eyes crinkling in the corners. "Why don't we get something to eat? I bet you've had nothing all night, right? And I bet those pants are getting uncomfortable. I'm sure I have something you can wear while I wash your clothes."

It wasn't until Erik had pointed it out that Nathan noticed how the semen in his boxers had cooled and was drying. "Would… uh… it be all right if I took a shower?" Nathan asked.

"Of course," Erik said while helping Nathan stand.

Nathan's eyes instantly dropped to the very hard bulge of Erik's crotch, and he could see a dampness there, which brought his gaze down to his own. A huge wet patch was obvious on the front of his jeans and Nathan let out a sound of dismay, covering the area with both hands.

Erik hugged Nathan. "Relax, Nate. It's okay."

Nathan lifted his head enough to stare at Erik.

"What?"

"That's the first time you've called me that."

Erik gave Nathan a quizzical look.

"You always call me Nathan, not Nate."

"Oh. I guess I just like the way Nathan sounds. Nate is cute, but Nathan is so much sexier."

Nathan's mouth dropped open, shocked at hearing his name described in such a manner. Erik laughed and slipped a finger beneath Nathan's chin, coaxing his mouth to close. "You'll catch flies like that," he teased, eyes twinkling.

Stammering, Nathan couldn't form words, and Erik kept one arm around his shoulders as he guided Nathan down a hallway to the bathroom. "Towels are under the sink. Hop into the shower, and I'll find some clothes for you to wear. Leave yours on the counter. Don't lock the door, okay?"

Nodding, Nathan watched Erik close the door as he left Nathan alone. It took several breaths before Nathan shook himself enough to move. He turned on the water and let it heat while he started stripping his clothes off, grimacing as his boxers stuck to his skin. *I definitely don't want to repeat coming in my pants again.* He folded everything and laid it on the sink, then stepped into the shower and closed the curtain. The hot water felt good, and he sighed as it rushed over him. Nothing about this situation seemed normal. The entire day hadn't turned out like he'd expected, and now he had another nail in his coffin on what to tell Alan the next time he saw the guy. Shit. He knew Alan had given him the go-ahead on being with Erik, but he still couldn't help the guilt spiking through him. Especially since he hadn't even gotten close to carrying out his promise to help Alan move on.

The sound of the bathroom door opening disrupted his thoughts and Nathan jumped, but the translucence of the shower curtain blurred most of Erik's shape as the man set the change of clothes on the counter and grabbed Nathan's. Nathan felt decidedly vulnerable considering the fact nothing except a thin sheet of plastic separated him and Erik.

"Come out to the kitchen when you're done. I had a rice casserole dish in the refrigerator. It's in the oven and should be almost heated by the time you're finished," Erik said over the running water.

"Okay, thanks," Nathan said. He didn't move again until Erik left, shutting the door behind himself.

Nathan finished washing and shut off the water. It didn't take long to dry off, and he dressed in the soft blue T-shirt and black running shorts Erik had left on the counter for him. His scars being exposed made him uncomfortable, but he didn't really have much of a choice. He stared at himself in the foggy mirror for a few minutes, wondering just what the hell he was doing. Why wasn't he leaving? Why couldn't he seem to stick to his resolve around Erik?

Leaning closer to the mirror, Nathan realized the dark circles under his eyes had faded a bit and the usual tightness around his mouth had loosened slightly. When had that happened? Nathan couldn't figure out what was so special about Erik. Granted, Erik was the first guy he'd met who had captured more than a passing interest from Nathan. He knew that much, at least. Nathan still hesitated to place much hope of Erik understanding or accepting his ability to talk to and see spirits. Especially once he knew Nathan could see Alan.

Sighing, Nathan pushed away from the cabinet and left the bathroom. He followed his nose to the kitchen, the scent of spices and cheese sauce drawing him and his empty belly. Erik stood at a stainless steel stove, his broad back to Nathan. He'd also changed into dark gray sweatpants and a white T-shirt, one which clung to every single muscle, sending strands of arousal and awareness trickling through Nathan, who nervously pushed his hair behind his ears. He'd lost the band he used to keep it tied back. Nathan cleared his throat, letting Erik know he stood there.

Erik turned to look at him, a smile stretching across his full lips. "Ah, good. Just in time. Have a seat at the table. Would you like soda, water, milk, or tea?"

"Water is fine. I can get it, though," Nathan said.

"Nope. Not tonight. Sit." Erik pointed at a gleaming oak wood table, already set for two, with four matching chairs. He picked up a small pan of piping hot cheesy rice casserole and brought it to the table, setting it in the center on a potholder. "If you want, I can make some garlic bread or a salad to go with, but you'll have to wait a few minutes."

Nathan shook his head as he slipped into one seat. "This is perfect. I'm not a big fan of bread or salads, anyway."

Erik raised a brow and removed the gloves he'd worn to carry the pan, setting them aside. "Really? Bread is the best part, I believe. Makes the meal usually, but I know you must be starving. You really need to eat better. I think I'll make it my life's goal to bring you dinner at work."

"You don't need to do that!" Nathan protested.

Erik sat and picked up a large spoon near the pan. "From what I've seen, you don't take care of yourself enough, and now that I'm around, I intend on making sure you do."

Nathan frowned. "Why?"

Picking up the plate in front of Nathan, Erik scooped two large dollops on it and set it back in front of Nathan before he replied, looking directly at Nathan. "Because I care about you, Nathan. And because I want to."

Nathan couldn't hold Erik's gaze and stared down at the table. He twitched in his seat, uncertain on what to say. His first thought was to protest, but he couldn't ignore the tendril of warmth curling through his belly and up into his chest, either. None of the times his aunts or Troy had wanted to do something for him had ever inspired him to roll over and let them. Quite the opposite, in fact. Nathan had always vehemently denied them the right to do so. He'd insisted on doing everything for himself, especially after he'd gotten out of the hospital.

"I can take care of myself," Nathan finally said.

"I'm sure you can. I just like to help you is all."

Eyeing Erik, Nathan opened his mouth to protest again, but Erik stopped him. "Now eat. It's late and I'm sure you have class tomorrow."

Nathan's teeth snapping shut sounded audible in the surrounding silence. He didn't move as he watched Erik take several bites. His natural reaction urged him to say to hell with it, stand, and leave. But the other half of him, the one that wanted to crawl onto Erik's lap and let the man take care of him, screamed at him to do as Erik said.

Nathan took a small bite of the casserole. Within five minutes, he found he'd consumed the entire plate Erik had given him. Erik had a smug expression on his face as he dished another smaller portion onto Nathan's plate, and Nathan glared at him but kept quiet while he worked on demolishing the next bit of food. By the time he'd finished, he couldn't quite stifle the yawn working its way out of him and he could only just keep his head off the table.

"Sorry," he mumbled.

"Don't apologize," Erik admonished gently, standing. He came around the table and helped Nathan stand. "Come on, let's get you to bed."

Nathan hummed, leaning heavily on Erik, who easily

supported him. They made it to the stairs, but when Nathan stumbled after the first couple of steps, Erik swept him up into his arms.

"I can walk!"

"Hush and let me do this for you," Erik grumbled.

Nathan swore he heard Erik mutter the word "stubborn," but he was too far gone to do more than press closer to Erik's chest and close his eyes, breathing in the woodsy scent of Erik's aftershave. "Smell good," Nathan murmured.

"Do I?" Erik chuckled as he set Nathan down on what he thought might be a soft cloud.

Blinking heavily, Nathan peered at Erik through his lashes. "Uh huh."

Erik pulled the comforter back and then Nathan was airborne again for Erik to slide him under the blanket. "Well thank you, Nate. I think you're adorable when you're sleepy, by the way."

Nathan wrinkled his nose at Erik and snuggled down into the pillow. "Am not," he struggled to squeak out past a yawn. Erik gave another small laugh. He felt Erik card his fingers through his almost-dry hair as sleep pulled him under, and then he sensed Erik's body heat briefly before a brush of lips across his forehead. Then blessed darkness swamped him.

CHAPTER 13

Nathan couldn't be sure what woke him: the knowledge of sleeping an entire night without the usual haunting nightmares or the unfamiliar sensation of a large, warm body wrapped around him. The only nights he had slept without dreaming of the accident were the ones when he had been doped up on meds in the hospital. So, knowing that he had gone the whole night without reliving the worst day of his life was monumental. It disturbed him on a deep level at the same time as making him aware of just how being held all night had kept the nightmares at bay. He felt a hard bare chest beneath his cheek and muscular arms holding him tight as he opened his eyes. It took him several breaths to realize the chin resting on the crown of his head belonged to Erik, the very man he'd planned to break it off with the night before, and he'd slept in the man's bed last night after having an orgasm in his pants just from a heavy make-out session with him.

Heat suffused Nathan's cheeks, which only deepened when he realized the object poking him in his soft belly was none other than Erik's morning erection. Nathan wondered if he could wiggle free of Erik's embrace without waking him. The thought went out the window when Erik stirred, and Nathan found Erik's brick-like thigh sliding between his legs to push against his answering hard-on. A moan stuck in Nathan's throat. Especially when Erik rocked his thigh along Nathan's cock, adding friction to the pressure.

"Er-Erik," Nathan murmured, hoping to wake Erik enough to let him go.

In a rustle of sheets, Nathan found himself on his back and Erik hovering over him, his mouth being plundered, morning breath apparently not a factor in Erik's mind. Nathan gasped, eyes opening wide before slamming shut, and he grasped at Erik's biceps, holding on as Erik ravaged him. The scrape of early morning stubble rasping over his chin and cheeks sent a delicious tremble through him.

Nathan moaned, sliding his tongue over Erik's, meeting his silent demand for Nathan's participation in the obvious attempt to leave him breathless. Erik slid his hand beneath the hem of Nathan's shirt, fingers deftly stroking over the quivering muscles of his belly. Nervousness settled over Nathan. He wanted Erik, but he couldn't quite stop the trepidation he felt at possibly disappointing him. After all, Erik had a lot more experience with sex than Nathan. The only thing Nathan had ever done was jerk off a few times.

Erik broke their kiss and pulled his hand away from Nathan's stomach. He rested his forehead on Nathan's shoulder. "I'm sorry," he said, voice husky.

Nathan hesitated and then brought his hand to the back of Erik's neck, running his fingers through his hair. "Sorry for what?"

"Getting carried away and scaring you."

Nathan may have laughed if the situation wasn't so damned pathetic. "You didn't scare me."

Erik lifted his head to look at Nathan, a frown gracing his kiss-swollen lips. "Don't lie to me, Nathan."

"I'm not lying," Nathan protested. He dropped his gaze to the whorl of hair at the top of Erik's chest. He hesitantly slid his hand down to tease it with his fingers, tugging gently. "I got nervous," he muttered.

"Nervous?"

Nathan flushed. "I've never… I don't…"

"Nathan," Erik breathed, and then he kissed Nathan within an inch of his life again. Until Nathan couldn't think, couldn't see anything beyond the two of them, and Erik's large, warm body left him a boneless, quivering mass of flesh. He tried to follow Erik when he broke the kiss, but Erik pressed him backward, splaying one hand across Nathan's collarbone with a chuckle. "If we start that this morning, neither one of us will make it out of this bed, baby, and we both have somewhere to be."

The endearment had Nathan's heart fluttering in his chest.

"But I promise you, we will finish—" Erik brushed his lips over Nathan's cheek one last time. "—when you're ready. I will never push for more than you are okay with."

Nathan looked up at Erik, loving the way his hazel eyes had changed to a liquid green in the early morning light peeking in from the blinds over the window. He nodded in acknowledgement of Erik's promise. The more he was around Erik, the deeper he found himself pulled under, and the harder it would be when shit went south, as it invariably would. Biting his bottom lip, Nathan considered ripping the bandage off right then and telling Erik the truth, telling him about Alan and how he could see spirits.

But Erik took the opportunity out of his hands by suddenly rolling out of bed and then reaching down to grab Nathan's hand with a grin. "Come on. Time to get up. Want to get some breakfast in you before I drop you off at school."

Erik wore only a pair of tight dark blue boxer briefs that hugged his ass and cock like a second skin, leaving absolutely nothing to the imagination. Nathan's mouth went dry as he stared while Erik grabbed his freshly laundered clothing from a nearby chair and went to hand them to him. All the toned, muscular, tanned skin made Nathan's cock perk up and he stifled a moan. It was the sound of Erik growling that brought Nathan's gaze from Erik's body to his face. A feral, lustful look dominated the masculine features.

"If you keep staring at me like that, I'm going to forget about everything else and we're going to end up back in that bed," Erik said, his tone silky with desire.

Nathan buried his face in his clothes, groaning. He felt Erik's arms wrap around him and then Erik pulled him from the bed and against his chest. "If for one second I thought you were ready for that, I'd spend the entire day fucking you into the mattress, baby, but I want you to be more than ready. I want you to be sure beyond any doubt when I take you for the first time," Erik murmured into Nathan's hair. "Now, get dressed before I lose my head. There's an extra toothbrush under the sink."

With a small push, Erik urged him toward the bathroom and Nathan scurried in and shut the door. He leaned against the wood and breathed in deep to soothe his nerves. When he'd calmed down enough to move, he went through his morning routine fast, relieving himself, brushing his teeth, and finger-combing his hair with a bit of water. He didn't bother with worrying about shaving, not really one for growing a lot of facial hair fast. He winced when he noticed the purple bruise on his throat. His shirt didn't cover but half of it, and he knew Troy would certainly notice it when he saw him on campus this morning. A red flush came over

Nathan's cheeks, but he couldn't help noticing a sparkle had replaced the usual haunted look in his green eyes.

When he exited the bathroom, Erik had mostly dressed for the day in a pair of faded blue jeans and a white T-shirt. His feet were still bare. He kissed Nathan's temple on his way into the bathroom like it was the most natural thing in the world, and Nathan couldn't help the flood of warmth that spread through his chest and down into his belly at the simple gesture. "Give me five minutes and I'll be right out," Erik said.

Nathan nodded and went to locate his shoes. He found them in the hallway by the front door. Perching on the edge of the couch, he pulled on his socks and shoes, tying them afterward. He didn't stand right away, nervously waiting there instead. He looked around and spotted a framed photo of Erik hugging Alan from behind, both smiling brightly, love for each other shining in their eyes. Guilt struck him straight in the chest.

Nathan swallowed hard as he picked up the frame from the small table next to the couch. He'd been too worried about ending things with Erik the night before to notice it. Alan looked so blissful and jovial in the image. Nathan couldn't stop himself from wondering how things would have been different if Alan hadn't died. Nathan certainly wouldn't be sitting on Erik's couch, and he wouldn't have spent the night in his bed.

"That was our engagement photo."

Nathan jumped, almost dropping the frame. He quickly set it down on the side table. "I'm sorry," he said immediately.

Erik came around to where Nathan sat, took his hand, pulled him to his feet, and smiled at him. "It's okay. I know you must be curious."

Shaking his head, Nathan tried to protest, but Erik stopped anything he may have said. "It's natural to want to know things, Nate. It really is okay. Let's go get some breakfast and we can talk about it."

"I don't think—" Erik gave him a look and Nathan shut his mouth with a sharp snap of his teeth.

"Come on. We have enough time to eat and then get you to school so you're not late." Erik released Nathan, and after grabbing his wallet and keys from the table by the front door, he motioned Nathan outside. Nathan slid his backpack on and preceded Erik out onto the porch.

Nathan waited while Erik locked the door and then followed him to his truck. It didn't take long before they were on the road. He tried to imagine doing this every morning and found it wasn't hard to see himself waking up beside Erik, getting ready, and heading out for breakfast. What surprised him was just how much the idea appealed to him. He wanted that. More than anything he'd ever wanted in his life.

On the heels of that thought came the sharp bite of guilt. What right did he have to desire anything? Especially anything that made him happy? Nathan drew the hood of his jacket over his head and leaned his forehead against the cool glass of the window, his thoughts morose and bitter. Another day had gone by where he hadn't kept his promise to Alan. Another evening had slipped by where he'd selfishly clung to the one thing he knew would drown out the anguish he'd felt since his parents' death.

The feeling of Erik taking his hand and twining his fingers around Nathan's caused him to jump. "Penny for your thoughts?" Erik asked casually as he trailed his thumb over Nathan's wrist in a caress.

Nathan bit his lip, closing his eyes. "They aren't worth even that," he muttered.

"I'm sure they're worth something. Talk to me, Nathan."

Shaking his head, Nathan attempted a smile. "It's nothing."

Erik lifted their joined hands and kissed the back of Nathan's. "You sure?"

"Yeah." Nathan didn't want to drag Erik down into his mess. He wouldn't stain Erik's wonderful life with the tragic chaos of his own. Erik seemed to accept his answer and let it go, content to hold Nathan's hand the rest of the way.

They had breakfast at the same Denny's as the morning before. Nathan once again opted for just a bagel with cream cheese, much to Erik's dismay. He tried to get Nathan to order more, but Nathan declined, not really a big eater in the morning, or at all really.

"Did Troy actually get you a cell phone?" Erik asked.

Nathan frowned. "How did you know?"

"Well, you said something about calling Troy to come get you at my house last night. I kind of figured that meant he had."

"Oh. Yeah. He did."

"Can I have the number?" Erik asked.

"Of course." Nathan took out the phone, along with a spare hair tie he left in his bag. He quickly tied his hair back. "I don't really know the number myself, but I guess I can call you and it should show in your call log."

Erik gave him his cell number and Nathan called it. He ended the call after a couple of rings. Smiling, Erik said, "Now I can text you to make sure you eat when I'm not with you."

Nathan rolled his eyes. "Yeah, I guess so."

He tried to keep the topic off Alan and the picture of him and Erik, but Erik either didn't take the hint or wanted to get the subject of Alan out of the way.

"I told you how I met Alan already and how he died," Erik began while they waited for their food.

Nathan shifted in his seat with discomfort. "You don't have to talk about it," he said, taking a sip of his coffee to hide just how uncomfortable he was talking about Erik's fiancé.

Erik reached out and set his hand on top of Nathan's—the one not holding the mug of coffee. "I want to. Alan's gone, and I want you to know that there won't be a ghost between us."

Nathan flinched, causing the hot liquid to splash over the side of the mug and spill over the back of his hand. He set the mug down immediately and grabbed a napkin to wipe his hand. The damage was already done. Erik swore under his breath and fished an ice cube out of the glass of water the server had brought him. He grabbed Nathan's wrist and carefully ran the ice over the pink skin. "I didn't mean to spring that on you like that."

"Not your fault," Nathan muttered, biting down on his bottom lip. He almost laughed at the irony of Erik's words. If only the man knew just how wrong he was about a ghost being between them.

The ice felt good on the burn and Nathan sighed as it melted over his skin. Once the cube was gone, Erik retrieved another one and repeated the motion. "I'm so sorry, Nathan."

"It's fine. No permanent damage," Nathan replied. He couldn't take his eyes off the way Erik's tanned fingers stood out against his pale hand or stop the light tremble at just how gentle Erik was being while taking care of him.

"Do you not want me to talk about him?" Erik asked quietly.

That brought Nathan's attention to Erik in a heartbeat. "What?"

"Every time I mention Alan, you seem to get agitated. Does it bother you if I talk about him?"

"No!" Nathan answered, horrified. He saw the hurt in

Erik's eyes. "Alan was a large part of your life. It's natural for you to want to talk about him, Erik."

Erik stilled, his fingers just holding the ice on Nathan's hand. He had a strange look on his face. One that made Nathan furrow his brow. "What?" he asked.

"I like it when you say my name," Erik said, eyes darkening.

Nathan licked his lips, suddenly nervous at the obvious desire on Erik's face. He didn't know how to handle being wanted like that. His entire being went hot and his body felt tight, too tight. "I-I—"

Before Nathan could form a reply, the server came over with their food. Nathan jerked his hand away, dropping it into his lap to cover the very prominent bulge tenting the front of his jeans. He could feel the heat in his cheeks and when he peeked through his lashes at Erik, he could see Erik still watching him with the same hungry expression. Nathan's belly twisted and his cock jerked in answer. God, there must be something wrong with him to jump to full-blown hard-on despite the mention of Alan mere moments ago.

"Eat. I don't want to make you late for class," Erik prodded, his voice raspy.

Nathan wasn't even sure if he could get an ounce of food past the lump in his throat now. Clearing his throat, he grabbed one of the small containers of cream cheese and started prepping half of his bagel. He took another sip of his coffee before attempting a bite. Surprisingly, he cleared his plate and sat back with a satisfied sigh.

Erik smiled at him, flashing bright white teeth. "Good?"

"Yeah," Nathan answered.

"Don't see how a single bagel can be enough to eat," Erik said. "Gotta have some meat in there, too."

A noise left Nathan, a snort at Erik's words. He knew

Erik hadn't meant it to sound so… dirty, but Nathan could only imagine the field day Troy would have had with the turn of phrase Erik had used. He couldn't help the peal of laughter that flowed out of him after the snort, or the full-on belly laugh that followed. Tears spilled over, trickling down his cheeks, and he swiped at them, still chuckling. "Sorry," he gasped out. "Just—"

Erik chuckled around a bite of hash browns. "I got the joke. A little foul minded this morning, are we?"

"Couldn't help it," Nathan managed. "Totally something Troy would have pounced on."

"You said you've known him since middle school, huh?"

Nathan nodded and grinned. "Since day one. He's my best friend. Couldn't live without him. He saved my life."

Erik tilted his head in curiosity. "Saved your life?"

Tensing, Nathan mentally berated himself for slipping up. He tried to shrug it off. "Yeah. He kept me sane after my parents' accident."

"Ah. Of course. I'm glad he was there for you. I'm sure having someone helped a lot."

Nathan frowned. "Did you have anyone to help you after Alan died?"

Erik set his fork down. "My dad came back for a while and my cousin Matthew really gave me a lot of support afterward. Really, if it wasn't for Matthew, I may have done something stupid." Erik's lips twisted in a sardonic smile. "I got lost in a bottle for a while. Matthew helped get me out of it."

"I'm sorry," Nathan murmured.

"It's okay. I was weak. I let my grief overwhelm me and it was easier to numb the pain with alcohol than to accept it. Matthew got me in to see a grief counselor, and even though it took me a long time, I finally accepted Alan was gone. I miss him and I don't think that will ever change, but—" He paused and looked straight at Nathan. "—I'm ready to move on with my life."

Nathan swallowed hard and dropped his gaze to the table. He started toying with his napkin. Erik's words had sent a sharp thrill through him, as well as a damning sense of guilt. He had so many things he hadn't told Erik, so many secrets, yet Erik seemed so sure he wanted to start over with Nathan. "You barely know me," Nathan said.

"But that's the best part," Erik replied softly. "Getting to know one another, learning everything about each other. I want to know all there is to know about you. Everything. The good, the bad. All of it."

The weight of what Erik was saying pressed down on Nathan and panic set in. They'd only known each other for a short period, and Nathan wasn't ready for such a heavy burden. He already carried so much.

"I scared you," Erik said, his voice flat. Some of the fear must have shown on Nathan's face because Erik seemed to have read his mind. "We can take it as slow as you need, Nathan. I'm not going to cut and run just because we go at your pace. I told you before, the moment I met you, I felt a connection, something between us. Tell me you don't feel it too. Tell me you haven't felt it from the second we met, and I'll leave you alone."

Nathan couldn't say the words because Erik was right. The moment Erik had entered the music store, Nathan had been drawn to him, wanted to be near him. It was why he couldn't fight the desire inside him to give in and stay by Erik's side, no matter how wrong it was. Nathan tore at the napkin, shredding the paper into bits and letting it rain down on the tabletop. He closed his eyes when Erik's hand came down on top of his, stilling his nervous motions.

"Nathan?"

"I can't," Nathan croaked.

"Can't what?" Erik asked.

"I can't tell you that."

Erik tightened his hold on Nathan. "I need to kiss you," Erik rasped.

Nathan nodded, unable to speak. He was barely aware of Erik paying the check or standing. As soon as they were outside, Erik had him crowded up against the side of the truck, and Nathan raised his face to Erik's, eagerly expecting the kiss. A moan rattled in his throat when Erik's mouth crashed down on his, his lips parting to allow Erik's tongue access to explore the deep recesses, no doubt tasting the coffee and remnants of cream cheese from his plain bagel as he could taste the hint of eggs and bacon on Erik. Erik snaked an arm around Nathan's waist, hauling him closer, aligning their chests to one another, and thrust his large hand into the hair at the back of Nathan's skull, holding him steady for the onslaught. Erik broke the kiss long enough to growl Nathan's name before capturing his mouth once more.

It didn't make a difference that they were out in public or that anyone could stumble on the two of them hidden between two vehicles. The only thing that mattered was the intimate connection between them, the slide of tender flesh over tender flesh, the rasp of early morning stubble over sensitive skin, no doubt leaving red marks behind. Nathan didn't want it to end. He wanted to remain wrapped in Erik's arms, tasting his kiss, for the rest of his life. The thought terrified him at the same time as making his knees weak, and if it wasn't for the hard hold around his waist, he would have collapsed at Erik's feet right then.

Nathan gasped when Erik broke the kiss, his entire body trembling with need and want. When Nathan finally opened his eyes, he could see Erik was just as affected by their kiss. His cheeks were ruddy, lips swollen, and Nathan saw at some point he'd messed up the perfection of Erik's dark locks with his hands. Reaching up with shaking fingers, Nathan tried to smooth them back into place.

Erik gave him a tender smile and caressed the side of Nathan's neck. "I want to forget all reason, say to hell with taking you to school or going to work. Just take you back to my home and make love to you for the next several days," Erik growled.

Eyebrows going up, Nathan gave an unsteady chuckle. "Days?"

Erik hummed and leaned his forehead against Nathan's. "I'm not even sure that would be long enough, Nathan. Every time I touch you, it's like touching a live wire. It stirs something inside of me, and I only want more. I don't want to scare you more than I already have, baby, but I can't stop thinking about you, the feel of your skin, the smell of your hair, the taste of your lips. When we're apart, I can't wait to see you again."

Every word uttered by Erik struck Nathan hard in his heart and he closed his eyes, his fingers curling over Erik's biceps as he tried to keep himself in check. He didn't want to freak out over Erik's confession. He wanted to be happy. On one hand, he was, but on the other, he felt terrified at how quickly he was becoming attached to Erik. Especially considering the secrets Nathan still hid from him. "Erik," Nathan breathed.

Erik slid his fingers through Nathan's hair, dislodging the tie Nathan had used to wrangle the annoying strands away from his face and allowing the silken sheath to cascade around his face. "I'm not asking for anything more than you're ready to give. Like I told you, we can go as slowly as you need. I just need you to know how you affect me. To understand how much I want you. We have all the time in the world, okay?"

"O-okay. J-just… slow, okay?"

"Anything you need, angel," Erik murmured before lifting his head to kiss Nathan's forehead. "We should go."

Nathan couldn't meet his gaze as Erik released him and opened the truck for him, but he didn't pull away when Erik took his hand again once they were on the road to the college. In fact, Nathan couldn't quite keep his lips from curling with a small smile and kept his head turned toward the passenger window as they rode in silence.

When they reached Webster's campus, Nathan went to open the door, but Erik stopped him and leaned over to kiss him, brushing his lips lightly against Nathan's. "I'll see you tonight," Erik said.

"I have to work."

"I'll pick you up afterward."

Frowning, Nathan replied, "You don't have to do that."

"I don't have to do anything, Nate, but I want to. Now get to class before you're late."

Nathan started to argue, but Erik pressed a finger to his mouth. "I'm picking you up, sweetheart, end of story. Go. Troy's waiting for you and he looks kind of antsy."

Swiveling his head around, Nathan spied Troy waiting in his usual spot with a scowl on his face and winced. He'd forgotten to tell Troy he wouldn't be home this morning, so most likely Troy had gone to his apartment to pick him up. Damn. "Shit."

"What's wrong?"

"I forgot to call Troy and let him know not to pick me up this morning."

"Might want to tell him not to bother tomorrow, either," Erik said.

Nathan gaped at Erik for a split second. Then he said, "I have to go home tonight. I need clothes."

"We'll stop by your place to get some clothes for you and then we'll go back to mine."

"Awful sure of yourself, aren't you?"

Erik shook his head. "I just want to wake up next to you again."

Nathan's irritation at Erik's high-handedness died an immediate death. After hearing that, how could he feel agitated? Nathan flushed and fumbled with the strap of his book bag. "I uh…"

Smiling, Erik patted Nathan's thigh. "Go. We can talk later."

Without a word, Nathan shoved open the door, climbed out, and slammed it shut behind him. He scurried toward Troy without glancing behind him. He could feel Erik's gaze burning a hole in his back and rolled his shoulders, attempting to dislodge the sensation. When he finally looked toward the curb, the truck was gone.

"What the hell, bro?" Troy growled and punched Nathan on the arm.

"Ow!" Nathan grunted and rubbed at the sore spot.

"I should be pissed as hell at you right now, but I'm guessing you finally got lucky, considering who dropped you off and the fact that you're wearing the same clothes you wore yesterday!" Troy exclaimed with a grin. "Congrats, Nate."

Nathan groaned as heat flooded his cheeks. "Shut up, Troy! Nothing happened!"

"Oh yeah, sure! And that hickey on your neck is nothing?" Troy challenged.

Horror flooded Nathan, and he slapped his hand over the spot Erik had been sucking on last night when he'd embarrassed himself by coming in his jeans.

"Or maybe those beard burns are just razor burns?" Troy taunted.

"Troy, shut the fuck up!" Nathan snapped. His face felt like it was on fire.

Troy cackled and slapped Nathan on the back before slinging an arm around his shoulders. "You'll have to tell me the dirty deets at lunch, bro. Well, not too dirty. I'm not looking for a play-by-play."

"Oh, for fuck's sake!"

Classes went by quickly. Nathan didn't see a glimpse of Alan, but he knew it wouldn't be long before he did. Troy caught up with him at lunchtime and demanded the details of what happened the previous evening. No way in hell was Nathan giving him any information about shooting off in his pants, and he convinced Troy he'd done nothing except a heavy make-out session with Erik.

"You trying to give the guy blue balls?" Troy mumbled around a bite of his sandwich.

Nathan almost choked on his own food. "Jesus, Troy!"

"He's not exactly inexperienced, Nate."

Wincing, Nathan brushed a loose strand of hair back from his cheek. "I know he's not. I'm just not ready to jump into bed with him."

Nathan didn't really want to explain to Troy that he was afraid of disappointing Erik. He didn't have any experience aside from his own hand, and he hadn't done a lot of that either, considering he'd spent so much time trying to keep himself sane during the last six years.

He'd seen a couple of porn movies, but those weren't based on fact, and the men in them had way more knowledge of sex than Nathan did. What if he couldn't last longer than sixty seconds like the night before? Oh God, what if he came in his pants again? Or if he couldn't satisfy Erik? The idea of not being able to sexually please him terrified Nathan more than even the idea of encountering a new spirit. A cold sweat popped out along his back and under his arms.

Troy raised an eyebrow at him. "Why the hell not? It's not like you need a commitment from him or anything to get laid."

"Because I'm not, okay? Besides, he still doesn't know about everything."

"It's just sex, bro. Someone has to pop your cherry someday."

Nathan scowled at Troy to cover his discomfort. "You're an ass, Troy. You know that?"

Troy shrugged. "I'm just stating the obvious. You don't have to get so defensive."

"Maybe I don't want to be just another notch on some guy's bedpost. Maybe I want someone to care about me before I let them *pop my cherry*," Nathan said. "Can we just drop it? I don't want to talk about this anymore."

"It's not like you got a hymen for crying out loud," Troy muttered.

Nathan stared at Troy, mouth open in shock at Troy's words. He dropped his sandwich onto the paper and stood, anger surging through him. "I don't know what the hell set you off. If it's because I forgot to call you, I'm sorry, but it doesn't give you the right to be such a fucking prick."

He started to stomp away, but Troy grabbed his wrist, stopping him. "Nate." Mouth set in a tight line, he refused to look at Troy. Troy sighed and stood, pulling Nathan into a hard hug. "I'm sorry, Nate. You're right. I *am* being an ass."

"Why?" Nathan asked stiffly.

Troy stepped back and ran a hand over the nape of his neck. "Ever since you met Erik, it's like you're slipping away from me. We hardly hang out anymore, and this morning when I got to your apartment and you weren't there..."

Nathan winced. It was true. Before now, they'd been

attached at the hip. Troy would always pick him up for school and they were never apart. "It's not on purpose. Things just seemed to move fast with him. I'm not even sure what this is."

A rueful smile crossed Troy's lips. "Come on, Nate. You really don't see it?"

"See what?" Nathan asked.

"You'd have to be blind to not notice that you guys are completely into one another. If it hadn't been a short time, I'd think you both were already in love with each other."

Nathan jerked, eyes widening. "What the hell, Troy? I barely know him!"

Troy held his hands up in a placating gesture. "I know, Nate, but it doesn't take long to care about someone. This isn't me saying you are, and I'd say you were crazy if you believed you were. I guess I'm just a little jealous of how much of your attention he has."

"Troy, we're best friends. No matter what. I wouldn't be here without you. No one will ever come between us. I'm sorry if you felt otherwise."

"And I know that. I'm happy you've found someone and you're finally willing to let someone in besides me. You deserve to be happy, Nate, despite what you tell yourself in your head." Nathan flinched and Troy grabbed his shoulder. "You forget how well I know you, bro. I know you blame yourself for your parents' accident and you think you have to spend your life paying for it, but you don't. It wasn't your fault. The guy was drunk. He ran a red light. End of story. Stop beating yourself up over it. Let it go. Be happy. Just… don't forget I'm here for you."

"Never," Nathan murmured, ignoring the rest of Troy's words.

Troy pulled him into another brief yet fierce embrace. "I love you, Nate."

Nathan's throat tightened, and he had to swallow several times before he could return the words. "Love you too, bro."

They broke apart and shuffled their feet in discomfort before Troy coughed. "So... uh... let's finish eating. I'll take you to work after school so we can hang out for a bit, huh?"

"Sure. That'd be great."

They both retook their seats to finish their lunch, and Nathan changed the subject to Troy's girl at the diner to ease some of the tension.

CHAPTER 14

After classes ended, Troy kept his word and took Nathan to the music store, which Nathan was grateful for—he didn't relish possibly catching the same bus with the spirit of the woman on it, searching for her baby. They chatted about homework and some new music on the way. Troy stuck around for a little, hanging out near the register, and Nathan realized just how much he'd missed his friend. They joked together while Nathan put away some returns and new arrivals or helped customers find what they were looking for.

Alan made an appearance an hour after Nathan got to work. Nathan was in the middle of ringing up a shopper when he noticed him over by the window. He almost dropped the vinyl record in his hand with how hard he flinched, but he caught it before it hit the floor and apologized to the customer. Once the store was empty aside from himself and Troy, Nathan sighed and called out, "Alan."

Turning, Alan gave him a sad look and floated a little closer. "Nathan," he said tentatively, as though not sure of his reception.

Troy came alert at hearing Nathan say Alan's name, his face darkening. "The ass wipe is here?"

"Enough, Troy," Nathan said. He watched Alan come toward them. "I'm sorry, Alan."

"Don't apologize to him!" Troy exclaimed.

"Stop, Troy." Nathan shook his head. He never looked away from Alan. "I promised to help you and I haven't kept my promise. I'm sorry about that. I'll try to help you as much as I can."

"Are you going to tell Erik?" Alan asked, hope clear in his eyes.

Nathan bit his lip. "I can't."

The hope died. "I see."

"Not yet. I'm sorry. Things… Things are different now. I…"

"You want to be with him."

Nathan balled his hands into fists on the counter as guilt ate at his heart. "Yes."

Alan gave him a sad smile. "I understand. I really do. He's a great guy, and it's obvious he wants to be with you, too."

"What's he saying?" Troy demanded.

He waved a hand at Troy. "Maybe if we retrace your steps before your accident, you can remember what you need to tell him. Maybe we can figure it out that way."

Alan shrugged, his form drifting between almost solid and a slightly ethereal appearance. "I don't know, Nate. Hell, I can't seem to remember anything from that day or the days leading up to the accident. I just know there's something."

"And we'll figure it out. We'll find a way."

"Maybe it would be best if I just left you alone. It's obvious he's happy, Nate. I… I saw him last night. The way he looked at you. When he came into the store and the way his face lit up. He used to look at me like that."

A sadness unlike any Nathan had ever felt engulfed him,

and he had to grab the counter as his knees weakened. He gasped, and his eyes watered. "Alan," he groaned.

Alan immediately flitted away from Nathan until he was across the store, almost by the front door. "I'm sorry, Nathan. Maybe it's not a good idea for me to be around you. I can't stop the way I feel. I'm sorry."

"Alan, wait!" Nathan called as Alan dissipated. It was too late. Alan was gone. "Damn it!"

"What? What is it?" Troy asked.

"He's gone. Shit!"

"Isn't that a good thing?"

"No! If I don't help him, who will? I can't let him wander around forever, Troy!"

"Why not? You don't owe him anything."

"Because I promised to help him. And because of Erik. How do you think Erik would feel if he knew I could have helped his fiancé and didn't?"

Troy scowled. "His dead fiancé, you mean?"

"Either way! Alan doesn't deserve to remain bound here. Obviously, something is keeping him here and we just need to figure it out."

Nathan moved to the computer they used for special orders and opened the internet. Stuart would have a fit if he knew Nathan used it for personal browsing, but he couldn't wait until he could stop at the library. He opened Google and searched Alan's name. The same article regarding the accident in the ravine came up, but he scrolled past that, looking for more. There wasn't much. He found an old Facebook profile and a blog Alan had started as a sort of personal journal.

He clicked on the link to the blog and then wished he hadn't. The first photo on the page caused his heart to freeze in his chest. The last post Alan had made was right before Erik and Alan's wedding, and the picture was a candid photo someone had taken of the two of them kissing. Nathan couldn't still the arrow of jealousy jolting through him. He knew it was irrational to be jealous of a ghost, but Alan had been a big part of Erik's life. If Alan hadn't died, Nathan never would have met Erik, and Erik sure as hell wouldn't be interested in Nathan like he was. The reminder once again sent doubt raging through Nathan, and he couldn't help but think maybe he should break it off. Or tell Erik the truth and let him end it by being disgusted with Nathan.

"Did you find something?" Troy asked, coming around the edge of the counter.

Using the mouse to scroll down the page enough to hide the photo, Nathan shook his head. "Just an old blog of Alan's. Was hoping there'd be something here."

There were dozens of posts, and it would take some time to read them all. Nathan figured it would be a good idea to read at least the ones in the last months before Alan's accident. Maybe there'd be something in those posts.

"You want me to help read through them?" Troy offered.

Nathan felt weird for invading Alan's privacy like this, but then again, the man had posted them publicly for people to read, right? "I think I should read through them so I can talk to Alan about them."

"Uh huh," Troy said, giving him a knowing look.

"It may be the only way to know what happened before he died!" Nathan protested. "I'll print them out and read them later."

Troy left the subject alone. He just showed Nathan the easiest way to print without using up too much ink. Stuart would kill him if he caught on how much Nathan had used as it was. It took about twenty minutes for all the posts to print, and Nathan immediately shoved them into his backpack. Alan didn't show up again, and Troy left about an hour after Quinn arrived for his shift. Nathan spent the rest of the night going through the motions, lost in thought over how he could help Alan without telling Erik, but nothing seemed to come to mind. He knew if he didn't give Alan what the spirit needed in order to move on, he'd not only feel guilty, but eventually it would bleed over into whatever he had with Erik.

A few minutes before closing time, Quinn prodded him on the shoulder. "Yo, Nate. Where's your mind been at all night?"

"Huh?" Nathan shook himself and looked at Quinn.

Quinn grinned and propped his elbow on the counter. "Is there a certain dark-haired hottie taking up all your brain waves or something? You've barely been here all night. Mentally anyway."

"Oh, sorry, Quinn." Nathan blushed. He hadn't really told Quinn about everything that had happened with Erik. It seemed rather embarrassing to reveal that information. "Just got a lot on my mind."

"Come on. Spill. How'd things go with Mr. Tall, Dark, and Handsome the other night? Did you get laid?"

"Quinn!" Nathan spluttered, his face hot. "What the hell, dude?"

Quinn burst out laughing and slung his arm around Nathan's shoulders. "You're so uptight, Nate. I just want to see you relax for a change. I think it would do you some good to have some fun. With the way he was drooling over you the other night, it's obvious he wanted to tap that."

Nathan groaned and slapped his hand over his face while shaking his head. Quinn had no shame. "You're as bad as Troy. You know that?"

The front door of the shop opened before Quinn could keep razzing Nathan. Nathan uncovered his eyes and saw Erik standing there. A bright smile broke over Nathan's face before he noticed a dark frown on Erik's. Nathan's smile dimmed, and he tilted his head a fraction, uncertainty flashing through him when he realized Erik was mad about something.

Quinn removed his arm from around Nathan's shoulders and moved away from him. "Oops. Think lover boy's jealous," Quinn murmured with a laugh.

Surprise caught Nathan unaware, and his mouth opened in a rush of air. Erik strode toward the counter, shoulders tight with tension. "Almost ready to go, Nathan?" he asked.

Nathan wrinkled his nose at the hard note in Erik's voice, but he couldn't help the delight racing through him at knowing Erik was jealous of Quinn. "Erik, I'd like you to meet my *friend* Quinn," Nathan said.

Eyeing Quinn for a moment, Erik thrust his hand out toward Quinn. "Erik Moore."

Nathan could see Quinn working at keeping a straight face as he accepted the handshake. "Nice to meet you, sir."

The handshake didn't last long. Erik released Quinn almost instantly and turned back toward Nathan. "I thought we'd grab something to eat after you finish."

"Sure," Nathan said, unable to help the small smile he felt curving his lips. "Quinn, why don't you take off? I'll see you tomorrow."

"Thanks, Nate. See ya tomorrow." Quinn dashed into the back room to clock out and grab his things. He came back out in less than sixty seconds and stopped near Erik with a wink. "No need to be jealous, big guy. I prefer my partners with breasts and girly bits."

Before Nathan could reprimand Quinn or Erik could respond, Quinn was gone. Nathan almost gave a nervous laugh but squirreled it away in his chest. His hands trembled as he started closing the register and he almost jumped out of his skin when Erik brought his hand down on top of his.

"I'm sorry," Erik said.

Nathan glanced at Erik through his lashes. "For what?" he asked quietly.

"For running your friend off. I was… jealous, as he so rightly picked up on." A small intake of breath was Nathan's only reply. He finally lifted his head to look at Erik directly. Erik leaned in until there was nothing but a scant inch between them. "Do you forgive me?"

Nathan couldn't do anything except nod. Erik closed the distance and pressed his lips to Nathan's. It wasn't a passionate or hard kiss. It was tender and sweet. Meant to be nothing but a greeting, a hello after a long day away from one another. Nathan sighed and opened his mouth, bringing his hand out from beneath Erik's to touch the side of Erik's neck. He felt the throb of his pulse and almost moaned when it leaped at the caress of his fingers over the sensitive skin there. It was the first time Nathan had initiated contact with him. He'd done it unconsciously, needing to feel the warmth of Erik's skin.

Erik slid his tongue over Nathan's bottom lip, tracing the full outline before breaking the kiss. "I missed you," Erik rasped.

A pleased smile slid over Nathan's features, and he ducked his head, flushing. "Me, too," he mumbled.

"Hurry and close up," Erik whispered close to Nathan's ear, nuzzling the tender flesh briefly.

Nathan almost dropped something several times under Erik's watchful gaze, but he still finished balancing the register and creating the nightly deposit in half the time he normally did. He dropped the bag into the safe and went to get his things from the stockroom.

Erik grabbed his hand the moment Nathan exited the back. He never let go, even as Nathan locked the store. Not until Nathan slid into the truck's passenger seat did Erik let go, but it was only a brief separation. The moment the truck merged into traffic, Erik entwined their fingers once more for the short ride to the diner. Nathan couldn't stop the butterflies fluttering in his stomach or the way his pulse raced as Erik's thumb stroked over his inner wrist. He knew Erik couldn't miss the hard beat of it against his skin and he felt embarrassed at how easy it must be for Erik to read his reaction to the older man.

They didn't speak during the five-minute trip to the diner —the silence was too comfortable to break with idle chitchat. Erik pulled the truck into a spot in front and turned off the engine. He brought Nathan's hand to his lips and kissed the back of it before setting Nathan free, an act which caused Nathan to blush in the cab's darkness. "If you keep looking like that, I'm going to forget you didn't eat dinner," Erik growled.

Nathan could feel his cheeks get hotter and he tipped his head forward, hiding behind his hair. Nathan gasped as a calloused hand slid over the back of his neck before he found himself yanked partway over the middle console. Then a pair of demanding lips crashed down onto his.

Fire rolled over Nathan, and he moaned. The blaze fanned higher as Erik plunged his tongue into Nathan's mouth, gliding over his tongue and teeth, exploring deep. Nathan instinctively gripped Erik's shirt, tangling his fingers in the folds and holding on for dear life. The stubble lining Erik's jaw scraped over the sensitive skin of Nathan's chin, and he whimpered at the assault of so many sensations. Erik stroked the fingers of his free hand through Nathan's hair and along his throat. He seemed intent on devouring Nathan right there in the diner parking lot, uncaring of anyone who saw. Nathan debated whether or not to crawl over the console and into Erik's lap, his cock harder than nails at the moment and dying to be touched.

Then suddenly Erik pulled away, and Nathan made a

noise of protest. He opened his eyes, unaware he'd even closed them, chest panting as he sucked in air to fill his lungs. Erik appeared as affected as he was. With ruddy cheeks and glazed eyes, Erik fixed his gaze on Nathan. Nathan tried to restart the kiss, but Erik stopped him, his hand cupping Nathan's cheek. Shame flooded Nathan, and he jerked back into the passenger seat, hurt at Erik's rejection. His fears from earlier resurfaced. Had his kiss been too inexperienced? Had he turned Erik off?

"Nathan," Erik said softly into the dimness, "we won't have our first time be in the front seat of my truck in the parking lot of a restaurant, and we won't rush it. I want us to take the time you deserve. Understand?"

Nathan raised his gaze to Erik. Honesty shone in his eyes, and Nathan bit his lip as he nodded. Erik gave him a tender smile as he brushed the backs of his fingers over Nathan's cheek. "Let's eat, okay?"

"Okay," Nathan whispered. His hard-on had wilted, thankfully, and he could get out of the truck without embarrassing himself further. Though he noticed a sizeable bulge in Erik's jeans when Erik met him on the sidewalk in front of the diner. The blush returned to his cheeks, and Erik chuckled as he took Nathan's hand and tugged him to his side.

"Can't help it, angel. Seems to be a constant thing since I met you," Erik said as he held the door open for Nathan.

Nathan almost swallowed his tongue at the endearment and the admission of Erik's physical reaction to him. He made a beeline for his and Troy's usual booth with his head down. God, he felt like a teenager in high school! What the hell did he know about an adult relationship?

Erik slipped into the booth across from him. "Did you have a good day?"

Nathan shrugged and toyed with the silverware the

servers laid out after a table was cleared from previous customers. "It was okay."

"Anything exciting happen?" Erik asked.

"Not really. Troy hung out at work with me for a bit. He was understandably upset that I forgot to call him this morning and let him know I didn't need a ride."

"I think you should call him and tell him I'll be taking you to school in the morning again," Erik replied.

Nathan looked at Erik, eyebrows raised. "Awful presumptuous, Mr. Moore."

Erik smirked and lifted one broad shoulder. "Hopeful."

Unable to help a smile, Nathan opened his mouth to reply but stopped, stiffening when he felt a wave of icy death rush over him. He didn't look around, didn't identify the source. He attempted to ignore it while Erik gave him a concerned glance.

"You okay, Nate?"

"Fine," Nathan managed.

"Are you sure? You went as white as a sheet." Erik turned and waved to catch the server's eye.

Harriet rushed over with a smile. "What can I get you boys?"

"I'll have a BLT with a cup of coffee. Nate?"

"Nothing for me," Nathan bit out through clenched teeth. He could feel a bead of sweat trickling down his temple and fought the urge to swipe it away.

Erik gave him a grim expression. "Get him a cheeseburger with fries and a cup of coffee as well, please, Harriet."

"Sure thing, sweetie. Be back in a second with the coffee. Food should be right out." Harriet bustled off to get their drinks.

"What is going on, Nathan?" Erik demanded the moment Harriet was out of earshot.

Nathan shook his head and shoved out of the booth. "I'll be right back."

He darted for the restroom at the back of the diner, discreetly seeking the source of the decay. An old man was perched on a stool at the end of the counter, his clothing nothing but rags. His skin hung from his bones, brittle and paper thin, and his scalp was practically bald, with only thin wisps of white hair trickling down from it. Half of his face appeared crushed, caved in, and Nathan could clearly see the back of his skull. The scent of sulfur and dead flesh emanated from the man and Nathan almost gagged on the smell. It was obvious the spirit had been dead for quite some time, and Nathan could only imagine how he had died.

Nathan shoved open the bathroom door and dashed into one stall, slamming the door and locking it behind him. He leaned back against it, breathing deep and even to stem the rising tide of bile pushing at his throat. Not now. Not when he was with Erik. He couldn't do this now.

There'd never been a spirit in the diner before. Nathan had always considered this cozy little restaurant his safe space. Why now? He wanted to rage, to rail at the old man and scream for him to leave, but Nathan knew he couldn't. He swallowed again and again, trying to force away the urge to throw up.

"Nathan?" Erik's deep voice bounced off the tiled floor and walls.

Closing his eyes, Nathan stifled a sob. Why couldn't he be normal? He stuffed his fist in his mouth and bit down on his knuckles.

"Nate? Are you okay?"

Tears burned behind his eyelids.

"Nate?" The worry deepened in Erik's voice.

Nathan yanked his hand from his lips and struggled to speak normally. "I'm fine," he replied, his voice shaky.

"Open the door, Nate."

"I-I need a minute."

"Open the door."

The determination in Erik's tone sent a shudder down Nathan's spine. He rubbed at his eyes, praying they weren't red-rimmed, and then took a deep breath before sliding the lock free and stepping out of the stall. Erik yanked him into a tight embrace immediately, surprising Nathan, his eyes widening. Nathan kept his arms at his sides for a moment, but when it seemed Erik didn't intend to let him go, Nathan capitulated and hesitantly wrapped his arms around Erik's waist. The feel of Erik's firm chest against him, the heat of his body, sank into Nathan, and he closed his eyes, resting his cheek over Erik's heart, listening to the steady thrum of it beneath his ear. He dug his fingers into the material of Erik's shirt at the waistband of his jeans and held on tight.

Sunshine and rain-wet earth filled his nostrils, erasing the smell of death and decay as Nathan breathed in the heady scent of Erik, and for the first time in over six years, Nathan felt safe. No matter how many times Troy had helped him, saved him, Nathan had never experienced the same sense of rightness as he did right there, right then, in Erik's arms. And it scared him. It terrified him to his very bones. Because he knew he could lose it. He could lose Erik. The moment Erik found out about his terrible gift he would turn away from him. Nathan clenched his fingers deeper into the fabric of Erik's shirt and swore he'd never tell him. He could never reveal the truth of his ability. Ever.

"Better?" Erik finally asked, chest rumbling beneath Nathan's ear.

Reluctantly, Nathan untangled his fingers from Erik's shirt, and without lifting his head, he nodded. "Thank you," he whispered.

Erik cupped Nathan's chin and tilted his head back,

forcing him to meet his gaze. He searched Nathan's face for several seconds, then smiled gently. "Someday you'll be ready to share your secrets with me, angel, and when that day comes, I'll be here."

Nathan bit his lip to stop the tremble he could feel beginning. The door of the restroom opening gave Nathan a reprieve from having to respond and he stepped away from Erik, giving himself some space. The man who entered gave the two of them a suspicious look, eyeing them as he moved to the urinal. He then seemed to think twice and walked into a stall instead, closing the door firmly.

"Would you rather we get our food to go?" Erik asked.

Nathan nodded. "Please?"

Erik smiled. "Of course."

He trailed after Erik as they exited the bathroom, skirting away from the counter as far as he could. The spirit stared at the two of them, the one good eye observing them, and Nathan knew the ghost sensed something but couldn't tell which one of them knew he was there.

Erik asked Harriet to pack up their dinner, and Nathan went out front to wait near the truck, studiously keeping his gaze averted from the large glass window of the diner. Erik joined him a few moments later, and the tension in Nathan eased the moment they were on the road toward Erik's house. He pulled the hood of his jacket up and rested his temple on the passenger door, gazing out at the passing houses, hands stuffed in his pockets.

"You sure you're okay now?"

Nathan grunted.

"You want to talk about it?"

"I'm fine," Nathan said.

Erik didn't push for more and Nathan couldn't have been more grateful. He didn't want to have to lie to him. They didn't speak again until they arrived at Erik's and Nathan tried to refuse to eat the burger Erik had ordered for him.

"You need to eat something, Nathan." Erik gestured at the plate he'd set out and placed the burger with the fries on it. Nathan hadn't sat down. He stood just inside the doorway of the dining area, staring at Erik.

"I'm not really hungry."

Erik scowled. "At least try. Please."

If Erik hadn't added the please onto the end, Nathan may have gotten frustrated. Sighing, he moved to the table and slouched into the chair. He snatched a fry and stuffed it into his mouth. He barely tasted it. If it had been Troy, he'd have told Troy to fuck off even if he had said please.

The realization of how quickly he was becoming attached to Erik and how much he was changing because of him twisted in his stomach like a sharp knife. The fry became ash on his tongue and Nathan almost choked. He toyed with the next one, staring at the limp lettuce hanging off the almost cold burger.

It wasn't as though he hadn't already known how close they were becoming, but facing the reality head-on seemed daunting. If he felt this way now, after only a little over a week of knowing the man, how the hell would he feel in two weeks? A month? Six months?

Nathan thought back to Troy's words from earlier in the day and his chest tightened. Was he falling in love with Erik? Was this throat crushing, heart clenching, gut twisting, all-consuming need to never disappoint Erik the emotion everyone called love? He almost whimpered aloud at just how terrifying the idea was. He hadn't had so much to lose in such a long time.

A sigh rattled him free from his thoughts, and Nathan looked up to find Erik watching him. Nathan realized Erik had finished eating, and he hadn't eaten anything more than the first French fry since he'd sat down. "Sorry," he mumbled.

"If you're really not hungry, I can put it away for later," Erik said.

Nathan shrugged. "I'm really not."

"I'll put it away then." Erik stood and took their plates into the kitchen.

Nathan listened as Erik moved around, packing his leftovers and then washing their dishes. He folded his arms on the table and rested his head on them, closing his eyes. He really was useless at knowing what to do with others. The concept of him being in a relationship seemed so far-fetched that he considered laughing and telling Erik they'd made a mistake and then leaving. What the hell did he know about being with someone? Hell, he felt selfish as fuck right then. Aside from not telling Erik the truth about himself and being able to see Alan, he also had no clue how to be open with someone else, how to give that part of himself to someone else.

The warmth of a hand on his nape startled Nathan, and he jumped but settled quickly. It wasn't as if anyone was in the house except the two of them. "You okay?" Erik asked.

"I'm good," Nathan mumbled into his folded arms.

"Look at me, Nate," Erik said. Nathan lifted his head, dislodging Erik's hand. Erik stood over him, a compassionate expression on his features. "Whenever you're ready to talk, I'm here to listen."

"I'm fine," Nathan insisted.

Erik took Nathan's hand and tugged. At first, Nathan resisted, but when Erik pulled again, he gave in and stood from the chair, Erik instantly bringing him in close. "Stay here tonight?" Erik asked.

"Yeah," Nathan replied without hesitation, despite knowing he shouldn't.

His arms tightened around Nathan for a brief second before releasing him. "Head into the bedroom while I lock up, okay?"

Nathan couldn't bring himself to look at Erik as he walked out of the dining room. Once in the bedroom, he shed his T-shirt and jeans and laid them over a nearby chair, leaving his boxers on. As he pulled the comforter back, it dawned on Nathan how he'd completely forgotten to be embarrassed about exposing the scars on his legs and chest to Erik. He became motionless and gazed at the cream-colored sheets, shocked by his own actions.

The sound of Erik's footsteps coming down the hallway disturbed Nathan from his musings and he quickly slid between the sheets. He covered his legs and then pulled his knees to his chest, looping his arms around them and resting his chin on top. Erik came in and shut the door behind him.

"I'll set the alarm early enough to take you back to your apartment for a change of clothes," Erik said as he started unbuttoning the shirt he wore.

Unable to help it, Nathan watched each button slide free from its hole, captivated. He swallowed hard as more of Erik's tanned skin appeared. Twisting the sheet between his fingers, he realized he hadn't really thought it through when Erik had asked him to stay. Did Erik intend on having sex with him tonight? Was he ready for that?

Nathan almost moaned when Erik shrugged his shirt off, hard muscles rippling in the soft glow of the bedside lamps. He felt his cock harden, and he squirmed a bit, coughing slightly to cover the rustling of the bedding.

Erik didn't even seem to be aware of the effect he had on Nathan while he continued to strip down to a pair of black briefs, which hugged every single inch of Erik's groin and buttocks like a loving second skin. If the bulge in the front was any sign, Erik's girth matched his physique to a T, and

Nathan tried to imagine just how big it would get when hard. Then he had to work to force those thoughts from his mind when his cock got even harder, throbbing at the idea of seeing Erik completely naked, aroused and ready to take Nathan in the very bed he lay in.

Erik approached the bed and pulled the sheets back. "I have a late dinner meeting with a potential client tomorrow night. Do you think Troy could pick you up from work?" he asked as he climbed onto the bed.

Nathan had to blink several times and shake his head. "What?" he finally asked.

"Would Troy be able to pick you up from work tomorrow night? I have a late dinner meeting with a potential client, and it may run long," Erik repeated, a knowing sparkle dancing in the depths of his hazel eyes.

Nathan flushed. "Oh. I can get home on my own."

Erik frowned. "I'd rather you not. You've already had the unfortunate experience of being mugged once."

"I can take care of myself," Nathan said, scowling at Erik.

"I know you can, angel, but for my sake, please let Troy take you home. There's no way I can concentrate tomorrow night if I don't know you're safe."

Nathan glared a hole into the sheet covering his knees. Damn. Why did Erik have to go there? He finally nodded. "Fine," he grumbled.

"Thank you," Erik said, giving a relieved smile.

The bed shifted and Erik leaned over, causing Nathan to stiffen, but all Erik did was kiss his cheek. Then he flicked off the lamp on his side of the bed before he settled back down to his pillow. "Good night, angel. See you in the morning."

Nathan's mouth dropped open in shock as he stared at Erik, who had already shut his eyes and appeared to be asleep. Disappointment warred with relief. What the hell? He couldn't believe Erik hadn't even given him a proper kiss.

Nathan snapped off the lamp next to him but didn't lay down right away. Instead, he remained leaning against the headboard, staring into the murky darkness that was broken only by the soft light fanning in around the edges of the curtains on the windows. Somehow, he hadn't expected Erik to not want to at least kiss him for a little while. What had he done wrong?

"Stop thinking so hard and go to sleep," Erik murmured, causing Nathan to jump. He'd thought he had already fallen asleep. Erik opened his eyes. "Would you rather talk about what happened earlier?"

"No," Nathan said.

"Then go to sleep." Erik closed his eyes again. Nathan continued to stare at Erik until he spoke once again. "It would help if you lay down, you know."

Finally, Nathan couldn't help it. "What did I do?"

Eyelids flying open, Erik stared at him, confusion shining on his face. "What are you talking about?"

Discomfort caused Nathan to shift under Erik's intense scrutiny. "I… You… Why didn't you kiss me?"

Erik sat up, turning his body toward Nathan. "You think I don't want to kiss you?" he asked incredulously.

Nathan started to get off the bed, uncomfortable, but Erik stopped him, tumbling him beneath him and pinning him in place. "No running away. Not this time," Erik said. "There is never a time when I don't want to kiss you, Nathan. I didn't want to overwhelm you after what happened at the diner."

Erik ran a finger down Nathan's cheek in a light caress. "Never doubt that I want you, angel." He rocked his hips forward and Nathan gasped when he felt the hard length of Erik's cock dig into his thigh. A smile curled the corners of Erik's lips. "I want you more than anything, Nathan, but I won't rush you. When you're ready for more, you'll make the choice."

Nathan blinked at Erik, darting his tongue out to wet his suddenly dry lips. He pressed his thigh tighter against the bulge between Erik's legs, enjoying the hitch in his breathing. His own cock had stiffened and Erik no doubt could feel it pushing along his abdomen. When he experimentally shifted his leg along Erik's cock, Erik hissed and shuddered, his eyes darkening. "Nathan," Erik rasped in warning.

"Kiss me," Nathan begged suddenly.

A groan rattled in Erik's throat and then he crushed his mouth down onto Nathan's, swallowing the sharp gasp Nathan released at the full body contact when Erik lowered himself on top of Nathan. Nathan grasped at him, seeking a port in the sudden onslaught. He opened his mouth and accepted the slick slide of Erik's tongue along his, granting entrance to the pink muscle. The heat of the kiss ratcheted higher as Erik coaxed Nathan's lips into an erotic dance, hotter than even the previous night. He couldn't stop his hands from running down the width of Erik's back to the top of his briefs and then up again, exploring the smooth skin beneath his palms. Every muscle underneath his fingers felt alive, and he never wanted to stop touching Erik. Nathan arched beneath him, whimpering in need and a quiet plea for more.

Erik never broke the kiss, drinking deeper from Nathan while skimming one hand over Nathan's side to the lightly furred expanse of Nathan's thigh. He yanked it high over his hip and aligned their cloth-covered cocks. Nathan cried out, pushing his pelvis upward in desire for more contact. A moan vibrated between them, wrenched from Erik and trickling through Nathan.

"Erik," Nathan panted, pleading for more with that single word.

Trailing kisses and gentle scrapes of his teeth over Nathan's jawline, Erik continued the delicious friction with subtle thrusts of his hips, but it wasn't enough, and Nathan sobbed in need. He wanted more, except he didn't know how to tell him. Only, Erik seemed to understand, and he plunged a hand between them, first releasing Nathan's shaft from his boxers and then his own, grasping both with one hot, calloused hand and then stroking them together. Nathan sank his fingernails into Erik's shoulders, his breathing harsh and loud in the bedroom's silence, while he undulated his hips, desperate for Erik's touch. Dizziness assaulted Nathan's senses. He'd never felt the hand of another on his cock before, and the sensation was beyond mind blowing. Nathan blindly sought Erik's mouth with his, sucking wetly on his tongue.

Slickness spread quickly over their shafts, easing the friction of Erik's fingers on Nathan's sensitive skin and adding to the pleasure mounting between them. "Nathan," Erik groaned against his lips.

Nathan released Erik's mouth to toss his head from side to side, loose strands of his hair sticking to the sweat on his cheeks and forehead. The muscles in his lower belly tightened and Nathan knew he wasn't far off from coming. Toes curling, Nathan almost screamed when Erik latched on to his throat, mouth working the flesh there, tongue swirling over the salty skin. But it was the feel of fiery streaks of liquid splashing over his abdomen and stomach and the sound of Erik grunting that tipped the scales for Nathan. A keening cry broke free from him as he came. Hard shudders ripped through him, and for several long moments, Nathan's vision went black. Heavy breaths wheezed from his lungs, and he could hardly hear as he collapsed amongst the sheets, Erik a warm weight on top of him.

The first thing Nathan noticed was the tender caress of Erik's fingers along his shoulder and the light brush of Erik's lips over his temple, cheekbone, and anywhere else the feathery wisp of flesh could touch. A shiver trickled through Nathan and he opened his eyes, blinking heavily to clear the lustful fog clouding his vision. His lungs labored to pull in air, and he wondered if he would ever breathe normally again.

"Don't move," Erik murmured, his voice almost an unwelcome intrusion into the hush around them as he disentangled himself from Nathan's embrace. Nathan wanted to protest, but he couldn't say a word as he watched Erik leave the bed and enter the restroom. The light flicked on and then he heard the water running in the sink briefly before Erik came back into the bedroom holding a washcloth in one hand.

A hiss left Nathan's lips when the cool damp cloth brushed over his stomach, clearing away the white liquid left behind by both of them. After he'd tucked Nathan's flaccid length back inside his boxers, Erik cupped his cheek and pressed a kiss to the corner of his mouth. Erik slotted his mouth over Nathan's, but he didn't deepen the kiss, merely suckling gently at Nathan's bottom lip briefly before releasing it with a light nip. Erik dropped the cloth on the floor beside the bed and pulled Nathan into his arms.

Nathan burrowed closer to Erik to hide his scars now that hormones didn't distract them. They were white lines that varied in thickness and ran across his chest and down some of his bicep. Only his doctors, aunts, and Troy had ever seen them. The lust which had risen between him and Erik had frazzled his mind and he'd forgotten about them for those few moments. He'd never known being touched by someone else could feel so good. Masturbating had never led to such an intense orgasm.

Erik nuzzled Nathan's temple. "You doing okay?"

Nodding, Nathan rested a hand over Erik's heart. "I'm good."

Erik hummed. "I hope better than good."

A grin curved Nathan's lips. "Definitely."

Erik's chest vibrated with a laugh before he nudged Nathan to roll onto his back. Nathan reluctantly went, but he tensed when Erik's calloused fingers trailed along his scars. "From the accident?"

Nathan nodded, not meeting Erik's gaze. He bit his lip when Erik splayed his hand across Nathan's collarbone near his shoulder. The warmth of his palm radiated through Nathan's skin and into his muscle beneath. "What you went through must have been awful, but I'm grateful you survived it."

Swallowing hard, Nathan peered up at Erik from beneath his eyelashes. For the first time in his life, Nathan was feeling happy he'd survived, too. "Me, too," he murmured.

Erik kissed his temple, settled back down beside Nathan, and pulled him tight to his side. "Good night, angel."

"Night," Nathan said.

Nathan tried to sleep, but he couldn't. The ever-present remorse Nathan lived with every single day bore down on him. He was racked with guilt over daring to be happy when his parents were gone, as well as from the knowledge that he'd sworn to help Alan but hadn't kept his promise. He remembered the blog posts he'd printed and wondered if there was anything in them which would help him find out why Alan was still here. Erik's breathing evened out and Nathan heard a gentle snore coming from him.

Nathan carefully slipped from under the covers and trod lightly out of the room and down the stairs. His backpack sat near the front door where he'd dropped it. He picked it up and moved to sit on the couch. The zipper sounded harsh in the silence and Nathan held his breath, listening to see if Erik was still asleep. When he didn't hear Erik's feet on the stairs, he pulled out the blog posts and started reading.

A lot of them were about Alan's college courses and his relationship with Erik. Nathan felt weird reading them, but the only way he could help Alan was to find out what he needed to tell Erik. When he got to one a few weeks before Alan's death, Nathan's breath caught. There were no specifics, but Alan mentioned knowing something Erik didn't and how he didn't know how to tell Erik without hurting him. Nathan quickly skimmed the rest of the post, but Alan didn't go into any further details. He just kept writing about being torn about what to do and fearing Erik being upset. Damn, why did Alan have to be so fucking vague?

He read through all of the posts until they stopped. Alan never revealed what it was or even mentioned the topic again. Shit. He'd been hoping there was something. Even just a hint. Maybe the post would remind Alan—if he ever talked to Alan again after the way he'd disappeared.

Nathan stuffed the papers back into his bag, closed it, and stood. He padded into the kitchen to get some water. Alan thought Erik was in danger, so whatever it was must have been important. Nathan opened cabinet doors until he found a glass, filled it with water from the door of the fridge, and took a long drink. Did Alan do something? Maybe he cheated on Erik? The idea of Alan cheating on Erik angered Nathan. But seeing how lost Alan was, knowing the emotions he felt, Nathan couldn't imagine it being that.

Before heading back upstairs, Nathan sent a quick text to

Troy about Erik taking him to school in the morning and that he'd see him in class. Erik remained blissfully unaware of Nathan having gotten out of bed, as he was still sleeping soundly. Nathan slipped in beside him and pulled the covers over his legs. Sighing, he closed his eyes and tried to sleep. He couldn't be certain when he did finally pass out, but it wasn't without dreams this time. Dreams of Alan and the disappointment of letting him down plagued Nathan. Those dreams developed into Erik being disgusted by him for not telling him everything. By the time the alarm went off, Nathan felt as if he hadn't slept at all.

Erik slipped from the bed and Nathan rolled over, burrowing into the sheets and pillows. He heard the bathroom door close and the sound of the shower cutting on before he dozed off again. It wasn't until Erik shook him that he actually opened his eyes. The scent of Erik's woodsy aftershave washed over Nathan, and he smiled as he rolled to his back. "Good morning," he murmured.

Smiling down at him, Erik perched on the edge of the bed. "Were you able to sleep?"

Nathan shrugged one shoulder. "A little."

"You were restless last night. Bad dreams?"

"Kind of." Nathan sat up, leaning against the headboard.

"Want to talk about it?"

He shook his head. "Nothing to talk about, really."

Erik reached out and touched Nathan's cheek. "Some day you will talk to me, Nate, but I can wait. You'll find I am a very patient man."

Not going to happen. "I still need to stop by my apartment to change."

Standing, Erik held his hand down to Nathan. "Then let's get going, hmm?" He tugged Nathan out of the bed and right into a firm hug. "Good morning, angel."

Nathan wrinkled his nose. "Why do you call me angel?"

"You don't like it?"

"Well, isn't that something a guy calls a girl usually?"

"Says who?"

"I don't know. Just never heard it used by a guy toward a guy."

Erik kissed Nathan's forehead. "If you don't like it, I can stop using it."

Nathan blushed and looked down at their feet while shaking his head. "No, it's okay."

"Come on, get dressed. We're going to be late if we don't leave soon." Erik nudged Nathan toward the bathroom, where Erik must have placed his clothing on the counter. "The toothbrush from the other day is still in the holder."

It only took Nathan a few minutes to relieve himself, brush his teeth, and get dressed in the clothes from the day before. Erik was already downstairs when he left the bathroom. Nathan found him in the kitchen, pouring coffee in a travel mug. "Coffee?" Erik asked.

"Yes, please."

Erik handed him an already prepared cup. "I picked up some creamer and sugar yesterday. Pretty sure I got it the way you like it."

Nathan took a small taste and sighed. "Perfect."

"Good."

Nathan grabbed his pack and they climbed into the truck. Once they hit the road, Erik reached for Nathan's hand, and he didn't pull away this time. His thoughts turned to Alan again though. He needed to find Alan. Maybe he'd be at school.

"Don't forget to let Troy know to take you home from work."

Nathan nodded. "I'll talk to him before classes."

"I shouldn't be too long after you're off work. Maybe I

can meet the two of you at the diner and you can go back to my house tonight?" Erik said.

"I really need to study. I think it would be better if Troy took me home."

Erik looked over at him for a moment. "You could study at my house."

Nathan lifted his brow at Erik. "Really?"

"I can keep my hands to myself."

"Somehow, I doubt that," Nathan said wryly.

Erik chuckled. "Okay. Maybe you're right. At least call me when you get home. So I know you're safe."

"Okay." It surprised Nathan at just how easily he accepted Erik's concern and directive. If Troy had said the same thing, he knew he'd have gotten belligerent instantly. But Erik being concerned for him made him feel warm inside, and for the first time in a long time, he wanted to let someone take care of him.

They got to Nathan's apartment building and Nathan slid from the cab. "Give me five minutes."

"I can come with you," Erik offered.

Nathan shook his head. "Really, I just need to change my clothes. I'll be right back."

Erik conceded and Nathan rushed up the stairs as quickly as his leg would allow him. He unlocked and opened his door. "Alan?" he called out. "Alan, we need to talk. Are you here?"

Silence met his query, and Nathan frowned. He went into his bedroom, stripped, and dressed in another pair of jeans and a black t-shirt. "Alan, if you can hear me, we need to talk. Please come to the store later."

It bothered him more than he'd care to admit, how he couldn't sense Alan and how easily he had disappeared. Had he given up and moved on? Could he move on? Nathan didn't think it worked that way, but what the hell did he know? Sighing in disappointment, Nathan closed his door, locked it, and headed back downstairs to the truck. Erik was on a call when Nathan opened the door and quietly tried to climb in.

"Just tell them I'll be there in an hour. Have Victoria give them coffee and set them up in my office." Nathan heard garbled noises through the cell phone but couldn't make out what was being said. "No, Matthew, I haven't. Look, I'll tell you about it later."

Erik grunted in frustration. "Fine," he snapped. "I'll be there in thirty."

Erik ended the call and took a deep breath. "I'm sorry, angel. We're going to have to do a quick drive-through for breakfast and then I need to get you to Webster."

"I can just get something from the vending machine," Nathan replied.

"No, you at least need something hot to eat."

"You know I rarely eat much for breakfast, anyway."

Erik grabbed Nathan's hand and squeezed gently. "I know, but it's not healthy for you to skip so many meals. At least let me get you breakfast."

Nathan wrinkled his nose. "It sounded like they really needed you at work. I don't want to hold you up."

"They can wait. Besides, it was just my cousin Matthew being his usual self." Erik put the truck in Drive and merged into traffic. "He doesn't enjoy dealing with clients or people. He's my accountant and spends his life behind the desk. My aunt asked me to get him out of his hole, but Matthew can be extremely stubborn. If you remember, I mentioned he helped me after Alan died, and I couldn't be more grateful to him. I just wish sometimes he would find the confidence in himself to handle things at the office whenever I'm not there."

"Did you have a meeting scheduled this morning?" Nathan asked.

Erik shook his head. "No. They just showed up. I knew they were looking to contact my company for a job, but there was no formal meeting arranged. It's not the first time a client has done that. It won't be the last, I'm sure."

He pulled into a McDonald's drive-through. "Anything in particular you want?"

"I really don't need any—" Nathan stopped speaking abruptly when he saw the consternation on Erik's face. "An egg sandwich is fine."

Erik ordered the meal that came with a coffee and hash browns, then ordered another for himself. He handed everything over to Nathan before getting back onto the main road. Nathan dug out his sandwich and set the bag on the console between them.

"It's not as nutritional as I would like, but thank you for appeasing me," Erik said.

Nathan shrugged, unwrapping his sandwich to take a bite. They reached the school a short time later. Nathan tossed the empty wrapper into the paper bag, then grabbed his pack and the travel coffee mug. He'd dumped the McDonald's coffee in with what had remained in the mug.

"Don't forget to call me to let me know you made it home safely," Erik said, leaning over to give Nathan a quick kiss.

"I will," Nathan said, then closed the door. Troy stood near the front entrance, his shoulder pressed to the wall as he messed around on his phone. He glanced up and smirked when he saw Nathan walking toward him.

"Spending a lot of time with him, huh? You get lucky yet?"

Nathan rolled his eyes. "You need to get your mind out of the gutter."

Troy laughed. "It lives there, Nate. You should know that after all this time."

Instead of responding, Nathan just kept looking around,

hoping to spot Alan. Disappointment and guilt struck him when his searching proved fruitless.

"You looking for someone?" Troy asked while they walked toward Nathan's first class.

"Alan."

Troy frowned. "Why do you want to find him? Wait, he really left?"

Nathan ran a hand through his hair in frustration. "I haven't seen him since he disappeared."

"Isn't that a good thing, though?" Troy asked.

"I can't let him wander forever! Especially when I've seen the way the ghosts who've been stuck here for so long end up! Even if I don't want to do it for him, I need to do it for Erik. He'd never forgive me if I let Alan just stay lost."

Troy grunted. "All right, all right. I get it. Maybe I can help. I've got a free hour later today. I'll try to do some more digging myself. But if it is a secret, without Alan's memories I doubt we'll find anything."

"Try looking up Erik. See what you can find out about him. Alan is worried about him, like he's in danger. Maybe Erik is the key to the answer."

"Okay."

They separated when they reached Nathan's class, and Nathan spent most of the day struggling to concentrate on the lectures. He knew he'd have to borrow another classmate's notes when he saw how little he'd taken himself. By lunchtime, his head was hurting.

When he met Troy for lunch, Troy hadn't found anything either. "Everything I could find on Erik was about his construction company and the projects he's done. Aside from work, the only thing was an announcement of Erik's engagement to Alan."

Troy dropped a paper in front of Nathan. Erik and Alan were standing together, arms around each other, smiling at the camera. Nathan's heart tripped, and he swallowed hard. "They look so happy."

"Maybe Alan's wrong," Troy said. "It's possible there's really nothing going on and he just can't let go."

"I don't think so," Nathan replied. "If I've learned one thing over these last few years, there is always something keeping them here. They don't stay just because they want to. There's a reason."

Troy grunted and took a bite of his sandwich. In between chewing, he said, "Well, the guy needs to just sack up and figure it out."

Nathan sighed. "I may need to take the day off from work. See if I can take him around to familiar places to jog his memory."

A scowl twisted Troy's features. "You shouldn't have to lose out on pay because of this asshat."

"If I don't do something, he's never going to be at rest."

"It's not your job to worry about him," Troy muttered.

"I won't argue about this with you. You know why I need to help him."

Nathan left it at that and finished the lunch he'd grabbed from the cafeteria. "I'm not going to Erik's tonight. I need to study."

"Then I'm picking you up from work."

Rolling his eyes, Nathan said, "That's why I told you. I need to get Alan to talk to me before I convince Stuart not to fire me for taking a day off. The usual time, okay?"

"I'm bringing you dinner, too."

They parted ways and Nathan headed to class, still praying Alan would appear somewhere.

CHAPTER 16

Alan never appeared at school. Not even in Professor Johns' class. Nathan prayed he'd see him at work. Troy dropped him off and said he'd be back around nine to bring him dinner and hang out until Nathan closed the store. Disappointment filled him when he walked in and didn't see Alan. The man wasn't even in the stockroom where Nathan clocked in. Damn. He'd really hoped Alan had heard him at his apartment. He settled in to work his shift, all while glancing around occasionally for the spirit.

It wasn't until after Troy brought him dinner and Quinn bailed early that Alan made an appearance. Nathan didn't notice him at first because he was busy taking inventory. When he'd made the final notation in the tablet he held, Nathan turned and almost walked through Alan. He gasped and stepped back. "Alan! Oh thank fuck!"

Sadness trickled over Nathan and he knew it came from Alan. "Where did you go?" Nathan asked.

Alan gave him a bitter smile. "Just wandered. I can't go where I want to go, where I need to go."

"I still want to help you," Nathan said. "Troy and I found

nothing concrete, but I went through the blog you had and found a post. You mentioned knowing something Erik didn't, and you didn't know how to tell him without hurting him. But there weren't any specifics. Does that bring anything to mind? At all?"

Alan shook his head. "No, it doesn't. I can't remember anything."

"Tomorrow, I want to go with you to places you're familiar with. See if anything jogs your memory."

"Don't you have to work?" Alan asked, frowning.

"I'm going to bail. I want to help you, Alan. If that's the only way to help you find peace and know what you needed to tell Erik, I want to help."

"You just don't want to feel guilty," Alan groused.

"I can't deny a part of me feels guilty, but I also know I can't leave you roaming forever. You're a good person, Alan. What happened to you was a tragedy, and it wasn't fair. I've seen what that does to a person's spirit. There's no way I can let that happen to you."

Alan eyed Nathan. "Okay. I guess we can give your way a shot. Not like I have anywhere else to be."

"Tomorrow, after classes, meet me at the front of campus. We'll start there."

Alan nodded and then disappeared. Nathan finished his shift, closed out the register, and locked up the store. Troy stopped for him to drop off the night deposit and then drove Nathan home.

After sending a text to Erik to let him know he was home safe, Nathan emptied his bookbag and sat down at his little table. He really hadn't been lying when he'd told Erik he needed to study, and he spent the next few hours reading over his notes, the notes he'd asked a fellow student for, and some of the test preparation materials.

He didn't stop until well after midnight, which is when he

took out his phone to charge. There were three texts from Erik, one of which caused his face to infuse with heat and Nathan almost dropped the phone.

Erik: *Thank you for letting me know you're home.*

Erik: *I hope you ate something!*

Erik: *All I can think about is how sexy you looked covered in my cum last night.*

Nathan figured Erik was already asleep and didn't respond to them. He'd answer him in the morning. Of course, that is when the reality of sleeping without Erik set in. He had gone two nights without his usual nightmares about his parents and the accident. Would he be able to make it through tonight without one? He closed his books, put everything in his backpack, and went to get ready for bed. The covers were cold on his skin when he slipped beneath them, and he shivered. He turned off the light and lay there, trying to will himself asleep.

The silence was deafening. There was no breathing next to him, no heat transferring to him from Erik's broader, larger form. He rolled onto his stomach and buried his head in the pillows. But that only lasted for a few minutes. He moved to his side, then his back again. Sleep evaded him, and Nathan sat up. Insomnia had been his best friend for the last several years. This was nothing new to him, yet it ticked him off. In less than two weeks, Erik had changed everything. He'd given Nathan hope, something he hadn't had in a long time. Not since his parents' deaths.

Sleeping alone, Nathan had known what to expect. He'd grown accustomed to it. Now, he'd glimpsed the other side of the curtain. Could he ever be happy on this side again? What if Erik found out about his gift and thought he was insane? Would he survive having the feelings Erik evoked these last couple of weeks yanked away? Nathan got off the bed and started pacing, muttering under his breath. These insecurities and emotions were why he hadn't wanted to believe he had a happy future. Because it would hurt like hell to lose it a second time.

He eventually wore himself out and collapsed on the bed, only to stare at the ceiling until the light of day crept in around the curtains. The alarm went off not long after and he dragged himself into the shower, dressed, and made a pot of coffee. He drank half before he had to meet Troy outside.

"Man, you look like shit warmed over," Troy said, raising a brow at Nathan. "Couldn't sleep?"

Nathan shook his head.

"Was *he* bugging you again?"

"No. Just couldn't sleep."

"Hmm." Once they were in the car, Troy asked, "You still planning on taking this afternoon off to help Alan?"

"Yeah."

"What are you going to tell Stuart?"

Shrugging, Nathan said, "Probably that I'm sick."

Troy glanced over at him with a raised brow. "You went to work with the flu last year. You really think he's going to believe that?"

Nathan shrugged. "He has no choice. He won't fire me because he knows he can't replace me that easily."

The conversation changed over to classes and the midterms they were facing. When they reached the school, they separated and headed to their respective classes. Nathan forced himself to concentrate on the lectures by his professors, taking notes of anything pertinent. He would need to study hard for the next few days to pass the exams. Nathan hadn't joined any of the study groups the others in class had formed. Work kept him way too busy during the hours they usually met. He'd trudged through the first three and a half years by himself instead.

His phone buzzed in his pocket. Nathan waited until after

class to see who'd texted him. A new message from Erik was waiting for him, reminding him that he'd forgotten to text Erik back before classes.

Erik: *Good morning. Did you get a lot of studying done?*

Nathan: *I did. Sorry for not texting back earlier.*

Erik: *Did I upset you?*

Nathan: *What do you mean?*

Erik: *With the last text, did it bother you?*

Cheeks heating with embarrassment at the remembrance of the text, Nathan ducked his head, trying to keep his face hidden.

Nathan: *No.*

Erik: *I'm glad. I miss you.*

Nathan's heart tripped a beat in his chest.

Nathan: *I miss you, too.*

Erik: *When can I see you again?*

He hesitated. He really needed to spend more time studying this week. Plus, he had Alan to deal with.

Nathan: *A couple of my midterms are Friday. I need as much time as I can to study.*

Erik: *What about dinner? You need to eat and then I'll go home... alone.*

Nathan grinned and shook his head. The idea of Erik wanting to see him so badly sent warm tendrils trickling through his chest and down to his belly. Maybe he could do dinner.

Nathan: *Dinner is good.*

Erik: *Can't wait. I'll pick you up from work.*

Panic set in. Erik would know he'd bailed on work and would want to know why.

Nathan: *I'm calling out tonight so I can study after classes. I can meet you somewhere.*

Erik: *Nonsense. I'll pick you up at your apartment then. Does 7 p.m. work?*

Nathan: *Yea.*

Erik: *7 it is. I'll see you then. Can't wait to see you.*

Instead of responding, Nathan stuffed his phone back into his pocket and walked as quickly as his bad leg would allow him to his next class. A minor headache pounded at the back of his skull by the time he exited his last class and made it to the front of campus. He called Stuart and gave him a story about having a migraine and not being able to make it in that afternoon. Then he spotted Alan standing near a tree close by. When he reached Alan, he stopped and bent down to pretend he was tying his shoe. "Any ideas where we should start?"

Alan seemed paler than usual, and Nathan frowned when he straightened. His cheeks looked a little hollower, and the bright energy he'd given off at first had dimmed. Forgetting his attempt to hide talking to thin air, he asked, "Are you okay?"

"Define okay," Alan said. "I'm dead, in case you forgot."

Nathan winced. "That's not what I meant. You seem… different."

Alan gave a listless shrug and replied, "Doesn't matter."

To Nathan, it mattered. He wondered if Alan choosing to give up had caused his energy to fade slightly. Maybe a spirit losing hope of ever finishing whatever kept them earthbound was why some of them seemed so malevolent. He couldn't let Alan become one of those. "We'll figure it out, Alan. I promise. Once we do, I'll tell Erik. No matter what. I swear it."

Alan eyed him, obvious skepticism on his face. "You promised you'd tell Erik I'm here but still haven't. How will this be any different?"

"Because I'll know what I need to tell him. I *will* tell him, Alan. You have my word."

Some of the energy around Alan brightened and Nathan

knew he'd keep his promise. Somehow. "Now, where do we go?"

Nathan realized he'd been talking to Alan in front of people again. When he glanced around, several students were giving him a concerned or frightened look. "Shit," he swore under his breath.

Alan waved his hand at Nathan. "Forget them. You'll never see them again after college."

"Easy for you to say," Nathan muttered. He pulled out his cell phone and put it to his ear. "I should have thought of this sooner."

"Great idea!"

"Thanks. Ideas about where to start?"

Alan frowned. "Well, I obviously have no reminders here on campus. I've been all over and haven't had a single memory. I still think I need to go home."

Nathan shook his head. "We can't go to Erik's. Not yet. Let's try something else. What other places did you go to often?"

"There's a coffee shop around the corner from here. I used to go there and write my blog posts. Erik's office, of course."

Nathan grimaced at the mention of Erik's office. He'd have to come up with an excuse to go there. "Anywhere else?"

"There's a park by our home I used to go to all the time, too. And my old apartment is about three blocks from here. Maybe we could try there."

He nodded. "Sounds good. Let's start with the coffee shop first."

Alan smiled. "Thanks, Nathan. I really appreciate this."

"Don't mention it." Nathan didn't put the phone away, just in case. He walked with Alan to the coffee shop. He hadn't even known this place was here. Practically every student from campus was waiting in line. The smell of freshly brewed coffee hit Nathan, and his stomach growled. He hadn't eaten anything since the night before. Bringing his phone to his ear again, he said to Alan, "Look around. See if anything jogs your memory. I'm going to grab some coffee and a pastry."

Even though the line seemed longer than a Black Friday sale line, the servers were fast and efficient. Maybe fifteen minutes had passed before Nathan found himself close to the front of the line. Alan came back to his side and shook his head. "Nothing. Everything looks familiar, but I don't get any sense of dread like when I think of Erik."

It was his turn to order, so Nathan waited to respond until after he'd ordered, gotten his coffee and the pastry, and they were back on the sidewalk. He held the phone to his ear again. "Your old apartment next?"

"Okay." Alan led the way this time since he knew the area better than Nathan. Meanwhile, Nathan sipped at his coffee and ate his pastry. The closer to the apartment they got, the more Alan's energy seemed to grow brighter. Maybe they were onto something. But when they reached the building, Alan floated there, eyeing the front. "Let's go inside," he said.

"There's no way to go into your apartment!" Nathan protested.

Alan shook his head. "No, I mean into the lobby. Maybe that'll help."

Sighing, Nathan opened the front door and followed Alan inside. The lobby had muted red clay tile flooring, some plants scattered around the small area, and there was a line of mailboxes to the left. An elevator was toward the back of the lobby. Nathan wondered how much the rent was for a place like this. His own was a little over a grand a month with utilities. This one had to be at least double what he paid for his shabby apartment. He almost felt out of place.

Alan wandered around the area and stopped near the elevator. He looked at Nathan. "We need to go up."

Nathan hurried forward, shaking his head. "No. We can't. You're going to get me arrested for loitering or something."

"Come on. No one's here. Please, Nathan?" Alan put on a puppy dog face. One Nathan found hard to ignore.

"Damn it, Alan," Nathan growled while punching the button. "If I get arrested, you're so dead."

"Would you relax?" Alan said. "You're not going to get arrested. It's not like this place has security roaming the halls or anything."

"What floor?" Nathan asked when they boarded the elevator.

"Fourth."

He stabbed the number four and watched with trepidation while the doors closed. Within thirty seconds, the doors opened to the fourth floor. The usual ugly carpeting lined the hallway outside of the apartments, softening Nathan's footsteps. "Which apartment?"

"412."

Nathan begrudgingly followed Alan down the hall and around the corner. He could hear televisions and a radio from two units. A door opening caused Nathan's heart to jump into his throat. "Can we hurry?" he whispered to Alan.

They stopped in front of the apartment. "Aren't you able to go through the walls?" Nathan asked. "See if you can go in."

Alan gave Nathan an irritated glance. "Jesus, Nathan. You're strung tighter than a well-tuned guitar. Just give me a minute here."

He wanted to snap back at Alan, but he bit his tongue and leaned against the wall. "Just hurry."

Alan ignored him and then disappeared into the apartment. Nathan kept nervously glancing around, watching for anyone coming. Alan wasn't gone for long. When he returned to Nathan's side, he said, "Nothing. The person who has it now redecorated in tacky colors and furniture." He visibly shuddered. "Who would mix olive green with neon orange?"

"Let's get out of here." Nathan beat feet down the hallway back to the elevator. He breathed a sigh of relief as soon as they were out on the sidewalk. The minor headache he'd had when he'd left his last class increased in tempo. "You're trying to kill me, aren't you?"

Alan snorted and rolled his eyes. "Has anyone ever told you how dramatic you are? You really need to remove that stick from your ass sometimes and relax."

"Hey! I'm trying to help you, but I don't need to get arrested and have to try and explain this shit to the cops!"

"You won't get arrested just for walking around the building. Now calm the hell down."

Nathan glared at Alan while keeping his mouth shut this time.

"Good boy," Alan said, smiling.

Growling, Nathan swiped at Alan, which of course was ineffective, since his hand went right through the other man. "I swear to God, I'm done with this shit once you've moved on."

Alan pouted at him, eyes twinkling with mirth. "I thought we were friends."

"Friends?" Nathan asked, flabbergasted. "You've literally turned my life upside down these last two weeks. Almost caused me to kill myself. Threatened me. Got me kicked out of class. Even got people looking at me like I'm insane. You think we're friends?"

"You know, you're cute when you're angry," Alan teased. "I can see why Erik likes you."

He let out a frustrated cry and turned to walk away from Alan. "Every time I talk myself into this shit and every damn time, I regret it. Come on, let's go to this stupid park."

Alan chuckled the entire way to the bus stop. Nathan grumbled under his breath the entire time. They had to hop a couple of buses and walk quite a bit to get to Erik's neighborhood. Nathan prayed Erik didn't drive by and see him. The man would think he was stalking him or something. He had no clue what he would say if Erik saw him.

Thankfully, they made it to the park without incident and he sat on a bench under a tree while Alan wandered around. Nathan watched Alan become more and more frustrated and disappointed until he came back to Nathan's side. "Damn it! I don't understand! Why can't I think of whatever it is I need to tell Erik?" Alan kicked at the nearby garbage can. Only, his foot went right through it. "And I can't even hit something! Gah!"

Nathan saw Alan's energy changing from a golden tone to a darker reddish color. "We'll figure it out, Alan."

"How? I can't remember. Nothing seems to help!"

An idea came to Nathan. "What if... well... What if we went to where you had the accident? Maybe that would loosen something?"

"Maybe. But how are we going to get there? You don't drive, and it's not like we can walk there. It isn't exactly around the corner."

Nathan took out his phone, dialed Troy's number, and hit the Call button.

"Nate, what's up?" Troy answered. "You okay? Did he remember anything?"

"I'm fine. No. Not yet. I was wondering if you could come get us." Nathan explained what they needed, and Troy agreed. He gave Troy the name of the park where they were.

"I should be there in twenty," Troy said, then disconnected the call.

Nathan remained where he was, watching the few others in the park. Alan kept hoping for something to spark a memory and continued to wander around while they waited. Nathan couldn't stop the thoughts that flooded him. Were his parents out there somewhere? Waiting for him to help them move on? Or were they already at peace and wherever it was spirits went to? He'd gone back to the accident site more than once, hoping and praying his parents' spirits were there, but they never appeared. Every night for months on end, he'd reached out to whatever god or overlord there was watching over them to beg him for a chance to see them. Just one more time. The overlord never answered.

Before he could get too bogged down in the depressing memories and thoughts of his parents for the billionth time, he saw Troy's car enter the parking lot. "Alan," Nathan called and stood from the bench.

Alan followed him toward the car. Troy had already exited and leaned against the side of the car. "He's here?"

Nathan grunted. "Wouldn't make much sense for us to go there without him."

"Can he even ride in a car?" Troy asked, skepticism shining clearly in his voice.

"We rode the bus here," Nathan pointed out while opening the passenger-side front door.

Alan floated into the back seat behind him. Nathan nodded to Troy, who got into the driver's seat. A few minutes later, they were on the road and headed toward the curve where Alan's car had crashed.

"Do you really think this will help?" Alan asked.

Nathan could feel his own emotions darkening as depression set in. They were stuck in proximity, so he tried to fight it. It weighed on his chest like an elephant stood there. "It's worth a shot. I'm out of ideas otherwise."

Alan didn't say anything else during the drive. Nathan's

emotions ranged from depression to hope to despair, and he couldn't discern whether any of it was his own or all Alan's. He couldn't contain a sigh of relief when Troy pulled the car to the side of the road. The city had repaired the guardrail and there was no trace of an accident. Two years was a long time for any evidence to remain undisturbed.

Nathan got out of the car and walked over toward the barrier. Alan trailed behind him, an icy presence at his back every step of the way. He just let Alan look over the area, but when he saw the frustration on Alan's face, Nathan wanted to groan. "Nothing?"

A cry of defeat left Alan, and he kicked at the barrier, even knowing his foot would only go through it. "Damn it!"

To avoid absorbing any more of Alan's emotions, Nathan stepped back several paces without thinking. The loud blaring of someone leaning on their horn caused him to jump back to the side of the road. A black SUV went roaring by and Nathan froze. Horror and fear crashed over him. He snapped his gaze to Alan to see the man staring after the SUV in abject terror. "It wasn't an accident," Alan whispered, his form shimmering for a split second. "Someone deliberately ran me off the road."

CHAPTER 17

"What? Who ran you off the road?" Nathan asked, struggling to hold back his own reactions to Alan's panic.

"I-I don't know. I don't remember if I saw their face. All I remember are the bright lights, high beams in my mirror, and the sound of a horn. They rammed the bumper of my car, and I lost control. I-I hit the guardrail, my car went through it, but my back tires caught on the rail itself. They, oh God, they…" Nathan saw tears racing down Alan's cheeks. He locked eyes with Nathan. "They forced me over the edge by hitting my car again."

"What do you remember about the other car?"

A sob caught in Alan's throat. "It was a big black truck."

"Do you remember what make or a model? Anything distinctive about it?" Nathan felt bad pressing Alan so hard after he'd discovered something so horrible, but they needed as much information as they could get.

Alan shook his head and then halted. "I… Wait. I remember something hanging from the rearview mirror. A chain. There was an angel or something with wings on the end. It hit the windshield when he rammed into my car."

Nathan repeated everything to Troy. "Jesus," Troy said. "Nate, this is serious shit. If someone murdered Alan, we need to tell the police."

"Oh, right." Nathan snorted. *"Hey, officer, this guy I never met was run off the road two years ago. How do I know that? Well, see, I can see and talk to ghosts.* They'd cart me back to the mental hospital, Troy!"

Troy winced. "Maybe we can come up with something else."

"Like what?" Nathan asked. "What exactly can we tell them where they would believe us? Also, we don't even know *who* did it. So, what are we going to tell them, anyway?"

Alan shook his head. "I can't ask you to get involved any further, Nathan. It's too dangerous."

"What? No. We started this. We need to finish it!" Nathan protested.

"Someone killed me. They wanted me dead. I don't know why, but if they find out you know anything, they could come after you. I won't risk you being hurt because of me."

"Alan!" Nathan cried when Alan suddenly disappeared. "Shit!"

"He's gone?" Troy asked. Nathan explained what Alan had said before he faded away.

"We have to find out who did it, Troy." Nathan ran a hand through his hair in frustration. He kicked a nearby rock and watched it skitter over the edge. He'd never even considered Alan having died in such a heinous way. What the hell could he do to find the person if Alan wouldn't let him help? "I'm not giving up," Nathan growled.

"What do you want to do?"

Nathan didn't know what to do or where to go next. Why had someone wanted Alan dead? Had Alan seen something he wasn't supposed to? Had he maybe pissed someone off and triggered a person's road rage? That happened a lot nowadays. People shooting each other in anger because one cut the other off or some shit like that. Maybe he could find out who Alan was friends with or knew from Erik? But the idea of pumping Erik for information on his dead fiancé sat like a stone in his stomach. There hadn't been many people mentioned in Alan's blog posts, but maybe looking them over again might give him some new ideas of people around Alan.

"Let's go back to my apartment. I need to look over the blog posts again. See if there is anyone Alan mentions at all who may even be worth a second look."

Troy gave Nathan a worried look. "Maybe Alan's right, Nathan. We aren't cops and if someone does figure out you know more than you should, they could target you next."

"Whatever is going on may be tied to Erik, too, Troy. I can't just let this go without knowing the truth. What if they are a threat to Erik? One of Alan's posts mentioned telling Erik about something. Maybe they're connected."

"And maybe they aren't. It's been two years and Erik is still alive and breathing. I don't think whoever it is could be a threat to him if they haven't done something to him in those two years."

Nathan walked over to Troy's car and climbed into the passenger side. "Please, Troy. I need to know. I can't let anything happen to Erik."

Troy sighed and got in the car. "You're lucky you're my best friend and I love you. I still say we should tell the police."

Ignoring Troy, Nathan looked out the window while Troy pulled away from the crash site. Someone had deliberately run Alan off the road. The coincidence of the accident and Alan's post just didn't sit well with Nathan. His nerves caused his leg to bounce during the drive and he hopped out of the vehicle the moment Troy pulled to a stop in front of his building. His leg almost gave out on the way up the stairs from the abuse he'd put it through that day. All the walking and then the attempt to rush up his stairs made his knee protest. He caught the railing, swearing, and hoisted himself up the last couple of steps.

Troy huffed behind him. "You're not gonna find anything out if you fall down the stairs and break your neck, Nate!"

He ignored Troy's words and frantically unlocked his apartment. Troy followed him in, closing the door behind them. Nathan hobbled to the table and picked up the pile of papers, divided them into two piles, and handed a stack to Troy. "Just look for names besides Erik's or Alan's."

For the next hour, the two of them read through the posts, setting aside any that Alan mentioned someone by name. They had a mere pittance of seven posts by the time they were done. Nathan wondered how many friends Alan had when he was alive. Seemed as slim as Nathan's own list. He took out a small notebook from his backpack and wrote each name. None of them contained the last names, which frustrated him further. "Richard, Tyler, Katie, Paul, Matthew, Becca, and Owen."

"How are we going to know who they are?" Troy asked, frowning.

"Richard, Paul, and Katie were people in one of his classes. Matthew, Becca, and Owen are in posts where Alan was at some event for Erik's company. Matthew is possibly Erik's cousin. I don't think Tyler is someone we need to bother looking into. The post about him is about someone he knew in high school, some guy he had a crush on. Let's start with Richard, Paul, and Katie. See if we might get any records of whoever was in Alan's classes two years ago."

"I know someone in the administration office. I'll see if

they can do a little digging," Troy said. "She works there during her free periods for the experience."

"Good. Can you call her now?"

Sighing, Troy looked at Nathan. "I still say we should let this go, but I'll call her."

"Thanks, Troy," Nathan replied. "I can try to find out more about the other three from Erik. We're supposed to go get something to eat tonight."

Nathan glanced at his watch and saw it was just after six. "Shit. I didn't realize it was so late. He'll be here at seven."

"On that note, I'll make myself scarce." Troy stood and stretched. "Promise me you won't do anything stupid, Nate."

"Like what?" Nathan frowned.

"Like try to talk to any of these people on your own."

He gave Troy an annoyed glance. "This isn't my first time doing something like this, Troy."

"Exactly my point. You never ask for help, even when you should. If you try to take this on by yourself now that we know Alan was murdered, I'm going to tell Erik."

"What?" Nathan demanded. "You wouldn't."

"I would. He cares about you and so do I. This is getting into some dangerous territory here. Promise me you'll let me help you with this, or Erik is my next phone call!"

Anger and frustration coursed through Nathan. He couldn't believe Troy would do something like that. But he saw the panic and worry in Troy's face and the anger slowly faded away. He sighed and nodded. "I promise."

"Thank you. Now, I'm going to get gone, since Erik is on his way here. Call me if you find out anything about the people working for Erik."

Nathan nodded and watched Troy let himself out of his apartment. Then he spent a couple minutes gathering all the papers and shoving them into his backpack. He didn't want Erik to see them. Afterward, he headed into his bedroom to change out of his sweaty clothes and into a new pair of jeans and a plain black T-shirt. Most of his clothing was band tees and jeans with rips in them. There were only a few items he owned which could be presentable. Aunt Becky always tried to get him to let her buy him some nicer things, but he always insisted he didn't need them.

A few minutes to seven, Nathan heard a knock on his door and smiled. His knee still protested heavily during the quick walk to his front door to let Erik in. Erik didn't even give him a chance to say more than a breathy "Hi" before he swept Nathan up in a tight embrace and a passionate kiss.

Gasping, Nathan grabbed hold of Erik and opened his mouth, accepting Erik's tongue inside. Erik's moan vibrated against his chest, sending a shiver of pleasure down his spine. Knowing he affected Erik so much made him forget how totally wrong he was for someone like Erik. When Erik broke the kiss, Nathan panted and his cheeks felt flushed. "Wow," he whispered.

Erik grinned and winked at him. "That good, huh?"

The blush in Nathan's cheeks got hotter, and he ducked his head slightly. Erik laughed and tightened his arms around Nathan briefly before letting go and stepping back. "You ready for dinner, my studious friend?"

Nathan nodded, afraid his voice would give out if he spoke right away. The kiss had caused desire to wrap around his body and his skin felt too taut, as if his body just didn't fit in it anymore. There was an obvious bulge in the front of his jeans as well. He prayed it would go away before they got to whatever restaurant they were eating at.

Erik led the way out of Nathan's apartment and waited at the top of the stairs for him to lock the door. He held out his hand to Nathan and he happily grasped it, following Erik down the stairs. His leg protested but thankfully didn't give out.

Once they were in Erik's truck, Nathan asked, "Where are we going to eat?"

"I thought we'd eat at my house. I make a mean steak and vegetables. If you don't mind the brief wait while I cook. If that's okay?"

"Oh, yeah. That sounds good." Nathan didn't have to worry about being out in public and possibly having another run-in with a spirit like at the diner.

"How were classes? Did you get a lot of studying done today?" Erik asked while maneuvering effortlessly through traffic.

Guilt stabbed Nathan, and he turned his head to look out the window, hiding the grimace he made. "Classes were the usual. Studying was good. Got through more of my notes today."

"That's good to hear. I'm sure you'll do great on your exams." Erik paused for a second and then asked, "Are you free the Sunday after next?"

Nathan had to think it over. His scheduled hours on Sunday were from eight a.m. to noon, usually, but he wasn't sure if he had anything else planned. "I have to work in the morning, but I'm off at noon. Why?"

"Your exams are over next week, right? We're having our annual company picnic on that Sunday, and I would love to have you there."

Surprise had Nathan turning his head to look at Erik. "Really?"

Erik furrowed his brow. "Of course, really. I want you there."

"But… you hardly know me."

Erik leveled a disgruntled expression at him. "I know enough. It's just a picnic."

It would give Nathan a chance to meet the people who worked for Erik. He was just surprised Erik already wanted to introduce him to people he knew. "Are you sure? I mean…"

"I'm sure," Erik replied, strength and determination in his tone.

Nathan bit his lip and then said, "Okay. Sure, I'll go."

Erik smiled widely. "Good. The picnic starts at noon. I'll pick you up at noon at the store."

"Don't you have to be there when it starts?" Nathan asked.

"Nope. That's why I have capable people who work for me setting everything up."

Nathan knew Troy wouldn't be happy when he told him, but Erik would be there with him. "How many people will be there?"

"About sixty. Mostly my employees and their spouses and kids."

"Wow."

"Are you nervous?" Erik asked, frowning.

"No. Of course not. Just a lot of people to meet at once."

Erik chuckled. "Don't worry. There won't be a pop quiz afterward."

Nathan gave a weak laugh, but he wasn't worried about there being a test. He was more concerned about there being a potential murderer there. But he couldn't share that with Erik. The longer he held on to his secret, the deeper in the hole he went. Would Erik ever be able to forgive him when he finally told him the truth?

The drive to Erik's didn't take long. When they entered the house, Nathan spotted the table set for two along with a bottle of wine and… He stopped when he saw the long-stemmed rose lying on one plate.

Erik placed a hand on Nathan's lower back and urged him toward the table. "Have a seat. Pour yourself some wine. I'll start getting the steaks and vegetables going."

"I can help," Nathan said. He wouldn't touch the wine.

He'd sworn off ever drinking alcohol after his parents had died.

"Nonsense. I invited you to dinner. Just have a seat. If you want to do something, talk to me." Erik opened the fridge and took a container out, setting it on the counter nearby.

"What do you want to talk about?" Nathan asked, leaning a hip against the counter while watching Erik.

"When are you playing at that café again?" Erik started the oven broiler preheating and put a dish with mixed vegetables on the stove.

"Saturday night and then again Sunday night."

"Do you always play there?"

"Usually. Things have been a little hectic lately, but yeah. Curtis has been letting me play there for a couple of years now."

"Curtis is the owner?" Erik asked.

Nathan nodded. "I met him when I did one of their open mic nights."

"When did you first get interested in music?"

"When my dad bought me my first guitar. I was twelve."

"Early starter. Did you ask him for it, or did he just give it to you?"

"My dad loved the greatest guitar players like Eddie Van Halen, Slash from Guns 'N' Roses, Jimi Hendrix. He used to listen to them whenever he was having a rough time with a case. He always said *Nothing soothes the soul quite like the sound of a B major on the E string at the 7th fret.* Of course, it took me a long time to even understand what he meant." Nathan laughed softly. "Every time I hear the chords, it reminds me of him."

"You miss him."

Nodding, Nathan swallowed to clear his throat, which had suddenly grown tight. "Yeah. Every day."

"Troy said you have an aunt you lived with after the accident. Do you still see her?" Erik opened the oven and slid the dish with the vegetables inside.

"Sometimes. Actually, it's my aunts, plural. My aunt Jessica married my aunt Becky a couple of years before my parents died. They took me in until I was old enough to get a job and eventually my apartment."

Erik frowned while setting a pan on the burner and turning on the heat. "They made you move out when you got a job?"

"Oh, no! Nothing like that. They gave me so much and I didn't want to remain a burden on them forever."

"I hardly think your aunts were going to think of you as a burden." Erik dropped a tablespoon of butter into the pan and slid it around with a set of tongs to coat the bottom.

Nathan crossed his arms over his chest and looked at the floor. "There's just some things that made them taking me in more stressful than just me being a teenager thrust on them."

"Like what?" Erik asked, obvious curiosity in his voice. The steaks made a sizzling sound when Erik added them to the pan.

He tensed and tried to think of a way to get around Erik's question. When he remained silent for too long, Erik set down the tongs. He approached Nathan and cupped the back of Nathan's neck. "You never have to be afraid to tell me anything, Nathan. Nothing you tell me will ever change the way I feel about you."

Nathan had to bite back a snort. Somehow, he wasn't sure he could believe that. It's not every day someone says they can see ghosts, including their boyfriend's dead fiancé. Finally, he ignored the small urge he had to tell Erik the truth. "I was just angry and depressed a lot."

"Did you ever talk to a therapist about what happened?"

This time, the snort broke free. "More than one. They just thought I was nuts."

Erik surprised Nathan when he slid a finger under Nathan's chin and urged his head up enough until their eyes met. "Then they weren't very good therapists. You are far from nuts, baby. Sad, maybe. Taking more on your shoulders than you need to by yourself, definitely. But you are not nuts."

"But you don't know everything," Nathan whispered, his heart in his throat.

"Someday you will trust me enough to tell me everything. Until then, just know that I am here for you."

A sharp sting hit the back of Nathan's eyes and he blinked furiously. He wanted to believe Erik so badly. Most of his friends had abandoned him after the accident when they'd thought he'd lost his mind from the trauma.

Erik dropped a quick kiss on Nathan's lips and stepped back over to the stove to flip the steaks. "Why don't you pour us both a glass of wine? The veggies have a little longer to go and then we should be ready to eat."

"Um, do you have anything else to drink?" Nathan asked hesitantly.

His question must have made Erik realize he didn't drink alcohol when Erik let out a small oath. "I'm sorry, Nate. I didn't think. There are a couple of sodas in the fridge, or I can make you some coffee."

"It's okay. You didn't know." Nathan went to the fridge and took out a can of Sprite.

"Grab me one of those, too."

"You don't have to because of me," Nathan protested.

Erik shook his head and went to the table. He took the bottle off the table and put it into a small fridge with a glass door underneath the counter. "I shouldn't be drinking and then driving you back to your apartment, anyway."

"If you're sure," Nathan said, eyeing Erik.

"I am." Erik smiled at him.

Before long, they were sitting down to eat, and Nathan just about died at the way the steak almost melted in his mouth. He couldn't quite stifle the moan he let out at the taste.

Erik gave him a heated look. "I certainly hope I can make you moan like that."

A blush flooded Nathan's cheeks, and he gasped, heat blossoming in his lower belly. The heat pushed farther down, causing his cock to harden slightly. "Erik," Nathan murmured, unable to meet Erik's gaze.

Erik's tanned fingers came into view when Erik touched the back of his palm. "I didn't mean to embarrass you."

Nathan shook his head. "You didn't exactly."

"Oh?"

Biting his lip, Nathan peered through the strands of his hair, which had fallen into his eyes. "I'm not good at this."

"Good at what?"

"Flirting." He wanted to sink through the floor when Erik smiled softly.

Erik took hold of Nathan's hand in his. "You're doing just fine, Nate."

He squeezed Nathan's hand briefly and let go. Nathan hemmed in any additional noises he may have made over the food. Erik continued to ask him about his music, his favorite songs and bands, and Nathan had relaxed by the time they'd finished eating. Erik refused to let him help with the dishes, instructing him to remain at the table while he cleared everything and filled the dishwasher.

Afterward, they moved to the couch and Nathan got nervous again. Would Erik expect more tonight? A shiver raced down Nathan's spine at the memory of their frotting session. He wanted more, but he also was afraid of disappointing Erik.

"Relax, angel. You're thinking too hard." Erik nudged him

with his shoulder. "You have some time to watch a movie before I have to get you back home, Cinderella?"

Nathan chuckled and wrinkled his nose. "I hardly think I qualify for Cinderella status."

"And why not?"

"Wrong parts for one."

Erik chuckled and slid his arm around Nathan's shoulders. "That's a fact I'm happy about."

Nathan leaned against Erik's side and rested his head on his shoulder. "What do you want to watch?"

"Anything you do."

He shrugged. "I don't really know many movies. Between work, the café, and school, I don't spend a lot of time watching movies or anything."

"What genres interest you then? Horror?"

Nathan shook his head. "No. No, horror movies." He had enough horror in his life that he didn't need to see any movies with it.

"What about action movies?" Erik asked.

"I'm open to anything you want to watch. You choose. Oh, except Lifetime movies. My Aunt Becky loves those, and she forever had them on when I was living there."

"Okay, I have an idea."

Nathan watched him scroll through several areas before landing on a movie called *A Knight's Tale*. Erik leaned forward to set the remote on the coffee table and then he tugged Nathan tighter to him. "There's some great music in this film. I think you'll like it."

CHAPTER 18

For the next couple of hours, Nathan cuddled with Erik while enjoying the movie. Erik had been right. The soundtrack of the movie was fantastic. He was smiling when the credits rolled, and he tilted his head back enough to see Erik. "That was great."

"I knew you'd like it." Erik brushed a strand of Nathan's hair behind his ear. "You know, you're beautiful when you smile."

Nathan wrinkled his nose. "I'm not beautiful. Besides, isn't that a word used to describe women?"

"First, the word beautiful can apply to anything and anyone. Second, you are beautiful. Gorgeous, actually, with your raven's wing black hair, stunning green eyes, and every tiny little freckle across your nose and cheeks. You steal my breath every single time I see you."

Nathan sucked in a breath at Erik's words, his heart beating faster. "I'm not all that," he whispered.

"Oh, but you are. You just don't see it, and that is part of what makes you so amazing."

"But my leg, my scars—" Nathan was cut off by Erik pressing his fingers against his lips.

"Those are nothing except a sign of how strong you are. You battled something so awful and lived to be here today, in my arms." Erik pressed a kiss to each of Nathan's cheeks and then the tip of his nose. "I'm so glad you did because I would never have met you, and that would have been a significant loss in my life."

He opened his mouth to protest again, but Erik stopped him by kissing him. Erik thrust his tongue deep inside Nathan's mouth, prompting a moan from Nathan as heat shot straight down to his groin. His cock hardened and he wrapped his arms around Erik's shoulders, holding on tight. He returned the kiss, tentatively swiping his tongue over Erik's. When Erik growled, a heady sense of power bloomed in Nathan to know he could affect such a sexy and virile man as Erik.

Erik slid a hand under Nathan's t-shirt and along the skin of his belly. The calloused palm rasped in just the right way, ratcheting Nathan's desire even higher. He reached down and tugged Erik's shirt up, wanting to feel the broad, tanned flesh of his body. Their kiss broke long enough for Erik to rip the offending article of clothing over his head, tossing it away carelessly, before yanking Nathan's off as well. He leaned back in to capture Nathan's mouth once more. Erik coaxed Nathan to his back, following him down to the soft surface of the couch.

Nathan ran his hands along Erik's naked back, mapping out the various bumps and curves of his muscles. Erik slotted one knee between Nathan's legs. He pressed his own hard length along Nathan's upper thigh, and he gently rutted against Nathan. The movement created sweet friction between them and caused Nathan to gasp. Every fresh sensation made his head spin. He didn't know which one to concentrate on and enjoy first.

Erik's five o'clock shadow scraped over Nathan's lower jaw as he licked, nipped, and kissed his way to Nathan's throat. This time, he didn't stop there. He traced the line of Nathan's collarbone with his tongue and down to the right nipple. Nathan couldn't stop the cry he let out when he sucked the light brown nub into his mouth. The feel of Erik's tongue swirling around his nipple set off a throbbing inside of Nathan. Grabbing hold of Erik's shoulders, Nathan dug his fingers into the hard flesh, trying to hold on in the onslaught of a storm he'd never been in before.

When Erik lightly bit down, Nathan arched his back and whimpered Erik's name. Erik switched to the other nipple, giving it the same treatment before following the line of his sternum down to his belly button. The sound of his zipper lowering sent a shiver racing down Nathan's spine, but it was the whisper of Erik's breath over his heated flesh which caused him to curl his toes. "Er-Erik."

No other legible words came out because the second Erik's warm, wet mouth closed over the tip of his cock, Nathan lost all coherent thought. Electricity crackled throughout his body, tingles racing along his nerve endings. But when Erik swallowed his entire shaft, Nathan couldn't hold back, and he tipped over the edge, coming down Erik's throat. "Oh God," he croaked, his hands instinctively gripping Erik's dark locks.

Embarrassment nipped in right on the heels of his orgasm. Once again, he'd shot off within minutes. Shame flooded him and he released Erik's hair to cover his face.

"Hey, what's all this, angel?" Erik murmured near his ear.

He hadn't even realized Erik had moved over him again. God, he was such a loser. Instead of answering Erik, Nathan just shook his head. Erik gripped his wrist and gently tugged one hand away from his face. "Talk to me, Nate."

Keeping his eyes closed, Nathan replied in a thin voice, "It was so fast."

"Open your eyes, angel." Nathan slowly complied until he could see Erik's face hovering over his. "There is nothing to be embarrassed about. It felt good, right?"

He nodded.

"Then that's all that matters." Erik bent and kissed him again, the salty tang of Nathan's semen on his lips. The kiss grew heated within seconds and Nathan got hard again. Erik smiled against Nathan's lips and said, "Best part about being young."

Nathan didn't have time to get embarrassed about his words. He became swept up in every brief touch and brush of lips by Erik. By the time Erik stripped away the last of their clothing, Nathan was a quivering, pulsing bundle of lust. His focus centered on nothing except Erik. The way his gaze ate him up was like nothing he'd ever known. Despite Nathan's flaws and the secrets he still held close to his chest, Erik still wanted him.

Erik reached a hand between the cushions and came out with a small bottle. "I told you I wouldn't press you for anything you weren't ready for, Nate. I want you. Every scar, every freckle, every smile, every frown. Everything that makes you who you are." He paused for a split second, pressing his hand over Nathan's heart. "Do you need more time?"

Biting his lip, Nathan looked at Erik and shook his head. "I want you, too," he replied softly.

Tenderness flooded Erik's features before he popped open the lid of the bottle. He spilled some of the clear liquid onto his fingers, closed the top with a snick, and tossed it onto the couch beside them. Erik lowered himself slightly to kiss Nathan. Nathan tensed a bit when he felt Erik's fingers beginning to probe at the entrance to his body.

"Relax, angel," Erik said.

He curled the fingers of one hand into the couch cushion and the other over Erik's bicep. One of Erik's fingers breached him, and Nathan tensed again. It was a strange feeling. Erik captured his mouth once more, distracting Nathan enough to where he barely noticed when Erik slipped the second digit inside.

His cock twitched when Erik scissored his fingers, slowly stretching him wider. "Doing okay, Nate?" he asked, never letting up on thrusting and moving his fingers.

Nathan couldn't speak, so he just nodded. When Erik withdrew from him, Nathan watched him reach for his jeans and take out his wallet. His eyes widened a fraction at the sight of a foil package. It brought home the reality of what was about to happen. His breathing increased as he watched Erik tear open the package, take out the condom, and slide it down the length of his very thick cock.

"Turn over, angel," Erik said. Surprised, Nathan glanced at him. "It's easier for your first time."

"Oh," Nathan murmured and attempted to turn over, but his knee protested the action and he let out a gasp and straightened out his leg.

Erik gave a mumbled oath behind him. "I'm sorry, Nate. I didn't think of that."

Suddenly, Nathan found himself airborne. He squeaked and grabbed hold of Erik. "What are you doing?" he asked.

"Moving this to the bedroom."

"I can walk!" Nathan protested.

Erik ignored his complaints and carried him up the stairs and down the hallway to his room. He placed Nathan on the bed as if he was breakable and then he slid in next to him. Erik tugged Nathan to him with his back to Erik's chest and began kissing along his neck and shoulder. "I know you can do things for yourself, Nate, but sometimes you don't have to."

Nathan reached behind him to grip Erik's upper thigh. "I'm not comfortable with anyone doing things for me."

"Oh, I know," Erik rasped, biting gently on Nathan's earlobe. "You're a stubborn man, angel."

The light nibble caused Nathan's flagging erection to rise yet again, but he couldn't stop his body from tensing when Erik's cock slid through the crease of his ass. Erik placed a hand on Nathan's shoulder and rolled him onto his stomach, then straddled his legs.

"What are you doing?" Nathan asked, uncertainty clearly echoing in his voice.

Instead of answering him, Erik began running his hands along Nathan's back, pressing into the tense muscles of his shoulders and down to the swell of his rear end. At first, the massage kind of hurt, but eventually Nathan lost the tension in him, his eyes closing. He couldn't still the moan he gave when Erik's fingers curled around his shoulders and his thumbs dug in. The only type of massage he'd ever had was on his legs during physical therapy. It had never felt pleasurable.

Erik bent down and pressed a kiss to the middle of Nathan's shoulder blades. He did it again and again, only lower and lower each time. When he reached the swell of Nathan's bottom, the slick glide of Erik's tongue over the middle of his lower back caused him to shiver. But Erik went farther, and Nathan gasped when Erik spread the cheeks of his ass to lick over the ring of muscles. "Erik!"

He tried to squirm away, embarrassed beyond anything, but Erik hummed and stilled his movements with both hands. Erik flicked his tongue out again and Nathan's cock jumped. Lust danced over his nerve endings with each swipe.

Nothing had ever prepared him for the sensation of someone pleasuring him the way Erik was. Every swipe had his dick leaking profusely.

He almost whined when Erik stopped and settled beside him, one hand rolling Nathan to his side. The warm heat of Erik's chest met his back. Erik nuzzled at Nathan's nape for a moment before pulling away from him. Nathan heard a drawer opening and then the snick of a bottle again. Nathan didn't brace himself from the intrusion of his fingers this time. Erik continued to kiss along Nathan's shoulder and the side of his neck to distract him. When Erik removed his fingers and replaced them with the head of his cock, Nathan gripped the sheets tightly. "Push out, baby," Erik said.

Nathan followed his instructions and then Erik breached him. He winced, but Erik held still. He ran his palm over Nathan's side and around to his belly. "Relax," he murmured.

Nathan released the breath he hadn't even realized he'd been holding and closed his eyes. Erik pushed a little farther into him and then held still, continuing to stroke and caress him. The pattern repeated itself until Erik's abdomen pressed against his ass. Nathan had never felt so full before. It was the strangest thing, yet there was pleasure mixed in with the odd feeling.

"You've got it all, angel. I'm going to move now."

Nathan nodded, and Erik retreated a fraction before surging forward again. His breath caught in his throat, and he couldn't suppress a moan. Erik shifted a bit and this time when he thrust inside him, he hit something which caused stars to explode behind Nathan's closed eyelids. "Oh God!"

Erik growled near Nathan's ear, thrusting a little firmer now. "You feel so good, baby."

A few heartbeats later, Erik went a little faster and harder. His cock nailed that same button over and over. So many feelings raced through Nathan, and he could barely hold on to his sanity in the onslaught of sensations. Nathan heard the sounds he uttered, but he couldn't have stopped them to save his life. Focused on every movement Erik made, Nathan barely heard the loud cries he emitted with each thrust from Erik. If he hadn't been so lost in every sensation Erik sent rippling through him, he'd have been mortified.

Erik never stopped touching him—his palms ran over every inch of flesh he could reach, fingers tweaked Nathan's hard nipples, and a hand stroked Nathan's stiff length. Every sensation pushed Nathan's pleasure higher. He didn't know how he'd survive the differing sensations bombarding him. Nathan stretched one leg outward, opening himself up for Erik's invasion. Like most teenage boys, Nathan had fantasized about sex before the accident. Nothing in those fantasies had ever prepared him for the onslaught against his senses. Every new experience—every new feeling—rushed Nathan closer toward his orgasm.

"Er-Erik," Nathan rasped, reaching his hand back to grip Erik's rock-hard thigh.

Never changing the motion, angle, or intensity of his thrusts, Erik coaxed him closer to the peak. He nipped at Nathan's earlobe, then soothed it with his tongue. Nathan dug his fingernails into Erik's skin, trying to hold on in the storm.

"Come, angel. Come for me," Erik growled, his voice hoarse.

If you could climax just from someone's voice, Nathan knew it would be Erik's. He arched his back slightly, issuing a keening cry as hard spurts of seed escaped him, coating the comforter in front of him, some splashing over his abdomen. Erik gave several more thrusts before falling over the edge with him. The hard pulses of Erik's cock inside of him sent rippling darts of pleasure along Nathan's spine. Sweat coated their bodies from head to toe. Nathan could smell the tangy scent of his release and the salty essence of their sweat, which increased the haze blanketing his mind.

Nathan lay panting and dazed, too out of it to move. Erik slipped free of his body and Nathan felt the bed shift when he stood up. He heard the soft patter of Erik's bare feet on the floor and then the sound of water turning on. A moment later, the bed dipped, and Nathan hissed when Erik slid a cool washcloth over his abdomen, clearly wiping up the semen streaking his front. Erik cleaned off the comforter, stood again, and took the cloth back into the bathroom. Then he climbed into bed next to Nathan again, looping an arm over his waist. The sweat on his body cooled, and a shiver went through him.

"Cold?" Erik asked, nuzzling at his neck.

"No," he replied.

"Did I hurt you?" He could hear the concern in Erik's voice.

"Not at all," Nathan murmured.

He sensed Erik smiling. "Does the silence mean I rocked your world?"

Nathan couldn't stop the chuckle he let forth. "You could say that."

Erik hummed and kissed Nathan's cheek. "As much as I would love to be selfish right now and use my ability to rock your world to get you to stay, I think it's time I got you home to study. I've taken up more than a couple of hours tonight."

The reminder made Nathan grimace. He really needed to spend more time studying, despite how much he'd love to remain wrapped in Erik's arms. "Yeah," he breathed.

Erik tightened his arms for a brief second and then he rolled away from Nathan to stand. "I'll go downstairs and get your clothes."

Without a single sign of hesitation, Erik strolled naked out of the room, Nathan watching him every step of the way.

Nathan sat up, wincing slightly at the protest of his bottom, and pulled the blanket across his lap. He ran his fingers through his hair to straighten what he figured had to be a mess after everything. A small smile slid across his lips as he thought about the last hour with Erik. Nothing he'd ever imagined could have prepared him for what it would feel like to be made love to so passionately. Uncertainty swirled in to make him wonder if Erik had enjoyed himself, too, especially since he had pretty much done everything.

Before his self-consciousness could get to him, Erik walked back into the room and put Nathan's clothes on the edge of the bed. He had dressed already in the clothes he'd discarded on the couch earlier.

"I'll be downstairs," Erik said, and then he left the room again.

Nathan dressed and went into the bathroom to wash up. He stared at himself in the mirror while soaping his hands. The haunted look he lived with had faded, and he almost didn't recognize himself. The usual dark circles were gone, too. Of course, that realization brought guilt in on its heels. He glanced away from the mirror while he finished rinsing the soap, shut off the water, and headed downstairs.

Erik was waiting for him in the living room, watching out of the window. He turned and smiled at Nathan. "Ready?"

Nathan nodded and followed Erik out of the house. Within minutes, they were on the road. Erik immediately took Nathan's hand in his, resting his arm on the center console. "Everything all right?" Erik asked.

"Yeah, everything's fine," Nathan replied.

He could tell his answer didn't satisfy Erik, but he didn't press, just squeezed his fingers gently. They talked very little on the way, and Nathan remained lost in his thoughts. There were so many things he needed to sort through. Finding Alan was top of the list. Nathan would get to meet Erik's coworkers at the picnic, so maybe he could eliminate them. Then he wondered if Troy had gotten any information about the three classmates of Alan yet. Probably not if he had to wait until tomorrow to talk to his friend in the main office.

Too soon, Nathan found them parked in front of his building. He opened his door, but Erik tugged on his hand. "Can I have a kiss before you go?"

Nathan flushed but moved closer. Erik cupped his cheek and covered Nathan's lips with his. The kiss was sweet and slow. "I'll see you tomorrow?" Erik asked, his voice tender, his thumb trailing over Nathan's cheekbone.

"Yeah," Nathan said.

"I'll come by your job with something to eat."

"You don't have to do that."

Erik gave him a patient look. "I want to."

"Okay." Nathan capitulated easily. Butterflies tickled his stomach, and he couldn't hide his smile.

"There's that gorgeous smile," Erik said, pressing another quick kiss to the corner of Nathan's mouth. "Now, go on. Before I change my mind and drive us back to my place."

Nathan climbed out of the truck and closed the door. He felt Erik's gaze on him the entire way to his apartment, and he didn't hear him pull away until he'd unlocked and opened his door.

The moment he entered his apartment, he called Alan's name. "Please, Alan. Come out. I need to talk to you."

Silence met his plea. "Whether or not you're with me on this, Alan, I'm going to find out what happened."

Nathan sighed and went over to the couch to take his homework and textbook out of his bag. He spent the next several hours poring over everything his classes had gone over in the last few months. By the time he sat back, his eyes felt gritty, and they were drooping with exhaustion. It had been a while since he'd done an all-night cram session. The clock on the microwave showed it was almost three in the morning. He rubbed his eyes with his pointer finger and thumb, trying to relieve the tiredness.

A strange sound caused him to drop his hand and open his eyes. He almost jumped out of his skin when he saw Alan standing near the open door to his bedroom. "Jesus, Alan!"

Alan had the grace to look chagrined at having scared Nathan. "Sorry."

"Where'd you go?"

Alan shrugged and floated a little closer, stopping a few feet from Nathan. "I've caused you enough trouble. I shouldn't even be here."

"Then why are you?" Nathan asked, wondering why Alan had shown himself now.

Sighing, Alan moved over to stare out the window. "I heard you. I can't let you do this alone. If someone really intended on killing me, I can at least have your back and help if I can. I don't want them to come after you."

Nathan eyed Alan for a few seconds of silence and then launched into what he and Troy had found earlier. He also explained what they were going to do. Alan turned to look at him, hope once again shining on his face. "Do you think you'll find them?"

"We're going to try. Do any of the names strike any kind of emotion at all?"

Alan shook his head. "No. I mean, yeah, I remember them. Especially Erik's cousin Matthew. But none of the names remind me of anything."

Nathan grunted. "I'll be able to meet Matthew and the others. Erik's company is having a picnic, and he's asked me to go."

A fond smile overtook Alan's features. "The annual picnic was so much fun. The food is always great. Erik hires the best caterers. Every year he brings in something for the kids.

One year he brought in ponies for them to ride." Sadness chased away the fond look. "I'm going to miss them."

"I'm sorry, Alan," Nathan murmured. "I really am."

Alan waved away Nathan's apology. "It's not your fault, Nathan. You weren't the one who ended my life."

"Tomorrow Troy is going to investigate the classmates we saw mentioned in your blog posts. I'll be taking Erik's employees you mentioned and learning what I can at the picnic."

Alan winced. "Just be careful. You don't want to risk tipping off whoever did this."

"The likelihood they're going to connect you and me is very slim, Alan. How can they possibly think I would know anything? You've been gone two years and Erik doesn't know, so how could I even have any clue?"

"I guess you're right. But I can't help except to worry. I'll be there on Sunday. Maybe seeing them will help jar something loose."

"Just try not to distract me. Remember, people can't see you. If they catch me talking to thin air, they're going to think I'm mad." Nathan stood and stretched, groaning as his back protested the hours spent over his books and notes. "For now, I'm going to get a few hours of sleep."

He walked toward his bedroom, only to stop when Alan called his name. Looking back, he saw Alan staring at him with a weird expression. "What's up?"

Alan floated closer. "Something's different. You seem… happier."

Nathan flinched. Guilt stabbed in again. Guilt at being happy when his parents no longer could be and at knowing he'd slept with Alan's fiancé. But Alan surprised him. "You deserve it, Nate. I know I haven't been the easiest to deal with, but you have so much weight on your shoulders. You carry more than any one person ever should on their own.

I'm glad Erik found you. You make him happy, and I'm grateful he isn't alone anymore."

Nathan's only reaction was a slight intake of breath, and he murmured Alan's name. Alan gave him a slight smile before dissipating. He didn't know how to take Alan's acceptance of the relationship he and Erik appeared to be building. Honestly, he should run as fast and as far from Erik as he could. He already knew he was being selfish. Dragging Erik into his nightmare of a life without warning him was even more selfish than throwing a tantrum to get his parents to leave the party that night six years ago. After he helped Alan, he would tell Erik the truth. Everything.

CHAPTER 19

The next morning, Nathan groaned when his alarm went off, slapping it in irritation. He rolled out of bed, did his usual morning ritual, and got dressed. Troy was waiting for him by his car, as always. On the way to school, Nathan explained what had happened with Alan the previous night. He left out the sex portion of the evening, but Troy kept looking over at him, a contemplative look on his face. Finally, Nathan asked, "What? Why do you keep looking at me like that?"

Troy stopped at a red light, turned slightly in his seat, and said, "You had sex last night, didn't you?"

"What?" Nathan squawked.

"There's a certain… glow about you. Come on, spill. Did you and Erik get nasty together or what?"

"Jesus, Troy!" Nathan groaned and slouched into the seat.

"You did! I knew it! Come on, was it good? Did he make it good for you? He better have, or I'll kick his ass."

Nathan covered his face with both hands and shook his head. Heat flooded his face, and he knew he had to be as red as a tomato. He didn't know how Troy could have even guessed. There were no new hickies, a fact Nathan confirmed this morning in the mirror.

Troy nudged him. "Come on, bro, spill."

Sighing, Nathan knew if he didn't at least tell Troy something, he'd never leave Nathan alone. "Yes, we did, and yes, he did." Troy whooped and took off from the streetlight like a bat out of hell. Nathan grabbed at the dashboard. "Slow down before you kill us both, Troy!"

"Finally lost the V-card! About time. I thought for sure you'd be an old man living in one of those facilities before you got lucky." Troy slowed down the car, finally. "Well, how did it happen?"

"I am not going into details!" Nathan protested, shaking his head.

"Did you top or did he? He did, I bet. You strike me more as a bottom."

"Oh my God, Troy!"

"What? There's nothing wrong with being a bottom."

Nathan sighed. "You just don't stop."

"Nope, but you still love me," Troy bragged, grinning widely at Nathan. When they pulled into the campus parking lot, Troy's smile faded, and he gave Nathan a serious look. "I'm happy for you, Nate. Not because you lost your V-card, but because I haven't seen you this happy since before your parents died."

Nathan squirmed in his seat, slightly uncomfortable with the topic. They didn't hide things from each other, and they talked about serious shit whenever the occasion rose. Especially the whole seeing ghosts thing. His discomfort came more from still feeling guilty that he was moving on from the life he'd lived for the last six years. "Thanks, Troy," he murmured.

Troy reached out and yanked him into a backslapping hug. "It's not a bad thing to be happy, Nate. I know you still blame yourself for what happened to your parents, but they wouldn't want you to stop living life because they're gone. They loved you."

"I know," Nathan whispered, tightening his hold on Troy for a moment. Somehow, Troy always knew what he was thinking. Maybe that came from knowing each other for so long. They broke apart, and Nathan gave Troy a wobbly smile. "You know I love you, right?"

"Of course. Who doesn't?" Troy blew across his fingernails and rubbed them on his shirt, a teasing glint in his eyes. They both laughed before exiting Troy's car.

"Did you talk to your friend in administration yet?"

"No," Troy said. "She didn't answer my texts. I figured I'd talk to her this morning before class."

Nathan grimaced. "Okay. If you find anything out, let me know."

"You know it," Troy said. They went their separate ways, Nathan heading for his first class while Troy went toward the main office.

The day passed pretty much as usual. He met with Troy for lunch, grabbing something small from the cafeteria. Unless it rained, they normally sat outside. Nathan dropped onto the stone bench at the table where Troy sat. He started unwrapping his sandwich and asked, "Did you find out anything about those three classmates?"

"It's going to take a little time. Since we don't have last names, Megan's going to compare the names on the roster for Alan's classes for that year with the names I gave her. She should have something by the end of the day."

Before taking a bite of his sandwich, Nathan said, "Tell her I appreciate it, and if there's anything I can do for her, let me know."

"She's just doing me a favor."

They spent the rest of their lunch chatting about the

music store and Troy's latest attempt to ask out the server at the café. It felt like the first normal lunch they'd had in a long time. Nathan had a smile on his face on his way to his next class. Even Professor Johns didn't get to him despite many attempts during the hour they were with the guy.

Alan's accident wasn't far from his mind at any point. Nathan needed to find out who the hell had killed Alan and why. Not only to help him move on but also because it meant Erik could be in danger if it was one of his employees.

After classes were over, Troy drove Nathan to work, dropping him off at the door. "Call me if Erik can't pick you up."

Rolling his eyes, Nathan replied, "Yes, Dad."

"I'm serious, Nate."

"Yeah, yeah. He said he was coming. I don't see why he wouldn't." Nathan waved Troy away and entered the store. Quinn greeted him and Nathan went into the back to drop his bag and clock in. He was glad Stuart wasn't there. He really didn't want the man pissing on his good mood.

"Hey, Quinn," Nathan said. "How's it going?"

"Good. You look different." Quinn frowned. "Did you cut your hair or something?"

Nathan tried to hide the blush he knew colored his cheeks. What the hell? Did he have, like, a big flashing sign over his head about having had sex? "Nope. Same as always."

"You're wearing something new?"

He shook his head while looking over the custom orders. Quinn would have taken care of the ones which were typical, but he always left the more unique ones for Nathan. Sometimes they had to go outside their usual manufacturer to get in some of the requested albums. "Nope, pretty sure you've seen me in this shirt and jeans a dozen times."

A woman came to the counter with a couple of CDs and a vinyl album and distracted Quinn for a bit. Once she'd paid and left, he turned back to Nathan. "So, you going to tell me how things are going with Mr. Tall, Dark, and Sexy?"

The blush had faded but came back with a vengeance. Quinn caught it this time. "Dude, really?"

"What?"

"You slept with him, didn't you?"

"Oh my God. You're as bad as Troy!" Nathan growled, glaring at Quinn.

Quinn grinned and shrugged one broad shoulder. "Sorry, but I've known you for over two years and to see you finally got laid is like catching Bigfoot. Congrats, dude." He clapped one hand on Nathan's back. "But seriously, I think I know what's different." Quinn paused for a second. "You look happy. You don't have the usual dark aura to you today."

Nathan didn't know how to respond to Quinn. Troy had said the same thing a few hours before. He'd even seen it in the mirror in Erik's bathroom last night. Quinn put his hand on Nathan's shoulder. "I'm glad to see you finally enjoying something in your life, Nate. I've never met someone who was always so damn sad all the time."

Surprised, Nathan turned his head toward Quinn. He hadn't realized the careless frat boy he worked with had more to him than Nathan thought. "Thanks," he murmured.

The moment passed and the two of them spent the rest of the shift joking around and talking like they normally did. Nathan didn't even notice the passage of time until Quinn was ready to clock out at closing time.

Erik entered the store as Quinn was on his way out. "Evening, Quinn," he said. "Just came to take Nathan to get something to eat after the store closes."

Nathan was too far away to hear whatever Quinn whispered to Erik, but not far enough to miss Erik giving Quinn a brief nod and a pat on the shoulder. "Have a good night, Quinn."

"What was that?" Nathan asked.

"What was what?" Erik replied.

"Just now. What did Quinn say to you?"

Erik gave him a confused look. "I don't know what you're talking about."

"Uh huh."

Instead of acknowledging Nathan's disbelief, Erik walked around the counter and tugged him into a hug. He captured Nathan's mouth with his, giving him a mind-blowing kiss. He was panting by the time Erik released him and had completely forgotten whatever they'd been talking about. "That's not always going to work, ya know?" Nathan said breathlessly.

Erik grinned and winked at him. "Hurry and close out the register. I want to get something in your stomach before dropping you at your place."

Nathan nodded and punched a couple of keys to print out the day's receipts. Erik didn't say anything else, just leaned against the counter while looking out over the store. Nathan got the register closed and the deposit ready for the night, and they were out the door ten minutes later. Erik drove him to drop the deposit, then they headed to the diner for a quick bite to eat.

After dinner, Erik drove him back to his apartment as promised. The short time with Erik hadn't been long enough and Nathan just wanted to say to hell with studying and beg Erik to take him home. But he knew he couldn't, or he'd fail his exams for sure. Nathan went to open the door, but Erik grabbed his hand, stopping him. "Don't I get a good night kiss?" Erik asked.

Blushing, Nathan leaned over and popped a quick kiss on Erik's lips. Before he could move away, Erik's hand snaked around the back of his neck and yanked him into a deep kiss. A groan slipped free from Nathan, and he carded his fingers through Erik's dark locks while his tongue battled with Erik's. Abruptly, Erik pulled Nathan over the center console and onto his lap. Nathan felt Erik's obvious desire beneath his ass and his cock throbbed in memory of the previous evening.

"Erik," Nathan rasped, moaning when Erik nipped at his chin.

Nathan shuddered when Erik slid both hands under his ass and repositioned him to straddle his lap. Erik thrust upward, grinding against Nathan. "You make me want to forget everything except being inside you," Erik growled.

Pure lust spiraled through Nathan at his words. He sought Erik's mouth blindly, running his hands along Erik's muscular chest and over his shoulders, grabbing hold to anchor himself. Erik squeezed his ass, fingers kneading the flesh. Heat engulfed Nathan, lashing at his nerve endings. He couldn't figure out which sensation to concentrate on first. Their breaths mingled between them, and Nathan could taste the sweetness of the soda Erik had with his meal.

When Erik sucked on Nathan's tongue, it tugged at an invisible line straight to his cock. Nathan whined, digging his nails into Erik's muscles, and squirmed in his lap, trying to increase the friction on his imprisoned shaft. A fine sweat broke out over both their bodies and Nathan couldn't stop himself from licking at the salty sheen along Erik's throat. Satisfaction spiked through Nathan when he felt Erik's chest vibrate with a moan. He moved over Erik's throat, along his jawline, and returned to his mouth. Erik slipped both hands under Nathan's shirt to caress along his spine and the sensitive skin of his back.

He almost cried when Erik broke the kiss. He tried to capture Erik's mouth again, but Erik stopped him by leaning his forehead against Nathan's shoulder. Nathan panted, fine tremors racking his body. He'd never been so aroused and his entire being waited at a precipice, anticipating the fall over the edge.

Erik lifted his head from Nathan's shoulder. "You need to go inside, angel, before I selfishly follow you upstairs and ravish this sexy body of yours until we both can't move."

Another shudder rippled through Nathan. Erik squeezed his ass once more and said, "After your exams, I'll spend hours buried inside you, but for now, go. I'll see you tomorrow night for dinner."

Erik helped Nathan back over the console and Nathan opened his door. He looked back at Erik and said, "Good night."

"Good night, angel. Sleep well."

Nathan climbed out and closed the door. Erik waited until Nathan had opened his front door before pulling away from the curb. There was absolutely nothing in his life to have prepared him for the level of attraction he had to Erik. Every day they spent together, talked to each other, left him wanting more of the same. The want was slowly becoming a craving and a need. The closer he grew to Erik, the more frightened he became of losing him. He remembered the all-consuming grief he'd experienced after his parents died, and he knew it would be just as painful, if not more, if Erik hated him when he told him the truth.

Closing off his thoughts about everything, he settled down to study. He wasn't entirely successful, but he studied for a couple of hours before he could no longer keep his eyes open. He stumbled to bed, falling across the mattress without changing his clothes, and passed out until his alarm went off at the usual time.

The pattern of Erik picking him up for dinner, then taking him home to make out in the front seat until Erik practically pushed him out of the truck, repeated itself for the next two nights. The first day of exams, Nathan woke earlier than usual to shower, dress, and have his coffee. Nervousness caused his hands to shake, and Nathan tried to bolster his confidence as much as possible. He wouldn't be able to relax until after the last exam for the day. Erik sent him a text a few minutes before he met Troy downstairs.

Erik: *Good luck today, angel.*

Nathan: *Thanks.*

Erik: *Tonight, we'll celebrate.*

Nathan: *I still have a couple more days to get through before celebrating.*

Erik: *Still cause to celebrate getting through your first ones then.*

Nathan: *I'll see you after work.*

Erik sent a kiss emoji, and Nathan grinned. He felt like a teenager in high school with his first boyfriend. He couldn't wipe the smile off his face when he went down to meet Troy.

"What are you so happy about?" Troy asked.

Nathan shrugged. "Nothing."

"Did you get lucky again last night?"

Nathan rolled his eyes. "Why does your mind automatically go toward sex?"

"Hey, I can't help it. I'm a guy. It's ingrained in our genes or some shit."

He burst out laughing. "I don't think that's a proven fact."

Troy gave him a wide grin. "Maybe not yet."

Nathan realized he hadn't told Troy about the company picnic, and he'd been so busy with school and Erik he'd forgotten to ask about Megan's research. "Did you find out anything from Megan about those three people?"

Troy sighed. "I was hoping you'd forgotten about this

suicide mission. She found their names, and I researched them myself. Richard Plant moved to Canada after he graduated from Webster, apparently for some job. Katie Winters started her own medical research foundation after her mother passed away from cancer. And Paul Grisotto dropped out during his last year at Webster and from what I could tell, he's been living in South America. He posts to Facebook infrequently, but the last one was a couple days ago about catching some, and I quote, 'gnarly waves.' Pretty sure none of these people would have killed Allen."

Nathan grimaced. So, the spotlight would still be on the three people who worked for Erik. He told Troy about the picnic and how Alan had shown up at his apartment a couple of nights before. "He is going to come with us to the picnic."

Frustration and concern blanketed Troy's features. "Nate, please be careful. If it is one of Erik's people and they figure out you're onto them, they could become violent. I don't want you to get hurt."

"I'll be fine. It's not like they're going to guess I know anything about it. I didn't even know Erik when Alan died. How would they even have a clue?"

Troy still didn't look convinced, but he dropped the subject. They reached the campus and split toward their respective classes. Nathan pushed everything out of his mind and tried to focus on just the exams. Thankfully, the day went by quickly, and Nathan breathed a sigh of relief when he handed in the last exam.

Of course, now that the first day of exams was over, all Nathan could concentrate on the rest of the day was being with Erik. He knew tonight they'd be doing more than just necking in the front seat of Erik's truck. Anticipation and nervousness both hit the closer it drew to ten o'clock. Friday nights were normally busy and kept Nathan from focusing too much on his thoughts. Which really was a good thing, because it would have totally sucked walking around with a boner all night. Though when Erik walked into the store, Nathan's body came alive.

"Okay, I'm out, Nate. Don't do anything I wouldn't do," Quinn teased.

Nathan rolled his eyes at Quinn. "Well, that should be a pretty short list, considering you'd do just about anything."

Quinn laughed on his way into the storeroom to grab his bag and clock out. "I'll see ya tomorrow. I had Stuart put me on the schedule. Need the hours."

"Sure, Quinn. Have a good night." Nathan watched Quinn leave while Erik came toward the front desk. "Hey," he said.

"Hey back, angel." Erik swooped in for a quick kiss. "How was your day? How'd today's exams go?"

Nathan shrugged while working on balancing and closing the register. "Won't really know until next week or so. They went okay, though. I think."

Erik moved around the desk until he stood behind Nathan, and then he wrapped his arms around him as he rested his chin on Nathan's shoulder. "I've missed you."

"We saw each other last night," Nathan said, laughing breathlessly. He had to grab a deposit bag but didn't want to move. Not yet. He leaned into Erik's embrace and tilted his head back against his chest.

"That was yesterday, though," Erik groused, turning his head to kiss Nathan's cheek. It amused and delighted Nathan with how teddy bear-ish Erik was being.

"But I don't have to study tonight," Nathan said.

A sexy humming vibrated on Nathan's back. "Don't I know it," Erik replied. He kissed the side of Nathan's neck. "I can't wait to get you all to myself."

"I need to get this finished so we can leave."

"Hurry," Erik growled near his ear, right before nipping gently at the lobe.

Nathan moaned and tightened his fingers on the paper in his hand. "If you keep doing that, I'm not going to finish because I can't think."

Erik sighed and released Nathan. "I'll be good… for now."

Nathan couldn't have wiped the grin off his face to save his life. He prepared the night deposit without further interruption, and then they were in Erik's truck on the way to the bank. Hopping out, he dropped it into the slot and got back in.

"Are we going to the diner tonight?" Nathan asked.

Erik shook his head and entwined his fingers with Nathan's. "No, I don't want to share you with anyone tonight. I have dinner waiting for us at the house."

Settling into the seat to get comfortable, Nathan turned his head to watch out the window at everything racing by. The lack of a full night's sleep for the last several days took its toll on Nathan. He fell asleep not long into the journey to Erik's. It wasn't until Erik opened the passenger-side door did Nathan stir. Erik slid his arms under Nathan and lifted him from the truck, using his shoulder to close the door. "You don't have to carry me," Nathan murmured, his head lolling onto Erik's shoulder so he could look at him.

"You can go back to sleep if you're tired, angel."

How Erik unlocked the front door and carried him inside without a single fumble baffled Nathan. But he also felt more awake now that they were in Erik's house. "I'm good," Nathan said. "You can put me down."

"If only to get some food into you," Erik replied. He carefully set Nathan on his feet and nudged him toward the table. "It's staying warm in the oven, so we can eat pretty quickly."

Nathan sat and watched Erik pull a couple of dishes out of the oven. He set them on the table, then grabbed a couple of soda cans from the fridge and handed one to Nathan. Erik had made lasagna and what looked like garlic rolls. "You made this?" Nathan asked, scooping a small piece of lasagna onto the plate in front of him.

"An old recipe of my grandmother's. I bring it into the office a couple times a year and the crew loves it. I also have chocolate-covered strawberries and cheesecake for dessert."

"You're determined I gain weight, aren't you?" Nathan took a bite of the lasagna and his eyes rolled into the back of his head. "Oh, man. This is even better than the lasagna my Aunt Becky makes. Don't tell her I said that, though!"

Erik chuckled. "When do I get to meet these amazing aunts of yours?"

"You want to meet them?" Nathan asked.

"Of course, they're your family." Erik made it sound so simple, but Nathan hadn't really thought about introducing them. Mostly because things had been so busy with studying, the situation with Alan, and his worry about being all wrong for Erik. He wasn't sure he wanted to before he told Erik about his ability.

"Oh, um, I'm not sure when I'll see them again, really. They were supposed to let Troy and me know when they were ready for us to move the furniture back. I hope they didn't move it on their own." Now he really was feeling awful. He'd completely forgotten to return and help them with replacing the furniture once the walls were dry. Everything with Erik and Alan had completely sidetracked him.

"I'm sure they know you've been busy with school and work. Maybe tomorrow after work, I can take you over there to help them out."

"I really should call them before we do that. It's a long drive from my job. Plus, tomorrow is my set at Java Bean."

"I don't mind," Erik said, shrugging. "You let me know what you need. I'd love to go with you to hear you play, too."

Nathan started asking about Erik's company, the people who worked there, and how Erik got into architecture at all.

He listened while Erik told him about having tons of Lego sets as a child, building anything he could make out of the little plastic blocks, and it grew into a love of the special flare some buildings had.

"Favorite building you ever designed?"

Erik didn't even hesitate. "This house."

The reminder of why he built it caused Nathan's heart to hurt. He ached for the grief Erik must have endured after losing Alan, but he also felt a little jealous of this being Alan and Erik's dream house. Of course, Erik hadn't a clue Nathan knew why he'd designed it and Nathan had to pretend. "You designed this?"

"Every inch," Erik responded while clearing the table and putting away the leftovers. "I knew what I wanted and exactly how it would look."

"That's amazing." Nathan stood to help with the dishes, handing things off to Erik one at a time. Every single day, he sunk deeper and deeper into the mud of his lies and deceptions. He could only pray he would come out clean on the other side.

"Are you ready for dessert?" Erik asked. Nathan's mind immediately went to the gutter, and he blushed. Erik grinned at him. "Cheesecake, you naughty boy."

Nathan's blush deepened and he shook his head. "No. I'm full right now."

"Mmm, excellent answer," Erik said, stalking the short distance to Nathan.

CHAPTER 20

Erik took Nathan by the hand and pulled him into an embrace. Cupping Nathan's cheek, Erik lowered his head to capture his lips in a sweet kiss. Nathan had thought for sure the kiss would be more hungry than soft. He opened his mouth to Erik, accepting the seeking tongue inside.

Erik reached down to cup his ass, lifting him off his feet to set him on the counter. The show of strength heightened Nathan's lust for him. He wrapped his legs around Erik's waist and pulled him closer, his hands tangling in the strands of hair at Erik's nape. Erik continued to kiss him, his tongue dueling with Nathan's while he slipped his hands underneath Nathan's shirt. The roughness of Erik's calloused fingers scraping over his back and stomach sent a shiver through him.

Erik broke the kiss long enough to strip the shirt from Nathan's body before removing his own. When Erik recaptured his lips, Nathan mapped out the muscles along Erik's shoulders and back, lightly raking his fingers over the tanned flesh along his spine.

"Fuck, angel. You feel so good," Erik groaned into Nathan's mouth.

Nathan arched into Erik, panting. His head swam with how much he wanted the man touching him, kissing him, and fucking him. He reached between them to unsnap Erik's jeans, desperate to feel his hard length in his palm. A ragged moan came from Erik when Nathan wrapped his fingers around Erik's cock. Nathan gently squeezed and stroked him, his thumb swiping over the weeping tip. The clear fluid called to him, and he brought his thumb to his mouth, lapping at the salty liquid. He locked gazes with Erik while tasting his lover. Erik's hazel eyes darkened to a gorgeous amber, pure heat blazing out of their depths at Nathan.

Gripped with the need to taste more of Erik, Nathan hopped off the counter, grabbed Erik's hand, and tugged him over to the couch. He'd have gotten on his knees in the kitchen if it hadn't been for his bad leg. Nathan dropped onto the cushions and leaned forward to slide his tongue over the mushroom-shaped head. Erik slid a hand into Nathan's hair, freeing it from its confinement, and he guided Nathan onto his cock, slowly pushing in deeper. Another groan rattled in Erik's chest and Nathan looked up to see his head tilted back, his eyes closed. Using the flat of his tongue, Nathan caressed along the steel shaft. He went a little too far and gagged, immediately reversing.

"Easy, angel," Erik rasped. "You don't have to take it all at once."

Determination set in. Nathan wanted to please Erik, to make him feel good. It took several tries before Nathan could take most of his cock. Erik tightened his hand on Nathan's hair slightly. The musky pre-cum came faster the longer Nathan worked at Erik's prick. He applied a couple of moves he'd seen in a porn film before, gently rolling Erik's balls in one hand while the other moved up and down the length of his shaft.

Erik gave a sudden hitch of his hips and Nathan felt the head enter his throat. He swallowed around it without thinking. He increased the suction, moving his head a little faster. It may not have been the most elegant or well-practiced blowjob, but Erik didn't seem to mind. A moment later, though, he grunted and pulled free from Nathan's mouth. "Fuck, you've got me so close."

He reached down and pulled Nathan to his feet. "Let's go upstairs," Erik said.

Nathan followed him to his bedroom. Erik quickly disrobed and then removed the rest of Nathan's clothing. He walked Nathan back toward his bed and coaxed him down to the mattress, immediately covering Nathan's body with his own. But Erik didn't jump into prepping Nathan. Instead, he began kissing Nathan again, trailing down his neck to his collarbone. His fingers traced over Nathan's ribs, causing him to squirm and chuckle. "Ticklish, hmm?" Erik teased.

"A little," Nathan panted. Erik nuzzled and kissed along Nathan's sternum until he reached his belly button. The slick slide of Erik's tongue pressing into his navel made Nathan's cock weep a thin line of fluid, which Erik lapped up immediately. Nathan tossed his head against the pillow as Erik followed the line to its source. He arched his back from the mattress when Erik licked along the entire length of his cock down to the sack beneath. Only, Erik didn't stop there. He went farther and Nathan almost jumped off the bed when Erik pushed his legs up and took a swipe at the tight muscles hidden in the valley of his rear end. "Oh my God, Erik!"

Erik continued to lap at his entrance, nudging it open a little more with each pass. Nathan gripped the sheets in his fingers, attempting to find an anchor in the storm threatening to drag him under. Small cries and whimpers echoed off the surrounding walls. When Erik slipped a finger inside of him finally, Nathan let out a high-pitched cry, thrusting his hips downward. His body craved the feeling of Erik deep inside of him.

"Erik," Nathan sobbed.

A second finger pressed in alongside the first one, leaving Nathan panting for so much more. Erik continued to batter Nathan's senses. By the time Erik moved away long enough to sheath his cock with a condom and drip lube on the hard shaft, Nathan could do nothing except watch with hooded eyes, his chest heaving with panting breaths. Erik stroked the length of his cock, coating it with the slick liquid, before he rose over Nathan again.

Nathan eagerly spread his legs wider, accepting Erik between them without thought or fear this time. Erik caught his lips in a thirsty kiss as he slid inside Nathan. They both groaned when he bottomed out. But when Erik moved, Nathan broke the kiss to cry out, clinging to him. He brought his legs higher up Erik's sides, encouraging him to go deeper. A sexy growl left Erik and the man bent over him, nipping and suckling at every place he could reach. Every sensation overwhelmed the last until Nathan couldn't separate them. All he knew right then was he never wanted Erik to stop.

Sweat built on both their skin, coating the fringes of Nathan's hair. The salty scent only inflamed Nathan's pleasure, stoking his craving for Erik higher. "Erik, I-I need..." He couldn't finish the thought, tightening his hold on Erik in hopes the man understood.

"I know, angel. I've got you." Erik grunted, fucking Nathan harder, faster. Both were gasping for breath when Erik shifted his hips, tagging Nathan's prostate. Nathan shouted, his climax ripping through him unexpectedly. Hard spurts of semen bathed their chests and bellies. Erik sat up, pulling Nathan with him until he straddled Erik's lap, never once leaving the tight sheath of Nathan's body. He grabbed hold of Nathan's rounded bottom to lift and drop him, impaling Nathan again and again.

Clawing at Erik's broad shoulders, he burrowed his face against Erik's neck. Nathan could feel the heat rising in him once more, another orgasm on the heels of the one he'd just had. Erik never faltered or stopped. Nathan locked his ankles behind Erik's back, his arms holding on tightly around his neck. "Erik," he moaned.

"You going to soar for me again, angel?" Erik crooned.

Nathan pushed down onto Erik with each motion. The sound of Nathan's ragged breathing only beat out the sound of skin slapping against skin. "Oh God," he moaned.

"That's it, angel. Let go. Come for me."

Nathan splintered again, shouting to the heavens. Erik gave another several thrusts before he let forth a loud groan, his fingers tightening on Nathan's ass. Nathan could feel Erik's cock pulsing inside of him, each one like the beat of a heart. Eventually, Erik slumped against him, his forehead resting on Nathan's shoulder. They remained locked together in silence. Their breathing was the only sound as they settled from the most amazing sex Nathan had ever experienced. Not that he'd had anything to compare it to prior to the previous time with Erik.

Erik carefully laid Nathan back down amongst the pillows and slid free of his body. He crashed down to the bed beside Nathan, disposed of the condom, and wrapped an arm over Nathan's waist to yank him close. The cooling sweat caused Nathan to shiver slightly. "You okay, angel?"

He really didn't want to speak, so he just gave a low hum in response. Erik gave a breathy chuckle. "Did I leave you speechless?"

"Uh hmm."

"So, I rocked your world again, huh?"

Nathan couldn't contain a grin. "Twice."

Erik gave a deeper laugh and pressed several kisses along the line of Nathan's shoulder. He started running his fingers over Nathan's arm and down his chest. Nathan tensed when Erik traced along the jagged scars he had where his shoulder had ripped open during the accident. "Also from the car accident?" Erik asked.

Nathan took a small breath and nodded. "Yeah."

Soft butterfly touches flickered over the scars, almost tickling Nathan. Erik rolled him onto his back, leaning over him slightly. He could see empathy, not pity, in Erik's gaze. "Will you tell me about it?"

For the first time since it happened, Nathan wanted to lean on someone besides Troy. It had been a long time since he'd even talked about any of it with Troy. He knew Troy would never stop him, but he hadn't wanted to continue to burden his friend once he'd gotten out of the hospital. But he was tired of going through it alone.

So, he started, and the words just tumbled out of his mouth. He told Erik everything. Except about his ability. How he'd wanted to go to the party with his friends, but his parents had insisted he go with them. He told Erik about how selfish he'd been in demanding they leave. "If I hadn't, they'd still be alive," Nathan whispered, turning his face away from Erik. "They wouldn't have been in that intersection and that drunk asshole wouldn't have hit us."

"Stop," Erik said. He gripped Nathan's chin gently and forced him to look at him. "You were a teenager, Nathan. You couldn't have known what would happen and you can't spend your life blaming yourself. That man's choice to drink and drive was his own. He is the reason your parents are gone. Not you."

Tears welled in Nathan's eyes. "But—"

Erik stopped him with a finger on his lips. "No, angel.

You are not at fault. No buts, no ifs, nothing. You need to stop blaming yourself."

The tears trickled down Nathan's temples, dripping into his hair. Erik pulled him to his chest again, wrapping his arms around him. "That's why you refuse to let anyone help you."

A sob caught in Nathan's throat. He swallowed hard to clear it away. "I don't want anyone else to be hurt because of me ever again."

Erik held him tightly, running a hand along Nathan's back in a soothing gesture. "Life is full of uncertainties, Nathan. There are no guarantees that we'll live to see tomorrow, even. All we can do is hope and enjoy the time we have on this earth."

Nathan rested his forehead on Erik's chest. Was he right? The guilt he'd carried around for so long didn't feel as heavy as it used to. He sighed and closed his eyes.

"Rest, angel. Tomorrow morning, I'll take you to breakfast before work."

Yawning, Nathan burrowed deeper into Erik's arms. Everything else could wait until tomorrow. As he drifted off, he felt Erik kiss his temple and he could have sworn he heard Erik murmur something, but he couldn't focus enough to understand it.

The following morning, Erik kept his word and took Nathan to CJ's Diner for breakfast. Nathan hadn't been in there during the morning hours before. Of course, Harriet wasn't there since she worked the late shift, but they still got into his usual booth. Thankfully, there were no more spirits in the diner. At least not that day. Nathan didn't want a repeat of the last time he'd been there with Erik. For that matter, he hadn't seen the one in the music store either. He frowned, his eyebrows drawing together. They had never left him alone before when a ghost had figured out he could see them. They'd always come back, begging him to help them.

"Something wrong, angel?" Erik asked.

"Hmm?" Nathan shook himself and realized the server had returned, patiently waiting for Nathan's order. "Oh, no. Just lost in thought."

Erik smiled. "Good thoughts, I hope."

He didn't answer as he ordered a glass of orange juice, a coffee, and his usual bagel with cream cheese. After the food came, Erik tried to ply him with some of his bacon, but Nathan declined. He really didn't enjoy eating a lot in the morning. Doing so usually made his stomach hurt. They talked about random topics and what time Nathan's shift ended. Erik told him he'd pick him up, treat him to dinner, and then take him over to the café for his gig. Nathan agreed, still trying to think of a reason the spirit in the music store hadn't returned.

When they were back in the truck, Erik said, "Penny for those thoughts?"

Nathan shrugged and shook his head. "It's nothing. Really."

Erik didn't look convinced, but he didn't push. Since the diner wasn't far away, it only took a couple minutes for them to reach the store. Nathan slid out of Erik's truck. "Thanks for the ride."

"I'll see you at five, right?" Erik asked.

He nodded. "I have to be at the café before seven."

"I'll get you there." Erik waited for Nathan to enter the store, then reversed out of the spot and left. Nathan watched the tail end of Erik's truck until he couldn't see it anymore. Once Erik was out of sight, Nathan turned and got ready to work.

~

The day went by quickly. Nathan didn't realize the time until Erik walked into the store. He looked at the clock on the wall in surprise. "I just have to clock out," he said to Erik. "I need to run to my apartment to get my guitar, though. If that's okay."

"Anything you need, angel."

Quinn didn't miss the endearment, and Nathan knew he was going to say something smart. "Aww. That's so *cute!*"

Nathan rolled his eyes at Quinn while trying not to grin. "Shut up, Quinn."

He heard Erik laugh as he went into the storeroom to punch his time card. A warmth he'd never felt before settled in his chest. Stopping in his tracks, Nathan wondered if what he felt toward Erik bordered on love. He knew he loved being around Erik, and he wouldn't mind repeating last night every night. But was he falling in love with Erik? In such a short amount of time? He'd never loved anyone outside of his family and Troy. How the hell did he know what love felt like? For so long, he'd cut himself off emotionally from everyone, even his aunts. His feelings had been frozen because he never wanted to feel the deep ache he'd experienced at the loss of his parents.

"Nate, buddy, you okay back there?" Quinn called from the front, and he shook himself mentally. Hurrying to the clock, he grabbed his card, punched it, and slipped it back into the box. Erik stood by the front desk, chatting with Quinn, and Nathan almost came to a halt once more. The man was utterly gorgeous, and Nathan was certain Erik didn't even know it. The deep cleft in his chin, a body to die for where most of the clothing he wore hugged him like a second skin, and the kind heart beating inside Erik's chest were only a few of the things that made Erik so damned special.

Erik looked over at him and smiled, obvious pleasure in his eyes. "Ready to go, angel?"

Nathan nodded, trailing Erik out of the store. The second they were on the road to Nathan's apartment, Erik grabbed his hand and entwined their fingers, not letting go until he'd pulled the truck into a parking space. "You can wait here. I won't be that long," Nathan said.

"I'll come up with you," Erik said, turning off the engine. Nathan didn't protest. He exited the vehicle, closing the door behind him. Erik met him around the front of the truck and then placed a hand on Nathan's lower back, guiding him toward the stairs. Once again, Erik stayed behind him to prevent the possibility of his knee giving out. Everything Erik did made Nathan feel special and cherished. He prayed Erik would still feel that way after he found out about Nathan's ability to see spirits.

He opened his apartment door and entered, setting his bag down by the kitchen counter. The guitar lay against the side of the couch and Nathan moved over to pick it up. Erik intercepted him, taking Nathan into his arms and giving him a deep, heated kiss. When he broke away, Erik said, "Grab your guitar and let's get out of here. I'm curious to meet Curtis, and I can't wait to hear you play."

Nathan blushed, suddenly nervous. He put his guitar back in its case and zipped it up. "I'm ready."

They were back on the road in a matter of minutes. Nathan gave Erik directions on how to get to the café. He spent most of the trip quietly staring out of the passenger window. Before he felt ready, Erik pulled the truck into a parking spot and turned off the engine. As usual, the café was bustling, causing another burst of nerves to slam into Nathan. He hadn't been anxious about playing in front of an audience since the first time he'd done an open mic night. "Curtis is probably in his office," Nathan said over the noise.

He led Erik through the café to Curtis' office. He knocked and heard Curtis call for him to enter. Curtis smiled at him when he saw it was Nathan. "Hey, Nate. Glad to see you're doing better this week."

"Yeah, sorry about last week."

Curtis waved away his apology despite being ticked off before. "We all have those weeks. Who's this?"

"Uh, this is my, uh, friend Erik." Nathan didn't know if he should introduce them as more than friends. They hadn't exactly defined their relationship. Though the idea of calling Erik his boyfriend sent butterflies tickling through his stomach and a thrill raced up his spine.

Erik shook Curtis' hand before placing his palm against Nathan's lower back. "Nice to meet you."

Nathan saw a knowing look in Curtis' eyes when Erik touched him, but Curtis didn't seem phased by the knowledge. "Always great to meet a friend of Nathan's. Is Troy with you tonight?"

"Not tonight."

"So, what do you do for a living, Erik?"

Erik and Curtis started chatting about the usual niceties when you first meet someone. Nathan slipped out of the office and headed to the small platform near the back of the café. He unzipped the guitar case and pulled out his guitar, ignoring the people already seated at the various tables. Everything faded away as he perched on the small stool and adjusted the mic down to his height. After ensuring the guitar didn't need tuning, Nathan played a cover song, one he'd done dozens of times. The lyrics came easily, and he lost himself in the warmth and joy playing brought to him. Singing was only a part of it. He didn't enjoy it anywhere near as much, but he'd always been told he had a pleasant voice.

He saw Erik come out of Curtis' office and make his way to the table closest to the small stage. His heart started beating a little faster, nerves hitting him again. But they faded when he saw Erik smile at him. Nathan barely looked away from Erik as he transitioned from one song to another. Everything narrowed down to the man who'd slowly started becoming his entire world. His words faltered for a split second when that thought occurred to him. He knew if Erik tossed him away when he found out about Nathan's scary as fuck ability, he'd never fully recover.

No one seemed to notice the slip, thankfully, and Nathan kept going. Halfway through his set, Nathan saw his aunts come into the café. They waved at him from the front and stopped at the counter to order. Every so often, they would come to the café to watch him. Afterward, they usually took him and Troy to dinner. He stifled a wince when he knew he was going to have to introduce them after his set. Hopefully, his aunts wouldn't bring up the hospital or accident.

When he finished his usual set, Nathan lingered, taking his time to put his guitar in its case. Erik came over to the platform and took the case from him, wrapping an arm around Nathan's shoulders and kissing his temple. "You were amazing!"

Nathan flushed at Erik's praise before glancing at his aunts. He saw the realization on their faces. Shit. They approached the two of them. "Nathan?" Aunt Becky said.

Erik looked at the two women. "You're Nathan's aunts?"

They nodded. Erik smiled and held out a hand. "It's nice to meet you. I'm Erik Moore."

"Are you two... together?" Jessica asked, her eyes assessing Erik closely. She shook Erik's hand lightly, followed by Becky.

"We are," Erik answered. "I was hoping for a chance to meet you both. Nathan's talked about you a lot."

"Well, I wish we could say the same," Becky returned with a side glance at Nathan. He'd already mentioned meeting someone, but he had given no details since.

"Aunt Becky, I'm sorry. I've been so busy with work and school and stuff, I didn't really have a chance to call you."

Jessica looked Erik over and gave Nathan a discreet thumbs-up. "How long have you two been seeing each other?"

Erik smiled. "A couple of weeks or thereabouts, hmm, angel?"

"About," Nathan muttered.

"How did the two of you meet?" Becky asked.

"He came into the music store," Nathan replied.

"Why don't we go get something to eat for dinner and we can chat?" Becky asked. "Give us a chance to get to know one another. Make sure you're a good addition to our nephew's life."

"Aunt Becky!" Nathan slapped a palm over his face.

Erik chuckled. "It's okay, angel. That would be great, Jessica, Becky. Maybe you can give me some stories about how adorable Nathan was as a child," Erik said, smiling. "Anywhere in particular?"

"There's an Olive Garden around the corner from here."

"I know it. We'll meet you ladies there?"

They agreed and headed toward the exit. Nathan trailed behind them with Erik. The moment they were in the truck, Nathan apologized. "I am so sorry."

"For what, Nate?" Erik asked. "They're your aunts. They love you and care about you. Of course, they're going to want to be sure anyone you're dating isn't out to hurt you."

"I just don't want you to think it's too much," Nathan mumbled, staring at his hands folded in his lap.

"What's too much?" Erik asked, frowning.

"Them. Me. Everything."

Erik pulled the truck into a space in the Olive Garden parking lot and turned off the engine. He shifted in his seat so he could look at Nathan. "Baby, I don't care if they give me the third degree, run a background check on me, or grab their torches and pitchforks. Nothing will ever be too much for me." He took Nathan's hand in his and pressed a kiss to Nathan's knuckles. "If I have to answer a thousand questions from your very loving aunts, I will. Hell, I'd show them my stock portfolio and finances if they demanded it. I want to be with you, angel. Nothing is going to change that."

Nathan shook his head, his breath catching at how adamant Erik was. "Okay," he said. "If it gets to be too much, just please tell me."

"It won't." Erik squeezed Nathan's hand gently. "You ready?"

Snorting, Nathan twisted his mouth in a sardonic smile. "Not really."

"We've got this. Now, come on." Erik opened his door and got out. Nathan took a deep breath and followed, praying his aunts didn't talk about the six months in the mental institution.

CHAPTER 21

Dinner wasn't as bad as Nathan expected. His aunts gave Erik the third degree, but they seemed satisfied with the answers. Thankfully, they didn't bring up the mental institution or the accident. Afterward, Becky stopped Nathan near the back of Erik's truck. She hugged him tightly. "I'm so glad to see you finally living again, Nate. Your parents would want you to live your life, and I can see he makes you happy. I can't remember the last time I've seen you smile so much. Please, both of you come by the house soon, okay?"

"Sure," Nathan mumbled. Then he frowned. "Who moved the furniture back? You never let us know you were ready."

"We got our neighbors to help. Don't worry, we didn't move it on our own." Becky kissed his cheek before joining Jessica in the car.

Nathan watched them leave the parking lot. Jessica tossed her hand out the window in a wave.

"They care about you a lot," Erik said, sliding his arm around Nathan's shoulders.

"I'm so sorry about all the questions," Nathan said.

Erik shrugged. "They're your family. It's normal for them to be concerned. I didn't mind answering their questions."

Tilting his head back to look up at Erik, Nathan said, "Thanks."

"For what?"

"Being you." Nathan couldn't stifle the blush he could feel heating his cheeks, but he wouldn't take back what he said.

Erik gave a tender smile, brushing a strand of Nathan's hair behind his ear. He leaned against the side of the vehicle, pulling Nathan against him before his hands settled on Nathan's hips. Nathan placed his hands on Erik's chest and rose on the tip of his toes to kiss him. He'd never instigated a kiss before, and he could feel the blush in his cheeks when he pulled back. Erik flexed his fingers on Nathan's hips, sliding his index fingers through the belt loops on Nathan's jeans. Tugging gently, he coaxed Nathan into another kiss, one which quickly grew heated. A moan vibrated in Nathan's chest when Erik slid his tongue over Nathan's bottom lip.

"Stay the night with me?" Erik asked when he broke the kiss.

Nathan nodded, and they climbed into the truck. Erik's reaction to his aunts' nosiness gave him hope that he'd take Nathan's ability in stride, too. Maybe, just maybe, Erik wouldn't think him completely nuts. He still felt trepidation at the idea of telling Erik, but the longer he went about saying nothing, the harder it would be in the end.

They settled into a routine over the days leading up to the picnic. During the remainder of his exams, Nathan stayed at his own apartment, studying, and after that, he stayed at Erik's house every night. Erik set up an area for him to study and do homework and would leave him to it.

During the days and some afternoons, Troy and Nathan would hang out and talk about Alan or the details they were still trying to figure out. Alan only showed twice, and only when Nathan was home. Both times, Nathan noticed his form seemed more transparent than the previous weeks. He didn't really know if that was because of how long Alan had been lingering after his death or if something else had changed.

Guilt also struck him because he could see and feel how sad Alan was. He avoided the subject of Erik when Alan was around so he didn't make him any sadder. They planned for Alan to come to the store on Sunday, before Erik arrived to pick him up for the picnic. Nathan asked Alan to talk as little as possible while they were at the picnic. He also asked Curtis for the night off, just in case something happened at the picnic or the stress triggered another migraine.

Saturday night, Nathan couldn't calm the nerves in his stomach. Not even playing at the café could distract him. The next day, he'd most likely meet the person responsible for Alan's death. The idea not only terrified him, but it also brought him one step closer to revealing the truth about everything to Erik.

Sunday dawned bright and clear, with not a single threat of rain anywhere. Nathan went to work as usual. He spent the four hours of his shift waffling between wanting Alan to remember and wanting the situation to fade away. Quinn tried more than once to joke around with him or engage him in a conversation. Each time, Nathan found a reason to change the subject to work or avoid the conversation all together.

Alan appeared ten minutes before Erik was due. Nathan gave a small nod to him but said nothing, since Quinn was standing a few feet from him. The knots in Nathan's belly just got tighter, causing painful cramps. A slight tension headache settled into the base of his skull. He prayed it wouldn't become one of the excruciating ones.

Some of that faded away, though, when he saw Erik, and Nathan smiled widely.

Erik came toward the counter, where he leaned in to give a quick peck at Nathan's lips. "Hey, angel. How was your day?"

"Better now," Nathan murmured, his cheeks heating at his bold words.

Erik's gaze grew dark, lustful. Nathan bit his lower lip, the embers of his need for Erik rising to the surface. They'd made love that morning in the shower, but Nathan knew he'd never get enough of the man. "Don't tempt me, angel," Erik rasped. "I don't even want to go. Not when all I want to do is spend the rest of the day ravishing every delectable inch of your body."

Fire flicked along Nathan's entire being. The blush in his cheeks grew hotter, and he dropped his gaze to the counter-top, embarrassment fighting with his desire for Erik to do just that.

But Erik didn't let him look away. He tucked a couple of fingers under Nathan's chin and lifted his head until their eyes met. "Don't hide," Erik rumbled, his thumb caressing over Nathan's bottom lip.

Quinn grunted beside Nathan, interrupting the intense moment between them. "Get a room, you two."

Nathan flushed even more and then shame hit him because he'd completely forgotten about Alan's presence. When he glanced over at him, Nathan saw utter devastation and so much pain on his face. Clearing his throat, Nathan pulled away from Erik's touch. "Need to clock out," Nathan mumbled.

He scurried into the back room to get his backpack and punch his time card. Alan said nothing as Nathan followed

Erik to his truck, but Nathan could feel his despair and anguish. It settled onto his skin like a heavy sheen of oil, making Nathan's guilt skyrocket even more. When Erik closed the door, Nathan said, "I'm sorry, Alan. I really am."

"It's not like I expected him to pine forever," Alan said, his tone somber and pained. "It's just hard seeing him falling in love with someone else. I… I'm glad he's happy, though. He deserves it."

Nathan would have said more, but Erik opened the driver's side and climbed into the truck. "Ready?" Erik asked, smiling as he started the engine.

Not in the damn least. "Yes."

The entire way to the park, Nathan couldn't stop fidgeting. He twisted his hands, watching out the window and wishing they had more time. He wasn't only nervous because of the possibility of running into the person who'd hurt Alan. No, he was meeting for the first time people who mattered to Erik. People who could point out just how unsuited Nathan was for the older man. People who may just finally open Erik's eyes to his flaws.

He jumped when Erik's hand came down on top of his. "Relax, angel. They're going to love you. There's no reason to be nervous."

Nathan chewed on his lower lip, staring at the dark tan of Erik's hand against his pale white skin. "I-I'm not nervous," he lied.

Erik glanced at Nathan, consternation obvious on his features. "Want to try that again?"

Sighing, Nathan picked at a thread on his jeans. "I'm just afraid they aren't going to like me. Stupid, I know."

Erik gently squeezed his hand. "Nothing you feel is stupid. Do you think I wasn't worried about your aunts? That they would think I was too old for you or wasn't good enough for you?"

Surprise brought Nathan's gaze to Erik. "Really?"

"Really. It's always nerve-racking to meet someone's family. But whatever happens, I'm not going anywhere, angel. You matter more to me than what anyone else thinks."

Nathan's breath caught in his throat, and tears stung his eyes, which he quickly blinked away. Pure agony washed over him—a pain so deep Nathan couldn't suppress a gasp at the intensity of it. His chest grew tight while his heart seemed to shatter. Fuck. He knew where the emotions had come from: Alan.

Erik frowned. "Are you okay, Nate?"

"I'm fine," Nathan said.

He didn't look convinced, but he let it drop. The headache that had started at the store came flaring back hard. Nathan winced and pulled in a deep breath. He couldn't change what Alan had heard or seen. All he could do was apologize again when they were alone.

They reached the park and Nathan's heart pounded harder when he saw the sizeable crowd. He could hear music that was muffled by the windows of the truck. People were laughing, chatting, and drinking beer. Smoke wafted from the grill next to the pavilion. Several kids were running around chasing each other with what Nathan could only assume were water guns. A bounce house sat off to the side, with several more children jumping around inside. There were even a couple of ponies, a karaoke stage, and several carnival-style food carts: cotton candy, funnel cakes, and snow cones.

"Don't worry, angel. Just have fun. Come on." Erik opened his door and climbed out.

Nathan sat there, trying hard not to hyperventilate. He glanced over his shoulder at Alan. "You're going to have to point out who Matthew, Becca, and Owen are. If you see or hear anything that triggers something, please try to wait until we're alone to talk."

Alan shimmered for a slight moment. Nathan furrowed his brows. "Are you okay, Alan?"

"I'm fine," Alan replied, his tone exhausted and low. "Maybe we should just call this off, Nate."

"No. I can't do that."

Erik opened Nathan's door before Alan could reply. "Nate?"

Nathan gave a strained smile and slipped down to the ground. "Sorry. Just a little overwhelmed."

"You don't have to meet everyone. I just want you to meet my cousin and a couple of others." Erik took Nathan's hand and tugged him toward the pavilion. Everyone kept calling Erik's name, saying hi or tossing a wave at him. Nathan tried to hide his limp, but his knee protested the movement and he stumbled slightly. Erik gripped his elbow to steady him while a flush heated Nathan's cheeks.

"Is your leg bothering you?" Erik asked, his entire focus on Nathan.

Nathan shook his head. "No. I just stepped wrong."

"Erik!" A dark-haired man around Erik's height and with muscles upon muscles came toward them, a broad smile on his face. The two men embraced in a man hug, giving each other a backslap before Erik placed his hand on Nathan's lower back once more.

"Thomas, I'd like you to meet Nathan. Nate, this is Thomas. He's my foreperson on the jobsites and helps keep the show running."

Thomas held his hand out to Nathan. "Nice to meet you, Nathan. You must be the reason Erik is smiling all the time."

Blushing, Nathan accepted the handshake. "Hi."

"We'll have to spend some time getting to know one

another," Thomas said. "I bet I can tell you all the good stories about our Erik here."

Nathan smiled. "I'd like that."

"Let's make the rounds first. Then you can listen to the no doubt embarrassing stories Tom is going to tell you about me," Erik groused good-naturedly.

By the time Nathan met Becca, Erik's assistant, and Owen, an assistant architect, his head was swimming. Becca seemed super sweet. She gave him a kiss on the cheek and insisted they get to know one another soon. Owen seemed more reserved. Despite that, he didn't strike Nathan as devious enough to commit murder. Of course, he didn't exactly have a measuring stick on how to calculate if someone was a killer or not.

His phone vibrated in his pant pocket when Erik went to get them both a drink. Nathan took it out and saw a text from Troy asking for an update on what was going on. Alan had kept quiet the whole time, just hovering nearby while Nathan met everyone. He'd felt nothing except the same pain, a touch of anger, and not a small amount of despair. His heart hurt for Alan.

Nathan sent off a quick message that everything was fine and nothing had come up yet. Alan floated closer, his gaze on some kids tossing a football around. "We were going to adopt."

Doing his best to keep his mouth from moving, Nathan replied. "I'm sorry, Alan. I really am."

"It's not your fault, Nate." Alan moved to Nathan's side.

"I know, but I'm still sorry. I can feel what this is doing to you," Nathan mumbled. "Maybe this *was* a bad idea."

"No. We can't stop now. What if whoever did this wants to hurt Erik, too?"

The idea had crossed Nathan's mind before, but he'd

brushed it off. If the person wanted to go after Erik, they'd had two years already.

Erik returned then and handed Nathan a soda can. "See? Nothing to worry about. Everyone has loved you so far."

Nathan popped the tab on the can and took a drink. "Everyone's been really nice."

"Come on. There's one other person I want to introduce you to." Erik led him over to the funnel cake cart. "Matt!"

A man—who you couldn't doubt was related to Erik—smiled widely at them. They had the same flared nose, square jaw, and full lips. The major difference was Matt had green eyes while Erik's were a gorgeous hazel. "I wondered when you'd get here, cuz. What took you so long?" Those green eyes turned to Nathan. "Is this him?"

Nathan's brows went up. Erik had told Matt about him? "Angel, I'd like you to meet my cousin and best friend, Matthew. Matt, this is Nathan."

Matthew held out his hand. "It's so nice to put a face to the name! Erik's done nothing but talk about you for the last two weeks."

"Hopefully all good," Nathan joked uncomfortably.

"Nothing but! You are definitely as gorgeous as he described, too."

Nathan's jaw hit his chest, and another blush worked its way over his face. "Matt," Erik growled. "Stop embarrassing him."

"Embarrassing him or you, cuz?"

Erik rolled his eyes at his cousin. "Time to change the subject."

Matthew laughed. "Erik also mentioned how good you are at the guitar and that you have the voice of an angel."

Nathan groaned and slapped his hand over his face. "Really?"

What Matthew said next didn't register. Fear beyond

anything Nathan had ever experienced, even when he'd first realized he could see spirits, crashed over him. It was so heavy it almost brought him to his knees. Black dots danced over Nathan's vision, and he wondered if he was going to pass out.

"Nate? Angel? Are you okay?"

He couldn't answer. His throat closed over in horror and Nathan knew Alan had remembered something. Something that caused him such terror Nathan could almost taste it. He was only vaguely aware of Erik leading him to a nearby table and having him take a seat on the bench. Someone thrust a water bottle into his hand and Erik rubbed the other one between the two of his.

"Talk to me, Nate. What's going on?"

Nathan took a sip of water and then another. Alan had moved far enough from him that the sensation of a hand at his throat, squeezing, faded away. He dragged in several deep breaths and let them out slowly. "I think I just needed a minute," Nathan finally said.

Erik cupped Nathan's cheek and turned his head toward him. "Talk to me. Please. What just happened?"

"Just overwhelmed for a minute," Nathan lied. He bit back a wince. He'd lied so many times to Erik. Would the man ever forgive him when he could finally tell him the truth?

"Do you want to go home?"

"No! I'm fine."

"Are you sure?"

"Yes, I'm sure."

Nathan glanced around, trying to find somewhere he could go to be alone so he could talk to Alan. He needed to know what the hell had just happened. "Is there a bathroom nearby?"

"Just that building there." Erik pointed to a small two-door building close to where they sat. "Do you need help?"

"No. I can make it on my own." Nathan stood and headed toward the restrooms, praying Alan followed him. He entered and locked the door behind him. Leaning his ass against the sink, Nathan crossed his arms over his chest and rubbed his upper arms. Alan appeared a second later.

"Get out of here, Nate!" Alan exploded. "It's him. Matthew. He's the one who ran me off the road!"

"What? Are you sure? Why would he want to hurt you?"

Alan shook his head. "It's still a little fuzzy. I was at Erik's office. Erik wasn't there, but Matthew was. I recall being angry with him and I-I can see myself yelling at him. He… Oh God. He had a gun!" Rubbing his temples, Alan stared at the floor, his face filled with absolute horror. "Somehow, I got away before he could shoot me. I-it was raining. I could barely see. Then I saw his headlights in my rearview mirror."

Tears streamed down Alan's cheeks. "He hit the back of my car. I couldn't stop. The sound of the metal on the guardrail was so loud. But it kept my car from going over the ridge. I couldn't get the door open to get out. It had jammed or something. Then all I remember is the loud sound of Matthew's truck crashing into the back of my car and the ground and trees rushing toward me."

A sob echoed in the tiled bathroom. Alan lifted his gaze to Nathan's. "Matthew killed me."

Erik's words describing Matthew as his cousin and best friend resounded in Nathan's head. How could he possibly convince Erik that Matthew had a hand in his fiancé's death? "Are you sure it was Matthew, Alan? Do you remember why? What were you arguing about?"

Alan ran a hand through his hair. "I'm trying. It was something about books, but I don't know why that would have made him so angry."

Nathan frowned. Books? What the hell could make someone mad enough to commit murder? Nathan's mind flashed to the ledgers at work. The ones he filled out at the end of every shift when he closed out the register. "Alan, isn't Matthew Erik's accountant?"

He could see the moment the realization hit Alan. "He was stealing from Erik," Alan whispered. "I remember now. He'd already taken over a million dollars. I found out by accident. I was in Erik's office, waiting for him to return from a meeting with a client. Erik let me use his computer sometimes to work on some of my classwork. He'd left a couple of spreadsheets open on his desktop and I got bored waiting, so I just started looking at some figures.

"I noticed a discrepancy in one column. A couple thousand dollars. Erik trusts Matthew, so of course he's not going to double check Matthew's calculations. I went to the folder where Erik had stored the sheets and started looking over the others he'd already saved there. Month after month, there was always a discrepancy. Sometimes a thousand, sometimes ten thousand. I went back to the beginning of the year and then opened a sheet from five years prior. The same thing."

Alan scrubbed his face with his palms. "I grabbed every file and copied them to my cloud storage where I kept my homework assignments. I didn't want to say anything to Erik yet, because I wanted to wait until I had all the details. Later that night, I went through every sheet for the previous years and the total came out at just over a million dollars. A million dollars! I couldn't believe Matthew would do that to Erik. They're like brothers!"

Rage crowded Alan's features. "I confronted Matthew the next night. I had to know why, to make him see reason and return the money. Matthew got angry. So angry. It was stupid of me to go on my own, but I couldn't imagine hurting Erik like that if I could get Matthew to stop. That's when Matthew pulled out the gun. You know the rest…"

Nathan wanted to hug Alan but knew it wouldn't be possible. He could feel the anger, the sadness, and the abject horror coming from the other man. "Did you save the documents, or did you erase them?"

"I didn't delete them. I wanted them as proof. But surely, by now, Erik would have discontinued my storage. No way the company would have kept anything over the free two gigs they provide when signing up for an account."

"But you don't know that," Nathan pointed out. "I'll have Erik drop me off at my apartment instead of staying with him. We'll see if the account is still active and if we can retrieve the files. Okay?"

Alan nodded. "Okay. Please… be careful, Nate. I don't want you to be hurt because of me."

"Erik needs to know the truth, Alan. It isn't fair to keep him in the dark out of fear. If the spreadsheets are still there, and we can prove it, I'll bring it to Erik. I don't know how we can prove Matthew killed you, though."

"It doesn't matter. At least they'll arrest him for stealing from Erik. It's all I care about."

"He shouldn't get away with murder, Alan!" Nathan shouted. "It's not right."

"Right or not, unless he confesses, there's no way to prove he did it, Nate."

Nathan wanted to continue arguing with Alan, but Alan was right. Unless Matthew told the truth, there was no evidence to prove it. He also knew he had no choice except to tell Erik about his ability now. How else could he explain how he'd gotten hold of the incriminating spreadsheets? "Meet me at my apartment tonight."

Alan agreed and then faded away. Nathan took a deep breath, opened the bathroom door, and stopped short. Matthew stood there, a strange expression on his face. His gaze flicked to behind Nathan, then back to Nathan's face. "Everything okay?"

"Yeah. Just needed a minute." Nathan gave a strained smile before hurrying back to where Erik stood near a picnic table, talking. Erik took Nathan's hand the moment he reached his side. Nathan felt awful for lying to Erik, even if just by omission. Things were getting so much more complicated, and his silence wasn't helping. He spent the rest of the picnic avoiding Matthew while trying to watch the man. He didn't know what he was even looking for. It wasn't like Matthew would wear a great big sign that said "I'm a murderer!" But Nathan couldn't stop staring at Erik's cousin, waiting for something to happen or the guy to yank out a gun and shoot Nathan. Which was dumb, too, because Matthew couldn't know Nathan even had a clue about Alan's discovery.

He didn't breathe easily until Erik asked if he was ready to leave. "Do you want to leave?" Nathan asked. "We can stay longer."

Shaking his head, Erik said, "It's almost four. The picnic should wrap up pretty soon."

"Okay. If you're certain," Nathan replied. "Do you need to say goodbye?"

"I already did." Erik held his hand out to Nathan. "Let's head out."

To Nathan's dismay, Matthew stopped them near Erik's truck. "You leaving already, cuz? Wanted to talk to you about the McMillan account."

"You know I prefer business to remain at the office. Is it critical?"

Matthew glanced at Nathan and then shook his head. "Nah. We can talk tomorrow." He turned to Nathan. "It was great to meet you, Nate. Hopefully, we'll have time to chat again soon."

Nathan nodded and gave a tense smile. Matthew gave him an oddly intense look before turning away and heading back to the picnic.

Once they were on the road, Nathan said, "Is it okay if you drop me at my apartment? I have some homework to work on with Troy before tomorrow."

Erik frowned. "He's more than welcome at my home if you two have a project together."

Nathan bit back a wince. "It's just easier at my place, is all."

Pulling to a stop at a red light, Erik looked over at Nathan. "What about after you've finished? I was hoping we could talk."

Anxiety spiked in Nathan. "Talk? About what?"

"About what happened back at the picnic." Erik turned his attention to his driving.

"Nothing. I was just feeling overwhelmed. That's all."

Erik didn't appear too convinced by Nathan's words, but he didn't press for more. They pulled up in front of Nathan's apartment building a short time later. The rest of the ride had been tense, and Nathan worried Erik grew tired of his half-truths. He fidgeted in his seat, fingering the strap of his backpack, and glanced at the windows of his building.

Maybe he should start backing off now, before the truth of everything came out. They were so close to the answers for Alan and, hopefully, Alan could be at rest soon. He hated to think of seeing Erik withdraw from him. Especially after everything they'd shared and how Erik made him feel. His heart hurt at the idea of seeing Erik's face filled with anger and betrayal. The idea of never seeing Erik again, never touching him, never feeling his firm hands on his body, the brush of Erik's lips over his, made his soul cry out in pain.

"Thanks," he murmured, his throat tight with emotion.

Erik grabbed Nathan's wrist when he went to exit the

truck. "Nate, what's wrong? Talk to me. I can feel you shutting me out. I thought we meant something to each other these last couple of weeks."

Agony burned in the depths of Nathan's belly. He lied for the hundredth time. "Nothing is wrong. I'm just tired."

Erik looked wounded by Nathan's words. "You're lying. What happened today?"

Guilt stabbed Nathan, hard. He shook his head. "Nothing happened. I really am tired."

Erik released Nathan's wrist and put both hands on the steering wheel, his fingers tightening until the knuckles turned white. "I guess I'll see you tomorrow night, then."

This time, Nathan winced visibly. "I may have to study with Troy again. I'll let you know."

"Fine," Erik ground out.

"Erik, I..." What the hell could he say? "I'm sorry," he whispered, then hopped out of the truck and took the stairs as fast as his bad leg would let him. He slammed his apartment door behind him and leaned against it. A sob broke free and tears spilled down his cheeks. He couldn't fall apart now. He would have to wait until this was all over and he said goodbye to Erik for good.

CHAPTER 22

Nathan sent a text to Troy and asked him to come over with his laptop. After Troy said he was on his way, Nathan went into his bathroom to wash his face and wipe away the evidence of his heartache. He didn't want Troy badgering him about why he was upset. His eyes were still a little red-rimmed when he'd finished, but he could blame it on lack of sleep. He stared at himself in the mirror, his mind still playing through the multitude of outcomes of telling Erik the truth. It always came back to Erik being angry and disbelieving.

Who the hell in their right mind would believe someone could see ghosts? Every other person he'd ever helped connect with their loved one after their death had thought him insane. They'd eventually believed him when he'd told them about things he couldn't have ever known about unless he'd been there.

Sighing, he pushed away from the pedestal sink in his tiny bathroom and turned off the light before leaving. Whatever happened, he couldn't find it in himself to regret being with

Erik. Even though the pain when Erik left him would bring him to his knees.

Troy walked into his apartment a few minutes later. Nathan was making coffee when his door opened. Troy frowned as he closed the door behind him. "What's wrong?"

He should have known washing his face wouldn't work. He shook his head. "Nothing's wrong, Troy. Just tired."

"Don't lie to me, Nate. After everything we've been through together, you can't lie to me. Did you tell Erik? Did the bastard not believe you?" Troy demanded.

Nathan gave a humorless chuckle. "I haven't told him anything. Not yet."

Troy leaned against the counter near Nathan. "Then why do you look like your dog just died?"

"I don't want to talk about it." The coffee finished dripping and Nathan poured a mug full before adding his usual sugar and cream to it. Of course, Troy never could let anything go.

"No secrets, Nate. We agreed, remember? Tell me what's going on."

Knowing he couldn't keep Troy in the dark, Nathan waved toward the couch for Troy to sit and followed him, dropping onto a cushion next to him. He recounted the story of what had happened at the park. How Alan had seen Erik's cousin and remembered everything. Then he told Troy about his fears. About Erik hating him when he broke his relationship with his cousin. About how he'd been lying to Erik since they met. And how he knew Erik would hate him when it was all finally over.

Troy scoffed. "That man loves you, Nate. Whether or not he's told you, it's clear as hell whenever he looks at you. He isn't going to hate you."

"Maybe. Maybe not. But our relationship can't possibly survive the lies or the way I didn't tell him about Alan. How can it? How could he ever trust me again?" Nathan rubbed his eyes with his thumb and forefinger on one hand, his coffee mug in the other.

"I'm not exactly the best to give advice about dating. I haven't had a relationship last longer than a month. But I know it takes a lot of work, and if both of you are willing, I'm sure he will get past this. Give him a chance, Nate."

Nathan blew out a breath and dropped his hand to his lap. "Let's focus on finding those files. Alan should be here soon. We're going to see if we can log into his cloud account. Hopefully, Erik or the provider didn't delete everything since he hasn't used it in two years."

"Ignoring this won't make it go away, you know. But for now, I'll shut up about it."

Troy opened his laptop, connected to the hot spot on his phone, and logged on. He checked some email while they waited. Nathan just stared off into space, trying to blank his mind out and not think about anything else right then. Of course, whenever you didn't want to think of something, your brain would decide that was all it would think about. A headache started at the base of his skull. He got up to take some aspirin, and he'd barely swallowed the pills when Alan appeared.

"He's here," Nathan said, moving back over to sit on the couch again. Troy grunted in acknowledgement.

"What service was he using for storage?"

Nathan looked at Alan. "Dropbox," Alan said.

He repeated it to Troy. "Do you remember your username and password?" Nathan asked.

Alan came closer as he provided the information. Nathan could feel anxiety and fear rolling off Alan. "There's a folder labeled Finances. The files will be in there."

Troy punched in the information and Nathan leaned over

to see. The account logged in without issue and Nathan saw the folder Alan had mentioned. "It's still there!"

"It is?" Alan asked eagerly. "There should be at least five years' worth of spreadsheets in there. I only went back so far. Matthew started working for Erik about a year or two after Erik opened the company."

Nathan relayed Alan's words to Troy and Troy opened several of the sheets. "How do I know what I'm looking at?" he asked.

Alan moved so he could see the screen of the laptop. "There's an Excel file in there labeled Calculations. I put together the different discrepancies for each month and then had a control sheet at the front of the file that calculated the total amounts taken. I think Matthew has been slowly trimming off the top or burying it inside expenses for the company and sending it to an unknown account somewhere. But I didn't know how to get hold of that information since I didn't have actual access to Erik's business accounts and wire transfer information."

"This should be enough, though, right? To prove to Erik money is being taken?" Nathan asked.

"What did he say?" Troy asked. Nathan did a quick recap of what Alan had just said. Troy located the file and opened it, clicking between the different tabs. He let out a whistle. "There's over a million dollars taken here. If he's had another two years to keep doing this, he's gotta be close to another quarter million by now, maybe more."

Troy had always been good at math. Better than Nathan ever was.

"I don't know if it is enough. Erik loves Matthew. He trusts him. But I have no way to get hold of the actual wire transfer records. I'd be willing to bet Matthew deleted them or is the only one who has access to them," Alan said.

Nathan relayed Alan's words to Troy.

"Kinda dumb to keep that kind of evidence," Troy said distractedly. They watched as Troy went through each of the sheets, highlighting some of the info. "I may know someone who can hack into Matthew's computer and get those records if they exist. But it's not cheap, and we'd have to get Matthew's IP address."

"Oh, like that's going to be so easy," Nathan replied sarcastically. "I'll stroll on into Erik's office and just ask Matthew for it nicely."

Troy gave Nathan a disgruntled look. "I wasn't being sarcastic. No need to be an ass. But you and Alan are probably the only ones who *can* get into Erik's building to get it."

"I can't go alone," Alan said. "I've tried so many times to get there on my own. It's like an invisible wall. You'd have to go with me, Nathan. I don't know why I can follow you but can't get there on my own."

"What about Erik's house?" Nathan asked, frowning. "You've never followed me there."

Pain exploded over Alan's features. "I couldn't be there. Not when I knew he wanted you."

Nathan winced. "I'm sorry, Alan."

"I followed you there. Once. I saw you both through the window. It was too much." Alan glanced away from Nathan.

"What's he saying?" Troy asked, brows creased in confusion.

"He can't get to the office on his own." Nathan explained about Alan being able to go with him. He left out the part about Alan's pain. Troy didn't need to know. "There's no other way for us to get Matthew's IP address? We have to get to the physical computer?"

"Every PC has its own unique address. It's kind of like your apartment. While you live in the building and that building has an address, your unit number separates your apartment from the others. Without that information, there's nothing he can do."

"He doesn't have any special ways to get it?"

Troy raised a brow at Nathan. "He's not a Jedi Master. Even hackers need information to penetrate people's computers and phones. Why do you think I'm always telling you to be careful when you read your emails and stuff?"

"What if we send him an email with a file that has a tracker on it, then?" Nathan asked eagerly. "We could use one of the spreadsheet files! He'd have to open it then. We could even hint at what's in the file. There's no way he could ignore it."

"I know his email address," Alan interjected.

A speculative look came over Troy's face. "Maybe. Let me give Gray a call."

Nathan felt giddy at having come up with a plan. One that wouldn't put all of them in the deepest of shit trouble.

"I don't like this," Alan murmured near Nathan. "What if he figures out where it came from?"

"How can he possibly know?" Nathan asked, brows drawing together. Troy had set his laptop aside and stood over by Nathan's kitchen sink. He only heard a portion of Troy's conversation with his friend. "We can create a bogus email address. Like in Gmail. We don't even have to use our actual information to create the account."

Alan still didn't look convinced. "I'm just worried he's going to figure out it's you, Nate. I don't want you to get hurt. Not for me." He paused, his features tightening. "And especially because of Erik. While it pains me to admit it, you make him happy. His face lights up when he sees you."

Nathan wanted to hug Alan but knew he couldn't. He looked down at his hands on his lap. "He won't be so happy when he finds out the truth."

"Give him a chance, Nate. You're underestimating him."

"What about my ability to see and talk to ghosts?" Nathan asked bitterly. "Who could understand that? He's going to think I'm insane."

Alan came closer and perched on the edge of the coffee table in front of him. "Troy understands."

"He's been my best friend for over half our lives. He doesn't count."

"Why not? He loves you. He accepts what you can do. Erik will, too."

"My aunts don't," Nathan responded, his chest aching. His aunts loved him, he knew they did, but they'd never believed him when he'd told them about the ghosts. "They were the ones who had me put in an institution for six months. Until I'd lied enough to convince them I no longer saw ghosts."

Nathan sighed and ran a hand through his hair. "I shouldn't be talking to you about this. It's not fair to you."

Alan snorted. "I may be dead, but I've been known to have a pretty good ear to bend." He brushed off one shoulder, his mouth twisted in a playful grin. "They're pretty tough."

"But it's about Erik," Nathan said. "I can feel how much it hurts you."

He waved away Nathan's words. "I'm not naïve. I knew he'd move on someday, and I'm glad it's with you. Of course, it hurts to see him doing it. After all, again, I'm dead and it isn't something I expected to witness. But you're good for him, Nate. You make him laugh."

"Is that enough?" Nathan asked.

"It's worth more than you know."

Nathan looked at Alan, hope warring with doubt inside of him. "Do you really think he'll believe me when I tell him about being able to see you and other spirits?"

"Honey, if anyone is going to believe you, it'll be him. Besides, when you tell him, I'll be there. I can tell you things you couldn't possibly know without me."

Nathan frowned. "I'm wondering if something is going on because for the last two weeks, I haven't seen a single damn ghost aside from you."

Alan gave him a brilliant smile. "That's because of me. I told the rest to take a hike."

Brows practically disappearing into his hairline, Nathan asked, "What? I didn't even know you could talk to each other!"

"Oh, yeah. It's not exactly the liveliest bunch of people around. I mean, everyone's dead and unable to move on. It's actually kind of depressing." Alan frowned. "That makes me sound like an asshole, but it's true."

"Where do you go when, you know, you disappear?" Nathan asked. He'd never really tried to learn anything from the spirits he'd helped over the last six years. "Is it, like, a giant room or something?"

Chuckling, Alan shook his head. "It's not a room or anything. More like a state of conscience that we are all stuck in. Some are more… aggressive than others and some are just ready to move on to wherever it is when we finally go."

"You don't even know where that is?"

"Nope. Mostly because I haven't been there." Alan shrugged. "None of the others really know, either."

"How many are there? Am I the only person alive who can see you?"

"I can't say for sure how many people are stuck. I'm not even sure we all go to the same place or if it's a numbers game or even just who died in this county. And as far as I know of, you're the only one." Alan gave him a speculative look. "Although I'm willing to bet you aren't the only one. People have near-death experiences every day. So why would it only be you?"

"Mine wasn't near-death. I died," Nathan explained.

"Still, other people die and CPR or other means bring them back."

Nathan had never thought about asking any of the others further questions. He'd just wanted to get them out of his life as fast as he could. But Alan's explanation made him want to help the others. They were stuck and couldn't move on. Wouldn't he want someone to help him? For the first time since he'd realized what he could do, Nathan felt as if his ability wasn't a curse. He had always believed that he had received it as a punishment for his selfishness in causing his parents' deaths. Alan's explanation pushed his train of thought to another track. Maybe he'd been more selfish at ignoring the others he'd refused to acknowledge over the years.

Another thought hit him. "Alan? Do you know all the others where you go?"

"Not personally, but I've had conversations with a few of them. Some I just know of by sight. Why?"

Nathan took out his wallet and pulled out the worn photograph of his parents that he carried with him. He showed it to Alan. "Have you ever seen either of these people?"

Understanding dawned on Alan's face. "These are your parents, aren't they?"

He nodded.

Sadness trickled over Nathan's skin, twisting his stomach into knots. He knew part of it was from him, but the other half came from Alan. "I'm sorry, Nate, but I've never seen either of them. That could be a good thing, though. It means they moved on. They aren't stuck here."

Disappointment bit deep, but he knew Alan had to be right. His parents hadn't lingered. "It's okay. You're right. At least I know I haven't left them suffering since the accident."

"You know the accident wasn't your fault, right, Nate?"

"Isn't it?" Nathan replied. "I'm the one who demanded they leave the party. If we'd stayed, they'd still be alive."

"Nate, who can say it wasn't meant to happen? They could have easily been in another accident the same night, even if they'd left later. No one knows what is going to happen. You can't predict the future. Stop blaming yourself. Forgive yourself. I guarantee your parents don't blame you, and they wouldn't want you to live your life doing that, either. They loved you, Nate."

Alan's words made sense. He knew his parents had loved him. His mother had even told him that right before the explosion. How could he let his guilt go without dishonoring the memory of his parents?

Troy interrupted anything else they might have said. "Gray said we can definitely add an extra passenger to a file. Matthew would have to open it for it to work, though. I can send Gray the file tonight, and he can have it ready for us by tomorrow morning."

"How much?" Nathan asked, recalling Troy's words about it not being cheap.

A wince cut over Troy's features. "Five hundred."

Nathan coughed. "Where the hell are we going to get that kind of money?"

"I can take it out of my savings," Troy said.

"No. Absolutely not. You're saving that to get a better apartment. I won't take your money, Troy."

"What about your aunts?" Alan asked.

"No! Besides, what would I tell them? Hey, Aunt Becky, Aunt Jessica, can I borrow five hundred bucks because see, we're going to bug this guy's laptop to prove he's embezzling from his cousin?"

"No need to get pissy," Alan said.

"I already paid him," Troy interjected.

"You what?" Nathan stood and started pacing. "You

shouldn't have done that."

"I want to help, Nate. You're my best friend, damn it! The sooner you get this over with, the sooner Alan can move on, and the sooner you can stop waiting for the other damn shoe to drop!" Troy shouted.

Pausing in his pacing, Nathan stared at Troy, surprised. "What's that supposed to mean?"

Sighing, Troy placed his hands on his hips. "It's been six years since I've seen you truly happy, Nate. Six long fucking years. You beat yourself up every single day over your parents' deaths. You've been through so fucking much since then with the surgeries on your legs. Then the hospital, when your aunts thought you'd cracked after what happened, and every single time you encountered one of *them*."

"Hey!" Alan protested.

Troy, of course, didn't hear him and kept talking. "I love you, Nate, and I can't stand how you push me away every time I try to help."

Nathan dropped onto the couch, shocked. He'd never realized he'd made Troy feel that way. "I'm sorry," he whispered.

Troy sat next to him and wrapped an arm around his shoulders, pulling him tight to his chest. "You don't have to go through everything alone." He released Nathan and pulled away. "These last few weeks since you met Erik, it was like I'd gotten my friend back. The one before your parents' accident. You were smiling, happy, and even the darkness you carried with you had faded some. Every time I see you now, it's gone just a little more. If five hundred bucks is all it takes to make that darkness disappear, it's worth more than anything I can ever give you."

He'd never thought his decisions were hurting Troy. Nathan gripped his shoulder, squeezing slightly. "I'm sorry, Troy. I didn't know."

Shaking his head, Troy gave him a sardonic smile. "I didn't tell you, but you should know by now, whatever happens to you happens to me. We're best friends. We stick together until we die, and even then, we'll be kicking up shit in the afterlife."

Nathan laughed, his chest tightening with emotion. "You're right. But I'm going to pay you back."

"Nope. I won't accept it."

He rolled his eyes at Troy. "Stubborn."

"Pot meet kettle!" Troy exclaimed.

Alan grunted. "He's got you there, Nate."

"Be quiet," Nathan growled without heat.

"What did he say?" Troy asked. Nathan repeated Alan's words. "First time we agree on something, jerk wad."

"Jerk wad!" Alan squawked. "He's lucky I can't affect the physical plane, or I'd put itching powder in his shorts or mayonnaise on his car door handles."

Nathan started laughing and couldn't seem to stop. "I wish we'd known you when you were alive, Alan."

"So not cool for you two to be talking shit when I can't hear!" Troy said, pouting.

Nathan laughed even harder. He calmed down enough to relay Alan's words to Troy.

"Let's see you try, asshole!"

"He already said he couldn't," Nathan pointed out, grinning so hard his cheeks hurt. "I think I'd pay to see that, though."

The image of Troy squirming and scratching his crotch brought forth more giggles, to the point tears started rolling down Nathan's face. "Oh my God," he said with a gasp.

"Glad you find it so funny, Nate."

"It's not like he actually did it," Nathan pointed out, breathless.

"Whatever. Let me get this file over to Gray and we'll get

a fake email address set up. Which file do you think would be best to use, Alan?"

Nathan looked at Alan, who shrugged. "They're all incriminating, so it doesn't matter, I think. Maybe the one with the most money missing?"

He told Troy what Alan said. Troy grabbed his laptop, combed through the sheets, and found the best one before emailing it over to Gray. Then he opened Google and started creating a new email address. "What should we use? We need something that'll catch his attention."

"What about something hinting about embezzlement?" Nathan suggested.

"We don't want the email to get flagged. They probably have their servers set up to catch email subjects, email addresses, and content to be blocked by a spam filter. We need something that won't be obvious to a filter yet will still catch his eye."

After some discussion, they settled on a generic email address instead, figuring they could always use the subject to grab his attention. Since Gray wouldn't have the file ready until the following morning, they called it a night. Troy left and Alan did his usual disappearing act. Nathan glanced at the time and saw it wasn't much after nine.

His thoughts turned to Erik and how they'd left things earlier. His guilt and fear had caused him to do the same thing to Erik that he'd done to Troy. After changing into a pair of lounge pants and a plain t-shirt, Nathan grabbed his phone and lay down in bed.

Nathan: *I'm sorry.*

If Erik didn't answer, Nathan knew it was his own fault. In some ways, he was beyond his years in maturity, and, in many others, he was still that awkward kid in high school. Mostly with relationships. What the hell did he know about being in an adult relationship? He'd never even had a boyfriend before Erik. They'd never really discussed what was happening between them and if they were at the stage of boyfriends. Maybe he was being stupid. His phone vibrated.

Erik: *What happened today?*

Nathan: *I really felt overwhelmed. I also got scared.*

Instead of a text message, his phone rang. Nathan jumped at the sudden sound in the silence of his apartment. He saw Erik's name on the caller ID, took a deep breath, and answered it. "Hi," he murmured.

"What are you scared of?" Erik asked. Nathan closed his eyes as the deep tone of Erik's voice washed over him. The timbre vibrated through him, straight to his groin. Could he tell Erik the truth? Maybe part of it?

"It's going to sound crazy. We've only known each other a few weeks."

"Tell me," Erik said.

Opening his eyes, Nathan stared across his room at his dresser. The dark wood stood out starkly against the white wall behind it. "Losing you," he answered. "You realizing I'm a hopeless cause and hauling ass in the opposite direction."

He heard sheets rustle on the other end of the phone. Erik must have sat up in bed. "There's nothing that could make me run from you, angel. You're all I think about. What happened today to make you think differently?"

Nathan didn't answer right away. He wasn't ready to tell him about Alan. Not until they had the evidence of Matthew's embezzling. When he finally did answer, he shocked himself because he truly hadn't grasped just how much it was true. "Seeing you with your employees, friends, family. You're successful and mature and beautiful. I've never been in an actual relationship, and I must have seemed so juvenile to the people who care about you."

"No one thought that of you, angel. No one. And if they did, it's nothing I care to know about. It doesn't matter if you've never been in a relationship before. Everything we learn comes from experience. It may sound exceedingly arrogant, but I'm glad I'm your first everything." Erik chuckled into the phone. "That sounded better in my head. You also don't give yourself enough credit. You're kind, sweet, and amazingly sexy, and that's all those people saw today. It's what I see every single time I look at you."

He didn't know Erik thought those things about him. "I-I don't know what to say," he whispered.

"I miss you. You shouldn't be so far away from me. Tell me I can come and pick you up. Bring you where you belong."

His breath caught in his throat and Nathan uttered, "Yes."

"Twenty minutes," Erik growled and disconnected the call.

Nathan got out of bed, pulled on a pair of sneakers, and gathered clothes for the next day, along with his backpack for classes. He sent a quick text to Troy to let him know he wouldn't need to pick him up in the morning like he'd thought. Instead of waiting in the apartment, he locked his door and took the stairs to the street.

He couldn't have kept the smile off his face when he saw Erik's truck pulling to the curb. Erik waited for him to climb in and settle his stuff on the floor by his feet before wrapping his hand around Nathan's nape and yanking him into a deep kiss. "Never shut me out again, angel," Erik snarled against his lips.

"Okay," Nathan replied, warmth flaring in his chest. He loved how gruff Erik sounded. "I won't."

Erik pulled away from the curb and turned the truck toward his house. Nathan settled into the seat and watched the world flash by, finally feeling content for the first time since the park.

Nathan woke the next day, sore and sated. Erik had been practically insatiable the night before. He'd taken Nathan three times and left him gasping for more. He got out of bed, pulled on a pair of lounge pants, and padded into the bathroom. After relieving himself and doing his usual morning routine, he got dressed in the clothes he'd brought with him and went downstairs to find Erik.

Erik stood at the stove cooking breakfast, and Nathan leaned on the doorframe to watch him. His broad back looked amazing in the light blue polo shirt he wore. But Nathan's gaze dropped to the firm, rounded bottom hugged so deliciously in a pair of dark wash blue jeans. Erik turned and smiled at Nathan, his hazel eyes sparkling. "Good morning, angel."

"Morning," Nathan said, moving to sit at the table. Erik dished some eggs and bacon onto the plate in front of Nathan and kissed his temple.

"I hope I didn't wear you out too much," Erik said, a knowing look on his face.

A flush worked its way over Nathan's cheeks. "Not at all."

Erik poured him some coffee, then prepared his own food before sitting across from him. "Do you and Troy still have to work on your project together tonight?"

"I'm not sure," Nathan replied. He knew Troy had told him his friend would have the file ready by morning, but he wasn't sure if they'd work on it at lunch or after classes. "I can let you know later on."

"Did you get a lot done yesterday?"

Once again, guilt stabbed Nathan. He gave a vague reply and changed the subject. They finished breakfast and left the house. Erik gave him a scorching kiss before Nathan climbed out of the truck in front of campus. Troy waited for him on the usual bench, a smirk on his face. "I see you still ended up over at Erik's last night."

Nathan shrugged, unable to erase the smile he wore. "And?"

"Nothing. Just glad to see you so happy." Troy stood and stretched, groaning as several bones popped.

"Anything from Gray yet?"

Troy shook his head. "Morning to him could be 11:59 a.m. I'll keep checking my emails. I moved all the sheets to a thumb drive, just in case. Once we get the rest of the evidence, you can give the entire thing to Erik."

Something Nathan completely dreaded. There was no way he could hand that off to Erik without an explanation of just how he'd come to have it or how he'd even known about Matthew. "I'll see you at lunch," he said as they parted ways.

The morning seemed to drag on and Nathan kept watching the clock. He dreaded Gray sending the file at the same time as being ready to just get everything over with. His nerves couldn't handle the constant suspense any longer. Even if they got the corrupted file over to Matthew, there was no guarantee the man would even open it. Then, if he did open it, Gray would have to dig through everything on

Matthew's computer to find whatever evidence was possible.

He met up with Troy at noon, and Troy confirmed Gray had sent him the file. They spent most of their lunch break working on the email and what to say. Nathan couldn't even imagine eating. His nerves had his stomach twisted so tightly into knots, he felt as though he'd vomit if he ate. Sweat broke out all over his body when Troy finally hit the Send button. Now all they had to do was wait. "How will Gray know if he opened the file?" Nathan asked.

Troy shrugged. "How does any hacker know when someone has opened anything they've sent? I didn't ask him, but I figured there's some kind of alert. He said he'd let me know as soon as Matthew did. I already told him what's going on, brief details, and what he should look for. He's going to send me everything he can find."

Nathan chewed on his lower lip. "Matthew won't be able to detect him in there?"

"No. I doubt a small company like Erik's has high-tech anything to detect him in there. Besides, Gray knows what he's doing. He actually said it would be one of the easiest jobs he's ever done."

They went their separate ways until their class with Professor Johns. Nathan couldn't concentrate in any of his classes and knew he'd need to borrow another student's notes again. Troy showed him the text from Gray, confirming Matthew opened the spreadsheet.

"I don't know if I'm going to survive this," Nathan muttered.

"Relax. There's no way Matthew can trace it back to us." Troy clapped Nathan on the shoulder. "Just concentrate on Professor Johns. The day's almost over and then I'll take you to work."

Nodding, Nathan tried to keep his focus on the professor,

but his mind kept wandering. He barely heard anything the man said and took zero notes. The end of class couldn't come soon enough.

Troy drove him to the music store afterward and hung around instead of leaving. "You aren't trying to get with that server still?" Nathan asked while restocking some returns.

"Nah. Turns out she has a girlfriend already," Troy said.

Nathan grinned at Troy. "Another strikeout, and there's not even a chance for overtime."

Rolling his eyes, Troy replied, "Shut it. We all can't be you and find our perfect match the first time around."

He raised a brow at Troy. "You've had several perfect matches. You just keep running."

Troy's penchant for bailing the second things got serious came from his mother. She'd been through at least a dozen boyfriends since the messy divorce from Troy's father. The fights and the distrust between Troy's parents had left a sour impression on Troy. He'd never come out and say it to Nathan, but Nathan knew Troy well enough to see him following in his mother's footsteps.

A scowl creased Troy's features. He fidgeted with a row of CDs. "I do not."

"You do, too." Nathan moved over to Troy's side, where he placed his hand on Troy's. "Not every relationship ends up like your parents', Troy."

"How would you know?" Troy bit out. "You met Erik, what, three or four weeks ago? Now you're an expert?"

Nathan flinched and pulled his hand away from Troy's, shocked at his attack. They rarely ever fought, and Troy's tone sounded downright mean. He knew the words were an automatic defensive shield, but they still hurt. "Shit," Troy cursed. "I'm sorry, Nate. I-I didn't mean that."

"Didn't you?" Nathan asked, stepping back from him. "You're not wrong. I don't consider myself an expert, but my parents had an amazing relationship before they died. My aunts? They've been together for as long as I've been alive and still love each other. So, maybe I don't know everything about being in a relationship. Hell, I've even doubted myself since things with Erik started."

He paused and looked away from Troy. "But I know what happened with your parents sucked. I've always known you've never stayed long with any of the girls you've dated because of them."

Troy stepped closer and yanked Nathan into a hug. "I'm sorry, bro. I didn't mean what I said. You know I love you, right? I'm happy for you, and as long as Erik treats you right, I won't have to kick his ass."

A laugh bubbled up in his throat. Erik had a couple of inches on Troy and at least thirty pounds of muscle. Troy had defended him in high school a few times when the jocks got it into their heads to pick on him, especially after he came out, but he didn't think Troy could take Erik in a physical fight. "I think I'd like to see that," he joked.

"You never will if he keeps making you happy."

Nathan hugged Troy tight and then let go. "I gotta get back to work."

Just like that, the spat was over, and they moved on to other subjects. Alan showed up two hours into Nathan's shift. "Any luck?" Alan asked, causing Nathan to jump.

"Fuck, Alan," Nathan growled. "Wear a damn bell or something."

Quinn glanced at him and frowned. "You okay, Nate?"

"I'm good," Nathan replied. He was getting too comfortable with not seeing ghosts anymore. At least while dealing with Alan. Nathan knew after he helped Alan, they'd probably come out of the woodwork again. Facing the front of the store, Nathan whispered, "We emailed Matthew a few hours ago. Troy's friend confirmed he opened it. Now we just have to wait until the guy digs through and locates whatever evidence he can find."

"How long is that going to take?" Alan asked.

"I don't know. It could be a couple hours or even a day or two." Nathan straightened some vinyl albums in their rack and moved a couple that were out of order into their correct placement.

Alan sighed. "I'm just ready for everything to be over. Do you know how long it feels since the accident? Decades. We don't exactly have a sense of time when stuck. The only way I could know the date was by looking at a computer screen or someone's phone. And…"

"And what?" Nathan asked. Alan's tone and entire aura had darkened. Usually, Nathan interpreted that as sadness. "And what, Alan?"

"I'm getting weaker," Alan murmured. "It's taking more and more energy for me to remain here. I don't know what will happen when I run out. I'm scared."

"Alan," Nathan whispered. He rubbed his chest, feeling Alan's depression like it was his own. "There has to be something better out there. Otherwise, where do the rest of people's spirits go? Maybe you'll move on. It can't all be a bad thing."

Alan sniffled. "I have a terrible feeling about it, Nate. If I don't finish this, I don't think I'll be going on to any place good. I've never been an overly religious person. Never grew up with it in our house and there are so many raised in the church who hated me, hate others like me, just because of who we are. Do you think there's a Heaven, Nate?"

The conversation had just taken a very serious turn. Nate sighed. "I don't know, Alan. I've wondered the same thing. But if there's a God, how could He let my parents die the way they did? How could He let me live and take them away? Maybe there is and maybe there isn't, but I have to believe there's something good on the other side of that veil. There has to be."

When he turned around, he saw Quinn standing only a few feet away from him with a concerned look on his face. "Who the hell are you talking to, man?"

"Myself," Nathan lied.

"You call yourself Alan?"

Shit. Quinn had heard the whole thing. "He's my alter ego," Nathan joked.

"If you say so," Quinn said, obvious skepticism in his tone.

Instead of replying, Nathan shrugged and went back to his task. Troy left for a little while to get some coffee and something to eat. He'd offered to grab something for Nathan, but he'd refused. The idea of eating still made him nauseous.

When Troy returned, Nathan asked, "Any word?"

"No. It's probably going to take him a while. If he finds anything at all. I don't think the guy would be stupid enough to keep records of his crimes."

"He sent the spreadsheets to Erik."

"Which Erik never really spent any time reviewing, apparently."

Nathan sighed and banged his head on the counter twice. "I just need this to be over."

"You both still need to be careful," Alan said. "If Matt finds out you sent the spreadsheet or that you have any of this stuff, he could come after you, too."

"How can he possibly find out?" Nathan grumbled. "It's not like we signed our names to the email."

"Matt's not stupid," Alan pointed out. "I never really got to know him well enough to know how much he knows about computers."

Nathan lifted his head to stare at Alan. "You think he could know how to figure it out?"

"How?" Troy asked. "There's no trail leading to us.

Anonymous Gmail account. No identifying information on the email itself. Pretty sure he won't have a clue."

Alan frowned at Nathan. "I don't know. I was never really into computers much beyond social media, my blog, and what I needed for school."

Nathan's nerves wound tighter. If Matthew murdered Alan to keep his crime hidden, he could only imagine Matthew would have no issue with killing him and Troy. "God, I hope he can't."

"Relax, bro," Troy said. "He's not going to figure it out."

Nathan's phone vibrated in his pocket, and he pulled it out to find a text from Erik.

Erik: *Tell me I can see you tonight.*

Nathan glanced at the clock. He still had three hours left before the store closed. "Do you think you'll need me tonight, Troy?"

Troy smirked at him. "Erik wanting his snuggle bunny, or he can't sleep?"

"Shut up," Nathan grunted, growing flustered. "Will you need me or not, Troy?"

"Nah. If anything comes up, I'll text you, but I'm pretty sure Gray won't have anything until tomorrow at the earliest."

Nathan: *Yes. The usual time.*

Erik: *Miss you. Can't wait to have you in my arms again.*

Smiling, Nathan closed his eyes for a second to savor the butterflies taking flight in his belly. He craved being around Erik, being touched by him, and Nathan didn't have a clue how he'd survive if Erik ended it when he found out about Alan.

Nathan: *Miss you, too.*

Erik: *Miss the sounds you make when I'm inside you.*

His face caught on fire, and Nathan turned away from

Troy, hiding the blush. Nathan's cock swelled when the memory triggered by Erik's words flashed through his mind.

Nathan: *You're going to cause me to embarrass myself.*

Erik: *Did that turn you on?*

Chewing on his bottom lip, Nathan shifted his stance, trying to diffuse some of the arousal in his groin. It didn't work.

Nathan: *Maybe.*

He watched the three dots as Erik responded. His next text caused Nathan to choke, and he gave a rushed excuse for using the restroom before hurrying to the back. He ran into the bathroom, slamming the door behind him.

Erik: *Do you know, right before you cum, you make this sexy mewling sound? I wish I could hear it right now instead of being in this meeting.*

Nathan: *You are trying to embarrass me! I had to go into the restroom, or I would have!*

Erik sent a devil face emoji. Nathan leaned his head back against the door, palming his hard cock through his jeans.

Erik: *Take your cock out.*

Nathan: *What?*

Erik: *Take out your cock.*

Oh God. Nathan used his free hand to unsnap the button on his jeans and slide the zipper down. The cool air brushing over his heated flesh caused Nathan to hiss. He wrapped his hand around his shaft, squeezing slightly. Nathan closed his eyes. He'd never considered doing something so sinful as jerking off in public.

Erik: *Stroke yourself. Imagine my hand on you, touching you. I can almost hear the sounds you make when you're close.*

Panting, Nathan licked his palm, then slid his hand up and down his dick. With his trembling free hand, he responded.

Nathan: *I've never done anything like this before. God, I wish you were here.*

He moved his hand faster, his breathing growing deeper. When his phone rang, Nathan jumped, surprised at the loud noise in the bathroom's quiet. He saw Erik's name and answered. "H-Hey," he moaned into the phone.

"Fuck, I wish I could see you right now," Erik growled. "Tell me what you're doing."

The rustle of fabric came through the line. "I-I'm touching myself."

"Your hand is on your cock? Stroking it? Imagining it's my hand?" Erik groaned.

His cheeks grew hot, but Nathan couldn't bring himself to stop. "Y-yes."

"Tell me how your cock feels," Erik demanded, his breathing getting shakier.

"H-hot." Nathan whimpered. "So hot and hard." He swiped his thumb over the head, smearing the clear fluid. His prick wept copious amounts, slicking the length of his shaft, driving his lust higher.

"Do you want my mouth on you? Taking you down my throat?" Erik snarled.

"Oh fuck, yes," Nathan said with a moan, tugging himself faster.

"Can you feel it? My tongue sliding over the smooth, heated flesh of your cock, angel?"

Nathan's balls pulled tighter to his body as he approached the edge of bliss. He couldn't have stifled the grunts and moans he let out with each hard jerk of his hand. The vein lining the underside of his shaft throbbed in tandem with the beat of his heart. He tucked the phone against his shoulder, freeing his hand to cup his testicles. "Erik."

"Are you going to cum, angel?" Erik's words sounded shaky, and Nathan knew the man had to be close himself.

The knowledge of such a sexy, gorgeous man like Erik masturbating to the image of sucking Nathan off pushed him right to the brink.

"So cl-close," Nathan panted.

Erik grunted in his ear. "Cum, angel. Cum for me while I swallow every drop."

The words were exactly what Nathan needed. His toes curled inside his sneakers as Nathan shouted and arched his back away from the door. Seed spurted from the tip of his cock and hit the vinyl floor in hard splatters. His chest heaved with every breath he sucked into his burning lungs. Head spinning, Nathan slumped against the door, his hand still holding his dick. "Holy shit," Nathan rasped.

Erik hummed in agreement, huffing right along with him. "You are amazing, angel."

Embarrassment hit Nathan hard. Not because of what he and Erik had done, but because he knew there was no way someone hadn't heard him. "I can't believe I did that."

"Next time, I want to see you," Erik said. "I'll be there to pick you up at ten."

"Yeah," Nathan murmured. They disconnected the call, and Nathan groaned as he cleaned himself the best he could with toilet paper. He stuffed his softened dick into his pants before wiping the floor clean, too.

When he exited the bathroom, he stopped to take a deep breath. The second he stepped out of the back, Troy gave him a knowing smirk. Quinn looked everywhere but at Nathan. Heat flooded his cheeks, but he kept his head high, ignoring them. Alan seemed to have disappeared. Shit. No way Alan hadn't heard either.

"Not a word," he snapped at Troy, who held his hands up.

"Not saying a word," Troy said, eyes twinkling with mirth.

The rest of the time flew by quickly. A half hour before Erik was due to show, Troy got a text from Gray letting him know he'd found what they wanted. Matthew really must have been stupid enough to keep the records. Nathan guessed he never intended to get caught, since Erik trusted him and the one person who'd known the truth was dead. Gray sent Troy the files to the same email they'd used to plant the malware on Matthew's laptop. Troy immediately saved those to the same thumb drive where they had Alan's files saved.

While in the inbox, Troy also found a reply from Matthew's email address. "Fuck," Troy murmured, reading it. "He wants to meet. He's offering fifty thousand dollars for the copies and to keep our mouths shut."

"Are you kidding me?" Nathan demanded, moving to Troy's side to read the email. "Jesus Christ."

"Maybe we can use this to our advantage," Troy said. "Talk to Erik. Tell him, Nate. The truth. Then Erik can be there to confront him."

Fear and anxiety slammed into Nathan. He hadn't expected to have to tell Erik the truth so soon. After what they'd done on the phone, Nathan couldn't imagine dealing with that right now. But Troy was right. Erik needed to know, as much as his heart hurt at the idea of Erik turning his back on him when he revealed everything.

"I'll be there, Nate," Troy said. "I can help him understand."

"You mean help him think I'm not insane?" Nathan asked bitterly.

"He won't think you're insane." Nathan almost jumped out of his skin. Alan stood a few feet from him, a sad smile on his face. "Erik will believe you, Nate. You must know by now, he loves you."

"What?" Nathan asked. "It's too soon. We've only known each other for a few weeks."

Alan shook his head. "It was fast with us, too, and I can

see it when he looks at you. Even if he hasn't told you yet, he loves you."

Nathan stumbled slightly, grabbing hold of the edge of one of the wooden CD racks. "How can he love me when he doesn't even know me?"

"He knows you, Nate. Better than you think. If there's one thing I am certain about Erik, it's that he knows you. He sees your heart. He's always been good at that."

"If he's so good at seeing someone, then how does he not know about Matthew's true nature?" Nathan challenged, afraid to believe such a kindhearted, beautiful man could ever love him.

"He's blind with Matthew because he believes Matthew is a good person. They've been there for each other since they were kids." Alan shrugged. "I wasn't even sure if I showed him the spreadsheets that Erik would believe me. I still had to try, but I never got the chance."

Troy glanced at the spot Nathan was speaking to. "I may not know everything he's saying, Nate, but I believe Erik loves you. I've seen the way he looks at you. The way he worries about you." Troy moved to Nathan's side and set a hand on his shoulder. "You're my best friend, Nate. We've been there for each other through a lot of bullshit. I would never tell you something that would get you hurt. Erik loves you. Give him a chance."

Tears burned the back of Nathan's eyes. He couldn't lose Erik. His life had finally started having meaning again. For once, he'd believed that maybe he deserved a future. One that wasn't saturated with death and guilt. "I do-don't wanna lose him, Troy," Nathan replied, his voice cracking in agony.

Troy shook his head and squeezed his shoulder. "You won't, Nate."

"How can you be so sure?" Nathan asked.

"I know this is a shitty way to answer that, but I just do. I can feel in my bones Erik won't hurt you by walking away."

Nathan searched Troy's gaze, looking for answers. Of course, there weren't any. Life didn't work that way, though God knew Nathan wished it did. He gave a shaky nod. "Okay."

Alan gave Nathan another sad smile. "I know he's right, Nate. Even though it hurts, I want you to know that I am glad you found each other. He's happy again. I don't want him to be heartbroken for the rest of his life. He deserves to be with someone who makes him smile and laugh. Even if that person can't be me."

Then Alan chuckled and winked at Nathan. "Even if I'm obviously more handsome than you."

Nathan gave Alan a trembling smile. "I may disagree with you there, but thanks, Alan."

Rolling his eyes, Alan said, "Now stop worrying. Everything is going to work out. If Erik even thinks for a minute that you aren't telling the truth, I'll haunt him for the rest of his life until he gets his head out of his ass."

He gave Alan a watery laugh. "Hopefully it won't come to that."

"It really sucks not being able to hear both sides of the conversation," Troy said in complaint.

Nathan laughed harder. "Would you rather be able to hear and see Alan then? You're already at each other's throats. Imagine him being able to haunt you."

Troy gave Nathan a horrified look and shuddered. "Hell no! Jesus."

He couldn't help it. Nathan threw his head back and laughed even harder. Tears began rolling down his cheeks. When he'd finally calmed down, Troy gave him a goofy grin. "It's good to see you laughing like that, Nate."

Nathan cleared his throat and glanced away. Troy was

right. He couldn't even remember the last time he'd laughed until he'd cried. He looked at the clock and saw only ten minutes remained until closing. "Wait here while I get started on balancing the register. Erik said he'd be here at ten."

"Is it cool if I bounce? I got a test tomorrow to study for," Quinn said when Nathan reached the front desk.

"Yeah, sure. I'll see you tomorrow."

Quinn headed into the back to clock out and grab his stuff. When he came back out, he stopped at the counter. "Nate, I'm not sure what is going on, but I heard some of the conversation between you and Troy. Be careful, okay? People who steal get angry when someone threatens the money they're after."

Nathan's mouth dropped open for a split second. He hadn't realized Quinn had heard all that. "Oh, uh, yeah, I don't plan on approaching the guy."

"If you need help or anything, call me, okay?"

"Thanks, Quinn," Nathan said.

Quinn smiled. "No worries, brother. I'll see you tomorrow, right?"

"Same time, same channel."

"I'm holding you to that, Nate." Quinn tossed a wave at Troy before leaving.

CHAPTER 24

Nathan began pulling the receipts for the night. "Troy, can you turn the sign to closed for me?" Nathan asked his friend when the clock hit ten.

Troy went over to the door, locked it, and flipped the sign. Nathan started doing his usual tasks to close out the register. He glanced up when he heard Troy open the door. Erik entered, looking sexy as hell in a tight white Henley and faded black denim jeans.

"Hey, angel," Erik said with a smile when he saw Nathan looking at him.

Nathan flushed, recalling their earlier stolen moments on the phone. "Hey."

Erik strode toward him, pulled him into a tight hug, and kissed his temple. "How was your day?"

"It was good. Same as usual."

"Did you get something to eat?"

He shook his head. "No. I wasn't hungry."

Erik gave him a stern look. "You need to eat."

"I really wasn't hungry. I'll eat later."

Nathan broke away from Erik's hold to finish his task.

Fifteen minutes later, Nathan went into the back to clock out. He turned off the lights and followed Troy and Erik from the store. Troy looked at Nathan, one brow raised. He knew he couldn't avoid the conversation with Erik.

"Is there somewhere we can go to talk?" he asked Erik.

Erik frowned. "Something wrong?"

"There's just some things we need to talk about."

"Sure, angel." Erik's brow furrowed. "We can go to my house."

"Troy is going to follow us there, okay?"

"Okay. You're worrying me, Nate. What's going on?"

"Just… We can talk when we get to your house." Nathan got into Erik's truck and closed the door. Erik glanced at Troy, trying to pick up on what was happening, but he didn't ask again before getting into the truck, too. Nathan felt more than saw Alan behind him in the truck. He must have gotten in while Nathan finished closing the store.

The ride to Erik's was tense, and Nathan could practically feel the apprehension from Erik. He wanted to take Erik's hand, but right now, he wasn't sure if he could do that and still have the courage to come clean with Erik.

Once they'd reached Erik's home, Troy sat on one recliner while Erik took a seat on the couch. Alan wandered the living room, pure sadness radiated from him. Nathan paced to the front window and back to the couch. He couldn't even imagine where to start.

"Talk to me, angel," Erik said, sitting forward on the edge of the couch cushion. "What's going on?"

Nathan stopped, picking at one of his fingernails, still not meeting Erik's gaze. "I told you about the accident when my parents died, but there's something else I didn't tell you."

Erik nodded and waited for Nathan to finish. "While they were trying to save my life, I died on the operating table. For six minutes. They almost couldn't get my heart to restart."

An intake of air was Erik's only response. Nathan swallowed past the lump in his throat. He started pacing again. "When I… When I came back, I came back different."

Erik frowned. "What do you mean, different?"

Nathan halted and gave Erik a pleading look. "Please… let me get through this before you say anything."

Erik nodded again while Nathan returned to his nervous pacing.

"I didn't realize it at first. I just thought they were patients or visitors to the hospital. It wasn't until I was talking to someone, and a nurse came in…" Nathan glanced at Troy, who gave him an encouraging nod. Sweat broke out over Nathan's body. "She asked me who I was talking to. I told her I was talking to the other patient standing by the window."

He peeked at Erik and saw confusion on his handsome face. "The nurse said no one was there," he whispered. "I kept insisting there was. She called the doctor in and the next thing I knew, they had a psychiatrist in my room."

True to his word, Erik didn't ask or say anything, but Nathan could see some comprehension coming over Erik's features. "I didn't understand how they couldn't see him or hear him. It wasn't until a few days later when I saw someone, a woman with ha-half her skull crushed in, that I realized they weren't seeing them because… they were dead."

Nathan wrapped his arms around himself and turned away from the couch. He couldn't stand to see the pity and disbelief change Erik's expression. "They said my mind was making things up to protect myself from the tragedy of the crash. From losing my parents. T-the only one who believed me was Troy. My aunts, they love me, but they agreed with the doctors."

He gave a harsh chuckle, no humor in it. "Aunt Becky didn't want to admit me to the psychiatric ward, but Aunt Jessica talked her into it. I spent six months there. Finally, I learned to stay quiet and pretend the ghosts weren't there in order to go home."

A warm hand coming to rest on his shoulder startled Nathan. When he looked up, he saw Erik standing beside him just before Erik pulled him into a crushing embrace. His voice vibrated in his chest beneath Nathan's ear when he spoke. "I believe you, angel."

Tears fell, trickling down Nathan's cheeks. "Y-you do?" he asked, incredulous.

Erik tightened his arms. "I do." He pulled away enough to look at Nathan. "That's why you were upset at the diner that night, isn't it?"

"You remember that?"

Smiling softly, Erik cupped Nathan's cheek, running his thumb over the smooth skin there. "I remember everything about you."

Nathan wrapped his arms around Erik's waist and burrowed against him. Erik believed him. The knots in Nathan's stomach didn't unravel, though. He still had to tell Erik about Alan.

"You still see them then," Erik said.

Pulling away and swiping at his cheeks, Nathan nodded. "Yes. It's been six years since the accident, and I still see them."

Erik took Nathan's hand and led him to the couch, where he sat and pulled Nathan down next to him. He didn't release Nathan's hand, entwining their fingers together instead. "Do they frighten you?"

Nathan shrugged. "Sometimes. They can't physically hurt me. At least, I've never had one try."

"Do they ever leave you alone?"

Snorting, Nathan said, "Not if they know I can see them." He glanced at Alan for a second, who had the grace to give him a chagrined smile. "The ones who do… the only way I can get them to go away is by helping them."

"Helping them?" Erik asked, frowning. "What do you mean, helping them?"

"They're stuck here because there's something keeping them here. Usually, they need help talking to their families. There's been a couple where they had me tell their wives about an insurance policy or something about their finances."

"Then they go away?" Erik asked.

Nathan nodded. "Yes. They go wherever people go when they die, I guess. After helping them, I never see them again."

He knew he wasn't getting to the point and Troy prodded him with his foot. "There's something else I have to tell you," he said.

Erik waited patiently. Nathan looked down at their hands lying on Erik's thigh. "Alan's with us."

Silence met Nathan's declaration. He took a deep breath before looking at Erik. Surprise, sadness, and pain warred for residency on Erik's face. "I'm sorry, Erik. I wanted to tell you sooner, but I didn't know how," Nathan murmured.

"He's here? With us now?" Erik asked, releasing Nathan's hand. Nathan bit back the pain Erik's action triggered. He couldn't blame him. The man he loved stood a few feet away from them. "Why? How?"

Instead of remaining at Erik's side to be rejected again, Nathan stood and moved away from the couch. He didn't approach Alan because he knew Alan's emotions were no doubt running high with finally being able to talk to Erik. "I met him the same day I met you," Nathan said. "He got me kicked out of my class because I made a mistake and acknowledged him."

Alan had tears in his eyes, and he gave Nathan a watery

smile. "Tell him I love him. Tell him I miss him so damn much."

A lump formed in Nathan's throat, and he had to swallow twice to speak past it. "He says he loves you and he misses you."

Erik jerked as though struck. Nathan's heart clenched at the utter wonder and love on Erik's face. "Alan?"

Nathan stifled the pain he felt. He'd fall apart later when he went back to his apartment. "He's here and he can hear you."

"Oh God, Alan," Erik rasped. "I miss you so much, too. All this time?"

Nodding, Nathan looked at Alan, who moved closer to where Erik sat. "He's been stuck here because there's something he needed to tell you. It... It took a while for him to remember what it was."

"What? What does he need to tell me?" Erik asked, eyes darting everywhere as if he could see Alan.

"He's standing by the couch," Nathan said. "To your left."

Erik turned toward Alan. He didn't even look at Nathan when he asked, "What is it? Tell me."

Nathan hadn't even realized Troy had moved until he stood next to Nathan and placed a hand on his shoulder. He gave Nathan's shoulder a slight squeeze in comfort and encouragement. "It wasn't an accident. Someone murdered him," Troy said. "Your cousin, Matthew."

Erik whipped his head around so hard Nathan almost found the situation laughable. Almost. "What the fuck?" Erik snapped. "Is this some kind of sick joke?"

"No!" Nathan protested. "He's telling the truth. Give him the USB, Troy."

Troy eyed Erik for a moment before heading to his bag near the recliner. He opened the side pocket and took out the drive. "Alan found out Matthew has been stealing from you for years," Nathan said. "He confronted Matthew with what he'd discovered, hoping Matthew would stop and tell you the truth. He tried to attack Alan, but Alan got away. Matthew followed him, ran him off the road, and Alan hit the guardrail."

Nathan stopped, needing a chance to breathe. He could see Erik vibrating with rage. "The g-guardrail stopped his car from going over the edge. He w-would have been fine, but M-Matthew rammed him with his truck, pushing him over and into the ravine."

Troy handed Erik the memory stick. "The proof is on there. Nathan's telling you the truth."

"How did you get this?" Erik demanded, standing from the couch.

"Nate, tell him I hated the pink flowers my mother picked out for the wedding," Alan said.

He gave Alan a puzzled look. "I don't think that matters right now, Alan."

"Just do it. He'll know."

Erik looked at Nathan. "What's going on?"

"Alan says he hated the pink flowers his mother chose for the wedding," Nathan repeated.

Erik stumbled back a step and dropped back onto the couch. "Jesus. He's really here."

Nathan hid how much his words hurt. Erik had lied only moments ago about believing him. The pain drove right into his heart, and he stifled a gasp. Nathan nodded at Erik. "He is."

"Matthew killed him?" Erik asked, his question almost too low to hear.

"He did," Nathan said. He knew there was no way Erik would want to be with him after this, but he hadn't expected anything different. No. Erik's easy acceptance moments ago had given him hope. Now… his hope lay shattered into a million pieces.

Erik got up, grabbed his laptop from the dining table, and moved back to the couch. He set it on the coffee table and opened it. Nathan watched as Erik reviewed the contents of the USB. Rage flooded his features. "How did you get this?" Erik asked, not looking at Nathan.

"When Alan saw Matthew at the picnic, he remembered everything. Including the spreadsheets he'd had on his cloud storage," Nathan explained. He went on to tell him the details about Gray and what they'd done. By the time he'd finished, Erik looked ready to explode.

"Matthew wants to meet with us," Troy said. "He's offering to give us fifty thousand dollars to keep our mouths shut and give him the evidence we have."

Nathan walked to the window, wrapping his arms around himself. He gritted his teeth to stave off the agony threatening to consume him. Alan came to his side, an empathetic expression on his face. "It'll be okay, Nate."

"No, it won't," Nathan murmured, keeping his voice low. "He hates me now."

"No, he doesn't. He's just hurt by Matthew's betrayal. He loves you, Nate."

Nathan closed his eyes, his chest feeling as though it would cave in because of Alan's words. "Stop," he begged.

Losing his parents had been one of the worst things he'd ever gone through. He would never trivialize losing them. Yet somehow Erik's anger and obvious distrust hit him so much worse. "I think we should agree to the meeting," Nathan said, not looking at the others. "Set up a time and place, and Erik can be there, out of sight, listening."

"What? Fuck no!" Troy shouted. "If he killed Alan, what's to stop him from trying with us?"

Nathan lifted one shoulder in a careless shrug. "It'll just provide the proof Erik needs. Besides, if he shows himself after Matthew makes the offer of the money, I doubt he'll try to kill us in front of him."

"It's too dangerous," Erik said. "We have the evidence we need here. We can take this to the police."

"Do you?" Nathan asked. "Is that enough to prove it was him who killed Alan? They're not going to believe me when you tell them I heard it from Alan's ghost. They're going to think I'm nuts." *Just like you did*, Nathan thought bitterly.

"Matthew will still go to jail for embezzling," Erik said.

"Matthew needs to pay for what he did, Erik," Nathan replied, still facing away from him. "He doesn't deserve to get away with Alan's murder."

"I don't want him killing you, too!" Erik exploded. "Damn it, Nathan. Think this through."

Nathan finally turned to look at Erik. "If you won't help us, we'll go without you. I can record Matthew's confession on my phone."

"God damn it, Nate," Troy growled. He stalked to Nathan and grabbed him by the shoulders. "Erik's right. We can't risk it. We don't even know if he won't just shoot us on sight."

Glaring at Troy, Nathan wrenched away from his hold. "I'm doing this. With or without you."

Erik stood. "No. You aren't."

"Why not? Why do you care?" Nathan spit, finally unable to stamp down the pain. "I'm crazy, right? Nuts? Because I see ghosts? You're just like the rest of them!"

Nathan couldn't handle the pain any longer. He shot past Troy and ripped open the front door, letting it slam against the wall. He took off down the front porch, his leg protesting his fast movements. Before he'd even made it to the sidewalk, he collapsed to the ground, his leg throbbing. Nathan gripped his leg against his chest, rocking at the agony tearing through him.

Curse words rent the air. Erik had followed him out of

the house. He rushed to Nathan and scooped him from the ground, gently carrying him into the house. Nathan clenched his teeth so hard that they should have shattered. He didn't want Erik touching him. It only reminded him of what he'd lost. Erik settled him on the couch, then sat next to him, his hand coming to rest on Nathan's thigh. "Do you have any pain meds?" Erik asked.

Scowling, Nathan refused to answer him. He glared down at the hand on him. Troy started rifling through his backpack. "The doctors won't give him any, but I have a few oxycodone left behind from when I broke my wrist. I left them in my bag in case I ever needed them again," Troy said. "He doesn't like to take meds at all. Especially if they make him loopy."

"Shut up, Troy," Nathan snapped. Erik squeezed his thigh and Nathan shoved his hand off him. "Don't touch me. My crazy might get all over you."

"Damn it, angel!" Erik growled. "You haven't given me any time to adjust to this. I don't think you're crazy. That has never crossed my mind, not even once."

Nathan stubbornly kept his mouth shut, staring away from Erik. His self-defense mechanism kicked in. Anger was the only way to stop himself from falling apart. Troy found the prescription bottle buried in the bottom of his bag. "I found them. I'll get you some water."

Troy set the bottle on the coffee table before heading into the kitchen. Erik sighed. "You took me by surprise. Not because you told me about seeing ghosts, but the whole Matthew thing. He's been my best friend since I can remember."

"And I'm someone you just met three weeks ago," Nathan replied, his tone icy. His shoulders slumped in defeat.

"That doesn't matter to me, Nate. Three weeks may not seem like a long time, but the last three weeks have been the best I've had since Alan died. I lost myself for a while after Alan. Matthew helped me through that. To know that he's the reason—I believed you about being able to see and talk to ghosts. When Troy said Matthew killed Alan, I couldn't even imagine how either of you could think that."

Nathan tensed when Erik cupped his cheek, coaxing Nathan to look at him. "I'm sorry for getting angry and not believing you about Matthew. But I never, ever thought you were insane."

He searched Erik's gaze for any hint of dishonesty, wanting to trust Erik so badly. Biting his bottom lip, Nathan closed his eyes and leaned into Erik's touch. Erik stroked his thumb along Nathan's cheekbone. "Do you believe me, angel?" Erik asked, his voice deepening.

"I want to," Nathan whispered.

Erik brushed his lips across Nathan's. "You can, Nate. I promise."

Nathan tilted his head forward, kissing Erik back. It was a kiss without heat or passion. Just one seeking comfort from another. Erik glided his hand down Nathan's neck to wrap around his nape. He broke the connection and pressed his forehead to Nathan's. "Do you forgive me, angel?"

"Yeah," Nathan murmured. "I'm sorry for overreacting."

"I understand why you did," Erik said. "It must have been hard when your aunts didn't believe you."

He moved until his head rested on Erik's shoulder. "Troy did. He got me through the last six years. Everyone else faded away because I made them uncomfortable."

Erik slid one arm behind Nathan's back, holding him tightly, and moved to pick up the pill bottle. Nathan shook his head. "I don't like taking them."

"You're in pain, angel."

"I'm used to it," he said.

"You shouldn't be. Please take one. For me?" Erik cajoled. "I hate seeing you suffer. Especially since this is my fault."

Nathan relented and took the pill Erik extracted from the bottle, swallowing it down with the glass of water Troy had set on the table. Troy hadn't stayed in the room, obviously giving them privacy. "Troy," Nathan called.

Troy entered the living room from the kitchen. He sat on the coffee table across from Nathan. "I think we should let the police handle this, Nate. Erik's right. It's too dangerous."

"But we can't let him get away with murder!"

"The police can still get him to confess. He doesn't know the email came from you two," Erik said.

Nathan glanced around for Alan, but with everything that had gone on, including Erik kissing him, Alan had disappeared. He winced at causing Alan more pain. "Alan? Are you here?"

Alan didn't respond. Nathan tried again. "Alan, please."

This time, Alan flickered into Nathan's vision, his form even more translucent than before. "I'm here," Alan said, sounding sad and exhausted.

"Was Erik knowing the truth enough?" Nathan asked.

"Enough for what?" Erik asked, brow furrowing.

"For him to move on. He's stuck here because of what he had to tell you. Or at least that's what we thought."

Alan shook his head. "I don't see a light or anything, if that's what you mean. Just feel weaker."

"Shit. There's gotta be something else. Maybe Alan needs justice for his death. I don't know. All the others I've helped were able to move on after they'd gotten their message to their families."

Erik kept glancing around as though he could see Alan. Nathan nudged him and pointed to where Alan stood. Erik zeroed in on the spot, staring hard. No matter how much he tried, Nathan knew Erik would never see Alan.

"The others, I'd like to hear about them sometime," Erik said. "If you want to tell me about it."

"You really want to?" Nathan asked.

"I do." Erik rubbed Nathan's back slowly. "Is it okay if I talk to Alan and you can tell me what he says?"

Despite knowing being their telephone would be the hardest thing he'd ever done, Nathan agreed. Erik turned his attention back to Alan, no longer touching Nathan. He shoved aside the bereft feeling and concentrated.

Alan moved closer to them. "Tell him I still love him," Alan said. "Tell him I've thought of nothing except him for the last two years, and I'm sorry for confronting Matthew instead of coming to him first."

Nathan repeated Alan's words to Erik, trying to detach himself from the situation. His heart ached at the obvious love on Erik's face. Erik had loved Alan deeply, and Nathan knew he could never compare to Alan. "I miss you so much, Alan. When they told me you were gone, I lost myself. I buried myself in a bottle and didn't surface for weeks."

Tears glistened in Alan's eyes. "I miss you, too."

Again, Nathan parroted what Alan said.

"I will make sure they punish Matthew for what he did to you, Alan. I swear it on my life. You'll always be in my heart, sweetheart, and a part of me will always miss you."

The tears in Alan's eyes spilled over, and he choked out a sob. "Tell him… I'm glad he's finally moving on, and I'm glad it's with you. He deserves to be happy and to live his life. Tell him to hold on to you and never let go."

Nathan shifted in discomfort, but he repeated what Alan said. His own throat tightened with emotion.

"I will, sweetheart. I truly hope wherever you are going, you'll be happy there. We'll see each other again someday."

Alan covered his face with his hands and Nathan struggled not to shed tears of his own. He'd helped so many people over the years since the accident, but he'd never gotten close to any of them. Not like he had Alan or Erik. "He —" Nathan stopped to clear his throat. "He's crying."

Erik shook his head. "Please don't cry, Alan."

Letting his hands fall away from his face, Alan smiled through the tears. "I know we got off to a rocky start, Nate. I know I was a bit of a dick when I tried to hurt you. But I want you to know I would have loved having you as a friend while I was alive. I-I hope you consider us friends now."

"We are," Nathan rasped. "I think we would have been great friends."

"No matter what happens, please, just tell him I moved on. Even if I don't."

"Alan, I…" He hesitated. Could he really promise to lie to Erik about the man who'd held his heart? But telling Erik anything else would only hurt him. Nathan knew that, but he still wasn't sure he could promise to keep hidden Alan still being stuck between whatever planes of reality existed.

"Please, Nate. I don't want him to be sad anymore."

Nathan finally nodded. "I will."

"What's he saying?" Erik asked.

"Just how we would have been friends," Nathan lied.

"I-I won't come back again," Alan said. "Please be careful with Matthew. He's dangerous."

"We will be," Nathan said.

Alan smiled again, moving closer. He reached out and gently rested his hand against Erik's cheek. Erik sucked in a deep breath, shivering. Nathan knew Erik had to feel the coldness of Alan's spirit against him. "He's touching your cheek," Nathan murmured.

Erik pressed his own hand to his cheek. Alan gave Nathan one last look before dissipating.

"He's gone," Nathan said.

"Gone?" Erik asked. "Like moved on or just left?"

"I-I don't know." Nathan could feel the pain pill kicking in. His blood seemed so warm beneath his skin and his mind became fuzzy. "I think he moved on." Nathan slouched into the back of the sofa. "We still need to come up with a plan to trap Matthew."

Shaking his head, Erik replied, "We are going to let the police handle it. I'm going to call a friend of mine, a detective. He'll take it from there."

He didn't argue this time. Mostly because the meds were making him drowsy, and he could barely hold his head up. It wasn't until Erik woke him by lifting him from the couch that Nathan realized he'd fallen asleep. The living room was dark, and Troy had left. "Go back to sleep, angel," Erik murmured. "I'm just taking you to bed."

"Okay," Nathan said. He yawned and burrowed closer to Erik, closing his eyes again.

CHAPTER 25

The early light of morning awakened Nathan. His leg throbbed slightly, but it didn't hurt as badly as the night before. He sat up and tested his weight on it, needing to use the bathroom. A sigh of relief slipped free when he found he could walk on it, albeit with a more pronounced limp than usual. After he relieved himself and washed his hands, Nathan opened the door to find Erik standing at his dresser, pulling clothes out.

"Good morning, angel," Erik said, his voice sleep roughened.

"Morning," Nathan said. He felt uncomfortable knowing Erik knew the truth about him. There was also still a little voice in his head telling him Erik hadn't believed him. Maybe that voice would never go away and maybe that voice was right. Erik may have greeted him good morning, but he also didn't look Nathan's way. He didn't even try to give Nathan a hug or kiss, something Nathan had begun to anticipate over the last couple of weeks. Instead of either, Erik brushed past him to use the restroom himself.

Nathan dressed in the same clothes as the day before,

then made his way downstairs instead of waiting for Erik. His heart ached. Even though Erik claimed to believe him, he treated him differently already. Clenching his jaw, Nathan refused to let Erik see the way it hurt him. He made coffee and texted Troy while he waited for it to brew. Instead of an uncomfortable ride to campus, Nathan would rather have Troy come get him.

The coffee finished brewing by the time he heard Erik's footsteps on the stairs. Nathan poured a cup for himself and added sugar and creamer. Erik seemed lost in thought when he entered the kitchen. His usual morning smile was gone, and Nathan waited for Erik to say something, anything, but Erik made his own coffee in silence.

Clearing his throat, Nathan said, "Troy is picking me up for class this morning."

Erik finally looked at Nathan, his brow furrowed. "Why? It's out of his way. I can drop you off like usual."

Nathan shrugged. "Just figured it would be better to have him take me."

The furrowed brow turned into a full frown. "What's that supposed to mean?" Erik demanded.

"It doesn't mean anything," Nathan muttered, looking away from him.

Erik stepped in front of Nathan, and with a finger under his chin, he coaxed Nathan to look at him. "What's going on, angel?"

"You tell me," Nathan challenged.

Surprise filled Erik's features. "What are you talking about?"

Nathan wrenched away from Erik and put some space between them, unable to stand Erik touching him with his heart breaking inside his chest. "You've barely looked at me this morning. You've hardly even spoken to me. I'm not stupid, Erik. I know that you still think I'm lying or that I'm nuts."

"That's not it at all, Nate," Erik said. "I believe you. I'm just trying to sort out the situation with Matthew in my head. That's all."

Hesitation and uncertainty kept Nathan where he was. He didn't want to continue to sound like an immature kid. Though he supposed compared to Erik, he was. Nathan studied his face, looking for any evidence the man lied.

Erik sighed and took a couple of steps toward Nathan. When Nathan didn't move away again, Erik closed the distance between them and pulled him into a tight embrace. "I'm sorry, angel. I didn't mean to make you doubt me. Truly."

The stiffness went out of Nathan's body, and he sagged against Erik, tentatively wrapping his arms around his waist. Erik kissed his temple. "I know you've been hurt by those who didn't believe you, baby, but please trust in me when I say I'm not one of them."

Nathan swallowed before whispering, "I do trust you."

He didn't release Nathan, only gripped him tighter. "I spoke to my friend Detective Holt Forrester last night. Holt is already working on the investigation. I emailed him all the files from the thumb drive. He's pretty sure they can make an arrest later today."

"I'm so sorry, Erik," Nathan said. "About Matthew. About Alan."

Erik ran a hand along Nathan's back in a soothing manner. "I've grieved over Alan. I still miss him, but at least now he'll have justice. Matthew's betrayal hurts. Since we were kids, we've always had each other's backs. To know he —" Erik's voice cracked.

Nathan nuzzled at Erik's throat, squeezing him a fraction more, hoping to offer some level of comfort. He said nothing else because what could he say? He still worried Erik would hate him for being the messenger that shattered his friendship with his cousin. Wasn't the phrase "Don't shoot the messenger" or something along those lines?

Erik broke the extended silence. "Text Troy and tell him not to come. Please. I'd like to take you to get something to eat before class."

"Are you sure?" Nathan asked.

"Always," Erik murmured before taking Nathan's mouth in a soft kiss. There was no passion behind the action, it was more an act of comfort. Erik leaned his forehead against Nathan's when he broke the kiss. "Whenever you're doubting anything, angel, talk to me. Ask me. Okay?"

Nathan nodded, closing his eyes for a moment. "Okay."

"Good. Text Troy."

Retrieving his cell phone from the counter where he'd left it, Nathan sent off the message and then stuffed the phone into his pant pocket. He grabbed his bag near the couch while Erik went for his keys and wallet by the front door. Once they were in the truck and on the road, Nathan asked, "Did your friend say when they expected to arrest Matthew?"

"Not specifically," Erik replied. "He just said sometime later this morning."

Nathan frowned. "Be careful. If he could hurt Alan, he could hurt you."

"I'd like to believe he wouldn't physically hurt me, but I won't be going straight to the office this morning. Going to check on a couple of jobsites, and Holt said it would be best if I weren't there when they make the arrest."

"I'm glad," Nathan said. "Will you text me when you know they took him into custody?"

Erik grabbed Nathan's hand, kissed the back of it, and laid it on his thigh. "The moment I find out."

A few minutes later, Erik pulled the truck into a space in

front of a small diner. He turned the engine off but didn't get out of the truck right away. Nathan looked over at Erik, confused. "Are we going inside?"

Shifting until he faced Nathan, Erik reached out and tucked a strand of his hair behind one ear. Then he ran his thumb over the ridge of Nathan's cheek. Erik's next words shocked him to his core. "I love you, angel."

Nathan couldn't find words, any words. He opened and closed his mouth several times.

Erik smiled softly. "You don't have to say it back, Nate. Not until you're ready." He leaned over the console and gave Nathan a light kiss, his thumb still caressing his cheek. "I can wait," he murmured against Nathan's lips.

Then Erik pulled away, opened his door, and came around to open Nathan's. He sat there, still blown away at Erik's declaration. "Nate," Erik said, finally rousing him from his thoughts.

"Oh," Nathan said and slid out of the passenger seat. Erik closed the door and Nathan followed him into the diner, where he spent most of the time lost in thought over Erik's words. He'd already wondered if he was falling in love with Erik—more than once—but he had never felt romantic love and didn't know how to tell if he was in love with Erik.

Breakfast passed mostly in silence. Nathan barely registered the food he consumed, eating on autopilot. Erik left him to his thoughts, only prompting him when the server came to the table. When they were back in the truck again, Erik took Nathan's hand in his and twined their fingers together. "I'll pick you up after work tonight like normal, okay?"

"'kay," Nathan said, staring out of the window without really seeing anything going by.

Erik squeezed his hand gently. "I didn't expect you to go monosyllabic on me. Everything good with us?"

"What?" Nathan frowned. "Oh, yeah, everything's fine."

Slowing the truck to a stop at the curb in front of campus, Erik gave Nathan another kiss, this time a little slower and with a little more heat. A flush warmed Nathan's cheeks when Erik broke away and leaned his forehead against Nathan's. "I'll see you tonight, angel."

Nathan nodded, grabbed his bag, and exited the truck, closing the door behind him. Erik smiled at him before pulling back into traffic. Troy waited for him at the usual bench, earbuds in, head moving to the music. When he saw Nathan, he took out his earbuds. "Hey, Nate. Any news about Matthew?"

Dropping onto the bench next to Troy, Nathan told him about the arrest and how Erik would let him know once it was done. "He… uh… He told me he loves me," Nathan murmured.

Troy's eyes widened, and then the biggest grin came over his face. He slapped Nathan on the shoulder. "That's amazing, bro! Did you say it back?"

"No. I-I didn't know what to say."

"Uh, I love you, too, seems like a brilliant response," Troy said, frowning. "Do you love him?"

"I don't know," Nathan said. "How do I know? It's not the same as loving family or friends. I don't know what I feel for Erik."

"Does he make you happy? Is he the first thing on your mind when you get up in the morning and the last when you go to bed at night? Can you imagine a future with him? Without him?"

Nathan thought over Troy's questions. Erik made him unbelievably happy. Every single minute of every single day, Erik was never far from his thoughts. It didn't matter what time of day—beginning, end, middle. The idea of losing Erik made his heart clench and his lungs ache for air. Did all of that equate to love?

"Ah, ah, there it is," Troy said, grinning and pointing at Nathan's face. "You love him, Nate. Now just fess up and tell him."

"I'll try," Nathan said, tilting his head forward so his hair hid his features.

"Have you seen Alan since last night?" Troy asked.

"No."

"Do you think he moved on?"

Nathan shook his head. "I don't think so. It wasn't the same as all the others. When they crossed over, I felt a release of energy. Like this giant wave crashing over me. With Alan… he just disappeared."

"Maybe once Matthew's arrested, he'll be able to let go."

Shrugging, Nathan ran his hand through his hair. "I don't know if it will be enough. Especially since there's no evidence of Matthew running him off the road. He won't go to jail for murder. He'll go for embezzling and theft. What if Alan can't move on until he has justice for his death?"

Troy sighed. "Unless Matthew confesses, I don't see a chance of that."

"I know!" Nathan's frustration bled through into his tone. "I wish I knew how to prove it!"

Troy squeezed Nathan's shoulder in comfort. "Do you need a ride to work after classes?"

"If you have nothing to do," Nathan said.

"No plans, bro. Probably hang out at the store with you for a bit."

They both stood and headed toward their classes. Nathan spent most of the day struggling to concentrate. When he hadn't heard from Erik by noon, he worried something had gone wrong. As soon as he could, he texted Erik to ask if the cops had taken Matthew into custody.

Erik: *Matthew didn't show up at the office this morning.*
Nathan: *Why?*

He paced back and forth while waiting for Erik to reply. Had Matthew somehow known? That was impossible, though.

Erik: *I don't know. He's always in on time and usually before me.*

Nathan: *Could he possibly know?*

Erik: *I'm not sure, angel. Don't go anywhere alone until we know what's going on. I'll pick you up from work tonight. Is Troy taking you in?*

Nathan: *Yes. He'll be with me.*

Erik: *Good. I love you, Nate.*

Nathan: *Be careful. Please.*

Nathan didn't want to tell Erik how he felt through a text message. He wanted Erik to see the truth in his face when he said it to him the first time. Worry and anxiety followed him for the rest of the day. Where the hell could Matthew have possibly gone? Would he go after Erik now?

After Professor Johns' class, Troy needed to stop in and see one of his other professors to clarify some information about an assignment. Nathan headed to the parking lot to wait by Troy's car. He checked his phone again, but there was still nothing from Erik. Sliding it into his pocket, Nathan leaned against the passenger door and sighed, crossing his arms over his chest. He thought about the last few weeks since meeting Alan and Erik.

It seemed almost surreal how he'd met them both on the same day. So many things would have been different if Erik hadn't had his CDs stolen or Nathan hadn't accidentally acknowledged Alan in class that day. His chest hurt at the idea that even a single change to the chain of events that day could have led to him never meeting Erik.

Being lost in his thoughts, Nathan didn't realize a truck

had stopped at the back of Troy's car until Matthew appeared next to him. Absolute terror crashed over Nathan, and he tried to move away, but Matthew stopped him by pointing a gun at him. Nathan froze, his heart pounding so hard he could barely hear what Matthew said.

"Get in the truck, Nathan," Matthew growled.

Matthew kept the gun low enough to hide it from anyone walking by, but he never took it off Nathan. He motioned toward his truck with the weapon. "Now!"

Nathan knew if he got in the truck, he'd end up dead just like Alan, but what choice did he have? "M-Matthew, wh-what are you doing?" he stammered.

"You know what the fuck I'm doing! Now get in the fucking truck!" Matthew grabbed Nathan's wrist in a hard grip and yanked him toward the truck. He shoved Nathan until he complied and got into the driver's seat before clambering over the console as best he could.

Matthew never let go of the gun as he got into the truck and put it in Drive. Nathan glimpsed Troy coming down the walkway toward the parking lot, and he hit the button to lower the window. "Troy!" he screamed.

Troy looked at him, his expression turning to horror, just as Matthew backhanded Nathan with the gun. Nathan cried out in pain, his lip splitting and his head hitting the door-frame. Matthew rolled the passenger window back up while tearing out of the parking lot, almost sideswiping another vehicle. "I don't know how the fuck you knew about Alan or the money, but you should have stayed the hell out of it, kid. None of this would have ever happened if it wasn't for you!"

Nathan's head throbbed from the hits he'd taken. He felt something wet trickle down his temple. His hand came away red with blood when he swiped at it. Memories of the accident crashed over him, and he whimpered. "I-I don't know wh-what you're talking about," Nathan lied.

Matthew snarled at him. "I heard you at the picnic when you were talking to yourself in the bathroom. You know exactly what the fuck I'm talking about. The only thing I can't figure out is how the hell did you find out?"

"Al-Alan told me," Nathan said. His words earned him another punch to the side of his face, exacerbating the already nauseated feeling in his stomach and the ringing in his ears. Nathan gripped his head, trying to quiet the sound, but he knew it wouldn't help.

"Alan's dead!" Matthew snapped.

Bile rose in Nathan's throat as the nausea got worse. He knew he probably had a concussion. "I can see and talk to ghosts," he murmured. "Alan told me."

The sound of a police siren penetrated the road noises and the squeal of tires as Matthew weaved in and out of traffic. Matthew beat the hand holding the gun against the steering wheel, swearing so badly Nathan could almost see the air turn blue. Hope at being rescued settled into his chest. Troy had to have called the cops.

The idea to talk Matthew into admitting he murdered Alan out loud while Erik listened popped into Nathans head. He reached into his pocket and hit what he hoped was the right speed dial for Erik. He could only pray Matthew didn't notice or hear if Erik answered.

Matthew's frustration at being chased by the police and his overall rage drowned out the tinny sound of Erik saying Nathan's name into the phone. "Why did you do it, Matthew? Why did you kill Alan?"

"Because the stupid son of a bitch wouldn't take the money that I offered him to keep his mouth shut!" Nathan's breath caught when Matthew wrenched the wheel to dodge a pedestrian stepping out into the street. The horrified look on the pedestrian's face registered briefly as they passed the man. "He was going to tell Erik. He would have ruined everything!"

"Erik's your cousin. Family! How could you murder the man he loved?" Nathan challenged, swallowing again to fight down the need to vomit. Fear, pain, and knowing that if Matthew lost the police car chasing him, then Nathan would join Alan in the afterlife, caused tremors throughout Nathan's entire body.

Matthew backhanded Nathan a second time, causing Nathan to cry out in agony as his head hit the window this time. Spots danced in Nathan's vision, and he knew another hit would knock him unconscious. "Shut the hell up! You're just as annoying as Alan was. Sanctimonious prick! He thought his shit didn't stink."

Nathan leaned his head back against the headrest, struggling to keep his eyes open. A new siren joined the one already behind them. The side mirror reflected the flashing lights from the top of the cop cars. Matthew cursed again.

"Where are you taking me?" Nathan asked, his voice strained. "You won't get away. Not with the cops right behind us."

"Just shut up!" Matthew screamed, spittle flying out of his mouth. "I need to think."

The guy had truly fallen off his rocker. Nathan knew if he didn't get away, Matthew would kill him, too. "Let me go. Please, Matthew."

"I told you to shut up!" Matthew swung the gun toward him, and Nathan cowered against the door as far as he could. He immediately dismissed the idea of opening the door and jumping out. They were going too fast for him to risk it. Matthew was stronger than him, so getting the gun away from him wouldn't work, either.

When he glanced out at the front of the truck again, he realized they were heading toward the same place Matthew had run Alan off the road. Praying Erik would hear him, Nathan said, "You're taking me to the same place you murdered Alan, aren't you?"

Matthew snarled in frustration. "I told you to shut up!"

Nathan snapped his mouth closed, not wanting to be hit again. Trees rushed by at an alarming speed as they approached the turn. Nathan barely had time to grab hold of the dashboard to keep from slamming into it when Matthew stomped on the brakes. The back end of the truck fishtailed a bit, forcing Nathan's heart into his throat. If the tires didn't catch, they could go over into the ravine like Alan had. Thankfully, at the last second they caught, and Nathan almost cried when the truck came to a full stop.

"Get out!" Matthew demanded, jerking the gun to show Nathan should exit the truck on his side.

Matthew climbed over the seat to follow him out of the truck. One police vehicle stopped several hundred yards away from the truck while the other went past and pulled across the road. More than likely to stop any other innocent people from getting close to the scene. Nathan flinched when Matthew grabbed his arm and yanked him in front of him, shielding himself with Nathan. Matthew wrapped his hand around Nathan's throat, holding him in place. The cops didn't approach, but they pulled their own guns.

"Sir, put the gun down and let him go," one officer shouted.

More police cruisers arrived, surrounding the area in a semicircle. Nathan's heart pounded in his chest, fear causing him to shake, and he squeezed his eyes closed. A few weeks ago, Nathan would have welcomed death and the chance to see his parents again. Death would have been a reprieve from the guilt and pain that had ridden him hard every single day. But now those feelings had dulled. Erik's presence in his life blunted the sharp edges of them, making him want to live, to see where their relationship would go.

The sound of a car coming to a screeching stop a few moments later caused Nathan to open his eyes. His breath caught when he saw Erik being held back by two police officers. Erik must have sped like crazy to get there so quickly. "Nathan!"

Tears welled in Nathan's eyes. All he wanted right then was to be in Erik's arms. Matthew tightened his hold on Nathan's throat, and Erik stopped fighting to get past the two officers. Even from where Nathan stood, he could see the rage and the fear on Erik's face.

"Why, Matthew?" Erik demanded. "Why are you doing this?"

Matthew sneered at Erik. "Because you've always had everything!"

"What?" Erik asked, incredulous.

"Everything came so fucking easily to you! Grades, athleticism, money, men. I had to fight and claw for every little thing I ever had! Your parents even loved you after you came out. Mom and Dad disowned me when I told them I was gay."

Erik's rage dimmed to be replaced by shock. "You never told me that. How did no one in the family hear about that?"

A harsh laugh tumbled from Matthew. "They were too proud and didn't want anyone to know. So, they pretend like everything is fine when they must." Growling, Matthew pressed the barrel of the gun harder into Nathan's temple. "It doesn't matter."

Nathan noticed movement in his peripheral, his heart pounding faster when he saw Alan standing nearby. His emotions shifted as Alan got closer. Pain, anger, fear. All of them crashed over him. "Alan," Nathan whimpered.

"What the fuck did you just say?" Matthew dug his fingers into Nathan's throat, nails breaking the skin.

Alan met Nathan's gaze briefly, affection in the look, before he rushed forward. Nathan shut his eyes again, a shudder racing down his spine when Alan's translucent form engulfed them.

"No! No! You're dead. You can't be here. No!" Nathan heard Matthew shriek before he released him.

A loud bang nearly shattered Nathan's eardrums, and a searing agony ripped through his back, sending him to the ground with a shout. The last thing he noticed before losing consciousness was the police rushing forward and a crashing noise behind him.

CHAPTER 26

*B*right light caused Nathan to squint. Where was he? There was nothing surrounding him except white. No doors. No windows. No people. He walked for several minutes, but it never changed. "Hello?" he hollered, a hand stretched out in front of him, hoping to touch something. "Is anyone there?"

Nathan stopped walking when no response came. Panic and anxiety set in. Was he dead? He remembered Matthew abducting him from the campus parking lot, and the police chasing them through the city streets until Matthew stopped where Alan had died. He recalled Alan rushing at him, Matthew yelling, and a loud bang. Then nothing.

A shadow formed several feet in front of him. His anxiety ratcheted even higher. What was going on? The shadow took the shape of a man, forming further by the second, until Nathan realized Alan stood before him. "Alan? What's going on? Where are we?"

Alan smiled at him, reaching out to take his hand. "Everything's okay, Nate. It's over."

"Am I... dead?"

Alan tugged him into a tight hug. "Thank you, Nate. For every-

thing. For being there for me, helping me find out the truth. And for being there for Erik now and in the future. I owe you so much."

Nathan couldn't help noticing Alan didn't answer his question. "It's over? You're truly able to move on now?"

Nodding, Alan released him. "I am. Please tell Erik I love him."

He opened his mouth to respond when a loud voice echoed through the empty white space. "Clear!"

Nathan slammed his hands on top of his ears at the deafening volume. Alan said something else, but Nathan couldn't hear him. "What?" he shouted.

An electrical charge surged through Nathan, and he arched his back, screaming at the intensity of the current. Alan gave him one last smile and then, using both hands, he shoved Nathan. Hard. A cry caught in Nathan's throat as he fell backwards, his stomach dropping out. Blackness engulfed him.

The indistinct murmur of voices and a steady beeping noise awakened Nathan. He blinked his eyes open, squinting. Once his eyes adjusted, Nathan saw the pattern of the hospital ceiling panels clearly. His heart clenched and his stomach knotted. He didn't want to be in the hospital. Not again. There was no way he'd be able to avoid the ghosts tied to there.

When he tried to move, a hand on his shoulder stopped him. "Relax, angel," Erik murmured.

Nathan turned his head to see a very haggard, very exhausted-looking Erik sitting in the chair next to the bed. Erik's eyes were red-rimmed and there were dark circles under them. A five o'clock shadow dusted his cheeks and neck. Nathan tried to speak, but his throat felt tight and scratchy. Erik stood from the chair. "Let me get the doctor, baby. Don't talk yet."

Erik opened the door and leaned out, calling for the nurse. "He's awake."

He didn't remain there long, returning to Nathan's side quickly and then brushing a strand of hair back from his forehead. "I'm so glad you're all right," Erik rasped. "I thought I'd lost you."

Nathan realized an IV ran into his arm and he felt sore all over. "Wh-what ha-happened?"

"Matthew shot you," Erik replied. "The son of a bitch shot you in the back."

Before Nathan could ask any more questions, the door swung open and a nurse came in. "Hi there, Mr. Bryant. I'm Nurse Kline, and it's good to see you awake. The doctor will be by shortly. Is there anything you need? Are you in pain?"

"Water," Nathan said.

"I'm afraid until the doctor sees you, you can only have ice chips." She checked the IV drop bag. "I'll be right back with those ice chips, sweetie."

The nurse left, and Nathan turned his head toward Erik. His breath caught when he saw tears in Erik's eyes. "Erik?"

Erik leaned over the bed, buried his face in Nathan's neck, and breathed deeply. A shiver trickled through Nathan at the feel of the sharp scruff against his skin. "When I heard the gun go off—" His voice cracked.

Nathan laid his hand on the back of Erik's head. "I'm here. I'm okay."

Erik's shoulders shook, and Nathan gently stroked the strands of hair at Erik's nape. Warm wetness dampened the skin of his throat, causing Nathan's heart to clench in agony at Erik's pain. "I promise I'm okay," Nathan murmured.

The sound of the door opening had Erik sitting back and scrubbing his face to wipe away the tears. A man in a white coat, who Nathan assumed was the doctor, came toward the bed. "How are we doing this morning? I'm Dr. Whitley."

"I'm fine," Nathan replied. "Just thirsty."

"That's to be expected after what you've gone through. Mr. Moore, I'd like to speak with Mr. Bryant, if you could wait outside for a few moments."

"No," Nathan protested. "I want him here. Please."

"Very well. We extracted several bullet fragments from your spinal column. During the surgery, you crashed and were unresponsive for several minutes." Nathan heard Erik suck in a sharp breath. "Are you feeling any pain right now?"

Nathan shook his head. "No. I feel all right." He tried to move his legs, wiggle his toes, but they were unresponsive. Slight panic set in. Even after everything with the accident and his time in the hospital with both legs being broken, he'd never not been able to move them. "I can't feel my legs. Is that normal?"

"After what you've been through, it's not surprising. We won't know if there is any lasting damage until the swelling goes down. No need to get anxious just yet."

"Okay," Nathan murmured, his heart racing despite the doctor's words. Erik took hold of Nathan's hand and squeezed gently.

"You are a very lucky young man, Mr. Bryant. We've had similar cases that didn't turn out so happily."

"I really want to go home," Nathan said.

"Patience. We'll have you out of here in no time." Dr. Whitley patted Nathan's shin. "I'll be back by a little later to check in on you again."

As the doctor left, his aunts and Troy entered the room. Becky scowled at Nathan before giving him a gentle hug. "You just can't help but take more years off my life, can you, young man?"

There was no true heat behind her words, and he saw the tears in her eyes. Remorse stabbed Nathan straight in his chest. "I'm sorry, Aunt Becky," Nathan said. "I wasn't trying to."

"We're just happy you're okay," Jessica said, leaning in to kiss his cheek. She brushed his hair back from his forehead.

Troy gave Nathan a fist bump. "You're like a cat. You've got nine lives, bro."

Nathan gave him a weak smile. "I think I've used them all."

Troy looked at Erik. "You better take care of our boy. You feel me?"

Erik chuckled and gave Nathan's hand a light squeeze. "As much as he'll let me."

The four of them stayed with Nathan until he started dozing off again. Becky, Jessica, and Troy gave him a half hug before they left. Erik remained at his side. "I'll be here when you wake up, angel," Erik murmured.

Nathan didn't know how long he slept, but when he woke, the room was empty, and he could see it had grown dark outside. Tension set in quickly. So far, no spirits had appeared to him, but he knew it wouldn't be long before one wandered into his room. Despite the promise he'd made to help others, he couldn't quiet the panic he always felt whenever he encountered one. Before his anxiety could get too high, the door opened and Erik appeared. A sigh of relief rushed from Nathan. "Where'd you go?" he asked.

Erik came straight to his side. "Sorry, angel. I was just stretching my legs and grabbing a coffee. Is something wrong? Do you need the doctor?"

He grabbed Erik's hand when Erik turned away to go get someone. "I'm okay." He bit his lip and dropped his gaze to his lap. "It's just…"

Using his foot to drag the chair closer, Erik sat, never letting go of Nathan. "You're worried about seeing the dead."

Hearing Erik say it so matter-of-factly felt strange to

Nathan. Alan hadn't been wrong about Erik. The big, strong, amazing man had accepted every facet of him without reservation. Emotion crashed over him and before he could chicken out, Nathan whispered, "I love you."

A sharp intake of air and the tightening of Erik's grasp on his hand sent uncertainty through Nathan, even though Erik had already said it more than once. Everything that had happened could have made him change his mind.

"I love you, too, angel."

The ball of fear in Nathan's chest released at hearing Erik say it again.

Erik stood, bent over the bed, and captured Nathan's mouth in a gentle kiss. Nathan sighed into the kiss, tilting his head back and opening his mouth. Lightly tracing Nathan's lips with his tongue, Erik coaxed Nathan's out to play. The kiss didn't last long, though. Erik broke away and leaned his forehead against Nathan's. "I'm not leaving you, Nate. If one shows up, I'll be by your side to deal with it together."

The calm acceptance, the promise to stay with him, shattered the last of the wall Nathan had erected around himself. His parents' deaths and then his friends and family not believing him had happened so close together, it had left him reeling. He'd spent so much of his time these last six years with a wall up to stop himself from being hurt again that he'd become so paralyzed. Not really living life. Not opening himself to the possibility of anything or anyone. Erik had entered his life like a wrecking ball, smashing into the wall and dragging him out into the light.

Tears spilled over and Nathan covered his face with his free hand.

"Hey, angel, what's the matter?"

Through several stuttered, choked words, Nathan explained the epiphany he'd just had. Erik smiled tenderly at him and tucked a strand of hair behind one ear. "Baby, I saw all of that the moment I met you. None of it deterred me from wanting you. All of us have scars. All of us have things in our past or future which may challenge us and leave us wondering if we can trust anyone again. I will never break your trust, Nate."

The tears fell harder, and Nathan couldn't stifle a small sob. Erik stayed quiet, seeming to know Nathan needed the cleansing cry, and he waited patiently until Nathan calmed down. When he'd settled, Erik sat back in his chair and handed him a tissue from the nightstand. Nathan wiped his cheeks first, then his nose.

"Better?" Erik asked.

Nathan nodded. "Thank you."

"No thank you needed, angel. I am here for you whenever you need me."

"Even… Even if I can't walk again?"

"No matter what, Nate, I will be here. For *your* sake, I hope you can, but if not, it doesn't matter to me. I meant it when I said I love you. That means we are each other's port in the storm. I'm not going anywhere."

Nathan gave Erik a wobbly smile. "I don't know what I did to deserve you. I can't believe you didn't just walk away with how acerbic I was to you at the beginning."

Erik gave a shrug. "I didn't see it as you being acerbic. You were only trying to protect your heart from more pain. Knowing everything I do now, I can understand why. Losing your parents, blaming yourself, and then to be abandoned by the people you call friends and your aunts not believing you… Anyone would have a hard time trusting after all of that."

"Alan was so right about you," Nathan murmured, a small smile tugging at one corner of his mouth. "He told me you'd believe me."

"He knew me very well."

A memory tugged at Nathan's mind, and he frowned. Alan... Eyes widening, Nathan sucked in a breath. "Erik. Alan... I remember being with him. In a white room or something."

Erik sat up straighter, frowning. "When were you with him?"

"I don't know. It wasn't before." Nathan furrowed his brow. "He told me everything was going to be okay."

"Wait... the doctor said you died for a moment, and they had to bring you back."

"Like the first time," Nathan whispered. "It must have been then. Alan was saying goodbye."

"Does that mean he moved on?" Erik asked.

Nathan took a steadying breath. "He wanted me to tell you he loves you. He told me everything would be okay. "I think he did what he'd been here to do. I don't feel him anymore. And he hasn't been in my room. At least not while I've been awake."

Erik stood and then sat on the edge of Nathan's hospital bed. "You said after the accident, you started seeing the ghosts, spirits, right?"

"Yes."

"They had to bring you back then, too, yes? What if this time it reversed it? You haven't seen any since you woke up, have you?"

Nathan shook his head. "No, but that means nothing. I didn't see them right away before either. And I haven't exactly been awake that long."

Erik hummed, lost in thought. Nathan picked at a small thread in the blanket. Was Erik right? There wasn't any proof in either direction. It had taken several days last time to realize he could see them.

"Let's just wait and see what happens," Erik said. "Do you

want me to get you anything? You slept through lunch and dinner."

Nathan's stomach chose that moment to growl. Erik laughed. "I think that's my answer. Let me go see what I can scrounge up, okay?"

He watched Erik leave the room and leaned his head back with a sigh. Hope warred with his usual dose of guilt. On the one hand, he would be ecstatic about no longer seeing the ghosts. But it also made him seem like an asshat because then he would no longer be able to help anyone.

Erik returned with a plastic-wrapped sandwich and apple juice. He handed the sandwich to Nathan and opened the drink, setting it on the rolling stand next to Nathan's bed. "What happened to Matthew?" Nathan asked around a bite of his sandwich.

Pain, anger, and sadness drifted over Erik's features. "He went over into the ravine."

The bite Nathan had taken sat like ash in his throat. It took several tries to swallow it. He set the sandwich down and laid his hand on top of Erik's. "I'm so sorry, Erik."

"You have nothing to be sorry for. I should apologize to you," Erik said.

"What? Why?"

"If it wasn't for Matthew, for me, you wouldn't be in here."

Nathan shook his head. "It's not your fault, Erik! You didn't know. Even if you hadn't come into the store that day, we still would have met because of Alan. Who knows what would have happened then? Matthew was still your cousin, your family. You loved him and trusted him."

"I had no idea he was going through so much," Erik said. "I thought we told each other everything. To know he thought so little of me..."

Giving Erik's hand a light squeeze, Nathan said, "Sometimes we can't see what the other person is going through because they hide it so well. If his parents really didn't want the rest of your family to know about disowning him, they hid it, too."

Erik sighed. "I guess so. It makes me wonder if I even knew him at all."

"Hey," Nathan said. "You knew him how you knew him. That's the memory you need to hold on to."

Giving Nathan a slight smile, Erik turned his hand over and intertwined their fingers. "Thank you, angel. For being here for me. Listening to me about the man who put you in here and may well have taken away your ability to walk. You're so much stronger than you give yourself credit for."

Blushing, Nathan traced a finger over the back of Erik's index finger. A tiny scar caught his attention. The roughness of Erik's palm and the blunt fingernails were a direct reflection of Erik's hard work while building his business. "I don't feel strong. I've spent so many years hiding out of fear that I've missed out on a lot."

"You can change, if you want to. There are so many years ahead of you." Erik slid two fingers under Nathan's chin and tipped his head up enough to meet his gaze. "I hope you'll spend as many of those with me as possible."

Nathan turned his head and kissed the inside of Erik's wrist. "I want to, more than anything."

"Good," Erik said. "Now, eat."

A couple of days went by, and Nathan hoped his curse had truly been lifted. He hadn't seen a single spirit during those two days. The doctor would give his final analysis of Nathan's injuries in an hour. Erik hadn't left his side for longer than a couple of hours. Mostly to go home, shower, change, and come back to the hospital. More than once, Nathan had tried to convince him he'd be okay on his own so Erik could go to work, but Erik had insisted on staying.

Troy came to visit every day, staying for a couple of hours. He kept Nathan entertained whenever Erik wandered off to talk on his phone to his assistant. Nathan told him about possibly no longer being able to see ghosts.

Of course, Nathan knew he wasn't supposed to move on his own, but he'd spent the last two days trying to move his toe, his foot, anything he could. His heart dropped into his stomach every time they didn't obey his thoughts. He finally had a chance at a normal life, and now this uncertainty hung over his head.

Tension and anxiety roared through Nathan when the doctor entered the room. Erik stood and grabbed hold of Nathan's hand in support.

"How are we feeling today, Nathan?"

"Good, Dr. Whitley," Nathan replied.

"That's good to hear. Now, let's see what we're working with, hmm?"

Nathan nodded. Dr. Whitley folded the sheet back, exposing Nathan's feet and most of his lower legs. "Excellent color," Dr. Whitley mused.

He took a pen out of his pocket and ran the end along the bottom of Nathan's foot. Nathan snorted out a laugh. Dr. Whitley smiled. "Tickles?"

"Yeah," Nathan said.

"That's a good thing, isn't it, Dr. Whitley?" Erik asked. He tightened his hold on Nathan's hand.

"It's a wonderful thing, Mr. Moore." Dr. Whitley poked Nathan's big toe. "Can you feel that, Nathan?"

"Yes!" Nathan said excitedly.

Dr. Whitley did more prodding and sliding touches with

his pen. He also requested Nathan to move his toes and feet. Elation replaced the anxiety and tension when Nathan successfully twitched his toes. "You'll have to go through some physical therapy, but I'm confident you'll regain full use of your legs."

Nathan released the breath he hadn't even realized he was holding. Tears of relief and happiness stung his eyes. Erik leaned in and kissed his temple, sliding an arm around Nathan's shoulders. "Thank you, Dr. Whitley!"

"It'll still be a day or two before we can release you, but after that, you'll be able to return home. I'll write up the referral for physical therapy and hopefully we won't see you back here for a very long time, Nathan. Please follow up with your primary care doctor for the aftercare for your wound once you're released." Dr. Whitley smiled, made some notations on Nathan's chart, and patted Nathan's shin before leaving the room.

"See, angel?" Erik said, kissing Nathan's temple again. "Just a little bit of faith and things will work out."

"I can't wait to tell my aunts and Troy," Nathan said. "Maybe I can go back to class soon, too. I don't want to miss any more than I have to."

Erik perched on the edge of the hospital bed. "There's something I wanted to talk to you about, Nate." Nathan gave Erik a questioning look. "Maybe it's time you live for yourself instead."

Nathan stiffened. "I am living for myself."

"But you aren't, baby. Music brings you to life. I see it every time you're playing at the café. You should see where that takes you. Just think about it, please. For me."

He'd spent so much time the last six years working toward paying his aunts back for everything they'd done for him. Where did he go from here? The possibility of concentrating on his music brought hope bubbling up inside of him.

But he still owed his aunts for everything. The hospital bills hadn't been cheap after the accident. He wasn't even sure how he would afford the current bill, which was no doubt getting higher while he was here. Not to mention the after-care and physical therapy. "I don't know if I can," Nathan murmured. "I owe my aunts everything. There's no way I'll be able to afford the bill right now either if I don't make money sooner than a career in music will give me."

"Your aunts love you. I'm sure they don't expect you to pay them back for taking care of you, angel."

They had told him that more than once, but it was his fault they'd even had to do any of it. Sighing, Nathan clenched his hands on his lap.

"And don't worry about this hospital bill because I'm going to pay it," Erik said.

"What?" Nathan asked incredulously. "No. It's going to be too much!"

Erik shook his head. "No, it's not. It's partially my fault you're in here. If my cousin hadn't shot you, you wouldn't be here."

"It's not your fault!" Nathan protested. "I was helping Alan. It could have happened no matter what."

Erik gave him a tender smile. "Did you hear what you just said?"

Nathan frowned.

"It could have happened anyway."

He still didn't understand what Erik was saying. "Okay?"

"Just like your parents' accident could have happened as well."

Nathan opened his mouth to reply but closed it abruptly. He didn't know how to respond. Erik gently unfolded Nathan's hands, spreading his fingers out and running his own index finger along the ridges of each of Nathan's. "I'm not trying to downplay anything that has happened. Whether the situation which landed you here now or the accident from years ago. But playing the what if or blame game won't change a single thing. All it does is make us question ourselves, question the people around us, and leave us with a heavy burden to carry. I love you, Nate. Whatever the future may bring, we're in it together. I want to help with the bill. Not just because it was my cousin who shot you, but because I can and because I want to. Please let me."

Stubbornness rose in Nathan, and he would have protested again, but before he could, Erik covered his mouth gently with one hand. "Please, angel."

Sighing, Nathan nodded. Erik gave him a blinding smile. "Thank you, Nate."

Nathan grumbled, but he didn't fight Erik any longer on paying the bill. He'd find a way to pay Erik back, too. The last few weeks had been such a whirlwind, Nathan could barely keep his thoughts in a straight line. Right now, all he wanted to do was concentrate on his recovery and loving Erik. Everything else could wait.

CHAPTER 27

THREE MONTHS LATER...

"Come on, Nate. We're going to be late," Troy yelled up the stairs.

Nathan put the finishing touches on his hair and walked down the stairs. "I'm coming!"

Troy stood by Erik's front door, arms folded across his chest. He rolled his eyes at Nathan. "You already bagged the dude. Why are you fussing over your hair now?"

He scowled at Troy. "That's not why, and you know it."

Troy opened the door for Nathan and motioned for Nathan to precede him. "Is Erik going to be there later?"

"Yeah. He had a meeting he couldn't get out of. Besides, the ceremony doesn't start until one, so there's plenty of time."

It had been three months since the hospital. Two months of twice weekly physical therapy sessions had taken place, and Nathan had spent those months getting to know Erik better and completing his degree. He'd only had a couple more months to get through, really, and didn't see the point in not finishing. Nathan had spent a better part of the three months thinking about Erik's words in the hospital. Maybe he wouldn't rush into a job in business. He wanted to take some time for himself to discover what he truly wanted to do with the rest of his life.

"Come on," Troy nagged. "Let's go already!"

Nathan grabbed his backpack from the front entrance, slinging it over his shoulder. He'd dressed in slacks and a button-down collared shirt Erik had helped him pick out for the ceremony. He'd stayed with Erik after being released from the hospital because he couldn't easily navigate the stairs of his apartment. It wasn't too long after that when Erik had asked him to move in with him. Nathan hadn't known if they were moving too fast, but he'd said yes immediately. Even before the incident with Matthew, he'd spent most of his time at Erik's anyway.

"We have hours before the ceremony! Why are you freaking out?" Nathan closed and locked the front door.

"Karen is going to be there," Troy tossed over his shoulder.

Nathan grinned while taking the porch steps down to the walkway. Troy had met Karen when he'd taken Nathan to his P.T. session. She'd been in a car accident where she'd broken her arm in three places. From the moment he'd seen her, Troy had spent every minute flirting with her, texting with her, or over at her dorm room. Turns out Karen went to the same school but was a year below the two of them. "She's not going to disappear just because we're graduating, Troy."

"She has to go back home for the summer, Nate. I don't want to miss my chance to say goodbye." Troy climbed into his car and started the engine before Nathan had even opened his door.

Laughing, Nathan shook his head and tossed his book bag at his feet before buckling his seat belt. Troy barely waited for Nathan to close his door. Maybe Karen would tame his playboy ways. Nathan just wanted Troy to be happy. She was a super sweet girl with shoulder-length red hair, pale skin, and big green eyes, and she was much shorter than both of them.

Nathan rolled down his window, letting the summer air into the vehicle while hanging his arm on the door. It took some time, but Nathan had finally become confident that his ability to see ghosts was gone. He hadn't encountered one since seeing Alan in the space between life and death. At least, he assumed that's what it was.

When they reached campus, Nathan separated from Troy to visit his counselor and say goodbye to a few of his professors. A new chapter of his life was beginning, and Nathan didn't have a clue what he intended to do after today. Erik continued to encourage him to work on his music while Nathan still worked at the music store. Maybe Nathan would see where his music could take him. He'd seen a flyer at the café where a band was holding auditions for a new guitarist. The idea of trying out had been niggling at him from the back of his mind for days. He hadn't told Erik about the opportunity, but he felt pretty confident Erik would encourage him to go for it.

The morning went by fast. Nerves settled in the closer it got to the graduation ceremony. Nathan picked up his cap and gown from the assigned room, then met Troy by the doors leading out to where the ceremony would be. Hands shaking, unable to believe he'd finished his degree, Nathan tugged on the gown and put on the cap.

"Relax, Nate," Troy said, bumping him with his shoulder. "This is the easy part."

He gave a small smile and dragged in a deep breath. Before he was ready, they were heading outside to the designated seats for the graduates. Nathan caught sight of Erik and his aunts. They waved and grinned in excitement. He returned their waves, but nervous energy still kept him from being able to truly smile.

During the ceremony, Nathan kept fidgeting. It wasn't until they called his name and he was up on the stage accepting his diploma that the nerves dissipated, and he couldn't stop smiling, tears threatening. He'd done it. He'd gotten through some of the worst years of his life and come out the other end in one piece.

His aunts and Erik met him after everything concluded, hugging the hell out of him and exclaiming over him.

"We are so proud of you, Nate!" Becky said, kissing his cheek.

"I knew you could do it," Jessica said, hugging him so tight Nathan struggled to breathe for a second.

Erik laid a kiss on him so passionately, Nathan panted afterward. "I'm so proud of you, angel."

Nathan couldn't stop the blush rising over his face. He pressed a hand to one cheek. "Thanks, everyone."

Troy came up then and grabbed hold of Nathan in a giant bear hug. "We did it, bro!"

"I couldn't have done it without you, Troy," Nathan murmured. He owed Troy so much. He had been there for him every step of the way after the accident.

"You're my brother from another mother, Nate. I wouldn't have missed a single second of our friendship." Troy hugged him tighter, slapped him on the back, and then released him. Nathan's aunts also congratulated Troy, giving him a hug and a kiss on the cheek. Neither of Troy's parents could make the ceremony due to his mother having a cruise scheduled for the week of graduation and his father was laid up in bed, having put his back out trying to do way too much on his own. Troy had missed a couple of the last days of school in order to help his dad out until he could arrange for a nurse to come in. He'd been disappointed his dad couldn't be there, but Troy knew it was unavoidable.

"Celebratory dinner!" Becky said, her hazel eyes sparkling.

"Actually, I planned on having everyone back to our house for food and drinks," Erik said. "My assistant is setting it up as we speak."

"That's too much trouble!" Nathan protested.

"Haven't you learned by now, angel? Nothing is too much trouble for you." Erik slid his arm around Nathan's shoulders. "You deserve to be celebrated, Nate. What you accomplished is no easy feat. Especially with everything you've been through."

Nathan flushed again, and he pressed his face to the side of Erik's chest. Everyone planned on meeting back at Erik's house and dispersed to their vehicles. Nathan and Erik rode in comfortable silence, with Erik holding his hand the entire way, as always. Nathan could barely wrap his head around how much had changed in his life in such a brief span of time. The more he thought about everything, the more he realized just how paralyzed he'd been since the car accident. He hadn't been living. He'd been surviving.

"Everything okay, angel?" Erik asked, interrupting his thoughts.

Rolling his head along the seat until he faced Erik, Nathan smiled. "Everything's great, babe."

Erik squeezed his fingers gently. "I really am so proud of you, Nate."

"I saw a flyer on the bulletin board in the café about a band looking for a guitarist. I was thinking about auditioning," Nathan said.

"That's great, angel! You definitely should! I know you'll blow them away."

"You think so?" Nathan asked.

"No doubt in my mind, baby," Erik replied. He pulled the truck into his driveway and turned off the engine before facing Nathan. "You have such a special gift for music, Nate. You need to share it with the world."

Biting his lip, Nathan dropped his gaze to his lap, still uncertain about pursuing something in an industry where many people never make it. "What if I fail?"

Erik reached out and cupped Nathan's cheek, urging him to look up. "You won't. Even if nothing comes of it, I'll be here. I just want you to be happy. When you're on that platform at the café, you come to life. You deserve the chance to chase your dream."

Nathan gave Erik a trembling smile. "I love you. So much."

"I love you, too, angel." Erik leaned over the center console and pressed a gentle kiss to Nathan's lips. "Let's get inside and get this party started."

Erik winked at him before opening his door to climb out. Nathan followed Erik into the house, only to stop just inside the front door. A huge "Congratulations" banner lined one wall and trays of food cluttered the dining room table. "Why so much food?" Nathan asked.

"I invited some of my people as well," Erik replied. "I want to show off my recent college graduate."

Over the past three months, Nathan had met several of Erik's employees more than once. He interacted with Thomas the most since they both loved music, and they had gotten into a verbal debate every time about which band had a better guitarist. "You didn't have to do all of this," Nathan said, uncomfortable with Erik spending so much money on him.

Erik kissed Nathan's temple. "Of course I did, angel. Relax. It's your day."

Nathan would have argued further, but people started

arriving. He didn't want to embarrass Erik in front of his friends and employees, so he kept his mouth shut. The party was in full swing before too long, and Nathan eventually relaxed. He ate a few bites of the various appetizers, talked to everyone, and thanked them all for being there. Some had brought gifts, while others handed him a card with either money or a gift card inside. Nathan spent a good portion of the time debating with Thomas yet again about the best guitarist of all time.

The party went on until late in the evening before people started trickling out of Erik's home. Nathan said goodbye to his aunts and Troy. Becca, Erik's assistant, was the last person to leave after making sure everything was put away or cleaned up—with his and Erik's help.

Nathan collapsed on the couch, exhausted. Erik sat next to him and tugged him against his side. "You continue to astound me, Nate."

"What? Why?" Nathan asked, frowning.

"You really don't know how amazing you are." Erik trailed the tips of his fingers along Nathan's arm. "You're beautiful, smart, talented, and so many other things which take my breath away."

Shifting in discomfort, Nathan shook his head. "I'm not all that."

"Oh, but you are, my angel." Erik nuzzled the side of Nathan's neck. "No matter what you believe of yourself, I will always see you for who you are."

Nathan shivered at the light rasp of Erik's five o'clock shadow on his sensitive skin. He tilted his head, granting Erik further access, almost moaning when Erik's lips skimmed along the same trail. Nathan settled one hand on Erik's chest, feeling the movement of muscles under his palm. Despite being together for four months and the number of times they'd made love, Nathan still blushed whenever Erik initiated anything intimate between them. "Er-Erik," Nathan muttered, biting his lower lip.

Erik's tongue lashed over Nathan's skin next, and Nathan groaned, his cock hardening. Nathan slid his hand along Erik's nape to tangle in the dark locks, holding on tight. Erik suckled at the skin while pushing underneath Nathan's shirt to settle against the softness of Nathan's belly. The warmth and roughness of Erik's palm sent electricity straight into Nathan's groin.

Erik aligned their mouths and took Nathan's in a tender kiss. Without hesitation, Nathan opened to Erik's probing tongue, eagerly sucking on the pink muscle. "Touch me," Erik growled.

Nathan moved until he straddled Erik's lap, instantly capturing his lips again while working frantically to unbutton Erik's shirt. He ran his hands over Erik's chest and shoulders. Erik leaned forward enough to allow the shirt to fall behind him and from his wrists before cupping Nathan's ass, drawing him tighter to him. The sound of their breathing seemed loud to Nathan in the living room. The only noise louder was Nathan's heartbeat. He couldn't prevent his heart from racing with excitement and passion. Nathan ground against Erik's hard cock, still trapped in his pants.

In the next instance, Nathan found himself airborne as Erik rose from the couch and carried him upstairs to their bedroom. Erik laid him down on the bed gently, almost reverently. He stripped away Nathan's clothing, leaving him naked, his shaft leaking profusely onto his stomach. A gasp wrenched from Nathan when Erik leaned down to lap at the small puddle and over the flared tip. Erik trailed the tip of his tongue down the length of his cock. But he didn't stop there —Erik continued down, bathing the sac beneath.

Nathan instinctively raised his legs, gripping the backs of

his knees with his hands to hold them up and open himself to Erik. The flick of Erik's tongue over his hole brought a moan bubbling forth from Nathan. "Erik," Nathan panted.

"Love the way you taste, angel." Erik slid his hands beneath Nathan's ass, holding him steady for an onslaught of licking and probing. Nathan writhed, head tossing back and forth at the pleasure swamping him the longer Erik feasted on him. His back arched from the mattress when Erik punched through, darting in to taste him. A finger breached the same muscle, adding even more to the overwhelming sensations racing through him. Erik thrust his finger in and out several times before adding a second one, scissoring them gently to stretch him wider.

Erik pulled away to reach for the lube sitting on the nightstand. Nathan watched with heavy-lidded eyes as Erik doused his fingers and his cock to prepare himself. Erik had gotten tested, wanting to take their relationship to the next level, and they'd gone without a condom ever since. A shudder raced through Nathan, knowing Erik would be inside of him soon, skin to skin.

Those fingers worked back inside of Nathan, scattering his thoughts and pushing the heat inside of him higher. "I need you," Nathan rasped.

"I'm here, angel," Erik said, pulling his fingers free and lining up his cock with Nathan's entrance. He worked his way in, carefully, taking cues from Nathan's expression. Nathan just wanted Erik inside him. He wrapped his legs around Erik's waist, his heels pressing against Erik's buttocks, and pulled him forward at the same time as thrusting upward. Nathan cried out, fingers clenching in the sheets again, when Erik slid balls deep into him. "Nate," Erik chastised without heat, not moving a single inch.

"It doesn't hurt," Nathan said, reaching up to grip Erik's biceps. "I'm okay. Please… move."

Erik leaned in to kiss him while starting a slow undulation of his hips, retreating slightly before thrusting inside of him. Nathan wrapped his arms around Erik's neck, holding on tight as the various sensations dragged him under. Their breathing became harsh, rasping into the silence of the bedroom. Sweat built over their skin, easing the friction between their limbs.

Tossing his head against the pillow, Nathan couldn't stop the small moans and cries he let forth. Movements became faster, pushing them closer toward the precipice they strove for. Erik broke away from him to sit back far enough to watch where they were joined. Need and lust glittered from Erik's hazel eyes, his face grimacing with pleasure. "Look, angel," Erik rasped. "Look at the way you stretch around me."

Nathan dropped his gaze to watch Erik's cock sliding in and out of him, his own weeping against his stomach. Biting his lip, Nathan slid two fingers along the outside of his entrance, feeling the hot flesh of Erik's length on each drive into him. "I can't get enough of you," Erik growled, giving a hard thrust. "You're under my skin, in my heart."

Erik fell onto him again, increasing the intensity of his movements. Nathan wrapped his legs once more around Erik's waist. "I love you, Nate."

Shattering, Nathan cried out as his seed spilled between them. Erik followed him, giving a guttural moan, his face buried against the side of Nathan's throat. Nathan felt each hard pulse of Erik's shaft, the slick feeling increasing as Erik continued with tiny ripples of his hips. Finally, Erik stilled completely, his body shaking with the heavy breaths he took.

Nathan gasped to fill his lungs, running his palms over Erik's broad, muscular back. "I love you, too," he whispered.

A shudder racked Erik before he lifted away enough to stare down into Nathan's eyes. He smiled gently, running his thumb along Nathan's cheekbone in a light caress. "I wish I could find the person who stole the CDs from my truck to thank them. I can't imagine my life without you in it, angel."

Nathan cupped the back of Erik's hand, leaning into Erik's touch. "You brought me back to life," he murmured, not breaking eye contact. He wanted Erik to know everything in his heart. "I don't know what my life would be like if we hadn't met, but I never want to find out."

A hiss issued from Erik as he slipped free of Nathan's body to climb off the bed and grab a cloth to clean them up. Afterward, Erik returned to bed, gathering Nathan close to him. "Tomorrow, you need to call the number on that flyer," Erik said, trailing his fingers lightly over Nathan's back.

"I will," Nathan said, smiling against Erik's chest.

"Good," Erik said before yawning. "Good night, sweet angel."

"Good night," Nathan murmured. The smile lessened but didn't fully go away. He lay there in the dark, listening to Erik's breathing. Nothing he'd gone through over the last six years had prepared him for Erik. He still felt he didn't deserve the amazing, sweet, mature man holding him while he slept, but he sure as hell wasn't letting him go. The guilt over his parents' deaths had lessened, but Nathan didn't know if it would ever truly fade away completely. He hoped they were happy and safe wherever spirits went after they crossed over.

Erik mumbled in his sleep and tightened his hold on Nathan briefly. Snuggling closer, Nathan smiled again and closed his eyes. For the first time in a very long time, Nathan looked forward to the future without fear or regret. He'd spent six years frozen in place, never really changing or moving, but now he wanted to rush toward whatever came his way. As long as he had Erik by his side, that was all that mattered.

~

Love freebies? Stop by J.R.'s website to subscribe for updates to receive a free friends to lovers novelette titled White Rain! Just enter your name and email address to subscribe! www.jrloveless.com

~

Love paranormal shifter stories? My True Mates series is perfect! Check out Book One Chasing Seth & Book Two Forgiving Thayne! Keep scrolling to read the first chapter from my True Mates novel Forgiving Thayne!

FORGIVING THAYNE

CHAPTER ONE

A N OVERWHELMING scent of earth and pine assaulted his senses the moment Nick Cartwright stepped into the Wolf's Den in the small town of Senaka. His eyes scanned the dim, slightly crowded establishment, seeking the source of the smell. Not even the sharp tang of booze dampened the earthy aroma, causing his cock to harden like a brick, and he clenched his jaw, knowing the only reason his body would react that way. His destined mate stood among the dozen or so men and women, several of whom were also wolves, who littered the bar. The only thing saving Nick from facing a room full of angry wolves was his ability to wrap his scent in his power as a true wolf. If they knew Nick's real nature, there'd be no doubt in his mind they'd believe him to be a Created One, much like Kasey Whitedove had believed his best friend Seth Davies to be.

Loud country music played from a jukebox in the far-off corner of a makeshift dance floor. Nick felt all eyes turn his way. He'd been in a few small towns before and knew how it worked. Strangers were noticed, especially ones entering a local tavern. He approached the bar, still searching for his true mate, but more discreetly.

The bartender lifted an inquisitive eyebrow at him, asking him without words what he wanted. "Whiskey, straight up."

The man placed a snifter on the bar in front of Nick and pulled a bottle from behind the counter to fill it with two fingers of Jack Daniel's. Nick tossed a twenty down and picked up the glass. He took a small sip while studying the other patrons in the mirror. A good percentage of the clientele were Native American, with perhaps two or three of Caucasian descent. It reminded him of Kasey Whitedove, Seth's true mate and the local sheriff, and the man's prejudice against white men. Kasey had believed Seth to be a Created One after discovering Seth was a wolf.

At the moment, though, Nick's focus remained on finding out which one of the locals was actually his true mate. Nothing else mattered except claiming him or her.

"What's a gorgeous guy like you doing in a place like this?"

Nick almost sneezed at the strong smell of a flowery perfume that bombarded his senses. Long red fingernails trailed over his arm, and he had to bite back the urge to toss the hand off. He turned on the charm and swiveled on his stool while giving one of his famous "fake" smiles. The woman, though gorgeous, wouldn't be able to hold his attention for long. Short dark hair feathered lightly around her naturally tanned face, accenting the dark eyes devouring his long, lean form.

"Just visiting an old friend in town for a few days. Stopped in for a drink or two."

"Oh? And who might your friend be?" she asked, pressing closer to him.

If it weren't for his wolf traits, he might have leaned far

enough back on the stool to fall off, but he managed to perch on the edge without ending up on his back. "The veterinarian, Seth Davies."

"I haven't had the pleasure of meeting Doc's replacement just yet, but I may have to go on over with my Georgia," she purred, leaning in even closer. "You wouldn't want to buy a thirsty girl a drink, would you, cowboy?"

Before Nick could think of a polite way to refuse her, the scent of his mate washed over him, and he sucked in a breath, knowing beyond a shadow of a doubt the person standing behind him was the one meant to be his. And he was a wolf. The scent of it clung to his skin, deep and primal. He lifted his gaze to the mirror and met a pair of eyes so dark they sucked him in. He couldn't look away, couldn't breathe, couldn't even think. His mate was stunning. Tall, taller than Nick by a good three to four inches, beautifully tanned, and well-defined muscles bulged beneath the gray T-shirt he wore. High, strong cheekbones complemented the firm chin and jawline, one Nick desperately wanted to follow with his lips. He swallowed hard as his gaze slid down the smooth skin of his mate's throat and farther still to the hollow at the base. When he brought his gaze back up to the dark eyes watching him closely, the answering lust caused his cock to jump in excitement. He wanted to dominate the man staring at him, to hold him down and mark him for the entire world to see.

The contrast between them couldn't be more obvious. Nick's own skin was lightly tanned but still pale compared to the other shifter. Blond hair versus raven's wing black hair, and emerald-green eyes snared by pools of dark chocolate stood out starkly against each other in the mirror. While the stranger's face was smooth, unmarred, Nick had a scar over his left eyebrow. Nick's body was more of a toned runner's form than the obvious boxer or weight-lifter size of his mate.

He wildly imagined how their skin would look tangled up on the nearest bed.

"Is there a problem here?" the man rumbled. Nick tensed, wondering if maybe he'd read the man's expression wrong.

"Go away, Thayne," she snapped. "He's not bothering me."

"I wasn't talking to you, Lilianne. I was speaking to him."

Surprise held Nick immobile for a split second before his mate's words sank in, and then he had to choke back a laugh at the woman's expression.

Murder shone in her eyes, and she glared at Thayne. "Don't make me tell your mother how you spoke to me, Thayne."

Thayne snorted at her threat. "Stop bothering the man, Lilianne, and go find some other poor sucker to leech off of."

Huffing in indignation, Lilianne stomped off toward the back of the bar.

Nick chuckled under his breath, hiding his grin behind his glass. He froze when Thayne sat on the stool next to his.

"She's been looking for husband number three for a while now. The men here in town know better than to mess around with her, so she's started in on any of the rare visitors we get. I'm Thayne."

"Nick," he murmured and took another sip of his whiskey. "You live around here?"

Thayne rested one arm on the bar while taking a long draught of his beer before answering. "Most of my life. Only back for a visit, though."

Nick breathed in his mate's scent, dying to ask questions about him, but held his tongue, not wanting to scare Thayne off. "Nice place."

"Not if you've lived here your entire life, it isn't. Everyone knows your name, and there are no secrets." Thayne set his empty beer bottle down on the bar. "I heard you tell Lilianne you're visiting the new Doc. He a relative?"

Nick downed the last of his whiskey, savoring the smooth burn of alcohol as it traveled to his belly. "Near enough. Known him a long time."

"How long you in town for?"

"Not too sure. He's going through some problems right now. I'm just here to help until he's okay." Nick sucked in a telltale breath when Thayne swayed in close to him, the tiny hairs all over his body standing on end at the almost contact.

"How about we get out of here?" Thayne purred right next to his ear. His breath whispered over the sensitive skin of Nick's earlobe, causing Nick to shiver in need.

Without a word, he nodded at Thayne, desire blazing through him. He wanted nothing more than to taste his mate, to feel his hard cock on his tongue as Thayne came down his throat. As he followed Thayne from the bar, he wondered if Thayne would react to his being a wolf the same way Seth's mate had reacted to Seth. Thayne disrupted his line of thought abruptly, shoving him into the darkness along the side of the building and slamming him against the wall. His lips crashed down on Nick's in a harsh kiss like no other he'd ever experienced. His tongue eagerly danced with Thayne's, twisting together in a sensual storm, sweeping away every thought except the desperate need to feel Thayne's cock buried inside him.

Thayne's hands slid down his sides, hips, and straight to his ass, cupping it in a strong grip before squeezing. Thayne growled low in his throat when Nick ground his hard flesh into Thayne's lower belly.

"I want to fuck you," Thayne rasped close to Nick's ear, his slick tongue flicking over the soft skin.

"Fuck, yes," Nick moaned, latching on to Thayne's neck and sucking deeply. His hands slid beneath the hem of his mate's shirt, palms gliding over the smooth skin of Thayne's back. The desire to feel Thayne's heated flesh on his ate at him. He yanked the shirt over Thayne's head, breathing in sharply at the well-defined muscles of his mate's chest.

Thayne reached for the front of Nick's jeans, tugging at the button and sharply parting the zipper. His big hand sank inside and cupped Nick's already-leaking shaft. Nick nearly howled in lust and pleasure, leaning his head back against the wall behind him. Thayne shoved the jeans down to reveal the small black briefs Nick wore, and he made a sound of approval. He dropped to his knees in front of Nick and buried his face in the fabric.

Nick shuddered at the hot breath seeping through the thin cloth. His fingers trembled as they wove through Thayne's dark locks, sinking into the lush strands, gripping tightly as Thayne sucked at him through his briefs. Nothing prepared him for the moment Thayne's tongue circled the tip of his cock, which peeked through the hem, and Nick gasped, panting in desire.

Thayne hooked his thumbs in his briefs and tugged them down, releasing Nick's straining length. It slapped lightly at Thayne's cheek, leaving a smear of precome along the tanned skin.

"Beautiful," Thayne breathed. He wrapped his lips around the tip, teasing Nick with tiny flicks of his tongue along the crown before delving into the small slit to gather the seeping liquid.

Nick swore, clenching his jaw to keep from losing control and jamming his cock down Thayne's throat. "Suck me," he snarled almost angrily when Thayne continued licking slowly.

Thayne hummed and slid to the root in one quick motion. Nick groaned and gave an uncontrollable thrust of his hips forward. Pulling off and chuckling, Thayne spun Nick around, pushed his pants down farther, and gripped his ass cheeks, parting them to bare his tight hole.

Nick jerked at the feel of Thayne's tongue swiping over the puckered flesh before spearing inside him. He clenched his hands into fists against the wall, his nails lengthening and digging into his palms to draw blood.

"Enough, inside, now."

After standing, Thayne quickly unfastened his jeans, allowing his cock free from the confining fabric, and pulled a condom from his back pocket. Nick spun around and snatched the condom from Thayne, ripped it open with his teeth, and quickly rolled it down Thayne's hard shaft. Thayne felt huge and hot in his palm. He squeezed the bulging prick, stroking for a moment. It disappointed him to have the thin latex between them, knowing neither of them could transmit diseases and wanting nothing more than to feel Thayne's flesh sliding over his.

"Turn around," Thayne ordered, his voice gruff and hoarse. Nick faced the side of the building once more and shoved his hips back, thrusting his ass at Thayne, who eagerly stepped forward to slide his cock along the crease. He nudged at the saliva-slickened hole and pushed in, piercing Nick's body, both of them groaning at the sensation. "So fuckin' tight," Thayne moaned in Nick's ear once he was seated deep inside him.

Nick clenched his muscles around Thayne's cock, milking the throbbing shaft. Thayne's fingers dug into the flesh at his hips as he pulled back until the crown caught just at the tight ring of muscle and shoved back in, expertly nailing Nick's prostate. Nick stifled a loud cry, biting down on his arm as Thayne fucked him, slamming into him over and over, rough and hard, just the way he liked it. Their bodies slapped together, the sound echoing in the empty alley. Nick's teeth elongated as he began to near his peak. His cock dripped profusely, drops staining the concrete beneath his feet.

"Harder."

Thayne slammed deeper and more violently, breathing heavily. When Nick tensed up, getting ready to come, Thayne's hips went into overdrive, pile driving deep into his ass. "Oh, yeah, baby. That's it. Come on my cock," Thayne ordered.

Nick splintered. His balls drew tight to his body, his spunk spraying the wall in front of him in thick, creamy spurts. He was dimly aware of Thayne's teeth biting down on his shoulder and the grunts Thayne made as he came inside Nick, filling the condom with his own essence. They slumped into the wall, bodies shuddering in mutual pleasure.

When Thayne finally moved, he carefully gripped the base of the condom and pulled free from Nick's body. He stripped the condom from his cock, tied it off, and tossed it into the nearby dumpster.

"Fuck, that was hot."

Grinning weakly, Nick nodded. He sensed Thayne mentally withdrawing from him now that he'd gotten off. "You're my mate," he blurted out once he'd turned to face Thayne again, his wolf desperate to keep from losing his destined partner.

Thayne stilled, his gaze piercing Nick. "What the fuck are you talking about?"

Nick quickly pulled up his pants, fastened them, and ran a hand through his hair. "Shit. I didn't mean to just come out and say it, but... you're my mate."

"How the fuck do you know about mates?" Thayne demanded.

Nick hesitated, but he couldn't keep the truth from spilling forth. "I'm a wolf."

Thayne's eyes narrowed at him, and he bared his teeth, now elongated slightly. "You're a Created One."

"No!" he protested, holding out his hand toward Thayne, who instantly backed away as if Nick would taint him. Nick's heart broke as he watched the look of satiation turn to one of hatred. "I was born a wolf!"

Before Nick could say anything else, Thayne shifted and launched himself at Nick. Nick felt time stop. He couldn't hurt his mate. He could only watch and wait for the impact. Their bodies collided, and Nick went down, his back slamming into the unforgiving concrete. He grunted, lifting his arm up to shield his face from the snapping teeth. Pain ripped through his forearm and radiated along every inch of his body. Thayne snarled, wrenching his head from side to side in an effort to tear at Nick's flesh. Nick cried out in agony, hot blood soaking his shirt.

Unable to take it anymore, he used every bit of his strength to shove Thayne away from him. Thayne crashed into the nearby dumpster, stunning him long enough for Nick to stand and shift. Thayne struggled to his feet as Nick gave him a sorrow-filled look. Thayne paused, watching him intently for a moment until Nick turned and ran. He darted between cars, keeping to the shadows to prevent anyone from spotting him. His chest hurt. It felt as if a huge gaping hole was left where his heart was meant to be. The accelerated healing ability of being a wolf left little to no mark when he finally shifted back to human a few blocks from Seth's place.

During the walk to Seth's, Nick made plans to leave Senaka the moment Seth's situation was settled. He couldn't bear the idea of remaining in the same town as his mate, not when he'd been rejected with such finality. His wolf cried out with every step, urging him to return to Thayne's side. Nick forced himself to ignore his wolf, to keep moving forward, one foot in front of the other. Each step broke him bit by bit until he felt he was nothing more than an empty, hollow shell. Nick knew he would never forget this night until the day he died.

. . .

Six Months Later

"HEY, NICK, is there anything left to handle with the Synergen project?" His friend and business partner, Ryan Driscoll, interrupted his musings and brought him back to the present. Nick blinked several times to clear his vision and glanced up from his computer monitor. He looked around to remind himself he was at his office in Emerald Lake Hills, California and needed to focus on work rather than the one night of heaven and the six months of hell since meeting Thayne.

Seth had settled well into his role as Kasey's mate and was well protected by his new pack. Nick no longer had to worry for his best friend's safety and found many excuses to steer clear of the small town, especially after finding out Thayne was Kasey's brother. Thayne still refused to accept him despite the discovery Nick wasn't a Created One. Knowing his mate truly didn't want him snapped something inside of Nick. He no longer found his world as colorful as he once had. He had tried unsuccessfully for the past several months to forget Thayne, to immerse himself in the bodies of others, but they couldn't make him forget the smell, the taste, or the feel of Thayne against him. He didn't allow himself much time to dwell on any of it, forcing himself to concentrate on projects and designs until all hours of the night, working himself into exhaustion, but sometimes his mind managed to wander to that time before he could stop it.

"Nick?" Ryan stood before him with an expectant expression as he waited for Nick's response. They'd known each other for eight years, having met during one of Nick's infrequent visits to the pack while helping to protect Seth. They'd even hooked up a handful of times, but it had never gone beyond sex. Mutual pleasure. Ryan was a dangerously attractive man. Two years older than Nick, six foot four, nice body, he kept in shape by swimming—not overly muscular but well defined. Dirty blond hair he kept in a neat fade, and hazel eyes that seemingly changed color with his mood made a gorgeous match.

Nick rubbed his eyes and sat back in his desk chair. Ryan knew something had happened when he'd gone to Senaka, but he wasn't one to pry unless Nick wanted to share, and for that Nick was grateful. Since he'd returned home, he'd worked himself into exhaustion almost every night. He'd even managed to complete two projects in a matter of a couple of weeks that normally would have taken a good two to three months to finish.

"Nope. Everything is ready to go. Kuraski should be quite pleased with the results."

"Great." Ryan hesitated a moment. He walked in and closed the door behind him. "Look, Nick. You know I wouldn't normally ask, but since you've been back, you haven't been yourself. You work until you almost drop, you've lost at least twenty pounds, and I never see you smile anymore. You ended up in the hospital a month ago from exhaustion, and considering you're a wolf, that's a pretty big deal. What happened in Senaka?"

Nick's face instantly became shuttered. "Nothing happened."

"Bullshit. Even Cole's noticed you're not the same person." Cole Ferris was the soon-to-be Alpha. His father, Elijah, would be stepping down in six weeks, handing the reins of the pack over to his son, so he could retire and take the time to see the world. "You know he expects you to become his Beta, but he's not sure if you can handle it right now. If ever, from the way you're heading. What's going on?"

Sighing, Nick closed his laptop, reached into his bottom drawer, and took out a bottle of Johnnie Walker Blue and two small glasses. He silently poured two fingers in each and pushed one of the glasses toward his partner. Ryan strode over, picked up the glass, and sank elegantly into one of the chairs in front of Nick's desk. He remained quiet, waiting for Nick to speak.

"I found my mate."

A broad grin broke out over Ryan's face after a moment of silence in which several emotions fluttered across his friend's features, one of which almost seemed like sadness. "That's great! Isn't it?"

Nick snorted and tossed back the entire contents of the glass, trying to gain false courage to put into words what silently tormented him for months. "Is it? He rejected me. Not only did he attack me, believing me to be a Created One, but he didn't want me even after he found out I'm a true wolf."

Shock flitted over Ryan's handsome face. Rejecting your mate isn't something normally done. Not only because of how unlikely you were to find them, but also because of the bond. It began to form the moment you met. Even now Nick could feel the strands of fate tying him to Thayne. Though unseen, they bound two mates as one. The longer you were apart, the more they "vibrated," pushing a wolf to seek physical contact. Nick figured it was the reason most wolves who'd lost their mates allowed themselves to shut down and cease to exist.

"How is that possible?" Ryan demanded.

Shrugging one shoulder, Nick poured another glass. "I don't know, Ry. But I know it fucking hurts. I know every day that goes by and I can't see him is torture. It feels as though a part of me is missing. I've never understood how a wolf could allow themselves to become so depressed they just give up. Now I get it. It's a struggle to get up in the mornings, at least on the nights I can sleep."

"That's why you've been working yourself to the bone." Ryan sighed, rubbing his chin lightly. "Do you know why he rejected you?"

"No. He refuses to even talk to me. Kasey, Seth's mate, says it's because Thayne has been saying almost his entire life that he doesn't want a mate. But I feel as though it's more than that. He wouldn't even let me near him. I finally had to just leave Senaka. I couldn't stand being that close to him and not having him." Nick stared broodingly into his glass. "I've always been told the mating bond is the most amazing gift. It's the foundation I was raised on. Granted, we haven't claimed one another yet, but all of the stories tell of it beginning from the moment you lay eyes on one another. The strings of fate begin to weave the souls of each wolf together. Yet he never even seemed affected by it. I knew it the moment I caught his scent."

Sympathy flashed through Ryan's gaze. "I can't imagine what it must be like for your mate to reject you, but the Nick I know doesn't give up so easily. Find him, Nick. Get the answers. Cole says the first summit is next month, the new moon. It's being held on neutral ground to cut down on the possibility of territorial fights breaking out. Maybe he will be there."

After Kasey's father revealed the existence of other wolves to his pack, they'd reached a truce and would gather once every six months, giving the members of each pack the chance of possibly meeting their destined mate. True mates were rare, since most wolves ended up restricted to their own pack due to proximity and the lack of exposure to others. Until recently, Nick had begun to wonder if he'd ever meet his own. Now he wished he hadn't.

"Not likely. He doesn't want a mate, remember? Why would he go to a summit designed to find one?"

"His father is the current Alpha, isn't he? Perhaps he will command him to attend to show good faith between packs?" Ryan pointed out.

"Doubtful. He's the type who won't be 'commanded.' I'm not certain I can take being around if others do find their mates among Jeremiah's pack. I'm happy they now have a greater chance, but I don't want to be forced to watch. Not when my mate hates my existence."

Nick's phone rang, interrupting any further conversation. "Cartwright."

"Nick!" Seth's voice came over the line.

"Hold on just a second, babe," he said quietly, covering the receiver with one hand before addressing Ryan. "If you want to schedule the wrap-up meeting with Synergen, I'll take care of the final presentation."

"Sure thing, Nick." Ryan stood and moved to the door. With his hand on the knob, he glanced back at Nick. "Don't give up, Nick. Don't let him go."

Nick waved his hand at Ryan and turned his chair around to face his window. He heard the soft snick of the door closing behind him. "How's the easy life in Senaka?"

"Easy life?" Seth snorted indignantly. "Living with the hulk of a sheriff called my mate is not easy. Did you know that Kasey leaves his clothes all over the house? I'm constantly cleaning up after him! I can't believe how much of a pig he turned out to be!"

Laughing, Nick leaned his chair back slightly, putting his feet up on the sill of the large window. Seth had always been a neat freak. After his experience living in filth for several weeks at the hand of a cruel and abusive Created One, his

OCD complex had gotten even worse. Seth even color-coded his socks. "Cut the man some slack, Seth. He's not only the town sheriff and future Alpha of the Senaka pack, but he's also got a Rho for a mate."

Seth was a rare wolf called a Rho. They were only born once every one hundred years and were gifted with an even rarer ability. Seth could heal other creatures, human or animal. It made Rhos one of the most coveted wolves in any pack, which in turn led to Kasey's constant watchful eye on Seth. Especially after the last incident where another wolf terrorized and kidnapped Seth, claiming to be his mate.

A grumble came over the line. "Blah, blah. So what if I'm a Rho? Kasey has every wolf in the pack practically trailing me wherever I go! It's getting a tad annoying."

"He's just worried, babe," Nick soothed gently. "He almost lost you. Give him some time. I'm sure it will get better after a while."

"How've you been, Nick?" Seth asked quietly, changing the subject.

Nick knew his friend worried about him after the rejection of his mate. He couldn't lie to Seth, not anymore. When Seth found out Nick knew about his past and how Nick had been sent to watch over him, he'd almost cut Nick out of his life. He couldn't take the chance of hurting Seth again and possibly losing the one person who meant almost as much to him as Thayne.

"It's been hard."

A sympathetic noise issued from Seth. "You sound tired. I hope you aren't working yourself to death."

It always surprised him whenever Seth saw straight to his heart. They knew each other way too well. Seth didn't know about his recent trip to the emergency room when he'd all but collapsed in exhaustion. He didn't volunteer the information. He didn't want to worry Seth further.

"I'm fine, Seth. I don't have any other choice than to be fine. It's not like Th… he is giving me any other option."

Nick could practically see Seth scowl over the phone as he responded. "I could kick Thayne in his balls for hurting you. Kasey still doesn't understand why his brother is so adamant about not having a mate. The bastard left town almost as soon as you did. He didn't even tell anyone, except his mom."

The sound of Thayne's name caused his stomach to clench, and he winced, rubbing at the offending area. "Can we talk about something else, Seth?"

"Of course." Seth launched into a detailed story of the Senaka pack's preparation for the upcoming summit. Both packs would be meeting in Kamas, Utah, at Bear River Lodge. The cabins bordered the Wasatch National Forest and provided the needed area for shifting, hunting, and running.

Zoning out, Nick flicked the touchpad on his laptop and studied the newest website he'd designed for Synergen, a company based in Los Angeles that custom built computers. The name flashed across the screen before giving the option of watching the slideshow on the prebuilt models or clicking a link to skip the slides, taking the viewer straight into the site.

"Nick! Are you listening to me?" Seth asked, irritation evident in his voice.

"Yeah, I'm listening," Nick lied. He didn't really care about the summit. At the moment, he found it hard to care about much of anything. "Seth, I have to go. I've got a big presentation to prepare for. I'll call you later this week, okay?"

Seth didn't reply for a moment before saying, "You know if you need to talk, I'm here for you, Nick."

"I know, babe. I promise I'll call you if I need you."

Nick hung up after saying good-bye and opened the e-mail from Ryan. He had an appointment Friday with the bigwigs at Synergen. His assistant, Annie, had already booked him a flight Thursday night and set him up in the Wilshire Grand Hotel, a few blocks from the Synergen building. He set the flight time in his BlackBerry. He'd stayed in the Wilshire several times and knew the exact location. At least there were night clubs in LA. Maybe he could find a warm body to fill his bed and make him forget, even if only for an hour.

It had been a week since he'd shifted, and his wolf prowled restlessly beneath his skin, causing him to feel on edge. Sighing, he stood and started packing up some items to work from home, including his laptop.

He hit the intercom button. "Annie?"

"Yes, Nick?"

"I'm going to head home and work from there. If anything urgent comes up, give me a call on my cell."

"Sure thing, Nick," Annie replied. She was a blessing in disguise for Nick. She kept him organized and neat to a fault. Also a wolf, she remained unmated because she believed she would find her mate. It had slipped out one night when they'd all gone out for drinks and Ryan left Nick and Annie alone at the table. He'd always hoped she would find her true mate, but now he wasn't so sure it would be the best thing for her. He knew lumping everyone into the same category as Thayne didn't exactly ring fair, but he couldn't stop the bitterness rising inside of him. It only grew stronger with each passing day.

Nick packed his laptop into his black satchel and slipped it over his head. After grabbing his keys, he left his office and took the elevator to the first floor. The front desk receptionist smiled at him as he walked past, and he managed a half-assed smile back. He exited the building and crossed the parking lot to the second love of his life: a black, fully restored 1967 Chevy Impala.

The car had belonged to his grandfather while Nick was growing up. He could still remember the joy he felt riding in it and had even told his grandfather that one day he'd have one just like it. His grandfather passed away while Nick was in college, leaving him the car. Nick had kept it in storage until he'd returned to Emerald Lake Hills to open his business with Ryan. Its gleaming black paint job and polished silver fenders were well maintained, and Nick made damn sure it stayed that way. His grandfather never would have forgiven him if he'd let it deteriorate after all the work they'd put into it together during Nick's childhood.

He opened the door, climbed in, and set his laptop bag on the passenger seat. The car started with a loud rumble, and he pulled out of the parking lot, heading for home. On the way, he tried to distract himself from the itch beneath his skin by thinking about his home and his pack.

Emerald Lake Hills had a small population compared to some of the cities in California. Just under five thousand people lived there, and a good hundred or so were pack members. The sleepy little burg had been named for the two beautiful lakes inside the city limits. The pack Alpha owned one of the large private homes on the Upper Emerald Lake shore. Due to the seclusion of the property, the pack meetings were normally held there before everyone headed to the park for the full moon run.

His own home—a single-story, two-bedroom house—sat on the border of Edgewood County Park, which ran along the edge of Pulgas Ridge Open Space Preserve. The park and preserve gave him and others in the pack miles of land to roam as wolves. They still ran the risk of humans spotting them, especially since wolves in California were rare even in the densely wooded areas, but it provided a modicum of coverage for their monthly pack runs. On occasion, like now, Nick felt the restless urge to run as his wolf, to let go and allow his animal instincts to overcome him. Sometimes he wondered what it would be like to remain a wolf forever, to let his humanity go. Those thoughts only increased after Thayne's rejection. Seth had given him a reason not to give in to his desire, but Seth no longer needed him. He had Kasey now.

The drive home seemed interminable, longer than ever. His wolf scratched at the surface, causing him to fidget in his seat multiple times. A sigh of relief slipped free when he finally pulled into his driveway and turned off the engine. He rushed inside, dropped his laptop bag and keys near the front door, and headed toward the back of the house. He barely managed to make it into the trees before he shifted, running the instant his paws met the earth. A long, lonely howl ripped free from him, echoing through the woods. In his true form, he felt the rejection more keenly than ever, his heart aching with need for its mate.

Nothing soothed him. He ran until his legs gave out. He collapsed beneath a tree, panting heavily and dropping his head to his paws. A light wind ruffled his fur, sending a shiver through the long length of his body. The same question he'd asked himself more than once over the past six months rolled around in his mind. Would the pain ever fade?

A NOTE FROM J.R.

Thank you for reading Paralyzed. If you enjoyed it, I would truly appreciate if you could let your friends know so they can also enjoy the relationship between Nathan and Erik. If you leave a review for Paralyzed on the site in which you purchased/read the book, Goodreads or your own blog, I would love to read it. Please email the link to jrloveless@gmail.com

ABOUT THE AUTHOR

J.R. Loveless began her adventure in writing at the young age of twelve. Her foray into creating her own worlds and telling her characters' life stories was triggered by her own love of reading. She currently resides in South Florida with her two dogs and one cat, and by day works as an application support analyst for a financial lending institute.

Her journey into gay romance began in 2005 when she began posting her original fiction on a forum for feedback and readers' pleasure. In 2010, a good friend urged her to submit to a publishing company, and the day she received the acceptance and contract was the best day of her life. Since then, she has been noted to be one of the most purchased audio books after Fifty Shades of Grey on Audiobook.com and received best gay romantic fiction for Touch Me Gently in the 2011 TLA Gaybies.

J.R. adores her fans and loves hearing from them.

Never miss out on an update or sale by by subscribing to J.R.'s Website. As a thank you, you'll receive a free short novelette called White Rain about two friends who become lovers!

J.R.'s Blog

J.R.'s Facebook Reader Group